S0-ARM-824

Also by Dick Couch

FICTION

SEAL Team One

Pressure Point

Silent Descent

Rising Wind

The Mercenary Option

NONFICTION

The Warrior Elite

The Finishing School

Down Range

DICK COUCH

COVERT ACTION

POCKET STAR BOOKS

New York   London   Toronto   Sydney

An *Original* Publication of POCKET BOOKS

A Pocket Star Book published by
POCKET BOOKS, a division of Simon & Schuster, Inc.
1230 Avenue of the Americas, New York, NY 10020

This book is a work of fiction. Names, characters, places and incidents are products of the author's imagination or are used fictitiously. Any resemblance to actual events or locales or persons, living or dead, is entirely coincidental.

ISBN-13: 978-0-7434-6425-3
ISBN-10:   0-7434-6425-7

First Pocket Books paperback edition August 2005

10 9 8 7 6 5 4 3 2 1

POCKET STAR BOOKS and colophon are registered trademarks of Simon & Schuster, Inc.

Cover design by Tony Greco

Manufactured in the United States of America

For information regarding special discounts for bulk purchases, please contact Simon & Schuster Special Sales at 1-800-456-6798 or business@simonandschuster.com.

To the 33rd Company Mets
Class of 1967
United States Naval Academy

Acknowledgments

My thanks to Dr. Bruce Kaplan, Dr. Steven Fagan (the real one), David Starr, and the many others who helped. And as always, any errors and inaccuracies are mine alone.

PROLOGUE

The two men sat just below a remote ridgeline in the Nyambene Hills, well concealed from anyone moving along the shallow valley below them. They had been there for the better part of two days. Behind them in a small clearing in the lush vegetation, they had made dry camp—just the bare necessities. If needed, they could be packed out and on the move in a matter of minutes. One or the other of them was always on watch, keeping the valley and the trail that wound through the drainage, under constant surveillance. But earlier that morning, they saw the file of men making their way over a rise to the north of their position. Now it would be a matter of time. They would soon be making their way down the sloping drainage, and events would take their course. This was the main route into the Kora National Reserve and one favored by those who came for the animals and the ivory. Sometimes, they came for more than animals and ivory. It was in the Kora that poachers had murdered park warden George Adamson, as they did his wife, Joy Adamson, in the nearby Meru National Park. The two Adamsons, Elsa the lioness, Pippa the cheetah, and all the others from their book *Born Free* were now gone. But the poachers still came.

While the two watched the valley floor, their Ndrobo tracker sat on his haunches back in the shade near the clearing. He would be there for the kill, but for now his work was done. Days earlier, he had ranged out to find the men. His experience and knowledge of the game trails had rightly predicted that this band of travelers would be coming this way. He swatted flies with a lion-hair quirt and dozed in the growing warmth.

The two on watch were very different, both in appearance and mind-set. One was a tall Turkana with ebony skin and a noble bearing—a powerfully built man with wide, useful shoulders and long muscles. Yet it was his features that defined the man; it was as if they were chiseled from black granite. He surveyed the area impassively, occasionally bringing a pair of Zeiss binoculars to his face to scan the terrain before them. The second man was smaller and more finely constructed, with an angular, aquiline countenance and nut-brown skin. He was Somali, and his eyes were ferretlike, as were his manner and movements—someone seemingly more suited to a bazaar than the bush. The tall Turkana was aware of everything—the wind, swampland at the foot of the valley, the pack of hyenas just beyond the edge of the swamp, the angle of the sun, the relationship of their position on the ridge to the terrain below. He missed nothing. The Somali watched only the trail that snaked into the valley. His was the patience of a bird of prey. Then they appeared.

There were twelve of them, and they moved in good order. They were tall and covered ground quickly with long, easy strides. Each carried an AK-47 assault rifle and a light pack. These were hard men, Sudanese, who could cover thirty miles a day or more on very little food or water. But in the Kora, in the shadow of Mount Kenya, water was never a problem. Since the lifting of the total ban on the sale of African ivory, a new and lucrative trade had sprung up, attracting poachers like these from the Sudan and as far away as the Congo and the Central African Republic. The shooting of elephants was banned in Kenya, but now illegal ivory could be passed off as that from sanctioned shootings. The Kenya elephant herd had stabilized at some estimated thirty thousand animals, but that number was now threatened with the resumption of trade in tusks. African poverty and men with automatic weapons again threatened the great herds, in Kenya and all over southern Africa. The bands of poachers, who were basically paramilitary units, now came south to kill elephants. And the park rangers charged with the protection of the great herds were, man for man, simply no match for these armed bands. The three men who waited carried papers that identified them as employees of the Kenyan National Park Service, but their charter and their duties were quite different from normal park ranger work.

As the Turkana saw the file of men keep to the game trail that would bring them past their position, he turned to his companion.

"You will stay here," he said in Masai, a language both men understood, "while I take on the head of the column. Let us do this quickly. *Awusipe namhla isinkwa.*" With that he filtered into the bush in a direction that would take him well in front of the advancing file of men. The Somali smiled and checked his weapon, a Belgian-made FAL automatic rifle. He settled into a comfortable prone shooting position and laid out two additional twenty-round magazines, far more rounds than he felt he would need. There was an audible click as he took the weapon off safe. The sound seemed to bring the Ndrobo from his dozing. He took up his AK-47 and found a shooting perch some fifteen yards down the ridgeline. This brought a scowl from the Somali. He knew the scout was not as good a shot as himself, yet he might just get one or two that might otherwise be left for him.

The Turkana got to his shooting position to the side of the trail, well ahead of the advancing column of men. He too had an FAL, and his extra magazines were in snap pouches on his vest. He knelt behind a fallen and decayed acacia tree that provided more concealment than cover. Five minutes later the first man in the Sudanese file appeared; he was perhaps a hundred yards away. The Turkana remained still as a statue and let the file approach the site they had selected for the ambush, where the trail cut through a short stand of grass. There was no place to hide, and any concealing vegetation was a fifty-yard run back up the trail. The leader carried his Kalishnakov at the ready, but the others had their rifles slung or draped across their shoulders, clutching them by the barrel. When he judged the file was in the most exposed position, the Turkana stood and in a single fluid motion shouldered his rifle. His first round center-punched the lead man in the file. He dropped as if he were poleaxed, dead before he hit the ground. A fraction of a second later, the second in the file took a big 7.62 round in the chest, just as the head of the last man in the file exploded from a well-aimed round from the Somali's rifle. The Turkana walked forward, taking each in turn, while his shooting partner on the ridge worked the column back to front. The little Ndrobo tracker blazed away at the center of the column on full-automatic fire, hitting no one.

It was over in ten seconds. One of the Sudanese poachers managed to get his rifle off his shoulder before he was cut down, and another had turned to run, which earned him a bullet between his shoulder blades. When they were all on the ground, the three men cautiously converged on the killing zone, changing magazines as they moved. There was some moaning but little movement. The Turkana surveyed the fallen men over the sights of his rifle while the other men moved among them, putting a bullet into the head of each. Now it was over and done. The tall man nodded, and the Somali and the Ndrobo began to search the bodies, looking for gold—gold in the form of bracelets, necklaces, and teeth. Then they collected the packs and weapons of their victims and ferried them to the swamp nearby, where they tossed them into the black ooze. The scout kept back a few of their quarry's magazines to replenish the rounds for his own AK. Otherwise, they took only pictures. The sun was well up, and the corpses would soon ripen. The vultures would get there before the hyenas, but not before the flies. The three executioners collected their gear from their dry camp and set off on a compass bearing that, in two days' march, would bring them to the town of Meru.

The office was a single room in a small cinder-block building in the center of town. Everything was shabby and mildewed, but there was a tattered orderliness to the stacks of paper and newspapers. The tall Turkana stood by the desk as a white man in slacks and a soiled white shirt downloaded the pictures from the digital camera into a laptop computer. He studied each of the images for a few moments, occasionally flipping back to a previous photo. His grisly task was to ensure that each of the macabre images was unique and that each documented a single human death. Finally, he rose from the desk.

"As I see it, you have twelve good kills here. That tally with your count?"

"It does," the African replied.

"Then here you go."

He counted out twenty-four American one-hundred-dollar bills. They were crisp, uncirculated notes. Several international charities contributed to the fund that exchanged money for dead poachers. This particular fund was administered by a Dutch wildlife trust called the Hans Wasmoeth Wildlife Foundation. There were many contributors, including, oddly enough, the Humane Society of the United States. The foundation's work in this regard was sanctioned and supported by several African nations. It was far and away the most effective antipoaching program in place. Those African nations who valued their wildlife resources knew that the only way to protect the game was to make the poachers game animals as well.

The Turkana signed a receipt, thanked the man, and gathered up the stack of banknotes. Outside, his two companions waited. Together, they made their way to what passed for a native tavern and found a seat in the corner. The other patrons studiously ignored them, as they were obviously hard men from the bush, and they carried guns. After a pitcher of warm beer was served, they drank and divided the money equally—six hundred dollars each. It was more than most Africans made in a year. Then the man from the foundation came in, spotted them, and made his way to their table.

"Sorry for the interruption," he apologized. They were in his view, after all, armed killers drinking beer. "But this came for you. I forgot to give it to you." He handed the tall African a telegram. "Well, I'll be off. G'day."

"Thank you for bringing this. Good day to you."

After the white man had left, the Turkana opened the telegram, noting that the seal had not been tampered with. As he read it, a hint of a smile crossed his handsome features.

"What does it say?" asked the Somali.

The tall man produced an easy grin, and the lines in the corners of his eyes showed genuine merriment. He laid the telegram on the table, but the other two ignored it. Neither could read English, nor any written language for that matter.

"It says," he replied with an uncharacteristic chuckle, "that we may no longer have to trek into the bush in search of dung-eating poachers from the Sudan."

Finally, the little Ndrobo picked up the telegram and stared at it uncomprehendingly. It read:

LOOKING FOR MEN WHO KNOW THEIR WAY IN THE BUSH.
WORK IS HONORABLE, PAY IS EXCELLENT, RATIONS ARE SUPERB.
REPLY THIS ADDRESS FOR DETAILS. AKR

1

AKR

Garrett Walker sat at a small table, enjoying the sun on his back and the gentle tug of trade winds that carried the sweet smell of oleander and frangipani. The Ballyhoo Restaurant was not the kind of watering hole he would normally choose; he preferred a workingman's bar, but right now, dressed as he was, he would have been very much out of place. At the Ballyhoo there was always a steady flow of tourists coming and going, and since he might have to be here for some time, it was an enjoyable spot to wait. The lunch crowd had thinned out a bit, only to be replaced by those who came to drink and socialize. His table had a clear view of the Fort and Banks Street intersection and the famous Circus Clock Monument, which dated back to the French occupation of Basseterre. There was enough activity below to hold his attention while he waited.

"Another, sir?" the waitress asked pleasantly.

Garrett glanced at his watch. "Why not?" He smiled. "And could you also bring me another mineral water?" A few minutes later she returned with a bottle of Perrier and a tumbler charged with Cane Spirits Rothschild and Tang. She gave him her best smile and retreated from the table.

Garrett grinned to himself, knowing that she had marked him as a "player," a wealthy visitor who might be a big tipper. He eyed the drink with some apprehension. CSR, a sweet liquor made locally from sugar cane, mixed with Tang, a grapefruit soda, was the national drink of

St. Kitts. He had already choked down one of the sweet concoctions for appearance's sake, but he was not so sure that he could do another. He would have much preferred a scotch. The whole charade made him uneasy, and it was not just the sweet drink. His normally straightforward military haircut was moussed and pulled back flat across the top of his head. He was dressed in a red T-shirt, a white linen sport coat with pleated matching slacks, and woven leather loafers—no socks. Everything felt a size too big. The heavy gold necklace and diamond pinkie were gaudy and made him feel awkward, as did the gold Rolex strapped to his wrist. His rich deep tan and wraparound sunglasses completed the look. AKR had suggested a diamond stud in one ear, but he had drawn the line with a definitive "not on your life." Garrett had his limits about masquerading in public in what he had come to call his gigolo cover.

They had arrived two days ago and tied the boat up in the Basseterre Marina. The fifty-five-foot Viking motor yacht had turned a few heads as they entered the harbor, but boats that size and bigger were not unusual. It was ostentatious, but all part of the plan. They had chartered the boat out of San Juan and made the run down through the Virgin Islands and the northern portion of the Leeward Island group, thoroughly enjoying themselves. Anchoring at night, Garrett free-dived for langouste and occasionally shot a small grouper. The Viking, named Ragtime, had an amply stocked bar. It had been a leisurely four-day run. If all went well, they would be finished in another day or so and be back on their way.

Garrett found himself thinking of Judy and how much she would have enjoyed the trip, especially the journey through the islands. It would have been great to have her along, but he would have wanted her well on her way before they got to the business end of their venture. Her presence would have been natural enough, even enhancing their cover, but knowing Judy Burks, she would have been hard to get rid of once the action started. AKR had been the one to propose this idea, and it was not a bad one, but Garrett had ruled it out. His employer, Guardian Systems International, would not have objected, but Garrett's time in the military had conditioned him differently. Men, at least men in his line of work, went overseas to do their job, and their women waited for their return. He had always felt that was as it should be, even though he seldom had a woman waiting at home for him. Despite the yacht and the elegant tropical setting, this was business, and perhaps it would become nasty business before it was over. As much as the lively Miss Judy would have added to the enjoyment of the voyage down to St. Kitts, there were issues that might come up that he did not want her to be a party to. They were on the same side, but not on the same team. Still, the thought of her and the audacious way she would have carried off her part in this venture brought a smile to his lips. His smile only deepened as AKR made his entrance onto the Ballyhoo deck.

He bent to say something in the waitress's ear, his hand casually dropping to her waist. She moved imperceptibly closer to him, smiling broadly. Then she squealed and danced away from him, heading for the bar to get his drink order. As he made his way to Garrett, every woman in the bar had her eye on him. He paused when he got to the table and gave Garrett an infectious grin.

"Tonight?" Garrett asked quietly.

"Tonight, mon," he replied, then gracefully swung into the chair across from Garrett.

Akheem Kelly-Rogers had joined GSI only five months ago. Except for some training exercises, this was his first actual operation—their first together. In the short time that Garrett had known him, they had become almost like brothers; they were so alike—and yet so different. Garrett was a team player, but not one to be easily given over to deep friendships. However, with Kelly-Rogers it had been different. Much to Garrett's surprise, they had become close in a very short time. Initially, he had been a little disturbed when Fagan had hired Kelly-Rogers without first consulting him. His résumé was impressive, and on paper he seemed ideally suited for the work they did. His military credentials were impeccable. But their work was dangerous and demanded absolute trust. Garrett more than trusted Steven Fagan, but he also found it odd that Steven hadn't talked with him before he actually hired AKR.

He vividly recalled the morning of their first meeting. Garrett had been up early, preparing for a morning run. They were at the field training site on the Big Island of Hawaii. GSI occupied a large tract of land on the western slopes of Mona Kea, midway between Kailua and Waimea. It was here that Steven Fagan developed the infrastructure and facilities to support the training of the Intervention Force, or IFOR. Garrett had come to work for GSI soon after the completion of the complex. It was a modern, compact military training facility and completely self-contained. Garrett knew that Kelly-Rogers had come in late the night before, and assumed that he would still be sleeping. The sun was just coming up as Garrett finished his stretching routine. Suddenly a tall man was standing before him, arms folded, regarding him quietly. He was dark, with chiseled features, broad shoulders, and a very narrow waist and hips. Except for an inch or two in height, he was built very much like Garrett.

"Mind if I run with you?" he asked. He spoke with a crisp British public-school accent.

"Not at all," Garrett replied, and they set off at a brisk trot. They were at three thousand feet, well above the lava fields of the Kona Coast, and the trail wound up the side of Mona Kea, gaining close to five hundred feet every mile. The chill in the air did not entirely mask the smell of decaying vegetation from the previous day's heat. The only sound was the padding of their running shoes on the crushed lava roadbed. In the growing light, Garrett glanced at his running companion. He was not really black, but more of a deep chocolate color, and he ran with ease and grace. Garrett was aware that the new man was in his early forties, the same as himself, but he carried himself as if he were much younger.

"How far do you want to go?" Garrett asked.

"How about until one of us drops?" Kelly-Rogers replied.

Garrett didn't say a word, but gently picked up the pace. Not another word was spoken, nor would there be until it was over. The two men were silently locked into battle, one that could only end when one or both of them had reached the end of his endurance. There are few men who can willingly turn a casual morning run into mortal combat, but Akheem Kelly-Rogers and Garrett Walker were two such men. In many ways, it was the basis of their relationship and their evolving friendship; neither was a man who would yield to another, which amounted to asking for quarter. When they arrived back at the base camp two hours later, both of them were out of breath and spent. Neither man could have maintained the wicked pace had the other not been there.

"Garrett Walker," he managed, holding his hand out.

"Akheem Kelly-Rogers," the newcomer replied firmly, taking Garrett's hand. "But my friends call me AKR."

AKR was an unusual man—a study in cultural contradiction. His father had been Sir Bernard Rogers, late of Her Majesty's Foreign Office. Sir Bernard was landed by birth and spent a lifetime of service to the crown, rising to the post of deputy home secretary just before his death.

He had met Rose Kelly during the war. She was a WAAF, working in one of the Home Chain radar stations, tracking incoming Luftwaffe raids, and he was a hurricane pilot. They married a week later, just the two of them at the home of a local magistrate near Biggin Hill. Rose had joined the RAF against her family's wishes. They were upper-middle-class Dubliners, and while they were not Nazi sympathizers, they were none too keen on their youngest daughter joining the British military, nor of her marrying what they regarded as some British Tommy. Rogers's family was mortified that he would take up with what they openly called "that Irish tart."

Following the war, Bernard took an advanced degree at Oxford and joined the Foreign Office. In the early 1950s he was posted to the embassy in Nairobi. After more than ten years of marriage, the couple were as in love as the day they met, but there were no children. Then fate intervened in the form of a maid who presented them with a month-old baby boy, before promptly disappearing into the bush. The prospective parents found the infant swaddled and lying in a basket on their kitchen table. Bernard fussed about the kitchen while Rose changed him. Bernard might have wavered, but when he saw Rose sipping her tea from a porcelain cup in one hand and cradling the baby in the other, he knew the decision had been made.

"What do you fancy we should call him?" he asked as if in passing as he unfurled the *East African Post*.

Rose paused, but only for a moment. "I believe Akheem will do nicely, wouldn't you think?"

When the adoptive grandparents were informed of the new arrival, there was stormy weather on both sides of the Irish Sea. In rare concert, the elders insisted that the child be given over to a Kenyan orphanage. Having weighed the concerns of their families and not wanting to slight either,

Bernard and Rose christened their new son Akheem Kelly-Rogers.

Akheem grew up in Africa and saw England only on those home visits when the Foreign Office periodically repatriated their diplomats for consultation and home leave. The young man followed his parents through postings in Botswana, Rhodesia, Nairobi, and a short stint in Pretoria. He spoke French and German fluently, as well as Swahili, Shangane, and a smattering of other African tribal dialects. When he was fourteen, Bernard and Rose packed him off to the Lucton School in Herefordshire. Bernard and his father had both attended Lucton, and Akheem was accepted on the strength of his family name, never mind his breeding. He was an instant success at Lucton, and due to the home schooling by his parents, he was more than prepared, taking honors in his first form. Akheem was very popular among his classmates; being black, bright, British, and affluent were all to his advantage at an upscale rural English boarding school. Tall for his age and an accomplished batsman, he was quite handsome in his blazer and school tie. But during his second year he became bored, and his grades slipped dramatically, a common occurrence among the sons of the service posted abroad. Rural England was quite mundane and dismal when compared with the adventure of living in colonial African capitals. Akheem might have been expelled for poor academics but for a chance meeting with a resident inmate of another boarding institution in Herefordshire.

During term break, when most of the other boys were home with their families, Akheem made his way into the village of Ross-on-Wye, looking for some diversion from the school dining hall. He was seated in a quaint pub in the village center, giving his order to the proprietor, when a group of skinheads stormed into the establishment. They were up from Liverpool, uniformly turned out in tight jeans, white T-shirts, jackboots, and tattoos.

" 'Ey there, gov'ner, leave off with that wog and get some pints around for us 'ere wots got a thirst."

"I'll be with you in a moment," the owner replied and turned back to Akheem, who was seated in a booth in the corner.

"At's not good enough by half, gov'ner. Ge' 'im over 'ere, Sharkey."

One of the skinheads grabbed the old man roughly to drag him back toward the bar, and Akheem was out of the booth in an instant. The ruffian was caught flatfooted, totally unprepared for the speed and power of the punch that snapped his head back and put him on the floor. It was not the kind of punch that one would have expected from a fifteen-year-old preppie. The proprietor retreated to the bar as the other four closed in around Akheem.

"So wot we 'ave 'ere is a cheeky kaffir needin' to learn some manners," the largest in the group snarled. "An' wer th' blokes 'at can do just that."

"Leave the lad be," a cold voice from across the tavern demanded.

The big man whirled in the direction of the new challenge. "So you be wantin' a piece of this as well? We can oblige that."

He faced a man in his late twenties, medium build and height, but with a singularly composed manner about him. The man eased himself from the stool but did not relinquish his hold on the pint of ale that he'd been drinking. He let the large man come to him, watching only his eyes as he approached.

"As I wuz sayin', you be wantin'—"

He moved like a snake, almost too fast for the eye to follow, whipping the ale in the glass directly into the big skinhead's eyes—too quickly for him to even blink. His next strike was a kick to the blinded man's crotch as he brought a forearm across his face, exploding the large man's nose like an overripe tomato. The skinhead went first to his knees, then forward onto the planked flooring on his face. His mates watched in stunned silence, disbelieving that their leader had gone down so quickly. Heads turned to a sharp, splintering sound as Akheem took a wooden chair and crashed it over the head of another of the skinheads. The one he had decked earlier attempted to get up, but Akheem kicked him hard in the ribs, sending him back to the floor. He curled into a ball and began to moan.

"I'm thinkin' that you boys had best be leavin' the premises," the proprietor said, brandishing a heavy burled walking stick, "while you're still able."

The five men collectively gathered themselves and made for the door. They helped each other into a Ford van and drove quickly away. The pub owner took the empty pint glass from the bar, refilled it with ale, and pushed it back across to the young man as he reclaimed his stool.

"Seein' as how the pint was only partway done," he said with a straight face and a twinkle in his eye, "I'll not be chargin' you for this one. Just this one time, mind you."

"Well, Gavin," the man replied, "that's quite decent of you." He took half the pint in a single draw, smiled in satisfaction, then got up and made his way over to where Akheem still stood by the booth.

The proprietor took up a dustpan and broom and begun to clear away the debris. He glanced up at Akheem. "And you, lad, given that you joined the fray unprovoked, I won't be chargin' you for the chair. But you'll have to eat elsewhere; kitchen will be closed for the rest of the evenin'."

The stranger looked Akheem over and, as if liking what he saw, held out his hand. "Simon Carter, here."

"Akheem Kelly-Rogers," Akheem replied.

He tossed off the ale with another long pull. "Looks as if we need to find you something to eat." He turned and headed for the door, and after only a moment's hesitation, Akheem followed.

"I'm not sure there's anything else open this time of day," Akheem offered, once they were outside.

"Well, then," Simon Carter replied, "I suppose there's nothing to be done but to head back to the mess. C'mon."

Again Carter led and Akheem followed. They rounded the corner and approached a battered Land Rover Defender, obviously a military vehicle from its light dune color, but lacking any markings. Carter motioned for Akheem to get in. The Rover started instantly with a smooth, powerful roar that was not in keeping with its shabby exterior. After a fifteen-minute drive they came to a gatehouse with a single sentry. He wore a British Army uniform with no insignia save for a parachutist badge.

"Evening, Simon," the soldier said, then bent to look into the Rover at Akheem. "What we got here, a new recruit?"

"Could be, Bertie. For now I'm just taking the lad up to the mess for some tack."

It was a large base, and it took them another ten minutes to get to a cluster of barracks. "Word of the altercation at the pub is bound to get around," Carter said as they pulled up to a nondescript building. "I'd be obliged if we could skip over the part where you dropped two of those goons and I accounted for only one." He then added with an easy grin, "Follow me, and we'll see about a bit of tea."

Carter led him into a large, comfortable pine-paneled room with swords and plaques covering the walls. One end of the room had a faded Persian carpet, dated leather armchairs, and floor lamps. The other had circular tables with casino-style lighting, ashtrays, and condiments clustered in the center. A half dozen men sat at the tables and that many more in the armchairs, smoking and reading newspapers. It had the smell of a private men's club, which in a way it was. It was the sergeants' mess of Her Majesty's Special Air Service. Akheem took it all in; it was an impression that he would carry with him for many years.

For the next several months Akheem took even less interest in his studies. All he wanted to do was join the SAS, and he would have left school for the army had he been old enough. He was on academic probation and just on the verge of being expelled when he was visited by an Oxford classmate of his father's. The Lucton headmaster had given over his private office for the meeting. Akheem was at that age when his parents and the headmasters of his parents' generation had little influence on him, but this visitor was a lieutenant colonel in the Army and a SAS battalion commander. He was a commanding figure, and Akheem jumped to his feet when he entered the room.

The tall officer took a seat at the headmaster's desk while Akheem stood before the desk at attention. The colonel took a long moment to appraise him. He made no motion for Akheem to sit down.

"I'm given to understand that you would like to join my regiment."

"Yes, sir."

"Life is not easy in the SAS. Are you prepared to make the necessary sacrifices for a life in the service?"

"Yes, sir."

"Beginning this very minute?"

"Yes, sir."

"Then sit."

The tall officer leaned forward on one elbow and looked at the boy straight on. Then he continued in a measured tone. "Have you ever heard of Sandhurst?" This question would change Akheem's life forever.

The transformation to model student was immediate and complete. Akheem Kelly-Rogers went on to graduate at the top of his class at Lucton and won an appointment to Sandhurst, England's West Point. After the mandatory five years in the regular army, he joined the SAS. Enlisted men in the SAS call their officers "Ruperts," a term that is not entirely complimentary. While at the SAS, Akheem became known as the Black Rupert, and his reputation was legendary. Those who served with him regarded him as the finest combat leader in the Special Air Service. One evening, in the very same SAS mess where Akheem had first dined, a young sergeant who had not served with Major Kelly-Rogers made a rare derogatory comment about the Black Rupert. He was promptly and unceremoniously knocked on his ass by a senior warrant officer named Simon Carter.

That evening Garrett was seated comfortably on the stern deck of the Ragtime. A cut crystal tumbler of tonic and ice sat at his elbow alongside a tray of papaya and passion fruit. It would be an interesting evening. Kelly-Rogers had left about thirty minutes ago in the RHIB, the small rigid-hull inflatable boat that served as the yacht's tender. It was mounted with a forty-horse outboard and crossed the blue-green waters between their anchorage and the Charlestown city dock like a scalded dog. Garrett was pouring himself another tonic when the RHIB returned. AKR brought it smoothly to the docking station on the swim platform and held it there as a portly man with a bad comb-over pulled himself aboard. He mounted the short ladder and stepped through the companionway in the stern rail to the stern deck. It was a few minutes before six, a time when most in the islands were on their second cocktail.

"Ah, Monsieur Lyle," he said, extending one hand while mopping his brow with a handkerchief clutched in the other, "it is a pleasure to finally meet you."

"Mr. Klein," Garrett replied, formally nodding his head, "welcome aboard. Please, this way." Garrett led him to a low, oval glass table and motioned for him to have a seat. "May I offer you something to drink?"

"Rum and tonic, tall, if you don't mind, monsieur."

It was a very warm evening, and while the Ragtime was air-conditioned, with ample generator power to keep the interior spaces cool and dry, Garrett had no intention of asking him inside. A little sweat would do Martin Klein some good. Kelly-Rogers stood to one side, awaiting further instructions from Mr. Lyle. Garrett snapped his fingers, indicating to him to build a drink for their guest.

That afternoon they had made the eighteen-mile run from Basseterre on St. Kitts to Charlestown on Nevis in a little under two hours. Nevis was a sleepy little island, circular in shape and between seven and eight miles in diameter. There was little nightlife, save for the entertainment at a marvelous Four Seasons resort. Garrett and AKR had elected to stay close to St. Kitts but had booked a suite for the week at the Four Seasons just in case. They were, after all, players, and no one knew that better than Monsieur Klein.

St. Kitts and Nevis had been possessions of Portugal, France, and England, with the English ultimately winning out for control of the two tiny islands. The island pair gained their independence from the UK in 1983, and now enjoyed federation status as a constitutional monarchy with a Westminster-style parliament. Basseterre is the little federation's capital and hub of most of the commercial activity. The two islands enjoy the same government and the same porous banking regulations, but Nevis has earned a singular reputation for financial flexibility. Depending upon which side of a given nation's tax code you happen to be on, it was a haven or cesspool for financial dealings. A lot of dirty money gets laundered on Nevis. For decades, both St. Kitts and Nevis had been way points for drugs coming up from South America to the United States and Europe. Those who value their banking relations, especially those with ties to Nevis, recently asked the cartels if they would not use the islands for drug transshipments. The drug cartels, who take direction from no one but who also understand the value of pliable banking relationships, were most accommodating. They rerouted their product through other islands.

Garrett was interested in the money-laundering activities on Nevis, but it had nothing to do with drugs or tax sheltering. Funds from wealthy Saudi and questionable Arab charities had been finding their way to and through banks in Nevis with some frequency. Garret, AKR, and the people they worked for did care about these dollars; they cared about them a great deal. Garrett would have normally handled this matter with Klein himself, but at the last minute, he had decided to put it in AKR's hands. Kelly-Rogers's military résumé was extensive, and during their field training over the past several months, Garrett had come to respect his military and paramilitary skills. But this assignment was different; this was not quite the normal military situation. It called for a different use of force—different from that which Garrett and AKR learned in the service of their countries.

For the past three months, Garrett Walker, aka Thomas Lyle, operating under the nominal cover of the Smithson Trading Company, Ltd., had been moving multimillion-dollar chunks of money through Klein's institution, the Leeward Bank. The transactions gave every indication of laundering activity, but a few quasi-legal concerns, such as offshore hedge funds, do move money in this fashion.

Smithson Trading had willingly paid the transfer fees a.
internal surcharges without question, making Smithson a
valued client. Klein's bank asked very few questions but
did require the name of a principal. Smithson, with of-
fices in the Caymans and Zurich, had listed one Thomas
Lyle as its chief operating officer. When Mr. Lyle sent
word that he would be calling at St. Kitts and Nevis on a
yachting vacation and would like to meet with Leeward's
managing partner, Mr. Klein was eager to accept. Martin
Klein and his anonymous partners catered to the likes of
the Smithson Trading Company, Ltd. Both Klein and Garrett had done their homework. Klein knew that Smithson
had relationships with other shady banks, and had the
ability to expand further on their business relationship. In
reality, Guardian Services International operated Smithson and several other shell companies to launder money
for no other purpose than to give the appearance that
these companies had lots of money to launder. GSI, with
its extensive intelligence liaisons, knew that Klein was
German by birth but had grown up in Paris. He had
moved to the French Antilles some twenty years ago.
There he was indicted for bank fraud, but the charges
were dropped for lack of evidence. From Basse-Terre on
Guadeloupe, he moved on to Nevis and a more accommodating financial environment. GSI's sources also revealed that Martin Klein was personally in debt, had been
skimming from his partners for years, and had a fondness
for young boys. GSI had provided Garrett with a complete
file on Mr. Klein's activities.

AKR had gone to Nevis several weeks ago to meet with
Klein to set up this meeting. He had given Klein every reason to think he was nothing but a gofer—a kind of personal aide to Mr. Lyle, and perhaps someone who doubled
as a bodyguard. Garrett lit a cigar, a Romeo & Juliette
Churchill, but he did not offer one to Klein. They talked

a while, about the hot spots in the islands
the action was on St. Kitts. Then Garrett
.KR.

y, why don't you get another rum tonic for our
guest, d while you're at it, feel free to mix one for yourself."

"Yes, Mr. Lyle. Right away, to be sure, mon."

He played the sycophant role so perfectly that, had
Garrett not been so intent on holding Klein in a condescending gaze, he would have broken out laughing. But as
Garrett held Klein with his eyes, he could not help but
think what a slimeball this guy was. What they were about
to do would not be pretty, but it was necessary.

"Lovely yacht," Klein said looking around at the teak
deck and tasteful appointment. "Do you have a captain or
crew aboard?"

"They are ashore. I thought it best if we could speak
privately this evening."

"Excellent," he replied, brightening at the prospect of
talking business. He took the drink proffered by AKR with
something of a dismissive gesture. "On behalf of the Leeward Bank," he began, "let me say it is a privilege to be of
service to your organization." He lifted the glass in a toast.
"We hope that this is only the beginning of a long and satisfactory relationship."

Garrett tapped the ash from his cigar and regarded the
Frenchman coldly. "Mr. Klein, we too look for a permanent and productive relationship, but our dealings may
run along different lines than you might have anticipated.
We will continue to do business as in the past, but we require some additional services from you personally." Klein
was now dripping with anticipation. "John, why don't you
lay out the special requirements we have for our friend
Martin here."

Kelly-Rogers pulled a chair close to Klein and carefully

seated himself in front of him. He regarded Klein thoughtfully, as a physician might a patient to whom he must give
some distressing news about his health. AKR's demeanor
and body language had taken on a whole different context;
there was now an air of authority and transcendence about
him. Johnny was gone. John, the man who had taken his
place, was both commanding and formidable. This transformation was not lost on Klein; it made the hair on the
back of his neck bristle. A feeling that something was
wrong—terribly wrong—settled over him. Garrett rose,
walked to the railing, and stood looking out to sea with his
back to them.

"What my associate Thomas has told you is quite correct," AKR began in a precise, educated British accent. The
singsong island slang was gone. "We will, for your benefit,
as well as for appearance's sake, continue to move funds
through your bank. But there is more. You will now respond to certain requests we may have from time to time
about other clients who do business with Leeward." Klein
started to protest, but AKR placed a firm hand on his arm
in a gesture of patience. "You see, we are not what you
thought us to be. We are, for want of a better term, a reporting organization. We gather information and provide
that information to our clients. Let me give you an example. We will provide you with a name or list of names
which represent single individuals or organizations that
use Leeward for banking services. If possible, we will even
give you the names of other banks where they also do
business. Your job is simply to provide us the information
and passwords you use at Leeward in your dealings with
these individuals." Klein would have been out of his chair
by now had it not been for the viselike grip that now held
him in place. "And, so you more fully understand us and
our new relationship, we are just as ruthless as we are well
financed. Now, this is what you will—"

"Who are you?" Klein exploded. "Who do you work for?" He was sweating profusely now, but managing to control himself. "The Mafia? MI-5? The CIA? The drug cartels? It does not matter; what you ask for will do you no good. It will gain you nothing. The internal passwords and coding we use for our banking activity do not control the account; they are only for internal processing. The passwords for our private numbered accounts that allow for the access and transfer of funds are known only to our clients. I do not know or even have access to your password, the one with which you use to control your own account. You control your account, not me." A look of frightened condescension passed over his face. "You see, your threats are meaningless. Even if I were to do what you say, it will gain you nothing."

AKR gave him a tired, patient look and rose to his feet. He gave every appearance of resignation and indecision. Klein now had a look of triumph on his face. He had started to speak when AKR slapped him with an open hand, one that stunned more than hurt the banker. But the vicious backhand that followed had much more authority. AKR leaned on an arm of his victim's chair with one hand and grasped Klein's jaw with the other, pinching his cheeks so his lips gathered in a quiver and groped for air like a freshly caught bass. Garrett had now turned to watch.

"You arrogant piece of shit! You think we don't know that? I ought to kill you right here and now. Nothing would give me more pleasure." Garrett cleared his throat as he regarded his cigar, and Kelly-Rogers seemed to take hold of himself. "Let me continue," AKR went on softly, switching to French, "and I want there to be no misunderstanding on this, so listen carefully. You will do exactly as you are told. If you do not, there will be serious consequences. We know of your homosexual activity. We know and can document, thanks to a cooperative Cayman banker, your personal financial difficulties. And your partners at Leeward may not be too understanding about the liberties you've taken with their money. On top of that, I will personally be very unhappy with you." He released Klein, and a six-inch boning knife seemed to materialize in his hand where a fraction of a second earlier, there was nothing. "You see, I will return to this miserable little island, or wherever you are, and I will find you. And when I do, I will use this on you."

The knife flashed, and a nick appeared in Klein's chin. It was no more than a cut that might have come from mishandling a safety razor. AKR ran the flat part of the blade across the cut and brought the bloodied knife up before Klein's eyes. Klein sat frozen, his eyes now wide with terror. AKR pulled his chair around so he could look more directly at the banker. He laid the knife on the table, and taking a clean handkerchief, he dipped it into Klein's drink and dabbed at the wound. The Frenchman was frozen, afraid to move, so AKR took Klein's hand and brought it to his face to hold the makeshift dressing in place. AKR sat back and cooly regarded the man over steepled fingers, a cruel smile fixed on the terrorized banker. Among the stench of sweat and fear was the sour, pungent smell of urine. Klein had soiled himself.

All the while, Garrett watched AKR. He felt he knew this man well, but this was the first time they had been on the job. This was the first time when it counted. AKR's military experience was not unlike Garrett's: both had seen combat; both had been wounded in action; and both had taken life. But that had been in uniform. Nothing in Kelly-Rogers's background gave any indication that he had done something like this before. This was terrorizing, not soldiering. The British SAS was a very capable unit, but this activity was more in keeping with an intelligence special operations unit. So far it had been a compelling performance. But was it a performance? Clearly Klein felt he was now in the hands of someone who could kill for personal pleasure. The intensity of AKR's actions alarmed Garrett. He had known several men, men with families who attended church regularly and who doted on their children who, when their blood was up, could become quite sadistic. Perhaps, Garrett thought as he watched the drama play out before him, there is some evil gene in all of us that, under certain conditions, overrules all humane consideration—something akin to a well-fed cat who will torture a mouse to death. GSI had no place, at least no place at this level, for anyone who genuinely enjoyed this sort of thing.

"Next week," AKR continued in French, "a technician will show up at your office with a replacement monitor for your computer." French wasn't Garrett's best language, but he could follow along. "He will make the installation and remove your existing computer monitor. It will function in all aspects like your normal monitor, but it will allow us an interactive link to your account base." Suddenly AKR's hand shot out like a snake's tongue and lashed Klein across the face. It was not a hard blow, but quick and vicious. "Are you listening to me?" AKR growled. "Are you?" Klein nodded numbly. "You will touch nothing after the technician makes the installation. From time to time, a man, who will refer to himself as Mr. Lenze, will call you with a request for certain information. You will give him what he asks for, do you understand?" Klein again nodded, but again, the hand shot out and Klein's head snapped back. There was now a trickle of blood seeping from one of his nostrils.

"Answer me!"

"Yes," Klein managed in a barely audible voice. "Yes, I understand."

AKR rose and towered over him. He genuinely seemed to be on the verge of losing control of himself. Klein cowered involuntarily, bringing his hands to his face.

"Do exactly as you have been told. Don't give me a reason to come back here. If I do have to come back, I will kill you very slowly. Do you understand me?"

"Y-yes," Klein croaked, now nodding his head vigorously.

AKR gave Garrett a look of disgust. "Get him out of my sight," he snarled, and with that he turned and walked to the rail near Garrett and looked out to sea.

Garrett helped Klein into the RHIB and took him ashore. He watched him closely on the trip in to the city dock. The man was clearly in shock. Occasionally he would glance at Garrett with a pleading look, but Garrett was careful to remain neutral.

"You must do as he says, you know," Garrett said once they were on the dock, easing into the good-cop role. "I'll do what I can to see that you are not compromised, and our firm will continue to move funds through your bank. Past that, it is out of my hands. If you do not do as you have been instructed, he will come back, and he will do exactly as he said he would do."

"Yes, but can't you—"

Garrett held up a hand to cut him off. "I can do nothing," he said coldly, "and neither can you. You cannot run and you cannot hide. Your only option is to do exactly as instructed." He then gave Klein a conspiratorial look and lowered his voice. "You must understand, he will look for any excuse to come back and carry out his threat. You must follow his instructions, or I can assure you that he will come for you. For God's sake, Klein, do as he says or you're a dead man!"

Garrett deposited Klein into a cab and gave the driver a fifty-dollar bill. He walked slowly to the dock without once looking back. When he climbed aboard the yacht and mounted the stern deck, he found AKR still by the rail, looking out to sea. They stood together silently for a moment before Garrett spoke.

"I don't know about you, but I could use a drink." He glanced at AKR. On his perpetually cheerful features was a look of sadness, one almost bordering on anguish. Garrett quietly went to the bar and poured them each a generous measure of scotch. He took the stairs up to the fly bridge and set the drinks on the cocktail table behind the control station. The sun was just above the horizon, and the wisps of high cirrus clouds strewn across the sky promised a spectacular sunset. AKR joined him a few moments later, looking a little more like himself. Garrett raised his glass.

"To soldiering."

AKR forced a smile and nodded. "To soldiering." They drank in silence for some time, watching the colors splash across the evening sky. AKR turned to Garrett, "What time does that plane leave tomorrow?"

"Zero eight thirty."

AKR again nodded. He set the half-finished drink down and rose. "I think I'll go take a long shower. See you in the morning."

Garrett Walker and Akheem Kelly-Rogers, traveling under false documentation, flew from Newcastle Airport on Nevis to San Juan. They called the yacht brokerage and said the Ragtime was having engine trouble, and they were done with the charter. The brokerage company was only too happy to send a charter captain and mechanic to Nevis to retrieve the boat and pocket the $20,000 deposit—no questions asked. Two days later, Garrett and AKR were back at the GSI training facility on the island of Hawaii.

For Garrett, flying into the Kona airport and making the drive up to the camp was like coming home—at least his operational home. He had been a warrior for well over twenty years. For most of that time he had been in uniform, the uniform of a Navy SEAL. Then home had been a Navy base, either Coronado, California, or Little Creek, Virginia. But home for a warrior, if he was a bachelor like Garrett, was usually a one-room apartment with very few personal belongings. The training and operational requirements of a Navy SEAL made for a lot of time overseas, and when you were not deployed and technically home, you spent a great deal of your time away from the house. In as much as Garrett could now call any place home, this facility on the side of Mona Kea was it. Given the dramatic isolation and quiet beauty of the camp, it was quite satisfactory.

Steven Fagan, GSI's chief executive officer, was going over Garrett's report when Garrett stepped into his office. Garrett had sent him the report from his Blackberry wireless handheld while they waited for connections in Miami.

"It appears as if you and Akheem had a successful trip."

"We'll know after the tech's visit, but I don't foresee any problems." Garrett poured himself a cup of coffee from the pot that was perpetually brewing on the credenza. He sipped it carefully and made a face. It was a dark Kona blend and a little strong for his taste. He took a seat across from Fagan.

"Did you want Akheem in on this?"

"I don't think it will be necessary," Fagan replied. "I know he was anxious to get back to his men and see how their training is progressing."

Steven Fagan was a quiet, understated man. He was about five-nine and a solid hundred sixty-five pounds, with good shoulders and thinning, wiry brown hair that still had something of a wave to it. It would be a slow process, but in the ten years it would take him to reach his early sixties, he would have more scalp than hair showing on top of his head. Yet on the sides and in back it would be as thick and rich as it was when he was in his twenties. He had soft hazel eyes and regular features. At first brush, one might peg him as an accountant or an insurance broker, or some nameless fellow you might sit next to in church. On closer inspection, there was a great deal more. People who met him briefly, even in a casual, social setting, came away from the encounter knowing there was something special about him, but if pressed to explain, could never say why. There was a quiet intensity about him, and he had an almost unconscious ability to get others to talk about themselves. But this was not uncommon for someone who had spent a career at Langley with his job description. At one time, Steven Fagan was considered one of the CIA's most talented covert action specialists. He had concluded an exceptional career at the Agency. During his tenure with the Directorate for Operations he had orchestrated more than a few events in sovereign foreign nations that were favorable to American interests but had no fingerprints of American involvement. His current job at GSI drew heavily on that background.

"And the boat was satisfactory?"

"It was a little cramped, and I think AKR resented the fact that I took the owner's stateroom, but we managed. After all, I have seniority."

"How did he like playing the bad cop?"

Steven leaned forward imperceptibly, watching Garrett closely. It was an important question, and both of them knew it. Steven was asking a great deal more than whether or not Kelly-Rogers was happy with his new job. Could their new man do this kind of work because it had to be done, professionally and dispassionately, or were there other motivations?

"He's every bit as good as you thought he might be, maybe better. He's a good gun in the file."

Both Steven and Garrett were former military special operations types—Steven had a tour with Special Forces before joining the Agency. A man who was a good gun was someone you trusted and with whom you were willing to go into harm's way. Steven considered this a long moment before he spoke.

"That's good to hear. We can use him, perhaps sooner than you think. I got a cryptic e-mail from Mr. Grummell yesterday afternoon." Armand Grummell was the current Director of Central Intelligence. The DCI was one of the few people in government who knew the purpose and some of the inner workings of Guardian Services International and IFOR. "He thinks he may have a problem and would like our FBI liaison officer to read us into the situation."

"Iraq? The Middle East?"

"I'm not sure. I sense it may begin there, but again, he was very vague. I think one of his key analysts has surfaced a number of indicators that may have triggered some concern." Steven paused, as he often did, before he continued. "He asked if we were capable of operating in Africa, but didn't elaborate. One thing is certain. He wouldn't be contacting us if he wasn't worried about something, perhaps very worried."

"Or there was no one else he could turn to," Garrett observed.

"That too." Steven smiled.

"When do you want me to leave?"

"The plane is ready when you are. If you leave sometime late this afternoon, you could be there for a breakfast meeting. That is, if you're up to it," he added.

"Oh, I think I can manage it, boss."

"Give my regards to our liaison officer."

"I'll do that." They shook hands warmly, and Garrett took his leave. He set his full cup of coffee on the sideboard as he headed for the door. No matter how good it smelled, it always tasted much too harsh.

Later that afternoon he relaxed on the gray tucked-leather lounger and tapped his code into the computer that swung into place at his elbow. He brought up the front page of the *Washington Post* and began to scan for items of interest.

"What could I start you with, Mr. Walker?"

He glanced at her name tag. "Cindy, how about a scotch, neat, with a twist."

"And something to eat?"

"What do you have?"

"Well, we have caviar or truffle pâté, with French bread or toast points."

Garrett smiled easily. "I think the day calls for caviar, but would you see if you can dig me up some Ritz crackers."

She smiled and headed back to the galley area. Garrett glanced out of the large oval window to a cloud-dotted Pacific Ocean below. The extended-range Gulfstream G550 had climbed quickly to 48,000 feet. Fuel economy was not an issue with an aircraft with this much legs. Hawaii to Washington, D.C., was an easy nonstop flight for a G550. They were well above normal commercial airline traffic, and the ride was so smooth that it seemed they were suspended in space. The two Rolls-Royce BR710 engines barely filled the luxurious interior with a gentle whisper, even as they raced along at a cruising speed of .87 mach.

"Luxury yachts, my own Gulfstream, and caviar," Garrett mused. "Helluva way to fight a war."

"I'm sorry, did you say something?" the attendant said as she set the drink on the arm of the lounger—an amber liquid in leaded crystal.

"I was just saying," he said as he swung the computer away from his lap, "that I'll bet I can kick your butt in cribbage."

She looked at him for a long moment, then turned and strode back to the galley. He watched her go, admiring the swing of her hips. It was, in fact, a terrific tush—worth far more than an indiscriminate kicking. She came back with a cribbage board, a deck of cards, and a plate of caviar ringed with Ritz crackers. There were only four on the plane—the two of them and the two pilots up front.

She sat across the table arm from him and began to shuffle the cards.

"What shall we play for?" she asked. She was drop-dead gorgeous; he almost said, "Sexual favors," but this was not where he was right now.

"Looser flies," he responded with a grin.

"All right, but it's only a soda for me. FAA rules."

He thought he detected a hint of disappointment in her voice.

2

STORM WARNINGS

The Gulfstream received immediate clearance to land at Andrews Air Force Base just outside Washington. The pilot was a little surprised at the approach vectors. Normally he was routed around the metropolitan area in a complex, low-level landing pattern, wasting time and thousands of pounds of fuel. Not this time. The Andrews controller brought him straight in with only one turn that put him on final. Once on the ground, he was directed to a patch of hardstand where a Lincoln town car was waiting. That made sense—a single passenger and a single car on arrival. While the attendant dropped the boarding ladder, Garrett stuck his head inside the cockpit.

"Great flight. Thanks for the lift, guys."

"You're welcome, sir," the pilot replied. "Have a nice stay in the D.C. area."

"I'll do my best," Garrett replied.

"What else do you do besides take advantage of young women at cards?" the attendant asked, stepping aside to allow him access to the aircraft exit door.

Garrett leaned close and in a low voice said, "Can't tell you, Cindy. If I tell you, I'll have to kill you." He winked, then added, "Thanks for the company."

They had been just over nine hours in the air. Garrett had napped, ate, drank, and thoroughly trounced Cindy at cribbage. He felt surprisingly refreshed. They had departed Hawaiian airspace at 5:00 P.M. and raced to meet the sun, landing at Andrews just before 8:00 A.M. Prior to landing, he had retired to the aircraft's well-appointed lavatory to get a shave and change—same blue jeans but a different aloha shirt. He carried only a small grip that held his dopp kit, slacks, a dress shirt, and a change of underclothes. Garrett wore a faded, wheat-colored corduroy sport jacket over the printed shirt and a pair of scuffed saddle oxfords.

Garrett Walker, Cindy pleasantly noted, looked a great deal like the actor Tom Selleck. Only he had green eyes, his hair was lighter, and at six-one, he was smaller than the six-foot-five Selleck. She also noticed that Garrett moved with the easy grace of an athlete. His wide shoulders and hands seemed outsize for his frame, and they were hands like those of a workingman. He had an even, easy smile that delivered crows' feet to the corners of his eyes. Garrett was a smooth article and could have been taken for a CEO of a major corporation. The intensity and charm were there, but something about his persona suggested he was someone who fought battles, but not in the boardroom and not for market share.

A damp breeze was blowing with the temperature in the low forties as Garrett stepped from the aircraft. He felt the chill, but temperature variations had little effect on him. He descended the boarding stairway and headed for the idling town car, a black sedan with smoke-tinted windows, and sprouting several small antennas. No one appeared from the interior to greet him. He opened the rear door and tossed his bag onto the floor of the rear compartment.

"Mata Hari, I presume," he said as he eased himself onto the pleated leather upholstery.

"The first thing you need to do," she replied coolly, "is burn that shirt. Well, maybe not the first thing." She then grabbed him and kissed him hard on the mouth.

The Gulfstream retrieved its stair-door and taxied back out toward the main runway. The only marking on the all-white aircraft was "GSI" blocked in black letters onto the tail. Immediately cleared for takeoff, it lifted neatly into the air.

"Do we have any idea who that guy was?" the copilot probed his fellow pilot. Their instructions were to drop him at Andrews, make the short jump up to Baltimore-Washington International, refuel, and wait. They were to stand by in a comfortable motel near BWI until Mr. Walker had completed his business, then take him back to Hawaii. A lot of Fortune 500 companies couldn't afford that much airplane for that period of time for a single executive. Guardian Services International was not a Fortune 500 company, nor was it listed on any stock exchange. In fact, it had been in business for only three years. The company was wholly owned by a philanthropist named Joseph Simpson. A number of entities operated under the umbrella and cover; Steven Fagan and his IFOR were just one such organization. The Gulfstream that had brought Garrett from Hawaii to Washington was only one of several belonging to GSI.

The pilot shrugged as he swung the plane onto his departure vector from Andrews. "Hey, we just pick up the packages and deliver them. GSI does a lot of business with the Department of Homeland Security. Maybe they have a big contract that needs to be worked out."

"You think that guy is here to negotiate a contract? He doesn't look like some corporate mouthpiece to me. Gotta be something else."

"Yeah, well whatever it is, it doesn't concern us. And if you keep asking questions, you'll be flying boxes for FedEx at a fraction of what you're making now."

The town car with Garrett and Judy was caught up in Beltway traffic, but the driver made skillful work of it.

They crossed the Woodrow Wilson Bridge to Old Town Alexandria and looped around to pick up the George Washington Parkway into the city. It was stop-and-go in Old Town.

"How about a bagel?"

"Love one," Garrett replied.

She said something to the driver, and he maneuvered to the right-hand lane and took a side street. After a few turns and dashes down narrow brick and cobbled streets, they pulled up in front of a storefront with no name. She led him inside, and they found a table along the wall. It was small, crowded, and smelled of yeast.

"You wait here," she ordered and dove into the queue at the counter. In an amazingly short period of time, she returned with two steaming mugs of coffee. His bagel came just as he liked it—sesame seed, toasted, with no topping. Hers was nuts and raisins, covered with a thick icing of cream cheese. She deftly managed the order like a waitress at a short-order house. Once seated, she raised her mug to him.

"Well, sailor. Welcome to the capital of the free world."

Judy Burks, as Garrett often mused, was a piece of work. She was not a tall woman, perhaps five-five in heels, but she exhibited a much taller presence. At thirty-something, she still had the wide-eyed enthusiasm of an undergraduate. She was pretty, not beautiful, with unremarkable, regular features, auburn hair, and a mouth that was just a little too big for her face. But her eyes were anything but ordinary; they were two dark pools of intensity. She ate like a longshoreman, but her figure was trim to the point of petite. Garrett worshiped at the altar of hard physical training and kept himself in top shape. Judy Burks, however, would not walk a block if there was a taxi stand nearby, but she gave every appearance of fitness and good health. She was, in fact, an accomplished tennis player and an excellent swimmer. They had become, according to Judy's term for it, an item, or as much of an item as their work allowed. Garrett often wondered why he was attracted to this spring-loaded wisp of a girl. But he had come to see that she was a lady with heart and spirit. Perhaps, he admitted to himself as he touched her mug with his own, he simply found her intriguing. Garrett never knew what she was going to do next. He had met her shortly before he joined GSI and IFOR, while she was on special assignment with the Bureau. Their paths had crossed under unusual circumstances—but then Judy Burks seemed drawn to circumstances that were unusual.

"So," he said in a low voice, "what's going on? A plot to kidnap the president? A secret terrorist cell in Congress? Or maybe a mole on the Supreme Court?"

"Could be any one of the three," she replied. "Or, maybe, I just wanted you back here so I could have my way with you."

Garrett considered this. "That works for me, but no concerts." The last time he was in the capital she had dragged him to the Kennedy Center for an opera. "Unless, of course, Willie Nelson is in town. Seriously, Judy"—again his voice dropped a notch—"what's going on? Steven seemed to think that there were some people in this town who are more than a little concerned about something. He used the word *scared*."

Judy Burks was an FBI agent whose current assignment was liaison officer for Guardian Services International. GSI was a worldwide provider of physical and consulting security services. GSI did many things. They provided counterterrorist training for commercial interests doing business overseas and to government agencies, including the FBI Training Academy in Quantico, Virginia. They had a reputation for being expensive and very competent. But Judy Burks's liaison assignment had nothing to do with GSI's training or consulting services. The Bureau nominally, and she personally, was the link between the U.S. government and the GSI subsidiary known as the Intervention Force. IFOR was buried deep within the GSI corporate structure, and for all but a select few in GSI and the government, it did not exist. The facility on Hawaii was simply a site where GSI trained bodyguards and security personnel. IFOR had been created in total secrecy. It was to be a response element for those situations that called for something stronger than a diplomatic protest and less visible than a special operations forces response. It was a force that operated without a portfolio or federal funding, and with complete U.S. government deniability.

Judy turned it over in her mind, hesitating just how to tell Garrett about why he had been summoned back to Washington. Had it been of more immediate concern to the national interest, someone far more senior to her would have met Garrett or his immediate superior, Steven Fagan. In the current lexicon, this one was in the "grave and gathering" category, rather than the "clear and present danger" one.

"Uncle Armand find some more loose nukes laying about?" he prompted. He was referring to Armand Grummell, the entrenched and unflappable Director of Central Intelligence.

"It's nothing like that, or at least, it doesn't appear to be. This one is more like a favor based on a hunch."

"Say what?" Garrett asked, lifting his eyebrows. A look of irritation passed over his handsome features.

"Now, take it easy. Your boss wouldn't have sent you here if there wasn't potentially a good reason."

Garrett rolled his eyes. "You know, we're not some global relief program or a cultural exchange. We deal with nasty people, and we do bad things to them. We move on hard intelligence, not hunches."

"Hey, don't blame me; I'm a liaison officer—a messenger. And if it makes you feel any better, this did come through the Director of Central Intelligence, okay? Well, from the DCI to the Bureau and then finally to me." She was feeling a little wounded. She knew that she herself would have taken just about any frivolous excuse to see him, but he was not that way. "Now, if you'll settle down, I'll tell you about it. You eat, and I'll talk."

Garrett reluctantly took up his bagel and leaned back in his chair to listen.

"Of course, I've only been told what I need to know, but as I understand it, there are some unexplained events taking place in Zimbabwe. We have no national interests there, just humanitarian concerns, but there could be something brewing that could develop into a security issue. At least, that's what the folks out at Langley seem to think. I assume you've read up on southern African geography and postcolonial politics?"

"Why, certainly, but how about you bringing me up-to-date? Uh, the executive summary will be just fine."

"Sure, no problem," she replied, warming to the subject. "When the colonial powers left Africa, Marxism and tribalism returned with a vengeance—usually one followed the other because the Soviets provided arms and advisers to any tribal thug who said he was a Communist. That's what happened in Zimbabwe. Zimbabwe was a British colony, then called Rhodesia. It was stable, productive, and racially segregated—not especially nice, but a functioning colony. Zimbabwe became independent in 1980. After a sham of an election, Robert Mugabe came to power; Rhodesia-Zimbabwe became Zimbabwe, and Salisbury became Harare. Mugabe, the then and current president, proceeded to mismanage the country on a grand scale. He and his cronies have run the nation into the ground, looted the treasury, and wired fortunes in cash to Zurich. To stay in power, Mugabe distributed all the land held by the white farmers, essentially driving them from the country. The rural provinces are now mostly run by tribal warlords, and the nation is a basket case. The country now has the highest incidence of disease and AIDS on the continent. The new African nations have had their share of despots, but few are in Robert Mugabe's league when it comes to lining his pockets. There's genocide, perhaps not on Rwandan scale, but he's killing his own citizens. He's firmly in control of the capital, but his influence really doesn't extend much past the city limits of Harare." She took a breath and another bite of her half-eaten bagel. "The country used to be the breadbasket of southern Africa. But now people are starving. The international community and any number of NGOs have tried to help, but it just isn't working. Zimbabwe is the classic failed African state. In late 2003, the British Commonwealth voted to expel Zimbabwe based on human rights abuses. It takes a lot to get kicked out of the Commonwealth, but Mugabe managed it."

"So," Garrett replied, "and I don't mean to sound insensitive, but there are some situations, particularly in Africa, that simply defy outside help. They're not candidates for intervention on any scale. When the European powers left, they took with them what they brought, the notion of a nation-state. In their absence, the tribal entities take over. The former colonies became sewers of corruption and lawlessness. There's really no way to bring relief to the suffering without military occupation. And we are not in the business of occupying African nations, especially after our misadventure in Somalia. Even the French have pretty much given up on massive military intervention."

"How about the UN?" she replied. "You'd think they could do something there."

"Right, send in the powder-blue berets. There are more

than a few African nations who are willing to offer their troops for UN duty. You know why? The UN pays their salaries, and the troops get to do a little quiet looting in the nations where they're sent to keep the peace. When they're not looting outright, they set up protection rackets on the side, extorting the people they were sent to protect. Even worse, they spread AIDS. And if there is a serious confrontation with the rebels, they break and run."

Judy Burks was silent a moment before she spoke. "So what's the solution?"

"Mercenaries."

"Mercenaries?"

"Yep. It's a brutal solution to a nasty problem, but whenever mercenaries have been sent in, peace and order are quickly restored."

"But what do they do that the UN or American troops don't do?"

"Three things, or three things in Africa," Garrett replied. "Mercenaries will take sides, take casualties, and fire preemptively."

"Fire preemptively?"

"That means that they will shoot first. Mercenaries will move into an area and say, for example, that there can be no one on the streets from sundown to sunrise. Anyone violating this curfew will be shot. Then when someone appears out after dark, they shoot him or her—no verbal challenge, no get your hands up, no nothing. Bang, dead. Any local who has a weapon is shot. Anyone who opposes them or interferes with their patrols or house searches is shot. The first few days, they shoot a few people. Then everything gets quiet. Any rebels in the area leave for the bush, and rebels don't do too well in the bush; they need communities to terrorize. In the long run mercenary intervention saves lives and restores order. It's not pretty, but it's effective. In Africa, it's the only proven solution."

Garrett watched as she took on a familiar semi-pout, something she did often when she questioned him and he gave her information she did not like.

"Well, then, why don't we just do what the mercenaries do; why don't we take sides and shoot first?"

He gave her a patient smile. "For the same reason the police don't go out into the hood and shoot guys they know are up to no good. It's not how we do business. Y'see, Judy," he said turning serious, "in the past we have ridden down the Plains Indians and massacred their villages, we have lynched Negroes, and we have put Japanese Americans in concentration camps. These are shameful incidents in our history; as a white-dominated culture, we have to carry a lot of guilt about those events. In some parts of Africa, brutality still rules. Tribalism is just another form of racism. This nation has had its share of that. We can't deal with it, and since we can't, we have no business going there. The kind of counter-brutality required to restore order in some of these places is simply beyond our reach. And the last thing I want is for some of our soldiers, even our special operations troops, to be put in that kind of a situation. It's bad enough in Afghanistan and Iraq. We have no national interest in Africa, and really no effective way to project force in that environment." He tilted his head, watching her closely. "Say, what's this all about, anyway?"

"You about done with that bagel?" Judy said as she rose from the table.

So it's going to be like this, he thought. He blotted his mouth with a napkin and tossed it on the table. "Lead on, madam liaison officer."

They drove into the District in diplomatic silence. Garrett had long ago learned not to try to pry information from Judy when she wasn't ready to volunteer it. And she probably hadn't been told all that much. A few things he did know for certain. As a liaison officer she would have some information, but not the whole picture, and certainly nothing of strategic or tactical value, at least not at this stage of the game. In all probability, only the wily Director of Central Intelligence, Armand Grummell, had a complete grasp of the situation, or at least as much as there was to know at the time. And Garrett knew he would not have been summoned to Washington if it were a matter that the Central Intelligence Agency or the U.S. military could handle. That most likely meant a difficult situation and one that had the potential to become critical. Since 9/11, the Special Activities Division at CIA had grown in capability and reach. They and the American special operations forces were able to handle a broad range of contingencies. *So why have I been brought into this? Is IFOR being considered for a tasking in Africa? Armand Grummell does not scare easily, and the Agency would not reach out to IFOR unless they were very worried.* Garrett concluded that there was little to be gained by speculation. In due course, all would be revealed to him, or as with Judy Burks, as much as he needed to know. As they drove across the Key Bridge and into the congestion of Georgetown, he settled back to enjoy the sights. Again, he was reminded of what a wonderful city this was to visit, and what a terrible place it must be to have to live and work.

The brownstone row house was a few blocks off Dupont Circle in a fashionable neighborhood of upscale residences and discreet businesses. They piled out of the town car, and Judy sent the driver off to hover; parking was out of the question. The brass plate to the right of the door read "Outreach Africa." Judy led them up the stone steps and gave the door buzzer a long, insistent ring.

"This is a do-gooder organization," Garrett said impatiently. "What the hell am I doing here?"

"Behave yourself," she said as she again stabbed the buzzer.

"Yes, can I help you," a haughty, clipped voice asked over the intercom.

"You certainly can. Judy Burks here to see Graham Burkett."

"One moment, please, and I'll see if he's available."

Garrett watched as Judy made a conscious effort to calm herself. He knew that if they were made to wait more than a couple of minutes, she'd have her shield out and attempt to kick in the door. Garrett was warming to the prospect when the heavy paneled door swung open. "Please come in," the same intercom voice commanded. The foyer was dated, intricate, and very well manicured. The woodwork was exquisite. You could reach a lot of Africans, Garrett mused, for what it cost for this renovation.

"If you'll have a seat, Mr. Burkett will be with you in a moment." She was fifty-something, styleless, and carried herself with a cool, aloof condescension. "Now, if you will excuse me, I have to return to my duties."

"Thanks," Judy remarked to the woman's retreating back as she disappeared into another room, "but we just had coffee."

Garrett grinned. "How does she know I'm not some well-heeled donor?"

"She knows. She can smell wealth, and you flunked the test."

They were admiring the soft colors of an African landscape when a side door opened.

"Oh, hullo. You must be Agent Burks and Mr. Walker. Thank you so much for stopping by. Won't you come in?"

Graham Burkett was probably in his late thirties, but racing headlong into his fifties. He had drab thinning hair, a sparse mustache, sloping shoulders, and the soft pear-shaped contour of someone who had gone sedentary many years ago. He wore a red knit tie loosely cinched around a button-down collar he had neglected to button down. The shirt bloused over his belt, meeting up with a pair of dark green corduroys. But the carelessness seemed to end with his physical appearance. After greeting Judy courteously, he gripped Garrett's hand firmly and held his gaze with sharp, intelligent brown eyes. He might have the appearance of a sloppy academic, Garrett inferred, but there was something more to this guy than met the eye. Burkett led them into a richly appointed office and motioned them to two leather wingbacks.

"Coffee? Tea?"

"None for me, thanks," Judy replied. Garrett smiled and shook his head.

Burkett pulled a brocaded armchair from along the wall and joined them around a low coffee table that was made of a crude hammered metal, obviously African. He was clearly a man who didn't like to talk to people from behind a desk.

"Zulu," he commented noticing their interest, "late nineteenth century. Oh, and my apologies for any rudeness you may have experienced by way of our Florence." He lowered his voice. "She's the spinster sister of one of our wealthy donors and came with a rather substantial endowment. We call her the gift that keeps on giving— kind of our own personal mother superior."

"But can she type?" Garrett offered.

"She can't do a damn thing," Burkett said, "but then the gift really was quite substantial. You're probably wondering why you were asked to come here, am I right?" Both Garrett and Judy nodded. "Well, to be quite honest, it has to do with my mother."

"Your mother?"

"That's right, Miss Burks, my dear mom. You see, she is a senior analyst at the CIA and, from what I gather, is quite well thought of in the Operations Directorate. A week ago last Sunday I was at her home in Chevy Chase for dinner. It's a second-Sunday-of-the-month thing. It used to be Saturday, but it seems that she's working most Saturdays these days. These are busy times at CIA, and she's very dedicated to her work. But since she can't talk about her work, we usually end up talking about mine—that, and why I'm still single. To get past the issue of my inability to find a wife, I told her about a recent concern we have about a region in Africa. This area seems to be experiencing some unusual travel restrictions that affect our work there, and we've encountered some puzzling medical problems. She questioned me pretty thoroughly, as only a mother and a CIA analyst can. A few days later she said this may be of concern to others as well, and then told me to expect the two of you." He smiled, a twinkle in his eye. "Given my mother's employer, I'll not ask who you are or why you need to know about this.

"Briefly, Outreach Africa is a nongovernmental organization that focuses on disease and the prevention of disease in Africa. We support and staff fifteen regional hospitals, and have one of the leading education and vaccination programs on the continent. So we're not in the intelligence-gathering business, but we do get very close to these people; their problems are our problems. It's a very challenging business, but we've had our share of success, and to be candid, not a few failures. We do what we can with the resources we have." He moved his hands in a helpless gesture. "What can I say? It's Africa. We're used to dealing with adversity, but we've had a little more than our share lately. You might even say, quite a bit more, and all of that is in northern Zimbabwe. Some strange things are happening there. We used to have two hospitals in the region. Actually, they're more like what we in this country would call clinics, but both of them were burned to the ground. Africa can be a brutal place, but the people there normally respect our facilities. We're not political; we just care. Before the burnings, the hospitals were reporting some strange deaths—people coming to the hospitals with symptoms they had not seen before. Some lived, but most died. It's our business to know why they're dying, but we hadn't a clue. Now we have no information coming out of this area. Of course, when you deal routinely with large numbers of AIDS-related deaths, it's often hard to determine if a death was brought on by something unrelated to the AIDS virus." He looked directly at Garrett. "How much do you know about Zimbabwe and the situation there?"

"Not that much, I'm afraid. We talked about it on the way over here, but only in generalities. It's a failed African state with a lot of problems and not many options. Robert Mugabe has ruined the country, and things are not likely to improve until he dies or is assassinated. And then it will be a long road to any kind of recovery. You said people are dying there, and you don't know what is bringing this on. Are we talking about some kind of epidemic?"

Burkett gave him a tight smile. "I know what you're thinking. The Ebola virus. That was what we first thought, but I don't think that's it. It's interesting to note that an outbreak of Ebola, even a relatively isolated one, is cause for great alarm in the West. Yet the AIDS epidemic kills hundreds of thousands each year, and it seems to be of little concern." He paused, lost within himself for a moment, then continued. "But that is another story. As for Ebola, the Africans know about it, and to some degree, they know how to deal with it. Total isolation and burning everything—the bodies, huts, and personal effects of those infected. Since the first documented outbreak in 1976, we've never had Ebola in a major city, just in outlying villages. They let the virus run its course, then go on with life. Most tribal societies are very stoic about these things. Drought, famine, Ebola, even AIDs; they carry on. These people can be very dignified in their suffering and misery." He paused a moment and swallowed, and for a brief instant, a look of pure sorrow and hopelessness passed over his soft features. Then, almost as if by an act of will, he cleared his throat and continued. "Usually under these conditions, our mobile medical teams are welcomed, especially in a region where a clinic has been forced to close, or in this case, burned. But in northern Zimbabwe, primarily in the Tonga Province along Lake Kariba, they have been turned away. Several times we have tried to send in a relief effort, usually a small convoy of Land Rovers with basic medical kit and supplies. They are turned back, politely but firmly. This in itself is very contrary to our experience, but there's more to it. We have reports that people are being taken out of villages at night. Some come back, usually sick and dying, and others are never seen again."

"Do you have any idea who may be doing this?" Garrett asked.

"Not a clue. The bits and pieces of information that we get come from Zimbabweans being treated at our hospital in Harare. These are patients who have relatives who live in the Tonga region."

"Any idea at all what may be the cause of the illness?"

Burkett leaned forward, elbows on his knees. His whole countenance became deadly serious. "Before the clinics burned, we had the chance to examine three individuals from the area. They were all Bantu. One had what looked to be anthrax. He recovered, but before we could investigate further, he left the clinic—fled in terror, actually. The other two died of what appeared to be some form of hemorrhagic fever. Before we could make arrangements to bring them to Harare for autopsy, the family claimed them and took them away. All three came into our facility in a small village near the town of Kariba. All three were seen by one of our field doctors on the same day. He could do little but make a preliminary diagnosis. His report did state that the families were terrified but would say nothing. The people in this region can be very superstitious. It was that night the clinic was burned, and we suspect arson. The headman of the village told our doctor that he was no longer welcome there. He also reported that the whole village was terrorized into submission. Midwives he had trained, young men he had befriended— all turned away from him. He could do nothing but leave. So he collected what personal effects he had in his quarters and drove away." Again Burkett paused. "I'm afraid that is about all we know."

Garrett considered this for a moment. "You said your medical teams trying to reenter the area have been turned away. How were they turned away?"

"The country is pretty open, with few roads. There are checkpoints along the roads manned by men with automatic rifles. They are what might loosely be called local police. Sometimes they are in uniform and sometimes not. Since President Mugabe's land redistribution program went into effect, much of rural Zimbabwe has reverted to tribal and clan control. They inspect all traffic that comes through. But they know of our work, and they usually let our people pass without a problem or with a token bribe. Since the burning of the clinics, our people are ordered to turn around and return the way they came."

Garrett had any number of questions. "Have you been able to question any of the locals about this? Has anyone from the area been willing to talk about it?"

Burkett smiled. "My mother asked the same questions. No one from that area will speak about it. The only people willing to talk seem to be out-of-area relatives, and they are very guarded. Our senior administrator asked several government officials in Harare about it, but she was told that it was none of her business. So as you can see, we know something is wrong, but little else."

Garrett was silent for a moment, digesting what Burkett had said. He was about to ask another question when Judy Burks began to stir in her seat, pointedly glancing at her watch. Garrett took the hint and rose from his chair

"Mr. Burkett, we'd like to thank you for your time. We'll be looking into the matter and getting back to you, or at least Miss Burks will be getting back to you."

"Thank you. It's been my pleasure to make both of your acquaintances," Burkett replied. He shook Judy's proffered hand and then took Garrett's. Once again Burkett clasped Garrett firmly, and there was deep concern in his eyes as he spoke. "Mr. Walker, my mother said to answer all of your questions, and not to ask any of you. So be it; I understand. But sir, please understand this. I know Africa, and I believe something is wrong in northern Zimbabwe—very wrong. I'd consider it a personal favor if you could be of any assistance to my people there."

"I'll do what I can," Garrett replied, meeting Burkett's intense gaze. He paused a moment, then added, "From what I can see, your organization does some much needed and noble work."

Burkett showed them to the door. Florence was organizing periodicals on the table in the reception area. Once on the street, Judy was immediately on her cell phone, and within seconds the town car slid to the curb. It was starting to rain as they climbed inside.

"Sorry to break that off, but I needed to keep you on schedule. Now don't say it; I know what you're thinking—why did I bring you to some do-gooders' organization? You're not in the relief or outreach business. Understood, but somebody thought—"

She was halted in mid-sentence by the look on Garrett's face. It was dark and set, one of pure concern.

"I'm no expert on problems in Africa," he said quietly after a moment, "but I can recognize when someone is concerned and very worried. Graham Burkett is in real pain. He cares deeply for those people—his people, as he put it—in Zimbabwe, and he's afraid for them. Few people truly care for others that deeply. He's quite a man—a very rare and very strong one." They drove on in silence for a while before he turned to her. "Where to next?"

She looked at him closely, trying to control her own emotions. Garrett Walker was the most capable man she had ever met—a true man of action. Yet he could be compassionate to a fault. And he was not a man easily given to compliment or hyperbole. He had seen Burkett as someone of strength and character, a man whom she had written off as some privately funded, blowzy bureaucrat with a poor sense of fashion. She wanted to reach out and hug Garrett, but simply placed her hand on his arm.

"There is a guy from Langley who wants to talk with you. I kind of guessed how you'd be dressed, so we're headed for a beer and burger place in the Virginia suburbs."

It was just after 1:00 P.M. when they pulled up in front of the Vienna Inn, on Route 123 in Vienna. Garrett got out, but Judy remained.

"You're not coming?"

"Nope. My liaison duties don't extend to this meeting. I'll be on my cell; give me a call when you're done."

Once inside, Garrett paused to allow his eyes to adjust to the interior. It was a gloomy day outside, but the Vienna Inn was a few shades darker. It was a warm, comfortable setting—lots of wood and red upholstered fake leather accompanied by the not unpleasant odor of fried food. A ring of tables surrounded an island bar. Past the tables there were booths along the walls. Most of the lunch crowd had left, but a good number of diners lingered over their beer or something stronger. Two older waitresses bustled about, shuttling drinks and bussing tables. Ignoring the Please Wait to Be Seated sign, Garrett crossed the room to a booth in the corner. Moments later a man appeared and slid into the opposite seat. In his early sixties, his gray hair combed straight back over his head, he wore a dated herringbone sport coat and an open-collared white shirt. His skin was mottled, and he had the look of someone who worked long hours and did not take particularly good care of himself. Yet the tired blue eyes showed a measure of intelligence and authority.

"Mr. Garrett Walker." It was not a question. Garrett nodded. "My name is Jim Watson." He smiled warmly and extended his hand across the table. "It is an honor and a very real pleasure to meet you. Thank you for coming to see me like this." He glanced around; at other tables men were gathered in close conversation. The older man smiled. "A lot of our business seems to get done in places like this. Probably too much, but then no one likes to talk in a hotel room or the back seat of a car." A waitress appeared with an order pad, pencil poised. "Are you hungry?"

Garrett sensed that this was not the time for food. "Coffee will be fine."

"Two coffees, then," Watson said. The waitress holstered her pad and, pushing the pencil into her hair, left without a word.

Garrett was a little stunned, but he felt that he hid it well. James Watson was the Deputy Director for Operations—the head of the Clandestine Service. He was the man responsible for most, if not all, of the espionage and human intelligence collection at CIA. Since the war on terror began with 9/11, Watson also directed the Special

Activities Division, which did a lot more than just gather information. More than a few senior Al Qaeda and Baathist leaders had been killed or kidnapped by SA operatives. The presence of Jim Watson took this African business to a whole new level.

"Mr. Walker—"

"Please, sir, call me Garrett."

"Thank you," he continued, "and it's Jim, here. Garrett, one of the reasons I wanted to see you was to thank you in person for what you and your people were able to do in Afghanistan last year. It was deeply appreciated at the highest levels. The resolution that you and Steven Fagan were able to bring about over there was nothing short of a miracle. You rendered your country an invaluable service. In a town with a notoriously short memory, it will not soon be forgotten by those who count."

Again, Garrett nodded. He had not considered what he did as a service, at least not service in the manner of when he was in uniform—when he was in the Navy SEAL teams. It had been a job, one for which he was very well paid. But it was a high compliment nonetheless, both in the sincerity of the words and the man who delivered them. Garrett had not recognized the face—few would outside the closed world of intelligence. Garrett did know that Watson had been the CIA chief of station in Moscow when Joseph Simpson had served as the American ambassador to Russia. During a portion of his career at CIA, Steven Fagan had reported directly to Jim Watson. According to Steven, Watson was a man of character and integrity who rose to the post of DDO through merit. With the exception of Armand Grummell, the Director of Central Intelligence was usually a political position. Deputy directors like Watson were there because they were the top men in their trade.

The coffee arrived, and Watson continued. "Under normal circumstances, we would bring you into the headquarters building and award you the Intelligence Star." Watson smiled, and there was a twinkle in his watery eyes. "Kudos from the Director and all that. Well, we think too highly of you and your organization to bring you in the front door and take your picture. And quite selfishly, we don't want to risk compromising a valuable national asset.

"Another reason I'm here is that those who know about IFOR make up a very short list. I don't want to intimate that my agency is a porous organization, but the fewer who know about your force, the better. The DCI is very adamant about that." Again he smiled. "So I'm your case officer. It's been a while, but I hope I'm up to the task."

"I'm sure you are, sir." Garrett found it hard to call him Jim, and Watson didn't correct him.

"And finally, I want to speak to you about this business in Africa. We are becoming increasingly concerned about what may be going on there. I understand you met Graham Burkett today. What did you think of him?"

Garrett noted that Watson asked about the man, not his story. He answered carefully. "I think our Mr. Burkett may at times let his heart rule his head. But I also think he is as intelligent as he is compassionate, and not given to overstatement. I believe him. If he thinks something is wrong in Zimbabwe, then something is probably wrong. Whether it's another African tragedy or a national security issue is not clear, or not clear to me."

"I agree," Watson replied.

"You must also think something is wrong, or we wouldn't be having this meeting."

Watson gave him a tight smile. "True enough. As you well might gather, we don't have as many assets in that part of the world. Our attentions and priorities are elsewhere. Even so, a great deal of valuable information and intelligence leads come from NGOs and citizens in the private sector. In Africa, as in Afghanistan, the best information comes from the locals and those with the ability to get close to the locals. We have managed to pick up a few things from time to time, primarily from our contacts with the French. At a national political level, the Francophiles in this administration are in a small minority, but at the working level we get on with the Frogs quite well." Garrett thought he detected some distaste in Watson's voice at the mention of the French, but the older man was skilled in managing his feelings. "But Zimbabwe was a former British colony, and the Brits are gone, so our sources there are limited. We have computer models that send up flags when certain parameters and conditions are met. But computers give us indications, and little else. Tell me, Garrett, does the term 'Sampson Option' mean anything to you?"

Garrett slowly shook his head. "No, sir, I can't say that it does."

"A little over ten years ago, Seymour Hersh authored a compelling book titled *The Sampson Option*. This well-researched work detailed the development of Israel's atomic bomb. According to Hersh, whose account we believe, the Israelis built secret underground laboratories in South Africa in the 1980s to conduct nuclear research. With this clandestine endeavor, they were able to process highly enriched uranium and build several atomic weapons. In total secrecy, even from us, Israel became a nuclear power. We had our suspicions, but not until they exploded a test weapon off the coast of Namibia did we really understand what had taken place. Whether or not we approved of Israel joining the nuclear club was beside the point; it happened without our knowledge. Can you just imagine the conversation between Reagan and William Casey, the Director at that time? Or the reaction of John Poindexter, the national security adviser, when he was told what had happened? Following that intelligence embarrassment, we been very mindful of secret events in Africa. In the 1990s we implemented a set of programmed indicators that would alert us to illegal or unusual events in Africa. Those indicators are updated and modified for various national security threats. As you might imagine, they are now tweaked for terrorism and weapons of mass destruction. Long story short, the alarms built into our monitoring systems are going off. Graham Burkett's concerns parallel our own. Something is going on there, and we'd like to know more. We can't afford another Sampson Option, nor can we let ourselves be on the wrong end of such a secret program."

Watson stirred his coffee carefully and continued. "We've had a report from our station in South Africa that may have some bearing on this. Garrett, have you ever heard of a military unit called the Selous Scouts?"

For a moment, Garrett was too taken aback to answer. "The Selous Scouts," he managed. "Rhodesian Army trackers, as I recall, but weren't they disbanded some years ago?"

"They were," said Watson, "supposedly in 1980, but they were something of a legendary unit. We now have indications that some of them may still be around."

They talked for the better part of an hour before Watson paused for a moment to frame his words. "Garrett, the Director would like your organization to look into this. It's not something that seems likely to respond to diplomatic pressure, and we have no assets that can respond in any reasonable time frame. We need some help. This may be one of those situations that we ignore at our own peril."

Garrett met Watson's steady gaze. "I see. Sir, when we tracked those nukes through Iran and into Afghanistan, we were operating almost as an extension of the U.S. military—

we are at war with the jihadists. The Middle East and Southwest Asia are in effect a theater of operations in that war. Going into an African nation like this, under these conditions, meets all the tests of a covert operation. This is a covert action."

Watson nodded. "It does, indeed. We need to investigate this without showing the hand of the United States Government. And if something should go wrong, neither the president nor the administration will take any responsibility—or come to your aid."

Garrett considered this a moment, then smiled. "I think I understand. Let me take this up with Steven. It may be within our charter and capability, but as I'm sure you know, his assessment of this is critical to any role we might play."

"Understood, and thanks in advance for taking a look at this matter." Watson consulted his watch. "Garrett, I'm afraid I really must get back to the office." He smiled ruefully. "Another meeting, as usual. I know your organization will need some time with this. Have Steven contact me when you've had a chance to review the matter. In the meantime, we will pass along anything we learn on our end. And once again, it's been a distinct pleasure to finally meet you."

"The pleasure is mine, sir. Just one more question." Watson gave him his full attention. "Graham indicated this matter was somehow surfaced or brought forward by his mother. Without presuming too much, what the hell does his mother have to do with this, even if she does work for the Agency?"

This brought a genuine smile to Watson's tired features. "Garrett, we are blessed with some very talented and dedicated analysts at CIA. Elizabeth Johnstone, Graham's mother, is one of them. She is a very perceptive lady. Her instincts regarding the nuclear weapons you recovered in

Afghanistan were spot-on. Candidly, without her intuition, we—you—would have been too late to prevent a catastrophe. And she enjoys something of a special relationship with the Director."

Garrett again thought he detected something of a twinkle in Watson's eye at the last comment, but the DDO was nothing if not a very controlled man. "We'll be anxious to hear from you after you've had a chance to discuss this with your people. Please give Steven Fagan my very best." They shook hands across the table, and Watson motioned for him to remain seated. "With your permission, I'll leave first. Once again, Garrett, it has been a distinct pleasure."

The older man rose and donned a topcoat and car cap. Then, plunging his hands into his pockets, he made his way through the tables to the door. Garrett glanced around; no one looked up, but a man seated by the door quietly followed Watson out. Garrett smiled to himself. Conventions, he mused, have to be observed, even in a meeting place for spies. He called Judy, took a last sip of coffee, and slid from the booth. Garrett started to reach for his wallet and stopped in mid-motion. He had not seen him do it, but James Watson had managed to slip a five-dollar bill, neatly folded, under the lip of his saucer.

The rain had changed to an oppressive drizzle by the time he reached the car. Judy Burks smiled sweetly at him as he crawled in.

"Everything go okay?" she asked.

"It was interesting," Garrett said evenly.

"Just interesting?"

"And informative," he replied

"Was it, now?" Garrett nodded, giving her an innocent grin. "Okeydokey, no more questions."

They were headed east on Route 123. "So what's next, madam liaison officer?"

"Ah, our next destination. I'm not sure I can tell you. It's a highly classified matter."

He pulled her toward him and began to tickle her. She squealed and made a show of fighting him off. The driver, from the Bureau motor pool, kept his eyes on the road.

"Okay, okay. Enough torture, you win. I have orders to take you to a safe house and to conduct a thorough interrogation."

"How thorough?" he said in a low voice.

Her voice was suddenly hoarse. "Very, very thorough."

The town car moved ahead of the afternoon traffic and made good time, clearing the beltway and sliding easily through the town of Fairfax and out toward Warrenton. They were on 66 West for only a short time before taking an exit onto a secondary road for about ten miles, then swinging onto a country lane. The road dwindled to a gravel turnaround that served a stately Victorian mansion. A small sign swung from a decorative metal arm: The Cedar Inn, circa 1810.

The driver pulled away without a word, and they mounted the steps. Garrett had his leather grip, and Judy a small overnighter slung over one shoulder. He had not noticed it in the car during the trip; she must have brought it from the trunk while he was with Jim Watson. They were expected, and a kindly older woman showed them to a two-room suite on the third floor—very private, spacious, and well cluttered with antiques. Garrett dropped his bag and tested the four-poster with his hand. Through the feather quilt, the mattress was surprisingly firm. On the settee was a tray of fruit, bread, and cheese, and a chilled bottle of claret.

"So now the interrogation begins?"

She came over and stood close to him, looking up with an impish smile. She gave him a gentle shove, and he fell back onto the bed.

"Now the interrogation begins."

While Garrett Walker and Judy Burks were making the most of a chilly winter evening in northern Virginia, a man in Rome was looking out the window onto his balcony and watching the first rays of the new dawn spread onto the western reaches of the eternal city. In the background, a throaty, gurgling sound from a bar across the small room announced his espresso was ready. He had not yet shed his striped Egyptian cotton pajamas, but had pulled on a satin robe and slippers against the morning chill. He padded across to the espresso machine and poured a measure of the strong brew into a demitasse. He seated himself at the table by the window, where he blew and sipped, enjoying the accompanying warmth and exhilaration of the drink. This brought on, as he knew it would, the desire for a cigar. In another hour, the sun would clear the hills behind the city, the same hills where Romulus and Remus were said to have suckled from a she-wolf. He would wait till then to have his cigar. This delay from coffee to cigar unvariably caused him to reconsider his choice of Rome in favor of some warmer city, but he was a man who simply could not live in a city without good opera and a decent orchestra. These necessities, he often reflected, seemed to bear a direct correlation with an increase in latitude. This was unfortunate for a man who enjoyed an early-morning cigar on the balcony. As he contemplated this, the cell phone on the table purred gently. It was programmed to purr at certain times of the day and ring at others. He glanced at the caller ID and considered whether or not to take the call. After a moment's thought, he pressed the speaker button.

"Yes, this is Jacques Drouet," he said in French.

"Ah, Monsieur Drouet, I am happy to have found you in the office. We wanted to let you know that the sum of twenty million Swiss francs has been deposited to your account. We will send the printed confirmation in the manner that you have specified."

"Very well. Thank you for the call."

"You are most welcome, monsieur. Have a pleasant day."

He sipped at his espresso, but he was not so pleasantly disposed as he had been before the call. It was not the deposit; it had been anticipated and expected. And the money would be there only a short time before most of it was wired elsewhere. Twenty million Swiss francs, nearly $16 million U.S., would, after making its way through a number of intermediaries, be deposited to a bank account in Riga. Sixteen million was a lot of money to pay for a small vial of pathogen, but the whole operation hinged on it. It was a lot of money for the man, a Russian, who would ultimately take ownership of this sum. He was not experienced in handling that kind of money. In all probability, he thought as he sipped the espresso, the man and the money would soon be parted, and it was highly likely that they would be violently parted. But he had met his obligation, and the money was his.

One reason he was not so pleasantly disposed was the business itself—the business in Africa. It was not something he felt very good about. He had always practiced his trade with some measure of ideology. Today it was sometimes a stretch to find something redeeming in his chosen field, but a man in his line of work did what he had to do. But he had not come to this point in time by his own hand. He had been stripped of his wealth, wealth he had carefully amassed by hard work and professional skill. One thing he was sure about; it was the Americans who had done this to him.

This business in Africa is not something I wanted to be a part of, he said to himself not for the first time, but what choice do I have? A man must have those things that his spirit demands. So I have no choice in the matter.

He took up another phone on his desk, a state-of-the-art system with embedded cryptology and frequency-hopping. Most corporations dealing in sensitive or proprietary information had this capability, and so did he. He dialed in a number from memory; he did not keep certain numbers in the speed dialer. His call was picked up on the second ring.

"Good morning, Dimitri," he said, shifting to Russian. "This is Pavel. How are you this day? . . . That is good to hear. Dimitri, I am calling to ensure that the delivery has been made before I wire the funds. . . . No, no, Dimitri, no other assurances are required. I need nothing but your word that it has been done. If you say the merchandise is in place, then the funds, per your instructions, will be there by the close of business today. . . . *Da,* and thank you as well. Good day, Dimitri."

He rang off and sat in silence before taking his second cup of espresso. There were few men whose word he would not question, and Dimitri Muschovia was one of them. In this business one needed intermediaries, and Dimitri was someone he could trust. But then, in the world in which he did business, was he not also a man others trusted? He smiled to himself. Trust was a commodity that was becoming increasingly hard to find. There were not many like Dimitri and himself, but then there were not many truly skilled former KGB operatives still working his side of the street.

He turned the project over in his mind again and once

more concluded that while it might be an unseemly enterprise, it was a professionally challenging piece of work. And it would hurt the West and possibly cripple America. He noticed that the sun had finally lifted over the crest of the hill and now bathed his patio. So Pavel Zelinkow selected a *robusto* from his humidor, carefully prepared it, and let himself out onto the balcony to properly greet the morning.

Garrett and Judy had spent the evening drinking wine, making love, and talking late into the night. The following morning they slept late, then made love again. They had worked up an enormous appetite. When they finally crept down the stairs, they were treated to a generous farm breakfast. Garrett contacted the flight crew and informed them that his business would be keeping him in Washington an extra day. It was the off-season, and there was only one other guest at The Cedar Inn, an elderly couple who packed off midmorning. The temperature dropped, and there was the threat of snow, but the innkeeper had a rack of old coats so they were able to bundle against the weather and walk about the spacious grounds. The inn had a small library well stocked with the classics and a cheerful, inviting fire. Judy had hoped that they would be extending their stay and had planned for it. They settled in next to the warmth of the fireplace to enjoy the cozy ambience. There was a steady diet of cheese, bread, fruit, and wine throughout the day, and sitting down to a regular meal never crossed their minds. The second night at The Cedar Inn was much like the first. The following morning, Garrett was up early, on the floor doing his exercises. The room was quite chilly and must have seemed more so to Garrett, coming from the tropical warmth of Hawaii. Clad only in his undershorts and not seeming to mind the cold, he moved quietly from one exercise to the other.

"Guess the honeymoon's over."

"What was that?" he said, finishing off another set of stomach crunches.

"Oh, nothing," she replied. The smell of coffee filled the room, and she realized that he had already brewed a fresh pot. The room was equipped with coffee service—and not just some prepackaged motel setup, but a canister of fresh-ground dark roast. Unable to resist the aroma, Judy leapt from the warmth of the down comforter, raced the chill across the room to fill her cup of the hot, dark liquid, and then, just as quickly, returned to the coziness of the bed. There, she nursed the steaming cup, content to watch Garrett complete his morning routine.

Judy Burks entertained fantasies of what it would be like if they were married, if she were Mrs. Garrett Walker. There was no one else in her life, and she was reasonably sure there was no one else in his. But they led very different, busy lives with a great deal of distance between them. Judy guessed that he would not soon leave GSI, nor had she any plans to leave the Bureau. Both of them traveled a great deal away from whatever place each might call their home. She also knew herself well enough to realize that spending weeks, possibly months, waiting while her husband was away on one of his adventures would be very difficult. She was equally sure that he wouldn't relish the idea of stoking the home fires while she was away on some case or at a stakeout. So once again she concluded that this was it, passing ships when their schedules would permit. It was the best they could hope for, at least for now.

Garrett was a passionate man, but not usually a morning lover. However, once again he slipped out of his shorts and was back under the covers, taking a sip from her mug and putting it on the nightstand. As his powerful arms enveloped her, *maybe someday* was her passing thought. For now, this was a slice of paradise sandwiched into their busy and sometimes violent lives. A town car arrived promptly for them at 8:30 A.M.

3

THE AFRICANS

Garrett's trip back to the Big Island of Hawaii was not unlike the one to Washington except that they were chasing the sun. The Gulfstream lifted off from Andrews shortly after eleven in the morning and let down at the Kona airport just before 4:00 P.M. local time. For part of the trip Garrett was busy at the aircraft's computer console, which was equipped with high-speed Internet access. His meeting with Jim Watson had brought up a number of issues he wanted to research. After five hours at the keyboard, he stretched and asked Cindy to bring him a scotch and the cribbage board. They cut for the deal and embarked on a rematch, but this time she beat him soundly. He could console himself that he could only play the cards dealt him to best advantage, but that didn't, at least for Garrett Walker, make losing any more palatable.

AKR was waiting for Garrett when he made his way through the private aviation terminal. Kelly-Rogers was dressed in shorts, shower shoes, a collarless shirt with the top three buttons unfastened, and wraparound sunglasses. His hair was approaching dreadlock length, and he wore a pooka-bead necklace. They shook hands warmly. AKR took Garrett's bag from him, and they headed for the car that AKR had left in the redlined fire lane along the curb of the terminal.

"You know, brother," Garrett said, "every day you look

more and more like a drug dealer and less like one of the good guys."

"What do the good guys look like these days? Hey, you never know, man," AKR said with a chuckle, "when you're gonna want me to go into the ville and score you some Kona gold."

"That'll be the day," Garrett replied. "You buying weed and me smoking it. Steven at the camp?"

"In his office and waiting for you. He just received an intelligence report forwarded from State in Harare. It seems that one of Outreach Africa's doctors got himself whacked in Zimbabwe yesterday. It's been confirmed by the French. And I understand it wasn't very pretty."

"An American doc?"

"No, Indian." AKR crossed Highway 19, which ran along the coast and headed east toward Mona Kea. Soon they began to climb into the foothills. "As I understand it, the guy got himself hacked to death by a machete. According to the reports we obtained from Doctors Without Borders, it was a pretty gruesome scene. All the NGOs have ordered their medical personnel out of the area. Langley tells us that bookings out of Harare International are way up."

AKR merged onto the Mamalahoa Highway, which took them in a northeasterly direction toward Wiamea. It was almost fifteen degrees cooler in the foothills than along the coast.

"Akheem, you're an African, what do—"

"Correction, sahib, I am an Englishman," he abruptly cut in, adding just a little more nasal tone to his public-school accent, "an Englishman who was born in Africa."

"How could I forget," Garrett replied. He sometimes found AKR's Bonnie Prince Charles act a little tiresome. "What do you know about the Selous Scouts?"

Kelly-Rogers gave him a sidelong glance before answering. "Steven asked me the same thing, and I'll tell you what I told him. They were the last and baddest of the Rhodesian Light Infantry. We left Rhodesia in 1970. Things were none too good then, but they really got ugly after that. My dad used to speak of them. The Selous Scouts were formed to counter the terror tactics of Mugabe and his Marxist movement. Originally they were trackers, and their mission was to track the terrorists after one of their raids back to their base camp. That often meant they would follow them across the border into Zambia or Mozambique. Then they called in the Rhodesian Air Force or the main elements of the Rhodesian Army. Sometimes they were known to slip into a terrorist camp to slit a few throats. There was butchery and atrocity enough to go around, although I think Mugabe and the Marxist-backed ZANLA rebels were probably the worst. Both sides were pointing fingers. For a while Dad thought that if the Rhodesian white farmers hadn't been so keen on groups like the Selous Scouts, maybe they could have cut a deal with the new government." AKR swerved to miss an oncoming car that was passing on a double yellow line. Garrett flinched, but Akheem kept up the narration. "But when Mugabe and his thugs took over, things changed. There were hard times for whites, and a lot of blacks for that matter—black Africans who were proud to be Rhodesians. Bottom line, you can't out-atrocity a Communist-backed insurgency. They were brutal beyond comprehension. Say, what is all this with the Selous Scouts? They're history, right?"

"Possibly. How's training going with the new men?"

AKR flashed him a broad smile. "Hey, you wouldn't believe how good these guys are. They get better by the day—by the hour. They've made a lot of progress since you saw them last, and best of all, they're starting to function as a team. That's something that doesn't come easy to these guys, but Tomba has them working as an integrated unit. And they're getting much better on their radio procedure, much more disciplined."

"How about their shooting?"

AKR shrugged. "Better, though I don't think they'll ever shoot like Brits or Americans. But I'd put them up against any of our special operations guys with a grenade launcher. They've taken to the M-203s splendidly." The M-203 is a 40mm grenade launcher slung under an M-4 rifle, the standard weapon of the IFOR fighters. "They're tough, and they're proud. Give me another two weeks, and I'll take them into the bush against anyone, even up against your Gurkhas." Garrett gave him a questioning look. "Seriously. These guys move in the bush like no one you've ever seen. Just wait until you go out with them. You'll see what I'm talking about."

It was late afternoon by the time they arrived at the camp. Garrett dumped his bag in his quarters, a spartan single-room studio apartment in the staff quarters. When he was not in the field or on overseas deployment, he had lived much of his life in places like this—bed, kitchenette, private shower and washstand, a bookshelf, a small desk, and plenty of locker storage for operational gear. The operations building was a short walk—nothing in the central area of the camp was far away. Garrett slipped into Steven's office and waited by the door for Steven to acknowledge him. Behind the desk, Steven hurriedly tapped out the reply to a secure e-mail and swung away from the computer screen. He rose and offered Garrett his hand.

"Welcome back. We expected you late yesterday, but I understand you got held over."

"Well, to tell the truth, I decided to hold myself over. Did some liaison work with our FBI liaison officer."

On the way back, Garrett had done a mental calculation on the one-day cost of a Gulfstream G550 and a flight crew. It was a serious five-figure number.

"Mission accomplished?" Garrett nodded, which brought a grin to Steven's face. "Then it was time well spent." Fagan leaned across the desk on his elbows. "I understand you spent some time with Jim Watson. Tell me about it."

Garrett recounted their meeting while Steven concentrated on him with his soft, patient gaze. Steven Fagan could listen like no one Garrett had ever met. He had the bedside manner of an elderly priest and the mind of a chess master. On top of that, he was perhaps the most experienced and knowledgeable covert action specialist in the world, at least in the free world. Fagan was a man of rare ability and intelligence, but what Garrett valued most in this quiet, unassuming man was his character. Garrett Walker had met few men he liked more than Steven Fagan, and none with more personal integrity. Issues of character were sometimes overlooked in their work, but for Garrett it was a crucial matter. When dealing in life-and-death issues, Garrett found comfort in the fact that others beside himself considered the moral implications of what they did. When Garrett finished, Steven leaned back, carefully digesting what he had just heard.

"Jim Watson is a good man, one of the best at Langley," he said, thinking aloud. "Watson is personally involved in this because Armand Grummell is concerned, and that means the concern goes straight to the White House. I think their worries are justified. If this were happening anywhere else in the world, we would be all over it diplomatically, either in bilateral discussions with that nation or through the United Nations. Or we would put a special operations team into the area to investigate. Africa, as we all know, is very touchy.

"And there is the particular case of Zimbabwe," Steven continued. "It's been kicked out of the International Monetary Fund, and it resigned from the Commonwealth of Nations before that body could kick it out. With the current government, it's just a step from reverting to tribalism. We have an official presence in the capital, but no real ability to move about the country to find out what's going on."

"What about CIA assets?" Garrett asked. "The Special Activities Division has some pretty impressive capabilities."

"They do, but they're also heavily committed in Afghanistan, Iraq, and Pakistan. They haven't really developed the personnel or assets to operate in Africa. No," Steven said, thoughtfully stroking his chin, "if I wanted to hide from satellite coverage and diplomatic scrutiny, and where white men can't easily move about, then that part of Africa would be a good choice. You see, we don't care much about Africa; nobody does. Undoubtedly, if there is an organization behind all this, and evidence suggests there is, then they know we have almost no intelligence and military capability in this area, and that our close allies are just as limited. Our focus is the Middle East and Southwest Asia right now. In the current war on terror, we put more time and money in Iraq in one day than we put in all of Africa in one year. Our country is stretched pretty thin right now, and Africa is well off the scope." He paused a moment, then continued in a measured voice. "Armand Grummell seems to be worried about this, and the DCI doesn't rattle easily. We need to put something together, and quickly. I've already asked Janet to work up some preliminaries on the situation. I'd like you and Akheem to be back here in an hour for a quick planning session."

Garrett wandered out into the compound. An hour would give him time for a light workout and a quick shower. On the way to his quarters, he saw AKR squatting on his heels in conversation with a man whose skin was so black it almost had a blue cast to it. He was dressed in sandals, loose cammie trousers, and a green T-shirt. His head was shaved, and as he addressed AKR, he spoke with gestures as much as with words. AKR rose when Garrett approached. His companion seemed to uncoil effortlessly as he also brought himself upright. He was handsome and serene, but his mild features did not altogether mask an underlying fierceness.

"I see you, my brother," the man said in his native Turkana dialect. He spoke very good English, but was aware that Garrett had a fascination and an ear for languages.

"And I see you, my brother," Garrett replied, unconsciously copying the manner and gestures of the Turkan. Garrett had a near-photographic memory for sounds, so he had quickly mastered the formal greetings that are so important in the Turkana culture. "Will my brother excuse this interruption?" When the tall warrior nodded, only then did Garrett turn to AKR and speak in English.

"Steven wants us in his office in an hour. Looks as if there's a growing interest in Africa."

"I'll be there," AKR replied.

Garrett bowed slightly and backed away as Turkana custom dictated, and headed for his quarters. He glanced back over his shoulder to see AKR and the tall African back in their stooped conversation.

The African's name was Tomba. Tomba and the others AKR had recruited had been in camp for about three months. Most of the new men were shy and polite, and they worked very hard. They were all warriors and immensely proud, but there was something very special about Tomba. Garrett had felt it in his presence and demeanor from the very first time they met. The Turkana were from northern Kenya and, like the Masai, had been influenced little by Western culture until quite recently. They had a well-earned reputation as fierce fighters. Tomba's father was a *laibon*, a ritual leader of the Turkana, and Tomba would have followed in his father's footsteps. But as with many young men in postcolonial Africa, drought, famine, and border wars had driven Tomba from his tribal lands. AKR had met him when his father was posted to Nairobi, and Tomba was a young park ranger at the Masai Mara National Park. In his early teens, he fought in the colonial wars, including a tour in the Rhodesian Army. Following the demobilization of the army, he served in the forces of Bantustan and sometimes worked as a safari guide, his employment usually determined by the fortunes of war. But he and AKR had remained in contact. IFOR had hired Akheem Kelly-Rogers to recruit and supervise the training of an IFOR contingent that could operate in Africa, much as IFOR's Gurkhas could move easily in many parts of Southwest Asia. He found Tomba in Kenya, working the national game parks in search of poachers.

An hour later Steven, Garrett, and AKR were seated at a small, circular conference table in Steven's office. The fourth member at the table was a face on a large flat-screen monitor. What she might have lacked in physical presence was more than made up for in the rich and authoritative voice that came across the speakers.

"Good evening, gentlemen. Can everyone hear me okay?"

Steven answered for them. "We hear you fine, Janet. How's the picture and audio on your end?"

Janet Brisco was the senior operational planner and controller for IFOR. When members of the intervention force were sent into the field, she would do most of the planning and serve as the focal point for command and control while they were on a mission. While on active duty in the Air Force, she had been the go-to ops planner of the U.S. Special Operations Command. She was recognized as the best in the business in the male-dominated special operations community. Steven had hired her with the understanding that she could do much of her work from her home in East St. Louis, where she nurtured and managed a large extended family. That is where she now sat at a console in her home office. On the split screen in front of her were the three familiar faces of Steven, Garrett, and Akheem Kelly-Rogers.

"I have your smiling, handsome faces in front of me, and hear you five-by."

"Excellent," Steven continued. "Gentlemen, I've had Janet working on this for the last day and a half. I'll let her give us some background before we get into the specifics. Janet?"

"Okay, here goes," Janet responded. She had notes in front of her, but she didn't need to refer to them. "Zimbabwe. British colony of Rhodesia turned African basket case when in 1978 white rule came to an end. Like most colonial turnovers, this one was very bloody. The first black prime minister elected to the new nation was Bishop Abel Muzorewa. The country name was then changed to Zimbabwe-Rhodesia. A decade-long guerilla war that preceded independence continued through Muzorewa's short tenure until new elections were forced by civil unrest, and the Marxist Robert Mugabe was elected prime minister. The British supervised the election, but it was thought that Mugabe had rigged the outcome right under their noses. In retrospect, the British made a real mess of it. They wanted out quickly so basically they cut and ran, handing the country over to the Communists. No offense, Akheem."

"None taken," AKR replied to the screen.

"Mugabe brought a lot of changes to Zimbabwe. He essentially ended democracy and any future for whites in the country. For over a decade, Mugabe continued to let the whites farm the large tracts of land they inherited from colonial rule. But then, about five years ago, he started appropriating the white-owned farms and distributing the land. With the seizures, farm productivity fell dramatically. Rhodesia and even Zimbabwe, in the early days, had a great deal of land under cultivation and were running modern, Western-style agribusinesses. Then things began to slip. Farming does not do well in a centrally managed economy. In a bid to build popular support for his embattled regime, Mugabe began a massive redistribution of the large farms. There is now only a handful of white farmers left in the country. People are starving, and the infrastructure is rapidly running to ruin. Mugabe, like Idi Amin Dada and Mobutu Sese Seko, has ruled only for his own personal gain. He has the nation in a state of economic collapse. The country is literally at the mercy of relief organizations and NGOs. The army, as in most failed Marxist states, is part of the problem. Extortion is becoming more widespread, and the Zimbabwe Republic Police are only capable of keeping order in the capital and some of the resort areas." Janet Brisco paused, looking at each of the faces on the screen. "With me, so far?" The three heads nodded. "Let me know if I'm going too fast for those of you who are taking notes.

"Now we come to this business in the province of Tonga." Janet continued. "We know something's going on there, but we're not sure just what. From the information that's coming in, we know that there are widespread kidnappings and that people have died under strange circumstances. And that the people seem to be terrorized. We also know that the government in Harare, which means Mugabe and his cronies, show no interest in what's going on there, nor are they disposed to help any of the NGOs who are concerned about the welfare of the people in that region. One can only assume that they are being paid to look the other way.

"The problem seems to be isolated within the boundaries of Tonga. Its population within the province is somewhere between a hundred and thirty and a hundred and fifty thousand. The largest city is Kariba, with some forty thousand. The people refer to themselves as Batonka or Tonga, but they are mostly Bantu. They were first discovered by Dr. Livingstone when he came down the Zambezi River in 1860. No white man came back until much later in the 1900s. In many ways, the Tonga consider themselves separate from the rest of Zimbabwe. There are really two Tongas. One is the city of Kariba and the area immediately surrounding Kariba along the shores of Lake Kariba. This region caters to the tourist trade that's grown up around the lake and provides workers and services for the Matusadona and Mana Pools National Parks. While the Shona is the dominant tribe in Zimbabwe, there is both Shona and Ndebele influence in Tonga. As for what is considered the other Tonga, it is the countryside in and around the national parks, and in the valleys that reach up from the lake. Its countryside ranges from inhospitable to unbearable. When the dam was built that created Lake Kariba, the Tongans were split into the Zambia Tonga and the Zimbabwe Tonga. The Zimbabwe Tongans are much more isolated than the Zambian members of the tribe. This only stands to reason, as the Zambian capital of Lusaka is closer to the lake than Harare. The Zimbabwean Tongans are also much worse off economically. They are and have always been a very superstitious people, and witchcraft is still a significant influence, especially in the rural areas.

"And finally, there is the lake. Lake Kariba is the biggest man-made lake in the world. It's some twenty-five miles wide and over a hundred miles long. It was formed when a huge dam was built on the Zambezi River in 1960. The creation of the lake displaced people and animals on both the Zambian and Zimbabwean sides of the river. The disruption caused by the creation of a lake this size was, as you could imagine, substantial. But it eventually spawned a lively tourist industry. Tourism is a financial sacred cow of southern Africa. In Zambia, Mozambique, and Zimbabwe, tourism brings in valuable foreign currency. It is also a barometer of the political climate and regional problems. Tours are still going to the Zambian side of the lake and into the Victoria Falls area, but not to the Zimbabwean side of the lake. Without tourism, the people in that area are back to substance living at best. The other sacred cow in the region is the power generated by two power stations just downstream of the dam. Electricity is shared equally between Zambia and Zimbabwe and managed by the Central African Power Corporation, or the CAPC, which is owned jointly by the two countries. The CAPC has an output of about fifteen hundred megawatts, and the revenues tend to find their way into the pockets of officials in Harare and Lusaka. So whatever it is that is going on in Tonga has affected the tourist industry. So far, it seems to have had no impact on the CAPC. My guess is that the people responsible for these deaths are paying off the government and scaring off the tourists, but they are not disturbing the power generation facilities. I went online this morning and tried to book a hotel room in Kariba or along Lake Kariba in Tonga and didn't have much luck. Many of them said there were no vacancies, which we know is not the case, or that they were closed for repairs.

"Also, one interesting note about the dam that made the lake. Just after construction began, a suspension bridge across the river collapsed and killed eighty-six Italian workers. Then the area experienced a once-in-a-thousand-year flood. Eighteen workers were swept away, many of them entombed in wet cement. The locals felt that the damming of the river offended the river god, a fish-headed, serpent-tailed creature called Nyaminyami. The tribes in the area say that Nyaminyami is still unhappy with the dam and the lake it created. As I said, the locals there can be very superstitious.

"As for access into the area, I've been looking for contacts within the tourist industry that are still active. I'm also checking for anyone within the CAPC who could help if we have to operate in the area. I've got some feelers out, but it may take a while to develop some dependable contacts. That's about it, unless you want a cultural lecture on the fauna and flora of the area, which are really rather spectacular."

"Thanks, Janet, for your report. Perhaps later on the fauna and flora." Steven turned his attention to Garrett. "Garrett, let's hear what you've got for us regarding the military aspects of what is happening there."

"As you all know, there is very little information coming out of the area. We have no reporting assets there on which we can rely for conclusive intelligence, but there is no doubt that there are some strange things going on in Tonga. We know that a nongovernmental armed force is moving in the area and, to some extent, terrorizing the locals. This paramilitary activity reaches throughout the province, but the focus seems to be the remote valley drainage leading up from the northeastern boundary of the lake into the foothills of the Mavuradonha Mountains. It's an unpopulated area, with a single road leading in and out. The road was built to serve a small resort hotel that was only marginally successful. It's very rugged country, with thick vegetation and hardwood forests. We don't have much satellite coverage in that part of the world, and the only mapping that's been done was by the Rhodesian Army when they operated there some thirty years ago. There are, or were, only a few bush camps there that catered to photographic safaris. What I've learned from the few available reports, and my recent briefing by Jim Watson, is that this new force in the Kariba area and east of the Zambezi River looks a lot like the old Selous Scouts. I know that sounds a little far-fetched, but the memory of Selous Scouts seems to be very much a part of this region. They are not so mythical as the serpent-tailed Nyaminyami, but the people in the area all have very strong recollections of them. When the Communist guerillas went into the Mavuradonhas to hide, the Selous Scouts went in after them. Most families in the area have at least one member who fought with the Scouts or against them, or had a family member killed by the Scouts. They left quite an impact on the area."

"You mean the Selous Scouts are *back*?" AKR exclaimed.

"That may be the case," Garrett continued, "or more probably, a force that patterns itself after the Selous Scouts. As a quick overview, the Selous Scouts were a group of trackers and bushmen culled from the Rhodesian Army. They were formed in the last days of white rule in Zimbabwe, when a decision was made to fight fire with fire. A Rhodesian Army captain named Ron Reid Daily, who was also a British SAS veteran, was tasked with developing a battalion-sized force that could track the Communist-backed terrorists to their bases and deal with them. Daily set up a training camp near Lake Kariba. The training is variously described as some of the most difficult and dangerous in the world. Men were killed in training. Captain Daily was looking for men who could live off the land and track their quarry for as long as it took to run them to ground. The force was mostly black; only two in ten were white. Volunteers came from all elements in the Rhodesian Army, but mostly the Rhodesian African Rifles. Perhaps only about one in ten of the volunteers made it through the training and qualified as a Selous Scout."

"Sounds like Navy SEAL training," Steven said.

"From what I've learned, this training was much shorter and much more brutal than SEAL training. The Communists under Mugabe were a pretty savage bunch. Villages that refused to support the insurgents could count on murder and rape at the hands of the rebels. But they met their match with the Scouts. For about eight years, they waged one of the most intense and bloody guerrilla counter-guerrilla campaigns of the colonial wars. Independence came to Rhodesia in 1978. Mugabe came to power in 1980, and the Selous Scouts were summarily disbanded. A few of the blacks stayed on, but not the whites. Many of the whites joined the South African Army, and moved on from there. A lot of the blacks found work in Bantustan and the Transkei Defense Force. But for eight bloody years, they were probably one of the most capable group of fighters on the continent. Their reputation over the years has grown and been exaggerated to some degree, but there's no doubt that they were good—probably very good."

"Akheem?" Steven asked.

"Garrett has it about right. Ron Reid Daily is still talked about in the SAS, but he was more a soldier of fortune and professional African hand than a career military officer." Then, turning to Garrett, "So what makes you think that there has been some sort of rebirth of the Selous Scouts?"

"As I understand it, we don't have much of an intelligence-gathering presence in Zimbabwe. Most of the reporting comes from State Department officers, and their activity has been restricted to interviewing people coming out of the area. So far, it's been mostly hunters and a few who were on walking safaris in the Matusadona National Park. These people reported seeing paramilitary units moving about the area in squad-sized units. One person, an American on shooting safari, was close enough to observe one of these units through his rifle scope. When he called it to the attention of his native guide, the guide said they were probably poachers. The American who reported this was little more than a trophy hunter. As it turns out, he had served a tour in the 101st Airborne, so he felt confident about what he observed. This guy said there were blacks and whites in the squad file. This alone marked the group as a non-Zimbabwe military unit. The whites wore bush shirts and hats and cargo shorts, and the two in this particular group had beards. He was pretty specific; some of them were carrying Belgian FAL rifles and others AK-47s. The blacks had a professional military look to them; they moved like soldiers. There have also been reports of terrorist-like activity in the Kariba area. Along the lake there are a few upscale hotels and marinas, but the town of Kariba lies some fifteen miles from the lake. It is spread out and very poor. One of the embassy officers talked with a Harare resident who has relatives in Kariba. The report said that this relative was very worried about his family there. He said people have been disappearing from their homes, both in Kariba and in some of the outlying small villages. Men come in the night and rob and kidnap people, and this activity seems to be happening throughout the northern part of the province of Tonga, mostly in the foothills that border the lake and along the Zambezi River.

"At first, they wrote it off to bandits or antigovernment activity. But with the hassling of NGO personnel and the exotic diseases that are popping up, Langley thinks it might all be connected. The Agency has asked the National Reconnaissance Office to step up their coverage, but they've yet to get anything specific from satellite imagery." Garrett paused a moment before continuing. "It's almost as if someone were trying to seal off the area and put a good scare into those who remain."

"What is the State Department's official position?" Janet asked.

"According to Watson, State and our embassy there have both written it off to banditry," Garrett replied. "And Langley doesn't dismiss that theory. The final stages of a failed Communist state are not pretty. A lot of things break down, and it's usually worse when it comes to Africa."

They were all quiet a moment, until Steven spoke. "I've traded a few e-mails with Jim Watson since Garrett met with him in Washington. The doctor who was just killed was an expert in epidemiology. His death was made to look like a random robbery, but some of our embassy people in Harare are not so sure. The matter is now before the National Security Council. This situation has some of the earmarks of biological terror, and these days, that gets a lot of people's attention. The question now is what to do about it. By charter, this is CIA territory, but they don't have a lot of options on this one. Langley recently sent one of their experienced officers there. As a visiting embassy staffer, he tried to arrange some official travel into the area, but was denied access by the Zimbabwe Ministry of Tourism. Langley talked about putting a few SA men in there under big-game-hunting cover, but neither the shooting nor the photo safari concessions are taking any new bookings. And even then, they would be restricted to the game preserves. When it comes down to it, white men just don't move too well in rural Africa. And for that matter, neither do American or Western blacks."

"Well then," AKR said with a sly grin, "this would seem to be a job for real Africans."

"Yeah, right," Garrett said, also grinning, "so now you're an African."

While Steven Fagan conferred with his key players, another staff meeting of sorts was taking place almost a half a world away. The setting could not have been more different from the IFOR compound and the Kona Coast of Hawaii.

The road between Harare and the town of Kariba stretches some 225 miles. Most of the land along the way is dusty high-veld African plain. Due east and north of Kariba the land rises gently to a series of mountain ranges with peaks approaching four thousand feet. The Mavuradonha Mountains look much like the foothills of the Rockies. Up one particularly scenic valley some sixty miles northeast of Kariba, the Japanese had built a small luxury hotel in the late 1970s. The Japanese consortium that built it called it Kubwa Msitu, thinking the name—"Big Forest" in Swahili—would draw Western tourists. While the upland forests are dense and beautiful, they lack the big game populations of the lower veld and the expansive vistas along Lake Kariba. Tourists come to southern Africa for the animals. They can find trees and mountains in much more convenient locations than this remote area of Zimbabwe. Shortly after the Japanese began losing money, they lost interest, and the hotel passed through a succession of British, German, and French resort chains until it was purchased by a wealthy Saudi prince. By then it had been renamed the Makondo Hotel. For a period under the prince's stewardship, the hotel was well stocked with luxuries prohibited in his country and by his religion. The prince and his entourage would fly into Harare on their private jet and transfer to stretch limousines for the trek into the veld. They would sometimes drive through Matusadona National Park for a chance glimpse of an elephant or a lion, but always anxious to reach the hotel for a few days of drinking and pornography, either on film or in the flesh— or both. However, the recent availability and convenience of the fleshpots in Bahrain eventually made the long trip to Zimbabwe unnecessary. The hotel had not seen the prince or a guest in well over two years, but a staff of Yemeni caretakers had kept up the grounds and were on hand to discourage looting.

Shortly after the Americans rolled into Baghdad, the prince was approached by an influential Wahabi cleric who asked about the hotel. The holy man seemed to know a great deal about the hotel and its history of who had visited there and what took place. After a short negotiation, it was agreed that the hotel would be an excellent choice for a retreat and school—a madrassa for the Muslims in northern Zimbabwe. The fact that only about 1 percent of Zimbabweans are Muslim did not seem to discourage the cleric. He was even able to get the prince to agree to pay for annual maintenance for as long as the school operated. Some months after the cleric and the prince concluded their agreement, the Yemeni staff was dismissed, and a new group of caretakers took possession of the hotel. One wing of the main building was converted into barracks, four men to a room. Men and equipment began to arrive, some from Harare and some smuggled across the border from Mozambique. Not all of the equipment was military. A number of Mercedes four-wheel-drive lorries and Land Rovers crossing the borders into Zimbabwe carried laboratory equipment and medical apparatus. Once everything was in place, a pair of limousines met a private jet at Harare Airport. Eight men in expensive Arab dress deplaned and filed into the limos. The plane had landed early in the day to allow time for a drive through the park before heading up-country. Only two of the passengers—

the security men charged with the safety of the other six—
were actually Arab. The other six were among the most talented and highest paid biochemists and microbiologists
that money could buy—three Germans, two Frenchmen,
and a Russian. None of them had ever been to Africa. As
luck would have it, they were fortunate enough to sight a
pride of lions and one of the park's rare and endangered
black rhinos on the way to the hotel.

The speaker was as different from Steven Fagan as Africa
from Kona. A middle-aged man with a coldly efficient
voice, he was seated at the desk of what had once been
that of the office manager of the Makondo Hotel. His
English betrayed only a hint of an accent. A trained ear
could detect that his native language was German, but he
spoke many languages. He dressed like many Europeans
in Africa, or at least like they used to dress—tan linen
slacks, white collared shirt, and woven leather loafers. The
desk from which he spoke, like his person, was neat and
orderly. His voice betrayed no emotion, but his question
was deadly serious.

Helmut Klan had been born in Argentina and raised in
an expatriate German community in Buenos Aires. His father told young Helmut of the horrors of his own child-
hood and the final days of the Third Reich. His maternal
grandfather, a ranking officer in the Waffen SS and a member of Himmler's personal staff, told him of the glorious rebirth of Germany after the humiliation of World War I.
Helmut was sent to the University of Lorraine, taking a degree with honors in civil engineering. From there he went
to America and in one year had acquired two master's degrees from MIT, one in engineering and a second in business, again with honors. He left Boston in 1985 and
journeyed south, where he spent five years with DuPont in
Wilmington, Delaware. Klan's duties included managing

and selling off unprofitable units within DuPont's extensive holdings. This often meant he had to deal with the restoration and adjudication of the unpleasant environmental aspects of DuPont's business. From there, he returned to Germany to take a position with Internationale Gesellschaft Farbenindustrie A.G., or I.G. Farben for short. The company had supplied the Nazis with fuel and war materials, and concentration camps with Zyklon-B gas. I.G. Farben had gone into receivership in 1952, yet the company and its vast holdings continued to generate revenue for another fifty years, funding its creditors and providing a rallying cause for generations of protestors. To Klan, Farben was like a noble, aging stag plunging through the forest, gradually being stripped of its strength and reserve by a pack of wolves. Helmut Klan stayed until the end, when Farben was finally dissolved in 2003.

DuPont, Klan often reflected, was never the company that I.G. Farben had been. Had they been competitors on a level playing field, Farben would have easily put DuPont out of business. But DuPont was on the winning side in World War II, and that had made all the difference. It never ceased to amaze Klan how America, and companies like DuPont, could have defeated Germany and the might that was I.G. Farben. Had a man like Hermann Schmitz, the brilliant founder of I.G. Farben, led Germany instead of the maniacal Hitler, the outcome would have been much different. But it was on the abilities and personalities of such leaders that the destinies of nations and corporations rested. Helmut Klan was contemplating such thoughts over lunch at an upscale restaurant in Berlin when he received a call from a Mr. Maurice Baudo from Rome. The caller said that he was due to arrive in Berlin that very evening and wished to meet with Helmut. Mr. Baudo conveyed to him that he had a project for which he was seeking a manager with Klan's qualifications. They met the following day. The discussion lasted several hours, and shortly thereafter, Klan found himself in Zimbabwe.

"So tell me again about the death of this doctor at the clinic near Karoi, and why it was so necessary to kill him."

The man to whom Helmut Klan now directed his question could not have been more different from himself. Klan had known the project would need security and perhaps even a bit of thuggery, albeit thuggery with some local knowledge. He had to admit that Claude Renaud was well suited to this unsavory task. Yet the man was unlike anyone he had ever had to deal with in his corporate universe. Renaud shrugged his massive shoulders in response to Klan's challenging question.

"Ah, the doctor, that was unfortunate business. We went there only to smash his clinic and frighten away those who sought treatment there—make it look like the work of vandals. We did not expect him to come back there so late at night. When he walked in, there was nothing to do but to make quick work of him. At first, we thought only to hurt him—put a good scare in him—but the boys got carried away. Once he was dead, I thought it best to make it look like a tribal bush killing." He chuckled mirthlessly. "Now the word will get out. These Western doctors can't come here unless they have help from the locals, and now they'll have a devil of a time finding drivers and clinic workers. In the long run it'll be good for us."

"But this doctor was an Indian—a Hindu."

"No matter. In Africa, those who are not African are Western, like you and me. Don't worry, doctors are often killed in the bush. In a week it will be forgotten. Trust me, in the long run this will work for us, not against us."

Klan was not so sure. Close to 40 percent of adults in Zimbabwe had the AIDS virus. That had attracted a lot of attention and money from the West. The Gates Foundation alone had spent millions in the country on clinics, medicine, and education. That kind of money was usually accompanied by foundation workers and administrators who asked questions. They did not need people asking questions. Klan cared little about easing the suffering of Zimbabweans and even less about the AIDs epidemic in Africa. He only wanted to get on with the work, deliver the product, and get out of this godforsaken place. Much of what he did not like about Zimbabwe and Africa was embodied in Claude Renaud.

Renaud fashioned himself as a mercenary soldier and white hunter of a bygone era. His father was French and his mother Dutch; he himself claimed Belgian citizenship but held several European and African passports. He was a big man, six-two and close to two-fifty, with a full dark beard that began high on his cheekbones. It gave him a wild look, which he cultivated. Renaud had unruly black hair that he tied in a loose ponytail and a brow that was wide and brooding. His Shonas called him Nyati, "the Buffalo," which he did not discourage. Invariably, he was dressed in a bush jacket with no sleeves, cargo shorts, and an old felt snap-brim hat. One of the lab techs referred to him as the Bwana Wannabe. As a young man in his late teens, Renaud had in fact served with the Selous Scouts for a while at the end of their short time in the field. From what Klan knew of this fabled Rhodesian Army scouting group, he had a hard time imagining Renaud surviving their brutal training. But he could well image that the atrocities of the colonial wars were certainly within his capability. For all his baggage and bravado, Renaud was just the man the project needed to guard the facility and to spread the required fear within the province. Now, it seemed, the killing of the Outreach Africa physician might have taken things too far.

"Perhaps in the long run," Klan acknowledged, "but in the short run, you may have brought us more attention than we want. People in Harare are not about to fuss over a few missing locals, especially if they are Ndbele or one of the other lesser tribes, but the killing of a white man is another matter."

Renaud gave him a tobacco-stained grin. "I thought you had those kaffirs in Harare in your pocket. And why should they care what goes on out here, anyway?"

"It's not the government I'm worried about, it's the international community. They can bring a lot of pressure to bear. We may need a month or more to conclude our business here, and I don't have the time to fend off a lot of inquiries. So for the next few weeks, I want you to keep a low profile. Keep your men out at night so the locals know you're there, but let's avoid any more killings."

"How about the snatches? You need more bodies?"

Klan considered this. They might have enough subjects, but given the incubation periods, he didn't want to run short of host material.

"Don't make a point of it," he told Renaud, "but if an opportunity presents itself, singly or in pairs, go ahead and bring them in. But be absolutely sure to make it appear to be a random disappearance." Rural Africans, Klan knew, were superstitious. When someone vanished into the night, it could be for any number of reasons besides kidnapping.

Renaud nodded and heaved himself from the chair. He pulled a cigarette from his pocket and stuck it into the corner of his mouth as he headed for the door.

"Claude," Klan called after him. The big man paused and turned in the doorway.

"We are getting close, so let's not screw this up. We both have a bonus due us, but only if the project succeeds. And I intend to collect that bonus."

"Understood, *Herr Doktor*," Renaud grunted as he lumbered through the door.

Klan didn't miss for a moment Renaud's attempt at needling him. Klan wasn't a doctor, but he oversaw a medical staff that needed human guinea pigs for their tests. Claude Renaud, he had to confess, was necessary for the project, but that made him no more palatable. They were both being well paid, and the bonus offered for a successful completion was substantial. Yet Klan sensed that Renaud was enjoying all this far too much. Bonus or not, Renaud was not so anxious to see this business come to an end. As an experienced and capable project manager, Klan couldn't help wonder what Claude Renaud would do once their work was done.

Klan's thoughts were broken by a knock on the door. He glanced at his watch, remembering that he had a meeting with the head of his medical team, and brightened as he rose and went to the door. "Come in, come in, Hans," he said, shifting to German. "I've been expecting you."

Garrett Walker did not enjoy this role. No doubt it was necessary, and someone had to do it, but it didn't go down easy. Furthermore, he knew that AKR took a perverse joy in assigning him this duty. But he also knew that realistic training required good role players.

"You seem a little anxious this evening, my friend. Your spirit seems restless."

Garrett gave a resigned shrug. "I guess I've always preferred being the hunter to being hunted."

"I understand, my friend," Bijay replied. "But it is a chance to learn. You know your role well as the hunter. Knowing the difficulties and misgivings of the quarry can also be valuable."

Bijay Garung was Nepalese, and one of more than two dozen Gurkhas that IFOR retained as a component of the intervention force. Bijay was a Gurkha leader of some stature and reputation. It was through him that this small band of warriors had been recruited and trained. The Gurkha element had been part of IFOR for a little more than eighteen months and operational for half that time. Garrett and Bijay had already taken them in harm's way, into Southwest Asia on an important mission, and they had performed magnificently. The reputation of the Gurkhas as tough, durable, loyal, competent soldiers was legendary. Garrett had found them to be all that and more. In Bijay he had found a brother in arms, as well as a man of immense talent and spiritual reserve. He often thought of him as a warrior monk, yet Bijay practiced no formal religion.

He and Garrett were stationed outside a small thatched hut on one of their training ranges. They walked their posts in and out of the shadows, bathed in lantern light that escaped through the windows. Inside two of the technicians sat at desks with portable radios. Garrett and Bijay were posted as guards at the "enemy" communications outpost. Night training evolutions like this were necessary to build the men into a functioning combat team. Usually this training was directed by a command and control element that would monitor and direct the evolution, as they would do on a real mission. Tonight's drill was a purely tactical exercise; there would be no C2—command and control—element directing the exercise play. Bijay and his Gurkhas had worked many of these training evolutions before they had gone on a real mission. They still did.

"What do you think of the new men?" Garrett asked.

In response to Garrett's question, Bijay picked up his rifle and began to pace. He was tall for a Gurkha, who were generally small in stature, and he carried himself with great ease and dignity.

"The Africans, they are not like us," Bijay said, carefully framing his words. "You and I are much alike, although we come from very different worlds. But we have been in uniform for most of our adult life—proper uniforms. As our British mentors would say, we have been in garrison. The formalities and patterns of Western military life are ingrained in us. This is not the case with our black brothers. They come from clans, tribes, and families. They have been conditioned to fight for their tribal group, not for their nation or for a cause." He was silent for a long moment before he continued. "They appear to be uncomplicated men, more like children than warriors, but this is not the case. I think it is because their souls—the essence of their being—are so closely linked with the earth and their native land. Our black brothers are spiritual and very connected to their environment. I know you wish they could shoot like my Gurkhas. I wish my Gurkhas could move in the bush like Tomba's Africans. But I sense that, like my men, they are loyal to their brother warriors, and that when called upon, they will be very brave—brave even to the death."

Garrett was about to answer when he saw Bijay's knees buckle and his body pitch forward. A fraction of a second later he too was on his stomach, his face in the dirt. There was a forearm levered into the back of his neck and a hand that felt like a baseball glove over his mouth. He could breathe, but all other movement was impossible. There seemed to be two of them, but Garrett could not be sure. He could hear muffled commotion from inside the hut, then silence. Suddenly he was jerked to his feet, but kept facing away from Bijay and the hut. The hand was removed from his mouth, only to be immediately replaced by a length of duct tape. Another strip sealed his eyes and wound around his head to block much of his hearing. He next felt nylon snap-ties as they encircled his ankles. Strong arms pulled him from behind, and he felt the bark of an ohi'a tree at his back. His hands were quickly bound behind the tree. Then all was quiet. It had taken less than two minutes. He would have felt foolish at being taken so quickly and easily, but his mind was instead drawn to the nylon snap-ties cutting into his wrists and ankles.

He did manage to reflect on the swift and professional action that had taken place. Neither had heard their attackers coming, and Bijay Garung was a man who was not easily surprised. He may have heard, but refrained from a reaction to stay in character, but Garrett didn't think so. There was no verbal communication, nor did they make much noise when they entered and secured those in the hut. They must have had their duct tape strips precut; there were no tearing sounds from the roll. And they seemed to have worked as a team, which was most important to Garrett. Teamwork sometimes did not come easy to cultures that championed the exploits of the individual warrior. They had left the area without a sound, taking their prisoners with them. The exercise called for them to neutralize the guards and capture the technicians. Impressive, Garrett thought, very impressive. Through the tape that bound his ears, he heard the approaching strains of "A Nightingale Sang in Barkley Square," very proficiently whistled. Then there was a soft snipping as jawed pliers bit into the nylon straps. He rubbed his wrists while his rescuer cut the duct tape. Garrett worked the tape from his mouth and head while AKR went over to free Bijay.

"This way," he said without preamble. "I want to watch them at the extraction site."

The three of them headed off at a trot to a jeep parked a short distance from the contact area. After a fifteen-minute drive they arrived at an open area dotted by low brush and hackthorn bushes. AKR parked the jeep well away from the clearing, and they walked to the edge and settled in. They waited in absolute silence under a quarter moon, AKR handing Garrett and Bijay each a pair of night vision goggles. They carefully surveyed the edges of the clearing but could see nothing. Garrett glanced at AKR. He could see the flash of his grin in the moonlight. A moment later they heard the rotor beat of an approaching helicopter. A single man moved into the clearing. With the low-light optics, Garrett watched as the man brought the H-60 in for a safe hover using infrared wands. Then an orderly file emerged from the bush and quickly boarded the helo. The captives each had a prisoner handler assigned to him. They handed the bound and gagged prisoners up to waiting hands in the hovering helo. The chopper lifted a few feet, then nosed over and began its run away from the clearing.

"Well," AKR said after the helo had cleared off, "what do you think of my guys now?"

Garrett smiled. "I'm going to reserve comment until after the debriefings and hot washup, but I haven't seen a thing I don't like. How were they on patrol?"

AKR had initially patrolled in with them, as they moved six miles over rough ground as a part of the exercise. "They moved well, and their noise discipline was excellent. They were rucked up with about sixty-five pounds per man, and I was clean. I had to work to keep up. They move through the brush like puffs of smoke."

"I too was very impressed," Bijay said. "I know you are working to build them into combat teams, but as your training permits, I would like my men to begin accompanying them when possible. There is much each can learn from the other."

The following evening, Garrett, AKR, Bijay, and Tomba sat around one of the outside tables after dinner. Bijay melded into the group with ease; they were professional warriors, and that cut through all cultural dissimilarities. But Bijay was held in a special regard by AKR and Tomba, who by virtue of his service with the Rhodesians was also a product of the British military. Bijay carried a distinction that merited him this special reverence: the Victoria Cross, Britain's highest award for bravery. He had won that honor while serving with a Gurkha contingent assigned to the SAS during the first Gulf War.

That morning and afternoon had been spent on the rifle and grenade ranges, and now the men were busy cleaning weapons. A few of Bijay's Gurkhas had been pressed into duty as shooting instructors. The rest of the Gurkhas were high up on Mona Kea, practicing rappelling. They would make an overnight mountain bivouac and return the following day. Garrett and AKR had wondered how the Africans and the Gurkhas would react to each other—would there be jealousies; would there even be racial tensions? Bijay and Tomba had talked for a long while when the Africans arrived, then each had spoken to their men. Both had tremendous sway with their men; there had been not so much as a hint of a problem. There was little interaction between the two groups, but Garrett noticed that there was much curiosity on both sides, for these were two very different kinds of warriors. He was relieved to see that there was also respect and acceptance. The two groups had never trained together. They were being groomed for work on two different continents. But it was a unique opportunity for them to learn different techniques from one another.

It was a soft evening, with the sweet smell of plant decay pushed up from the lower elevations by a gentle onshore breeze. They were four veterans, men who had known fighting in one form or another for several decades. In the case of Tomba and Bijay, due to their cultures, it had begun at a very young age. Both had been warriors for more than three decades. They had all fought different battles, taken life in the name of different causes, and believed in different deities—or no deity. But at this moment, they were four warrior leaders in garrison after a day in the field with their men, and that made them brothers. Each savored the moment in his own way. They were drinking warm beer that Tomba's men had begun to brew soon after their arrival, a thick, bitter-sweet, malty concoction with a delicious aftertaste. Garrett and AKR relished it, and Bijay sipped it with polite enjoyment. One of Tomba's men brought them a fresh pitcher and shyly retired.

"They are shooting much better, Tomba," Garrett said, placing his hand on the big African's shoulder. "I think we are ready to move Konie and Mumba to the sniper weapons. They are steady and seem to have a good shooting eye. They'll make excellent snipers."

Tomba nodded. "I agree," he said in his precise, halting English. "They are good with their assault rifles, and they pride themselves on their marksmanship. They will be honored to carry the long guns. Neither of them will disappoint you."

"And it is not just Konie and Mumba who are doing well. All your men are performing well." Garrett searched for the right words to frame his compliment. "We knew you were great warriors when you came to join us. But our ways and cultures are different, and our way of fighting is different. What I mean to say is that we appreciate their hard work, as well as your own. You have learned our ways of battle very quickly."

Tomba smiled and lowered his head in thanks. "*Nkosi,* I appreciate your words. But it is I who should thank you—all of you—for you have allowed us to continue to follow the path of a warrior. For us, it is a path of honor. Our homelands are not what they were. The whole of Africa is in constant change. We are moved about, made to live away from our tribal lands, and made to serve men who are not our tribal leaders—often men who have never tasted battle. We were warriors, but without a warrior cause, so we were without honor."

Tomba looked at each of them, holding each with his gaze, his eyes dark pools of intensity. None of them, save for perhaps AKR, had heard him speak with such emotion. They said nothing, waiting for him to continue.

"You see, my brothers, my men and myself are warriors without land—without a home. I fought in the colonial wars, and most of my men were orphaned by them. I am Turkana. Among the fourteen men who left Africa with me, there are Masai, Luo, Samburu, and Turkana from the north. There are Matebele, Shangere, and Zulu from the south. And of course, our single Somali. They are all men who were born in the bush or on the veld, served in some national army with officers of a rival tribe, then were discharged to find their families scattered and their lands confiscated. We are warriors in search of honor; you have provided that. We will serve with you; our allegiance is yours. My men will save what you are paying us, and someday, they will return to their various homelands with wealth and honor. As a group here, you call us Africans, and we are that. But we are more, and we each have our place in the land you call Africa. My men want to find their tribes and clans, or what is left of them, when they return. It is then that they will be able to buy wives and cattle and have the comfortable life of an old warrior. Or they will perish in the process. Both are worthy goals. You have given us much." He sipped his beer. "You have given me much. We will not disappoint you."

"And what about you, Tomba?" Bijay asked quietly. "Will you save your money and return to buy wives and cattle?"

He looked at Bijay, and a smile cut his handsome features. "Perhaps. Perhaps not. Or perhaps, like you, I am at home only when I am in the company of other warriors, preparing for the next battle. Only the gods know for sure."

For some time they remained in companionable silence, sipping African beer and watching the Hawaiian dusk turn to night.

4

PREPARATIONS

The sun had just cleared the lower reaches of Mona Kea when Janet Brisco strode into the operations office and tossed her handbag onto the chair by her desk. Steven felt the African issue could move easily from the assessment phase to the planning phase, so he had asked that she come to the Kona facility as quickly as possible. Brisco had taken a late-afternoon flight from St. Louis to Chicago and the last flight out of Chicago the night before, waiting out the early-morning hours in the VIP lounge at Honolulu International. During the four-hour layover, she had poured over the intelligence summaries and classified reports that streamed into her notebook computer, a secure, encrypted machine with a state-of-the-art wireless modem that connected her to the Kona facility's local area network. She caught the first Aloha Airlines flight over to the Big Island. Steven had offered to send the Gulfstream to pick her up, but she had declined. A single black woman climbing onto a corporate jet was not a common occurrence in St. Louis, so she elected to travel by commercial jet—first class, of course. What she really needed most was time to read herself into the problem, and she could do that on any airplane. Janet Brisco was known in the St. Louis area, and for that reason, she had always been careful to keep her family segregated from her work. She had done this well before terror came of age in America—well before 9/11.

Janet Brisco now stood behind the desk, hands on her

hips, surveying the maps and current message traffic that had been laid out for her attention. She was a tall, imposing woman, and strikingly beautiful. Janet was forty-six, brilliant, impatient, and aggressive. These gifts did not always endear her to those around her. She was often a source of exasperation to her parents, teachers, coworkers, and an ex-husband from a brief and stormy marriage. But it was her uncompromising attention to detail that had made her the best tactical special operations planner in the free world. Those who had worked with her on an operation were forced to overlook her abrasiveness because of what she brought to the mission. Unconsciously, she lit a cigarette and began to reorganize the paperwork on her desk.

"Are these the most current overlays?" she asked, not looking up.

"Just over six hours old, and I've annotated them. As you can see, we're focusing on the hotel complex. There were a few changes since the last satellite pass, but not many. Mostly vehicle location changes. If there is anything going on there, it's inside, where we can't see it."

"How about the cell phone and land line intercepts? Any unusual activity? Patterns?"

"None that we can detect. There is far more encryption than would be normal from some hotel in the bush. The open conversations we've monitored are businesslike and guarded. They're not giving us much, but I have to believe that something is going on there."

She put down one report and took up another. "Okay, how about that contact with the regional power company?" She finally looked up. "Are they going to be able . . . Say, what in the hell happened to you?"

Dodds LeMaster was IFOR's chief technician, a Cambridge-educated electrical engineer who had made a fortune designing video games and interactive Web sites. Dodds was also responsible for the design and construction of many of the military information systems that allowed tactical controllers real-time interaction with units in the field. He had fashioned the same command, control, and communications suites for IFOR that he had built for the military. Only given IFOR's requirements and near-unlimited funding, he had been able to dramatically miniaturize these systems. Thanks to Dodds LeMaster, they had a portable, flyaway tactical control package that was well beyond anything in use by any nation's armed forces.

LeMaster could be described as a super-geek, and a very patriotic one. He was also something of an Anglophile, but knowing that the defense of the free world rested squarely on America's shoulders, he had left England a decade ago. He had placed his genius at the disposal of the U.S. military, and now IFOR, because he believed in what they were doing—that they could make a difference. Janet Brisco's arrogance and intelligence often made her short with others, but that was seldom the case with Dodds LeMaster. If not her tactical peer, he was her intellectual equal, and then some.

Janet had finally looked up from her desk to see that LeMaster had a huge shiner.

"Billy and I were acting as role players in a training exercise a few nights ago. I was part of a body-snatch scenario, and I got a little banged up when they tossed me into the helo."

She came around the desk and gently removed his glasses to better inspect the damage. "Look at me," she commanded.

LeMaster was reedy thin, with a deceptively round face and reddish brown hair. He wore glasses that perched on top of his head when not in use. His left eye now had a fleck of blood next to the light green iris, and the skin around it and along his temple was blue-black. Janet's head snapped to look over at where Bill Owens sat at a computer console. Owens was older than LeMaster, and seemed to have a perpetual sickly pallor. He was an unkempt man with a sparse mustache and a bad complexion, one of those people who always looked anemic. All the fresh air and sunshine in the world could not make him look healthy. A master forger, he created all of IFOR's documents. Fortunately for the U.S. Treasury, he had used his exceptional skills in the service of the CIA. Within the Directorate of Science and Technology, he had been known as an artist of rare talent. When the Agency put him out to pasture, Steven Fagan immediately snatched him up.

Janet Brisco stomped over to where Owens sat, and he looked up owlishly from his computer screen. He had a swollen lip.

"You too?"

"Yeah." He grinned. "Me too." Owens wore the fat lip as a badge of honor. It was probably as close as he would ever get to being one of the boys. He sucked on the stub of a cigarette pinched between a nicotine-stained thumb and middle finger. "But we were volunteers." He leaned back in the creaky swivel. "It gets a little boring around here, and we wanted to get out and be with the operators, just for one night. Right, Dodds?"

LeMaster reached over to toggle the ventilation system, which was quite sophisticated and efficient. Both Owens and Brisco were chain smokers.

"That's right. We may not get a chance to volunteer again, but it was kind of fun, except for the blindfolds and getting drug around."

Owens and LeMaster watched as she came to a full boil. "You two hear me on this," she said in a low, menacing voice. "You are my technicians, and you work for me.

You are far too valuable to be out playing cowboys and Indians. From now on, you are restricted to the office. If I ever catch you out in the field again, God help your sorry butts. Do you get my drift?" Owens swallowed hard and bobbed his head; LeMaster just shrugged. "Did Steven know about this?"

"Well," LeMaster hedged, "he may have known that we were going to help out, but I'm not so sure he really knew what we would be asked to do." His voice trailed off as Brisco glared at him.

"A bunch of goddamn adolescent schoolboys. Well, I'm going to get to the bottom of this."

She stormed out of the ops building just in time to see Garrett going into the armory. There he joined AKR and Tomba, who were prying open two crates that had just come in from the mainland. These contained the new sniper weapons. GSI had contracted with Knights Manufacturing for specially built Stoner SR-25 semiautomatic sniper rifles matched with Leupold 10X scopes. The rifle could send a heavy .308 round downrange to kill a man at half a mile. They were anxious to take the new weapons to the range and get them sighted in.

"All right, I want to know who was in charge of the operation that got my two techs roughed up. Which one of you is responsible?"

"C'mon, girl," AKR replied, "it was not intentional, and the guys were okay with it. I mean—"

"Don't you 'come on, girl,' me, Mr. Hyphenated-Last-Name. Those men are absolutely critical if and when we mount an operation. They are way too valuable to be out serving as training dummies for the likes of you and your ruffians."

"Hey, Janet, take it easy," Garrett interjected. "We thought it might be good for their morale to get out and—"

"Morale! Don't hand me that crap. Did you *see* their faces? They were *brutalized!*"

"Look, Janet—"

"Were you in charge? Were you?" Garrett took a deep breath and looked away. "I didn't think so." She wheeled on AKR. "What gives you the right to take my people and use them like that? Answer me that?"

AKR shot Garrett a glance. It was the look of one truant to another, just after they had been hauled into the principal's office. He quickly assumed a penitent look as Janet Brisco continued to reprimand him. This was not the first time that she and AKR had clashed. When AKR was hired, Garrett was curious how the two might take to each other. Janet was older, but not by much. They were both single, AKR being a lifelong bachelor. They were both outgoing, intelligent, cultured, and in Garrett's judgment, two of the handsomest black people he had ever met—make that two of the handsomest, period. But from the first time they met it was fire and ice, oil and water. Janet Brisco, along with an off-the-chart IQ, was born with a chip on her shoulder. AKR could be charming and urbane, and could turn every woman's head when he walked into a room. But not Janet Brisco's. She was about to launch another verbal attack when Tomba stepped forward. He did not speak; he simply waited until she noticed him. Tomba was not a man who was all that easy to ignore, but she was so focused on venting at AKR that his presence failed to register until he had moved close beside her.

"Yes, what is it? What do you want?" After the words were out of her mouth, she suddenly realized that they were inappropriate.

He stared at her for a long moment. There was nothing menacing or threatening about his manner, just an infectious aura of strength and serenity.

"Please, miss, excuse this interruption, but I believe the incident to which you are referring happened just the other night when we took Mr. LeMaster and Mr. Owens as prisoners on a training exercise. Is that correct?"

"Well, yes, it is, and they were hurt." He now had her full attention. "Do I know you?"

For the first time, he smiled. "I have not had the pleasure, miss. I am Tomba, and the Africans are my responsibility. There are fourteen of us. If we were a traditional military unit, I would be their sergeant. May I know your name?"

"Yes, of course. I'm Janet Brisco, the IFOR operations officer."

"Ah, yes, Miss Brisco," he said, nodding solemnly. "I have heard a great deal about you. Now I understand your concern for Mr. LeMaster and Mr. Owens."

She seemed unaware that his hand was now on her elbow as he guided her away from AKR to a nearby table. He held a chair for her, then seated himself across the table. Garrett and AKR shot each other surprised glances. Both held their breath. Tomba was like some compassionate teacher who had just entered the principal's office to stick up for them. Neither of them moved a muscle.

"You must understand, Miss Brisco, that so much of this is all very new to us. By that, I mean the fighting with the support of technicians like Mr. LeMaster and Mr. Owens. We are warriors, and we know war. My men have fought for their tribes, for their lands, for water, for the British or the French or the Portuguese, and some of us, for the Communists. Or sometimes for the tribe that the Communists decided to provide with arms and ammunition. We mustered in ranks, often thousands of us. Orders were given, and we were marched off to do the fighting, often to be betrayed. Most of us have fought purely for money; we were what you call soldiers of fortune.

"But this is different. We now fight for the chance to return to Africa, with dignity and on our own terms. Of course, we accept Mr. Fagan's generous wages, and that still makes us mercenaries. So be it. But I believe that there is honor here, that the cause for which we offer our guns and perhaps our lives will be a just one." He paused a moment to frame his words, but his gaze never wavered; she sat motionless. "With the money we earn, my men will be able to go home, perhaps even purchase a portion of what were once their tribal lands. You see, Miss Brisco, what they want is the dignity and peace that are due an old warrior who leaves the field. I tell you all this because *Nkosi* Akheem tells me that you too are a warrior, so you know about honor."

Tomba again paused for a long moment, then gave her a soft smile. "There are things we do as a part of our trade—stalking, tracking, patrolling, walking long distances with heavy kit. As professional soldiers we do these things very well. But your ways are different. You use electronics, small radios, computers, and binoculars that allow you to see at night. And you have people who are not in the field who control us, who tell us what to do and when to do it. That has been hard for us to understand. But when those same people come out at night and help us train, and willingly let themselves be taken hostage to improve our training, that is important to us—very important. We did not intentionally hurt Mr. LeMaster and Mr. Owens. Truthfully, we did not understand how frail they were. But they freely chose to be with us, and we now know they are brave and good men. We don't trust the computers, but we now trust them. They are warriors, like us; they just fight with different weapons. They have earned our respect, and for my men, respect, is everything." He was again silent for a moment. "I am sorry for their pain. I am sorry for yours. Will you forgive us?"

In a most un-Brisco-like gesture, she reached across the table and put her hand on Tomba's. Then she stood up, and he rose, as well.

"Tomba, I did not have all the facts. You have nothing to apologize for, but perhaps you will forgive me for losing my temper." He inclined his head politely. "Thank you for your explanation of the matter. And now I need to get back to my office." She paused in front of Garrett and AKR and gave them a cold look. "In Steven's office in half an hour. We need to think about getting an advance party in place."

It was a run day for Elvis Rosenblatt, as opposed to a lifting day. So he was on the streets of Atlanta, pounding out his six miles on a seven-and-a-half-minute-mile pace. He glanced at his heart monitor, noticing that it hovered comfortably at 148 beats per minute. Rosenblatt's objective was not so much cardiovascular fitness as it was to burn excess fat, and for that, his optimum heart rate was 148. Most of Rosenblatt's nonwork waking hours were devoted to burning fat and building lean. He'd much rather be in the gym lifting, but this was a necessary part of his training regime. Several years ago he had gone the full distance in Atlanta's famous Peachtree Marathon, and not done too badly, but it cured him of long-distance running as a goal. So three times a week he pounded out his six miles. As much as he had come to dislike the running, it was efficient. Nothing burned calories and fat in as short a time as running on a heart monitor. There would come a time when he could take himself down to a seven-fifteen-mile pace at 148 beats, but he was not there yet. He had just made the turnoff at Tenth Street into the Charles Allen entrance to Piedmont Park when a dark sedan began to pace him along the park drive. It followed him a short distance, then accelerated ahead to where the path crossed the drive. A uniformed security guard emerged from the front passenger seat.

"Dr. Rosenblatt? Excuse me, sir."

Rosenblatt stopped and immediately touched his wrist stopwatch. Whatever this was, he did not want to lose count of his time over distance.

"Yeah, what is it?"

"Uh, sir, do you have any ID for positive identification?"

"Do I what? You got it right, the name is Rosenblatt. You're gonna have to take my word for it, or meet me at my car down at the park entrance." He held out his arms to indicate he had nothing on him. It was a chilly day, but he ran in a T-shirt and shorts; cold weather burned more calories. "What's with you guys, anyway?"

"Sorry, sir. We're from the Center, and we were told to find you. We just wanted to be sure. Here you go, sir. Just press the green send button."

Rosenblatt snatched the cell phone and took a few steps away from the sedan. He refused to wear a pager or carry a cell phone when he was taking his workouts. That issue had come to a head a few years ago when he was ordered to at least carry a pager. "You can fire me if you want, but I'm not wearing a goddamn pager." He hadn't been fired; a man like Elvis Rosenblatt, for all his quirks, was not easy to replace, but this was not the first time they had sent a car to find him when he was working out. It was answered on the first ring.

"Yeah, Tina, this is Elvis. Sure, I'll hold. . . . Lou, this better be an Ebola outbreak in Manhattan. I'm right in the middle of my goddamn workout." He listened for a full minute. "So what do they want us to do about it? . . . Oh, so they want to brief me. I thought I was the guy who did the briefings. . . . Right now—this afternoon; you're shitting me. . . . Oh, yeah, they're right here." Rosenblatt looked up to see a second sedan pulling up behind the first. "I guess I'll see you in a few minutes."

Rosenblatt tossed a set of car keys to a surprised security guard who had just emerged from the passenger side of the second sedan. Rosenblatt climbed into the rear seat of the first. "That's a brand-new BMW," he said to the driver as they sped off. "Tell the guy not to lug the engine." The second man up front got on the radio and relayed the message to the second car.

Dr. Elvis Rosenblatt had two passions in life. One was physical fitness, and the other was the detection and containment of contagious disease. He had been at the Centers for Disease Control and Prevention in Atlanta, or CDC, since he graduated from Johns Hopkins, and he was an authority on viral diseases. Dr. Rosenblatt was also good with bacteriological contaminants and genetic disorders, but viruses were his thing. He endearingly referred to them as bugs. The war on terror had provided him the job security of an emergency-room doctor in Baghdad. He was compulsive and a little weird, too weird to live with, if you were to ask his ex-wife, but he knew his bugs, perhaps better than anyone else at the CDC.

Rosenblatt grew up in Detroit, a skinny kid with acne, below average in every major adolescent category except school. Then the summer before he began junior high, two things happened to him. His dad, who was a science fiction buff, brought home a copy of *War of the Worlds* by H. G. Wells. He had few friends, so he spent much of his time reading and rereading the book over that summer. The idea that microbes could fell giant Martian fighting machines was incredible. So he began to study microorganisms and realized at a very young age what microbiologists the world over knew; in the world of living things, if you can see it with the naked eye, it doesn't count for very much. It was what you couldn't see that was fascinating and important. He also discovered weight lifting. By the time he entered high school, his room was filled with scientific journals and bodybuilding equipment and magazines. There are two important dates in the life of Elvis Rosenblatt—the day he graduated from Johns Hopkins School of Medicine magna cum laude, with an emphasis in viral pathology, and the day Arnold Schwarzenegger was sworn in as governor of California.

A guard at the CDC gate waved the car through. Rosenblatt was dropped at the rear entrance, close to the fitness facility. Security knew him by sight, and he was immediately motioned through the door. Five minutes later he was toweling himself off in front of his locker and hurriedly dressing. In his late thirties, Rosenblatt had been at the CDC for twelve years and still thought of himself as fresh out of med school. Dressed in blue jeans and a crisp oxford-cloth shirt, and preferring clear-plastic-framed glasses over contacts, he was handsome in a Buddy Holly sort of way. This better be good, he told himself as he quickly combed his hair; in another forty minutes I could have been back here *and* have completed my workout. He slipped into the stairwell and began to take the steps two at a time. Most employees at the CDC used the elevators; Rosenblatt always took the stairs. He paused at the top landing window to check out the parking lot just in time to observe the security guard pulling his BMW into one of the VIP slots.

The head of the Viral Epidemiological Department at the CDC was Dr. Louis Alexander. He was a talented virologist, but his real skill was ego management. Elvis Rosenblatt was not the only hotshot, self-centered epidemiologist on staff. Rosenblatt cruised through the outer office and into Alexander's without knocking.

"So what's going on, Lou? What was so important that you had to send the Mounties out after me?"

Alexander thought it was probably a poor time to bring up the issue of the pager, so he plunged ahead. "I have an FBI agent down in the conference room who has come to us with a rather unique problem. It seems a few people in high office have a concern. I was sent a rather cryptic message from the Bureau's executive director. He wanted us to receive this agent and hear what he had to say."

"The FBI, huh. So there must be an imminent threat of a domestic biological terrorist attack. But why drag me in here? I'm not the only guy who is working this problem."

"No, no, you're not," Alexander agreed, "but you are one of the few virologists on staff with a final top-secret clearance that is endorsed for SI—sensitive information. Uh, I didn't know that until the agent arrived. When it was learned that the matter was of that classification, well, I could do nothing but send for you. And there was a second request. They asked that the staffer who would be read into this problem not only have an SI clearance, but also be physically fit." Alexander quickly rolled his palms open. "Don't ask me why. I was directed to put my best man on this, someone with both qualifications." His instructions didn't specifically call for his best man, but Alexander felt Rosenblatt would enjoy hearing it.

"Aw, for Christ's sake, Lou, what's with the physically fit crap? These are bugs. You don't wrestle them; you study them under an electron microscope. You examine the bugs and the symptoms of those infected. Lou, you should have told those pencil-necks in D.C. to kiss your ass."

Alexander just shrugged. Rosenblatt's reaction was totally what he expected. So he played his ace.

"This request came from the FBI, but it was routed through the National Security Council with a copy to the

Surgeon General. From the context of the message, it seems that none of them know exactly what they're dealing with, but from our end there is not a lot of wiggle room. Go and meet with the nice FBI agent and let me know, in unclassified terms, how we here at CDC can be of service. Those are the CDC director's instructions to me; those are my instructions to you. It would appear that this is a potentially critical issue, and no one in this building will be told about it but you."

"Shit," Rosenblatt mumbled and left Alexander's office.

He found Judy Burks pacing in the conference room, and she was not happy. Agent Burks had been sent to do a job without really knowing the whole story. That was the problem with compartmentalized information. You were only told what was needed to accomplish your part of a given mission. The more sensitive things were, the more compartmentalized they were. Judy could only assume this disease business in Africa was turning into a major flap, but no one had really said as much. She had been told to hop on the next plane to Atlanta and brief some medical disease snooper about what might or might not be going on in Zimbabwe. It was something that could have easily been done by the Atlanta Field Office, but because it could potentially involve Guardian Services and IFOR, they wanted her to do it. It had come down from the top and, as far as she knew, the only Bureau people who knew about IFOR were the Director, possibly the Executive Director, and herself. She had raced for the airport and barely made the flight with seconds to spare. Along the way she was asked to show her shield four times to local cops and security guards and had almost missed her flight. Judy Burks lived for any chance to display her shield in one hand, wield her Glock 23 .40 caliber in the other, and shout, "FBI! Get your hands up." But to have to produce her credentials on demand for some local cop or

Pinkerton nitwit—accompanied by, "You don't look old enough to be an FBI agent"—*really* pissed her off, especially when she was running for a plane.

Then she arrived at the CDC and immediately found herself in a confrontation with a security guard about handing over her piece before they would let her in the door. She was close to drawing down on the guy when a senior-level CDC administrator intervened. She was then escorted to a conference room, with her Glock, and asked to wait until they located the individual she had traveled all this way to see. After close to an hour, Rosenblatt walked in.

He paused inside the door and looked around. "Uh, where's the FBI agent?" he demanded.

Judy Burks stared at him. I really don't need this crap from some frat-rat wannabe, she thought.

"You're looking at her, pal."

"You. You're an FBI agent?"

"I don't see anyone else in this room," she said, holding her arms out in an open gesture and feeling like Robert De Niro or Tony Soprano in a mobster scene. "Do you see anyone else in this room?"

"Ah, do you mind if I have a look at—"

"Not at all, pal." She tossed her shield on the table in a theatrical gesture, only to have it slide across the polished table and fall to the floor. She started to retrieve it, but Rosenblatt held up his hand.

"Let me get it."

He retrieved the shield and studied it for a long moment. "You sound like you've had a hard day, Agent Burks."

"You don't know the half of it."

"I think I know where you're coming from. Please, have a seat, and maybe we can get this over with."

They sat across from each other, and he handed her a key ring with several picture IDs attached to it. They detailed his status as a CDC employee and his various security clearances. She studied each one, front and back.

"Elvis?"

"Yeah, well, my parents were a little conflicted when I was born. It's part of belonging to a synagogue in Motown. They chanted Barry Manilow jingles during the service."

"No fooling?"

Rosenblatt rolled his eyes. "What is so important that a Bureau agent needs to speak with me personally?"

Judy Burks studied him a moment and came to a decision. "Okay, I'm going to dispense with the security lecture—loose lips sink ships and all that crap. You're a smart medical doctor; you know the deal. The information I'm going to talk about is classified, but the medical part is not really all that classified. It is pretty scary, though. We have a problem that involves a potential threat of bioterrorism. There is also a nongovernmental organization that may become involved with this problem. Their activities, and even their existence, carries the very highest security classification. The reason a lowly agent like myself is here is that I am the government liaison officer for this organization. Not many in or out of government know about this unnamed secret organization; I just happen to be one of them. The reason that I have traveled here to see you, as you can imagine, is that we need an expert on bioterror. The problem, or potential problem, is in Africa. At least for now."

"Africa?" Now she did have his attention. More than a few of the biological nightmares envisioned by the CDC came from Africa.

"That's right, Dr. Rosenblatt. Do you prefer Elvis or Dr. Rosenblatt? Or Dr. Elvis?" They both smiled.

For the next half hour, Judy Burks read Dr. Elvis Rosenblatt into what they knew about the situation in Zimbabwe. He listened carefully but asked no questions.

"This morning, the folks at Langley who are in the business of tracking nasty people found that two microbiologists with spotty reputations have been missing for several months. They feel this might raise the ante."

Before she could continue, he held up an index finger. "Which two microbiologists?"

She reached into her briefcase and retrieved a slip of paper with two names typed on it.

"Oh, shit," he said in a low, serious voice. "If these two bastards are missing, something is very wrong. And if they are missing and are working together, then this is not good—not good at all. Have you yet confirmed that they are together? Are they in Africa?"

"I'm told we have people working on that."

"Well, Agent Burks, you—"

"It's Judy, Elvis."

"Judy, you had better tell whoever you report to that these two characters are among the most capable and dangerous bio-thugs in the business. If these guys are together in the same lab, then your problem is probably bigger than you ever imagined. What do you want from me?"

"We want to send you data and keep you read into this thing as events unfold. You have a SIPRNET computer for classified material, right?" He nodded. The secret Internet protocol routing network, or SIPRNET, maintained by the Department of Defense, allowed for Internet transmission of secret documents. "Good. The information will come through CIA in Langley. And," she said, consulting her notes before looking back up at him, "there is also the chance that we may want you to travel to Africa with this unnamed organization to be on scene for any action taken there. Will there be a problem with that?"

He did not speak for a moment. "Just myself, or would I be with a CDC medical team?"

"I really couldn't say. I'm sure they will want your recommendations, but it may be just you. You will undoubtedly be briefed further on this as things unfold, but I do know that few people are cleared for this level of information."

This is very odd, Rosenblatt thought, but he shrugged his shoulders. "Why not? I go where the bugs are. But the equipment I will need is expensive, and if it is portable, very expensive."

"E-mail or fax me a list of what you might need. The cost of this will not be a problem and will not be an expense to the CDC, okay? I understand that we may have a physical location where this sickness is originating, but we want to be sure. My guess is that if we do have to put people into the area, we'll need you on hand to evaluate the dangers they may face. I will be your point of contact for now." She handed him a card and a cell phone. "Use this phone and the number written on the back of my card to reach me. It has a top-of-the-line scrambler. The e-mail address is rated up to secret. Questions?"

Rosenblatt slipped the card into his shirt pocket and sat back to again study the two names she had given him. "Not for now, but I'm sure there will be plenty."

She glanced at her watch. "Damn. Wouldn't you know it, the last direct flight to D.C. leaves in less than an hour. That slug of an official driver who brought me here will never get me there in time."

There was a sudden sparkle in his eye. "You need a speed run to the airport, Agent Burks?"

She caught the gleam and smiled. "You can arrange that, Dr. Elvis?"

A few minutes later the uniform at the CDC main entrance leapt back into the guard shack as the BMW tore through the gate and careened onto Clifton Road, heading for the I-75 interchange toward Hartsfield-Atlanta International.

Garrett and AKR started for Steven's office a few minutes ahead of their scheduled meeting. They wanted to arrive early and let Steven know that Janet was less than happy with the role of LeMaster and Owens in training the Africans. Although the storm seemed to have blown itself out, they still wanted to give Steven a heads-up.

"Man, did you see the way Tomba handled her?" Akheem said. "I couldn't believe it. That guy could sweet-talk a crocodile. Next time she comes after me, I want him around."

Garrett grinned. "Maybe that's Tomba's secret. It's not sweet talk. Guys like us are smoke and mirrors. He's the genuine article."

Steven was on the telephone when they arrived. He motioned them to seats around a small conference table while he finished the conversation. When he hung up, he did not immediately take his hand from the receiver. His face was very grim.

"Trouble, boss?" AKR said, immediately abandoning the issue of Janet Brisco's displeasure.

"Yes, there seems to be. The indicators that something is brewing in Zimbabwe are mounting. There is now concern at the CDC, as well as Langley. We may be asked to deal with something that is very dangerous, both tactically and biologically."

Janet came into the room, and the three men rose. She set her coffee mug and a notepad on the table and took the remaining empty chair. If she carried any resentment or anger from their previous encounter, there was no indication.

"Welcome back, Janet. Glad to have you aboard. I was just telling Garrett and Akheem that the 'observables' coming from Africa are not good. It's Langley's assessment that they are too dangerous to ignore, but the question of what to do about it is still on the table. We have not been asked to take action, but from what I've seen, it looks as if this issue may be laid at our door."

He paused and pulled a hand over his mouth. Steven Fagan was a tidy person, in his manner and his personal grooming. This morning there were bags under his eyes, and he hadn't shaved. Steven and his wife Lon enjoyed a quiet, comfortable bungalow just outside of Wiamea. He was the only one associated with IFOR who lived outside the camp. He also had quarters on-site, but it was obvious that he hadn't had much sleep in either place.

"I spent most of last night reading intelligence summaries and threat assessments concerning biological weapons and genetic research. Candidly, I had no idea such potential existed in these areas, or of the accelerating technologies that are driving this threat." He grimaced and shook his head. "While the suicide bombers are taking out shopping malls with conventional explosives strapped to their bodies, the genomic revolution has quietly been pushing biotechnology into an explosive growth phase. Along with the low-tech threats we read about in the papers and the nuclear proliferation issues we've already been called on to deal with, we now face a new and growing problem in the area of bioterrorism. I don't think I can overstate the danger here, nor how unprepared Homeland Defense and our clinical resources are to meet this threat. I don't scare easy, folks, and this scares the hell out of me. Here at IFOR we are interventionists, not biologists, but there are some things about this science that we need to understand, since we may be asked to enter an area where there are biohazards.

"Knowledge of genes and how they work is one of the most promising areas of life science. But this burgeoning knowledge base has potential for evil, as well as for good. This information may cure some of our worst diseases, or it can be used to create bio-weapons of frightening and devastating proportions. This knowledge can be used as well to make current diseases more resistant to drugs. It can also be used to depress our immune systems so existing pathogens can kill us. It can even be used to create whole new diseases for which there is no current cure."

He pushed himself to his feet and began to pace. "What I'm saying here is that this business in Africa may be the first of a series of biological bomb factories that spring up around the world. The information that drives this technology is expanding exponentially. It will only get easier for the bad guys to manufacture this stuff. But one thing at a time. If we are asked to take on this mission, and agree to it, how do we go about it? How do we get in, and how do we neutralize the threat once we do get in? Janet, you're our planner; what do you think?"

"Your assessment of this seems to be about right, Steven. My reading on the subject is no more encouraging than yours. First of all we need to start getting people and equipment ready to move into the region so we can respond if we get a mission tasking. And since we are dealing with a new and very dangerous issue, we need to give ourselves as many tactical options as possible. They haven't made it too easy on us. Initially, I think we should base our operations out of Lusaka. If those behind this in Tonga Province are paying off officials in Harare, we may have trouble working out of that capital. The Zambian bureaucracy is only a little less corrupt than its counterpart in Harare. We should be able to buy what we need in the way of cooperation or pay to have the authorities look the other way. It's a little closer to the target area as the crow flies, but then there's the issue of the border. That problem doesn't seem to bother the smugglers, so it shouldn't bother us. Since NGOs like Outreach Africa are pulling their people out, we have no international agencies to use for potential cover. The Central African Power Corporation, which operates the power stations below the Lake Kariba Dam, uses a German consulting engineering firm. They provide a range of technical services at the hydroelectric generation stations as well as throughout the distribution network. Maybe we can use them as a cover organization. If these people are where we think they are, then they have chosen a very remote and inaccessible site; it's going to be difficult to even get close to them, or even stage assets close by, without some kind of cover story."

"So we think we know where they are, and maybe why they are there, right?" Garrett asked.

Steven nodded. "The intercepts, satellite coverage, and intelligence all point to this one location. That said, we have no hard information yet."

"And it seems," Garrett continued, "as if they've created a biological research facility in the middle of nowhere. Wouldn't it have been more convenient to co-locate this activity with some existing facility? That would have been a whole lot easier than coopting a whole country, even a shell of a nation like Zimbabwe."

"That's a good point," Steven replied. "There is often little observable difference between authorized research and the creation of weaponized biological agents. From what little we know, it may be that they wanted to test their pathogens on human beings. That would account for the reports we have that people are getting sick and dying. You can only do this kind of thing in Nazi Germany, or someplace where life is cheap or the local population is poor and superstitious. In some ways, it's almost as if Josef Mengele has set up shop in Africa and is conducting some monstrous human experiment. I know it sounds far-fetched, but that may be what we have here."

"Then why don't we just put a couple of two-thousand-pound JDAMs on the place? Kill everyone there and incinerate whatever they're working on," Garrett offered. "Carrier-based aircraft shouldn't have much problem penetrating Mozambique airspace to get to Zimbabwe, or they can call in a B-1 from Diego Garcia."

"That's certainly one option available to the National Command Authority," Steven acknowledged, "but there are higher-ups who want to know who is doing this and exactly what it is they are doing. And there is the chance that this place is doing something totally unrelated to bioterrorism. For all we know, it could still be a sex palace for deviant Middle East types, or just another drug reprocessing facility. But the indicators tell us that it is a whole lot more."

"Steven." It was AKR. "Do those in Washington who know about us and what we do, know that we have an African contingent?"

"They do. Periodically, I provide Jim Watson an update on our capabilities and personnel. It's a very general laundry list, but something he can keep in his desk drawer for when a threat surfaces."

"So," AKR continued, "they assume that we can get our people into the area undetected. And they also assume that if during the process our people acquire some incurable disease, there will be no loss of life to officially account for—no next of kin and no accounting for collateral damage."

Steven gave him a long, careful appraisal. "That has been the premise on which IFOR has operated since its inception. And, unlike a regular American military unit or special operations team, we can decline a mission or tasking if we so choose. It cuts both ways. But that does bring us to the next point of discussion. However, before we take the poll, there is one additional piece of intelligence I need to share with you. Our FBI liaison has made contact with the Centers for Disease Control in Atlanta to get their preliminary take on this. As we expected, they know nothing. But Langley keeps tabs on potential rogue chemists, microbiologists, virologists, and the like. Two on their most-dangerous list have gone missing. We don't know where they are, but it seems that one of these guys is on extended vacation, and the other just plain vanished. The folks at the CDC shudder to think what these two may be capable of if they put their heads together and are properly funded and equipped. Langley asked, and I agreed, to let one of their cleared and vetted epidemiologists be read into the problem. That has been done. To date, he has not been made aware of the existence of IFOR. That may change if we go forward; we are eventually going to need someone with that skill set, to protect us if we go in and to evaluate what we may find when we get there."

Steven paused and looked at AKR. "Akheem, are Tomba and his men ready for operational tasking?"

Kelly-Rogers did not answer immediately, but finally he nodded. "We could use more time, but tactically, they're good to go. A few of them have fought in Zimbabwe and Mozambique. They know the territory."

"Garrett?"

"I agree with AKR, Steven. Furthermore, there is probably no more capable force for this mission."

Steven looked around the table. "Then I need a vote. Given what we know at this stage of the game, is this an appropriate and suitable IFOR tasking? Janet?"

"Yes."

"Garrett?"

"Yes."

"Akheem?"

This is the first time AKR had been asked to participate in what Steven called a "Department Head Resolution." As an IFOR element response leader, AKR had now earned a vote on this informal panel. There was no written or formatted criteria for this, nor did Steven want any. Simply put, was this a problem or mission within IFOR's unique capability and did this threat or problem justify the risk of their force—no more, no less—yes or no? If it was unanimous, Steven would take the vote to their employer for a final decision. If it was not unanimous, they would talk it out. Steven had hired each of them for their professional expertise, but he also wanted them to function as a moral compass for IFOR. Their recommendation, and the ultimate decision to undertake a mission, would commit resources and place people in harm's way. It could place them personally in harm's way. Everyone at the table had been in the military and had made tactical life-and-death decisions. But the more senior command level, go no-go choices, had been made by others. Now that ball was in their court.

"Yes," came AKR's answer.

"And I concur. This is doable and in keeping with our charter. Janet, I want you and Garrett to begin the planning process in earnest and get me some timelines for equipment and personnel flow. Akheem, put your personnel on standby and do what you can to train them for the conditions in the area. It seems we will be operating in southeastern Zambia, in the Zambezi River Valley, and in northern Zimbabwe in"—Steven paused to consult his notes—"in the Mavuradonha Mountains. I'll take this to the boss for confirmation and authorization. Questions?" He visually inventoried each of them. There were none. "Okay, thanks for your time and for your consideration. I'll let you know if and when we get a solid green light."

No one moved, as they all sensed Steven was not finished. "I don't mind telling you that this whole business worries me. Let's all of us do what we can to be thorough in our preparation. This could be the big nasty one."

Late that afternoon, Janet Brisco and her planning team were able to get a preliminary mission concept into Steven's hands, along with an outline of the major logistical requirements. That evening it was his turn to fly east. There was not a GSI Gulfstream available to him, but there was one waiting for him when he got into LAX. There it took him directly to the Edgartown Airport on Martha's Vineyard, the one that John F. Kennedy Jr. tragically failed to reach. They touched down just after 11:00 A.M. The weather was blowing sleet and rain with marginal visibility, but the Gulfstream's instrumentation was well up to the task. When Steven emerged from the small terminal, a tall man in a sheepskin coat stood waiting for him, leaning against a dated red Jeep Cherokee. He seemed impervious to the inclement weather. Steven was surprised that Joseph Simpson was there to meet him in person, but only mildly so. Like many who chose to spend time on Martha's Vineyard in the winter, Simpson was a wealthy man who liked to do for himself.

"Good to see you, Steven," Simpson said, shaking Steven's hand with one hand and reaching for his bag with the other.

"A pleasure to see you again, sir," Steven replied.

Simpson tossed Steven's grip into the back seat while Steven scrambled around to the passenger door. It was an ugly day, more so if you had just flown in from Hawaii. There were few people in the terminal, nor did they pass many cars on the way to Simpson's property. On Martha's Vineyard, summer and winter were day and night. For all his public notoriety, Joseph Simpson was a private man who sought solitude. He seldom came to the Vineyard in the summer, but was often here after Labor Day, once the tourists had left. Steven's feeling of isolation only increased as the automatic gate rolled back to admit them to the private drive that led to the house.

On the way from the airport, they talked about improvements at the Kona facility, the training of the Africans, and the other enterprises of Guardian Services International. Steven asked about the foundation. Joseph Simpson, just into his sixties, was a fit, handsome man with tanned features and a cap of thick, close-cropped gray hair. His eyes were so deeply blue and so intense it seemed as if they were backlit. For those who measure success by accomplishment and money, Simpson had done very well indeed. His long and innovative career in the international beef and poultry business had made him a billionaire many times over. During his four years as the U.S. ambassador to Russia, he had won praise as a skilled and accomplished diplomat. Yet, as with so many highly successful men, his life had been punctuated with tragedy. Prudence, his wife of thirty-five years, died in a horseback-riding accident in 2000. Then barely a year later, his son was killed in the collapse of the World Trade Center towers. Both were buried on Martha's Vineyard, which was one of the reasons he was here as often as possible. Of his immediate family, only a daughter remained, and he was estranged from her. Shortly after his son was killed, he turned his extensive business empire into cash and threw himself into the foundation named after his son. Under his skilled direction, the Joseph Simpson Jr. Foundation had in short order become an active force in relieving suffering in troubled parts of the world. A modern fleet of aircraft served the foundation, and were particularly useful for flying relief supplies and medicines into areas torn by civil and ethnic strife. Foundation help was welcome in parts of the Middle East and Africa where other Western and U.S. NGOs were not. It was an organization that could move quickly. Unlike most nongovernmental organizations, it was hampered by no internal politics, nor by the cumbersome oversight of a board of directors. Simpson ran the organization like a business, and his subordinates had the authority to take the initiative. His work following the tsunami disaster in the Indian Ocean had saved tens of thousands.

Guardian Services International had been Steven Fagan's idea. He still retained the title of chief executive officer, but his primary duties were the ongoing operations of IFOR. Guardian Services was initially set up to act as a holding company for IFOR and to provide a broad range of security consulting activities. They did a lot of things in the field of executive and corporate security. So far, they had avoided security contracts in Iraq, as those activities were becoming too controversial. GSI wanted a low profile so as to better serve its true mission as a cloak for the activities of IFOR personnel and the Kona operation. The Gurkha contingent, the first ethnic force stood up by IFOR, was occasionally contracted out for security and executive protection services. This provided some measure of plausibility for paramilitary activity on Kona. In time, the Africans would be contracted out as well, subject to maintaining the cover to the Kona training base. But it was not an economic issue, not with the wealth of Joseph Simpson behind the venture. To date, the only people who came snooping around the Hawaii operations were DEA agents. But GSI had needed to grow quickly to give it legitimacy. Because of the funds at his disposal, Steven had been able to buy several small, highly regarded security consulting firms. Then he hired an executive director to manage the day-to-day operations of GSI and the home office in Washington, while he concentrated on IFOR. It had proved to be a satisfactory arrangement, and although it was not part of the business plan, GSI was profitable.

Once inside his home, Simpson took Steven's coat and hung it beside his own on the hall tree. Simpson's house was a fairly modest saltbox, a type seen all over Cape Cod, and as comfortable as an old pair of bedroom slippers. The main house was served by a barn and two smaller outbuildings, all situated on an impressive tract of land. The interior was frozen in time, left exactly as it was on the day of Prudence Simpson's death.

"Let's go into the kitchen. I have a plate of sandwiches made up." Soon they were across a butcher-block table from each other, with tuna on rye and iced tea. "I've not been included on all the traffic or the details, nor do I wish to be, but I did speak with the Director early this morning. I think Armand's got some real concerns about this one. It's my impression they need us to find out exactly what is happening over there, and they need us to do it quickly."

"Then we have approval from the National Command Authority to proceed, sir?" Simpson had been a businessman and an ambassador, and Fagan had been a spy. Both were men to whom discretion came easily and naturally. Neither would say outright, "Does the President know?"

Simpson smiled. "Inasmuch as we get approval for what we do, yes, we have it. Or at least, we have what they will deny they gave us if we get caught. Bring me up to speed. Where are we with this?" He rose to put on some water for coffee.

"My people are putting together the details as we speak. This is our preliminary mission concept." Steven laid it on the table and continued, knowing Simpson would want a verbal report. "The target seems to be a small upscale hotel in northern Zimbabwe. It's a remote area, one road in and out. It's very rough country. The information is sketchy, but this hotel seems to be the locus for some strange and illegal activity. Two top European medical personnel with suspected links to bioterrorism have gone missing, and I just learned while I was airborne that we have identified a third. We've reason to believe, primarily from Langley's product, that this hotel in Zimbabwe may be a base for biological weapons development and testing. We have nothing concrete, but a lot of indicators point to that. And the Harare government is being very uncooperative. We think they're up to no good, but we'll have to put a team in there to find out. It could get messy, militarily and, if it's what we suspect, biologically."

For the next half hour, Steven outlined how they proposed to move, from Hawaii to Lusaka, and across the Zambezi lowlands into Zimbabwe. There were no U.S. or friendly government assets in the region they could use, and more than a few they wanted to keep in the dark about their presence in the area, including U.S. embassy personnel. Since surprise was essential, it was going to have to be an entirely black operation. It would be a covert action.

"Is the foundation currently involved in Zambia?"

Simpson had to think about this for a moment. The Joseph Simpson Jr. Foundation did a lot of work in Africa. So did any number of NGOs. "It seems to me that we make periodic deliveries of medical supplies for the Aambia National AIDS Network. And we are one of the primary supporters of Aqua Aid, a very worthy NGO that specializes in community participation in water projects. We provide help to others on a case-by-case basis, and when we have assets in the area. Let's go into my office."

Steven followed into a richly appointed study, anchored by an enormous wooden desk. The screen saver was a portrait of a young man Steven recognized as Simpson's son. Simpson entered the foundation Web site and punched through several screens.

"Ah, here it is." He read for a moment before looking up. "It looks like there is only one other organization to which we contribute on an ongoing basis: the Zambia Media Women's Association."

"What do they do?" Steven asked.

"If it's similar to other groups we support, they work through media outlets to promote gender issues, literacy, and advocate for women's rights in the country. As in most developing nations, women fall somewhere between chattel and farm animals. In many of these areas, even places like Zambia where there is a small Muslim minority, women are the nation's greatest untapped resource. In most African tribal cultures, a woman's role is to have children and work, period. I don't even want to get into the female circumcision practices; they are beyond barbaric. We have a department within the foundation that works women's issues in developing nations. I'll get you a point of contact."

"That may be helpful. Needless to say, we will make judicial use of the foundation's interaction with these local NGOs, but so far, it's probably the best cover we have there."

"I understand, Steven, and we trust your discretion. After all, that's one of the foundation's collateral duties. Whenever possible, we provide cover and support for your activities." The Joseph Simpson Jr. Foundation and IFOR were both the visions of Joseph Simpson. The foundation was his passion, but he wanted to do more than just good works; he wanted to oppose evil, the kind of evil that had killed his son. While he was ambassador to Russia, Jim Watson had been the CIA station chief there. The two had worked well together; Simpson allowed Watson to do his job, and along the way, he acquired a feel for clandestine operations. When he envisioned standing up a secret organization like IFOR, he prevailed on Watson for a recommendation. He needed a man with a background in paramilitary operations and covert action, and he needed a man with a great degree of character. Watson immediately recommended Steven Fagan. So Fagan and Simpson had been together from the beginning.

The relationship was based on personal and professional respect. The two men, with vastly different backgrounds and experience, got on quite well. Simpson had long given up on trying to get Steven to use his first name; it was always "sir" or "ambassador." For Steven, it would be like calling your father by his first name. But this little convention only seemed to stimulate the affection the two men felt for each other.

"So we have your permission to proceed?" Steven asked. This was also part of the protocol that would commit the IFOR to a mission.

"You do indeed, Steven." He held out his hand. "Good luck, and good hunting."

"Thank you, sir. I'll have the executive summary of the operations plan and support requirements to you in forty-eight hours. As you know, we have a crack operational planning team, but the planning does take time."

Simpson didn't ask Steven to stay over, nor did he expect to. For some men, being in the same house, even a large one, was like sharing a double bed with another man. They needed their space. And both men knew that long trips were not all that tiring when you had on-call executive jet aircraft. The Gulfstream took Steven back to Hawaii. It was necessarily smaller than the 550, to allow them to get into Edgartown Airport, but it was no less luxurious or well equipped. After setting down in Las Vegas just after dark to refuel, they raced the dawn west and were on the tarmac at the Kona airport just before sunup.

On the trip back to Hawaii, Steven spoke at length with key members of his staff and again with Jim Watson. Like all GSI aircraft, this one was equipped with a secure electronics suite and communications package. He enjoyed a delicious meal, with lobster bisque and a superb lamb chop, and managed a few hours of sleep. With the sound-canceling headphones in place, it was as quiet as a still evening at his home in Wiamea.

5

THE SCOUTS

Pavel Zelinkow had a nagging feeling that someone or something was not as it should be. He had been engaged in covert undertakings long enough to feel when things were wrong. During the many years he was with the KGB and for the few months he remained with its successor, the Federal Security Service, he had come to respect the CIA and other Western intelligence services. Out of that respect, Zelinkow had developed a sixth sense that warned him of trouble—when the other side might be plotting something or preparing to move against one of his own operations. The Federal Security Service, or FSS, had neither the teeth nor the professionalism of the old KGB. There would, he reflected, probably never be another organization like it. When most in the West thought of the KGB, they thought of Beria, SMERSH, Lubyanka, and the like. Or saw them only as thugs or the puppet masters of the Czech and East German services. Few today understood the reach and capability of what had been the KGB. There had been dignity and purpose and service to the motherland. Some of his mentors were among the most brilliant intelligence professionals ever to play the game. They had taught him his craft, but a great deal more; they taught him to be cautious and to try to anticipate the moves of the opposition.

"You have a nose for this business," one of them had told Pavel early on. "We can teach you a great deal about the mechanics and tradecraft, but never abandon your instincts. Your instincts are what separate the army of spies from the true intelligence professionals."

Zelinkow's instincts were now telling him that something was indeed amiss. He had long ago learned to spot the fingerprints and subtle overtones of opposition services—the CIA, Mossad, MI-6, but primarily the CIA. If not always the most accomplished, they certainly had the most resources. He had the distinct feeling that some organization or force was now playing the game with a little more skill and a little more flair than a state service. He understood this. After all, he thought, have I not taken my game up a notch or two since leaving my post and office at 3 Dzerzhinsky Square? Those of us who engage in covert activity evolve, just like technologies and species.

Zelinkow had been with the KGB's Ninth Directorate, the directorate responsible for terror and diversion, where he had made quite a name for himself. When Gorbachev began to dismantle the KGB, he began first with the Ninth Directorate. This had proved to be a blessing in disguise, for it launched Zelinkow into the world of private intelligence work ahead of the horde of out-of-work KGB officers coming behind him. He was on his own now, but that didn't mean he couldn't use some assistance from time to time or an occasional helping hand from his former organization. Zelinkow was browsing through the French-language edition of the *Times* of London when an attendant approached him.

"Monsieur Boulez, there is a gentleman at the front desk asking for you."

"Merci," Zelinkow replied in flawless French. "I'll come at once."

Zelinkow's guest was a wizened, shrunken man with alert eyes and a perpetual, playful smile. He had to be well into his seventies, but his sturdy Tartar genes made him seem ageless. The man wore a greatcoat, fur hat, and sturdy shoes. He appeared very much out of place standing here in the United Premier Club at Orly Airport, though he would have easily fit in with other travelers passing through the Moscow Airport. Zelinkow embraced the old gentleman with real affection.

"Boris Zhirinonovich," he said in Russian, just loud enough for the older man to hear, "welcome to Paris. It is good to see you again. Thank you for coming."

The older man held him at arm's length for a moment to take him in. "And you, Pavel. You are looking well."

"Please, come up to the lounge," Zelinkow said, reverting to French. "I have a table for us."

He led the older man up the stairs to a private table off to one corner in the expansive lounge area. Once seated, he ordered coffee, vodka, and a plate of sausages. They conversed easily in French, and could have done so in a half a dozen other languages. When the waitress had left them, they reverted to their native Russian.

"So tell me about yourself, Boris. You have managed to stay out of retirement, from what I gather?"

"In a manner of speaking," Zhirinon replied. "I am what the American attorneys would call 'of counsel.' I am called in to advise on matters of policy and occasionally for an operational matter. Vladimir still deludes himself that if a few of us old-timers are around, the old organization is still what it was. Nothing could be further from the truth, but it does allow me to keep my hand in the game. Although, as you well know, the game is nothing what it used to be."

"But, old friend, there is very little that goes on in the FSS that you do not know about."

"Or cannot find out," the old man said with a smile.

"That too. And tell me, how is your family? You have what, five grandsons, or is it six?"

Zelinkow drew him out, but carefully. Boris Zhirinon was not a man to be flattered or manipulated. He had, at one time, been head of Ninth Directorate and the head of the Russian Foreign Intelligence Service when it became a separate entity from the KGB. He had been "retired" for more than a decade, but old spymasters, East or West, never totally come in from the cold. Furthermore, Zhirinon had been not only Pavel Zelinkow's superior and mentor; he had been Vladimir Putin's, as well. Putin had been a colonel in the KGB and a fifteen-year veteran of the service. With the old Soviet Union facing collapse, he retired and began his meteoric political career. At only fifty years of age Putin became head of the Russian state, highly impressive in a country governed so long by an entrenched oligarchy. But Putin did not forget his roots, nor those who had helped him along the way.

"It is said, Pavel, that you had a hand in the stealing of two nuclear weapons from the Pakistanis. Of course, when that question has been put to me, I say that nothing could be further from the truth. I tell anyone who asks that Pavel Zelinkow, not unlike myself, is retired from the business—that his interests are in the theater and the opera, not international weapons theft." The older man smiled and sipped cautiously at his coffee, looking fondly at his young protégé. Zhirinon also enjoyed letting Zelinkow know that his recent activities had not gone unnoticed.

Zelinkow's features remained impassive, but he was taken aback that Zhirinon could have any way of knowing about his activities. "It is true that I have a passion for the theater and the opera, my friend. But like yourself, I do try to keep my hand in the game. Would this be wrong, so long as the small amount of work I do does not hurt Mother Russia? Or perhaps even helps her?"

"What is wrong and what is right these days?" Zhirinon

said with some resignation. "The West grows stronger, as do the Chinese. And to the south, the Muslim states snap at us with impunity. There are enemies wherever we turn."

"Then," Zelinkow offered, "perhaps our only strategy is to make sure that our enemies remain the enemies of each other. America became a great power by allowing Nazi Germany and Soviet Russia to spend themselves on each other." Zhirinon remained silent, so Zelinkow continued, aware he was on dangerous ground. "Had the nuclear weapons taken from the Pakistani arsenal been detonated in Afghanistan with loss of American life, then would not the West have responded by moving forces into the area, possibly even into Pakistan? Would that not lure them into a move that would prove costly and divisive, much as it has in Iraq?"

"Possibly," Zhirinon replied, "and possibly not. Playing games with the Americans is always dangerous business. The deepening of the rift between America and the Muslim world is not a bad thing. The trick is that the hand of Islam must be plainly shown in any move against the West. American politicians are led by American public opinion. The Americans can be terribly complacent, or they can be swift avengers." Then the old man smiled slyly. "They can also be manipulated, but manipulating America is like guiding a bear into a small room—a bear is not as stupid as he looks and can move much faster than would seem from his lumbering appearance."

Zelinkow considered this for a long moment. The old fox obviously knew more than he was saying. It was hard to know whether he carried an official or semi-official portfolio, or none at all. There is only one thing of which Zelinkow could be certain. Boris Zhirinon loved his country and would do all he could in its defense.

"What do we fear most, Boris? What is Mother Russia's enduring concern?"

They both knew the answer: China. With an economy three times as strong as Russia's and five times the population, how much longer would it be content to sit on its own side of the Siberian border? The undeveloped resources and land China so desperately needed were simply too tempting. Only force of arms could ensure that those resources remained under Russian control, and those resources alone were the motherland's only path back to her former greatness.

"What if," Zelinkow continued, "the Islamists were so foolish as to attack America in such a way as to bring about a massive retaliation? I am speaking of an attack so heinous that the moderates and the fundamentalists in all of Islam would come under siege. Would not such an attack allow us to then secure our southern borders and free us to turn our attention to the East?"

What Zelinkow now implied was that this would allow Russia to repatriate Georgia and Ukraine back into greater Russia, and permit them to once and for all deal with the Chechens. Russia had finite military resources. Chechnya and the "Stans" along their southern border tied up far too much of those resources. If the Muslim nations on Russia's border were forced to look south, not north, then those resources could be deployed to better advantage along the Sino-Russian border.

"Just what kind of foolish attack are we talking about?"

They talked for another hour. They spoke guardedly, often obliquely, but were honest in the way of spies who have slightly differing agendas. Neither told the other exactly everything, but they did agree that a deepening rift between the Muslim world and America would benefit Russia. And this would not be their last conversation on the matter. They were also forced to agree, with much reluctance, that the Western vodka they were drinking was superior to that distilled in the motherland. When their flights were called, they again embraced and parted for different concourses. Zhirinon caught an Aeroflot flight to St. Petersburg, continuing on to Moscow. Zelinkow flew KLM to Berlin and on to Rome. Neither traveled under his own name, nor with a Russian passport.

The small cocktail lounge of the Makondo Hotel was intimate, well appointed, and well stocked, but there was no one behind the bar. At the Makondo, which meant "eagle" in Shona, services were kept to a minimum by a reduced contract staff from neighboring Mozambique. They were paid in cash, treated well, and totally intimidated by Claude Renaud and his men. They occupied separate quarters and came to the hotel in shifts to prepare food, clean rooms, and keep the premises in order. They tended to everything on the upper floors, but were forbidden to go into the basement on penalty of death. If the rumors circulating among this captive, resident staff were accurate, it was a penalty worse than death. The patrons in the bar might have to serve themselves, but the absence of a bartender allowed them to speak more freely. The lounge was the exclusive province of the hotel's clinical personnel.

The Mozambicans and Renaud's security contingent had been told that this was a private research effort to develop cures for AIDS, Ebola, and other Africa-centric diseases. At the top of the agenda was AIDS, and many of those brought to the hotel-turned-clinic were already infected with the AIDS virus. It was further explained that the families of these unfortunates were paid a fee for their loved ones volunteering for this research, with the added bonus that they might in fact be cured of the disease. Neither the small housekeeping staff nor the soldiers really believed this story, but it kept them out of the off-limits areas.

Helmut Klan helped himself to a generous dollop of schnapps and found a table in the corner. He was soon joined by a man in a white lab coat. Klan had always wondered why laboratory personnel were so fond of lab coats when off duty. Most evenings the bar looked like a Good Humor convention. There were perhaps fifteen of them altogether, but they all seemed to need a drink at the end of the day. Perhaps, Klan reflected, it was the work that they did. He rose to meet his guest.

"Hans, my friend, how goes the battle?"

"We are close, Helmut, very close. I want to set up another series of tests to confirm the incubation period. Then we can move to manufacturing and packaging. If all goes well, perhaps another few weeks—three at the outside." English was spoken in the lab, as its personnel represented a half dozen nationalities, but when these two spoke in hushed tones, they naturally reverted to their native German. "I hate to ask this of you, but I will need another group of hosts."

"How many?" Klan asked.

"Ten, but preferably a dozen." In reality, he needed only six, but with the prevalence of AIDS in Zimbabwe, that many were needed to find at least six free of the virus.

Klan nodded. He had no choice. "But you think this will be it; this will be the last of the testing?"

"There are no givens in this venture, Helmut, you know that. But I see nothing further after this." He held up a tumbler half filled with whiskey. "We need to wrap this up; my liver can't take much more." He took a large swallow from his glass, drawing his lips back along his teeth. "I need to get back to a cooler climate and some good Munich beer."

Dr. Hans Lauda was the head of the medical team. He had been a top geneticist at the University of Bonn when he had a falling out with the dean of the medical faculty over stem-cell research. Once you were sacked at a German university, there was little else to do but look for work in the private sector. He worked for several small pharmaceuticals, one of which asked if he'd like to work abroad on a classified project. Lauda's wife, who missed the trappings of the academic life, had long since run off with an economics professor, so he took the job. For four years he had lived well in a villa just outside Baghdad, engaged in biological weapons research for Saddam Hussein. In late 2002, with the threat of the American invasion on the horizon, he had been paid off and asked to leave. His laboratory and the results of his work had been packed up and shipped off to Damascus.

With a nice stash of euros in the bank, Lauda had gone to the south of France to, in his words, de-Arab himself. After a year of good wine, plump women, and a thorough cleaning at the tables in Monaco, he returned to Berlin to look for work. But there he found that the pharmaceuticals were offering only journeyman clinical wages. Lauda's appetites had grown well beyond that kind of pay. He was then contacted by Helmut Klan and asked if he would like to go back overseas. Klan seemed to know a great deal about his work in Iraq. He didn't say exactly where overseas, but the job would only be for about six months, and the money was good—very good, even by Baghdad or Berlin standards. Lauda was paid a retainer and told to wait until the rest of the "research team" was assembled. Dr. Lauda fully anticipated that this research would be highly illegal, judging by the money offered, but then he was accustomed to that. He had worked for four years in Iraq for General Ali Hassan al-Majid, better known as Chemical Ali. There were no illusions about the research he would be doing or what that research product might be used for.

"Keep me posted on your progress, Hans. We all want out of here as soon as possible. I'll see about the hosts."

Klan knocked back the schnapps and took his leave, glancing around the empty lobby as he crossed the foyer to the front door of the hotel. Some hotel, Klan mused. In reality the place was a little shop of horrors. He could easily have put this off until the following morning, but he wanted to get it over with. It was a pleasant enough evening, so he set out to complete his mission. He was anxious to return to his suite for another schnapps and a good book. The Makondo Hotel had an elaborate spa, massage room, and juice bar in a separate building from the main hotel complex. Klan suspected that the Japanese and then the Saudis had used it for a whole host of carnal pleasures, but Claude Renaud had turned it into something of a noncommissioned officers' club. They had set up a few dart boards and carried in a billiard table. Instead of juice they had an ample supply of the local sweet African beer. It was quite different from the Munich brew that Hans Lauda longed for.

On his way to the spa complex, Helmut Klan considered the leader of his security force. He could understand Hans Lauda and the other members of the clinical staff, but Renaud was an entirely different species. He stepped through the screen door and closed it quietly behind him. From the entranceway he paused to watch Renaud. The big mercenary was commanding attention over a group of his men, who were mostly white. All were dressed in veld patrol attire—shorts, short-sleeved bush shirts, and rough-out boots. His voice boomed above the others; he clearly enjoyed the limelight.

Men like Claude Renaud, who have served in special military units at a very young age, tend to mature very quickly. They soon acquire a confidence and self-assurance well beyond their years. They can find themselves the object of respect, even envy, to civilians and conventional military units. All this is a powerful cocktail for a young warrior. For most, it becomes a personal yardstick by which they take measure of themselves, and it drives them to improve and extend their warrior skills. Knowledge of self becomes an engine for growth that allows them to succeed in any number of personal endeavors. But occasionally, it freezes a man in place, at a single point in time; he never moves beyond it, nor has any desire to. Claude Renaud was such a man.

Renaud grew up in Durban, South Africa, at a time when being white conferred a great many advantages. Yet as a young man he failed at many things. His father was a mining engineer, his mother a heavy drinker. An only child, he attended a private school, as did most white children in Durban, but struggled with his studies. Renaud was not dull, but tended to be more cunning than intellectually curious. Since he was bigger than most of his classmates, he easily assumed the role of bully. Before he was expelled from school at the age of fifteen, he had a taste of what it was to have others fear him and to curry his favor to stave off his wrath. No other experience gave him such pleasure or sense of self-worth as the physical domination of others. His father managed to get him a job at a mining concession, and since he was white, he was given a junior overseer's position. He immediately became abusive to his crew, physically and verbally. But these black men were very stoic about his excesses, denying Renaud the ability to intimidate them. This only encouraged him to further denigrate them. Most mine owners worked their blacks unmercifully, but in their own fashion they did take care of them, much as a hunter cares for his gun dogs. Few mine owners tolerated mindless abuse of their workers. It wasn't even a racist issue for Renaud; he simply had a need for others to fear him. After repeated warnings, he was fired, and personally escorted from the concession by the mine foreman.

"You're not capable of working with other men," the foreman told Renaud, "let alone being in charge of them. Now beat it, and don't come back."

Renaud's next move was the wrong one. In his rage and humiliation, he swung on the foreman. The big Afrikaner, like Renaud, had been a bully in his youth, but he had grown out of it and was now a tough but responsible mining foreman. He easily slipped Renaud's punch and then proceeded to beat him within an inch of his life. The beating was not personal, but it was physical and emotional, as the foreman knew it would be for a young man like Renaud. The foreman hoped that perhaps this might cause him to reflect on why it had come to this, and perhaps help him to see things differently. The effect was just the opposite. It convinced Renaud that he was not tough enough, or perhaps not brutal enough. He returned to Durban in complete humiliation, his face swollen and distorted from the pounding he had taken. People stared, and their looks of pity, along with a few smirks, seared his soul. That night he met a middle-aged black man on a side street, a minor municipal employee on his way home from work. Renaud dragged him into an alley and beat and kicked him to death. It was the only tonic for the rage that burned inside him.

Renaud immediately left South Africa and made his way north to Salisbury. He was only sixteen, but he lied about his age and joined the Rhodesian Army. During basic training, he worked hard, for he was someone who, when motivated, could focus his energies on a specific goal. He graduated at the top of his recruit class and found himself in Rhodesian African Rifles. At last, Claude Renaud felt he was where he belonged. The struggles for succession to the colonial powers was just beginning to heat up, and that meant the Communist-backed guerillas were moving against the European rulers still in power, as well as the fledgling black democracies. The white men were leaving, and power would evolve to the strongest, which in Africa meant the most brutally persistent. Government by consent of the governed was an idea with little traction on the continent. Rhodesia held on longer than most because of its superb army. This holding action was a little more vigorous because the Rhodesians, whites and blacks alike, were highly professional. They also could be almost as ruthless in the field as the Communist-backed insurgent forces vying for control of the country. But even during the brutal counter-guerrilla sweeps, where the killing and burning could often be indiscriminate, Corporal Claude Renaud had to be repeatedly cautioned by his sergeant and lieutenant. One day, after he shot some guerillas who were trying to surrender, the battalion sergeant major took him aside and said, "I'll give you a choice, Renaud. I'll see you up for court-martial, or you can join the Scouts."

The Selous Scouts ran their own training facility at a bush camp called Wafa Wafa, some forty miles from the town of Kariba. The name came from the Shona phrase *Wafa wasara*, "If you die, you die." It was a good name for the facility. The training itself lasted only three weeks. It was more a testing than training, designed to summarily weed out those who hadn't the heart or the temperament to fight in the bush. Claude Renaud, who could on occasion summon within himself a tenacity and vitality, managed to complete this grueling entrance exam. The proudest day of his life was when he was allowed to wear the coveted chocolate beret with the silver osprey badge. Like most elite forces, the Scouts kept pretty much to themselves, but Renaud loved nothing better than going into a bar in Kariba wearing military bush attire and his beret. He was a Selous Scout, and no one could ever take that away from him.

But the Selous Scouts were not parade-ground soldiers. They spent long periods of time in the bush, living off the land and tracking insurgents to their base camps. They often fought vicious, bloody engagements where they were heavily outnumbered. It was a difficult and dangerous business, one that required skill, patience, and a great deal of courage. A man, black or white, was treated with the respect he earned in the field. The Selous Scouts were one of the few fully integrated elite military units where whites served in the minority. The backbone of the Scouts were the warrant or noncommissioned officers, men who had spent years in the bush and had earned their leadership positions on the battlefield. Most of these hard, capable men were black. Following a raid into a ZANLA base camp area where the resistance had been particularly stiff, Renaud shot and killed several bound prisoners—executed them, in fact. Not only was this brutal, it was tactically unsound. Many of those they captured were "turned" by the Scouts and served the government cause, often with great distinction. When Renaud's warrant officer called him on this, he said something to the effect that the only good kaffir was a dead kaffir. After the company returned from the raid, the warrant asked Renaud to step out onto the dirt parade ground in front of the barracks. For the second time in his life he was beaten half to death, only this time it was by a black man in front of his company mates. The black warrant officer was as tall as Renaud, but just a fraction of his bulk and very fast. Following the thrashing, Renaud was dragged before his company commander and summarily dismissed from the Selous Scouts. This beating and abasement became a burning coal in the pit of his stomach that could never be extinguished. Every few years someone, somewhere, would bring it up, and he was forced to relive the humiliation. He never forgot the beating, nor the man who had given it to him.

From there, Renaud made his way back to South Africa, where a former Selous Scout, under any circumstances, was welcome in the South African Defense Force. After four years of undistinguished service in the SADF, mostly in Namibia fighting UNITA guerillas, he took a job with a Johannesburg security firm. He was assigned to guard the homes of wealthy white South Africans, a line of work that suited him; his size and presence was enough to discourage most casual thieves and burglars. It all ended when Nelson Mandela and his African National Congress came to power in 1994. It wasn't that whites were persecuted in postapartheid South Africa, but the traditional advantages afforded whites were rapidly disappearing. Renaud and any number of ex-military security guards found themselves out of work when their patrons took what was left of their personal wealth and headed for Europe, Australia, or America. With the South Africa he knew disappearing around him, Renaud learned that an organization for former SADF personnel with experience in the colonial wars was hiring—a private military force called Executive Outcomes. They payed well, and between jobs he could hang out in Johannesburg with other white mercenaries while they waited for work.

Something in Renaud sensed that the sporadic mercenary contracts were his last chance to remain in some kind of uniform—and the only work he knew. So when he was on the job, he did what he was told and no more. He was capable enough, and few whites in the mercenary trade were model soldiers. Most had something in their past they preferred not to talk about. Renaud still wore the silver osprey badge of the Selous Scouts on his beret. The reputation of the Selous Scouts and the Rhodesian Army still inspires fear and awe in central and southern Africa, and Renaud traded heavily on that reputation. He could always find work as a hired gun, but no more than that. Any chance at something more than journeyman's mercenary wages was quickly extinguished when some-one mentioned his exile from the Selous Scouts. Like honor among whores, those who paid for mercenary serv-ices wanted only to deal with those they could trust— military leaders who had a reputation for honesty and discretion. Leadership skills and integrity were essential in riding herd on a group of mercenary soldiers. Renaud had long wanted to contract for his own force, but while his spotty reputation was good enough for an occasional hir-ing and tall talk in the bars where expatriate mercs hung out, no one wanted him as a principal. No responsible government or mining consortium would contract for an unreliable mercenary leader. Mercenary intervention was dicey business at best, without the risk of an overzealous or excessive force. The contracting sources looked for reli-ability and integrity, and for those who managed merce-nary undertakings, reputation was everything. If they found themselves on the wrong side of an issue, or if the forces under their direction used excessive means, it could spell disaster, financially and in the court of world opin-ion. As they said in the trade, it would "ruin the brand," and they would not see another contract. Most mercenary contracts in Africa involved securing and guarding min-ing properties; it was about the ore—that and attracting as little attention as possible.

Claude Renaud was quite surprised, therefore, when he was contacted by a Frenchman named Georges Frémaux. At the time, Renaud had been drinking his way through his meager savings while living in a sleazy flat in Maputo. Maputo, the capital of Mozambique, was much cheaper than Joburg. Frémaux asked Renaud to meet him in Harare to discuss a project, and had made all the arrange-ments, including round-trip airfare from Maputo. During the hour-and-a-half flight, in one of the 737's four first-

class seats, Renaud managed to throw down four Crown
Royals on the rocks. At Harare Airport, a waiting car
whisked him to the Hotel New Ambassador. Following the
written instructions left for him at the desk, he took a cab
that evening to the Crown Plaza Monomatapa Hotel,
where Monsieur Frémaux was waiting for him in the dining room. There, over dinner and coffee, Frémaux, aka
Pavel Zelinkow, laid out his project. He wanted Renaud to
recruit and train a force of sixty men to provide security
for a medical experimentation project in Zimbabwe. It
seemed that a small, well-financed research group that
Frémaux represented was very close to perfecting an AIDS
vaccination. In order to bring their product to market,
they wanted to bypass animal testing and go right into
using the test vaccine on humans.

"I want you to understand that this is clearly illegal,"
Frémaux told him. "We have no right to test this vaccine
on humans. But in Zimbabwe, especially in the remote
Tonga Province, we have an ideal situation. Perhaps one
in three Zimbabweans have the AIDS virus, so any cross-
section of test cases will give us a control group and an infected group. And given the remote location of our facility
in this province, we will have little outside interference
while we conduct these vital experiments. You see," he
said, carefully lowering his voice, "this is about human
suffering and about money. If we can move directly to
human testing, then we can make this vaccine available
perhaps two or even three years sooner than if we go
through channels. But not if we go through the silly procedures imposed on us by the bureaucrats." He leaned forward, taking the measure of Renaud. "And most of those
bureaucratic requirements are imposed on us by the
American and European pharmaceutical companies. So
you see, it's about money. A lot of big pharmaceutical
companies are working on an AIDS drug. If we get there

first, we beat the big guys to the bank. But we need security, and we need discreet security, so we can perfect our drug. I want them to be well trained and able to protect and defend the project if necessary. And we may need you and your men to assist in looking for volunteers among the local population."

Frémaux did not have to spell it out for Renaud, but the former Scout did have one question. "What about the Zimbabwe Republic Police? What's to keep them from interfering with the operation?" Renaud was asking if he was expected to pay off the local police or any army unit that might come snooping around with his own funds.

"That has been taken care of," Frémaux replied. "And if more funds are required to ensure their lack of interest in the project, then we will take care of that as well. As you can see," he said as he handed the contract across the table to Renaud, "all expenses associated with the project will be carried by the project, and you will have broad discretion as to the hiring and management of your retainers." Frémaux watched closely as Renaud leafed quickly through to the page that detailed his compensation package. He saw Renaud swallow hard, and his eyes dilate.

"Here is a packet of information that covers the site in Zimbabwe, which is in fact a small luxury hotel, and the basics of what you will need to recruit your force. You will be able to conduct sustainment training on-site, but we prefer that you set up a bush training camp for your initial interviews, testing, and basic training. You will have to be sure of your men once you bring them to the operational site, as the secrecy of the work there must be absolute. Any breach of security could lead to compromising the site and endangering the project. And as you can see, there is a sizable bonus to be paid at the completion of the project, but only if security is not breached. I too will enjoy a comparable fee on completion, so I am trusting you to do your job and do it quietly. I hope, Monsieur Renaud, I have chosen the right man for this task."

Renaud assured this precise, serious Frenchman that indeed he had chosen the right man. Frémaux had given Renaud an encrypted cell phone and a single international number, making it clear that Renaud was to call if he had questions and provide ongoing status reports. Frémaux handed over a check made out to Renaud personally, drawn on a bank in Zurich, and gave him account information for a second bank in Bern on which he could draw operational expenses. With that, Georges Frémaux bid him a good evening and excused himself.

The next morning, when Claude Renaud presented his draft to the Bank of Zimbabwe, he was expected. He was paid in South African rand and walked out of the bank with more money than he had ever seen in his life. Rather than use his new cell phone, he called the Crown Plaza from a pay phone and asked for a Mr. Frémaux, only to be told they had no guest registered by that name. Renaud flew back to Mozambique. He had not been back to his dingy flat in Maputo more than an hour when the cell phone rang. It was Frémaux, phoning to ask if he had a pleasant flight back and if their arrangements were satisfactory. Over the next four months, as the recruiting and training progressed, they talked often. Renaud was aware that Frémaux seemed to know a great deal about him and the progress of his work, but Renaud knew absolutely nothing about his employer. The personal checks continued to come, however, and were honored when he came in from the bush to cash them.

With this mandate to raise and train a force, and more importantly, the funds to make it happen, Claude Renaud set out to create his version of the Selous Scouts. Perhaps one day, he told himself as he bent to the task, they will call us the Renaud Scouts. The first thing he did was to visit the site of the original Scouts training camp at Wafa Wafa, about an hour by Land Rover from the town of Kariba. In the thirty years since Captain Ron Reid Daily formed the Selous Scouts, the huts of the camp had been taken over by squatters. Renaud thought of moving them out, but the camp was too close to the lake for the kind of training he had in mind. Further inland from the Wafa Wafa, he found a disused game preserve, one that had been used for the breeding of native species for export to foreign zoos. With a modest payment to an official in Kariba who was responsible for land reallocation in the area, Renaud leased the property for a year. He now had a hundred square miles of bush, several thatch-roofed huts, and a large prefab metal barn. He hired some local labor and set them to cleaning the buildings. The barn he turned into a barracks with military-style, metal-framed bunk beds. One of the huts would be used for equipment storage, while the other would serve as a cook house. He hired two of his cronies from Executive Outcomes to mind the work on the buildings while he booked himself on a flight from Harare to Johannesburg.

South African law prohibits the recruitment of mercenary soldiers, just as laws in the United States prohibit the sale of illegal drugs. But mercenary brokers can be found in South Africa, just as drug dealers can be found in the United States. Renaud knew just where to go and who to talk to. After he cleared customs at the Johannesburg airport, he rented a car and drove two hours east to the town of Ventersdorp. There he arranged a meeting with Moses Shiabe, who had contacts with veterans from the famous, or infamous, 32nd Battalion of the South African Army. Disbanded soon after Mandela came to power, the 32nd had fought for years in the Angolan and Namibian wars, and were considered the best bush fighters in the South African Army, or any army, for that matter. These black veterans were used to working with, and taking direction from, white officers. Most spoke Afrikaans and English as well as their own tribal dialect. All were professional soldiers—hard men not given to bragging or bravado. They were also brutal men, used to the harsh life in the bush. If so directed, they would kill anyone of any age or gender, without hesitation and without remorse.

Renaud met Shiabe at his ramshackle home on the outskirts of Ventersdorp, and for a fee of 1,000 rand, about $160 U.S., he was allowed to look at a roster of available candidates. There were hundreds of names. Renaud ticked off thirty-five and told Shiabe to select fifteen more. Of the thirty-five, Renaud had soldiered with most in the South African Army or on a contract with Executive Outcomes. Others he knew by reputation. He gave Shiabe a generous bonus and admonished him to make the final selections with care. His only direction was that none were to be Shona or Matebele, the two dominant tribes in Zimbabwe. The fifty men were to be given a signing bonus and plane ticket from Johannesburg or Pretoria to Harare. Shiabe would arrange for their visas as laborers or construction workers. He had done this many times before, and these soldiers were quite used to filtering into black African capitals under false documentation. From the Harare airport, they would be met and ferried to the training site.

Once back in Johannesburg, Renaud was free to do what he had always dreamed of doing. He went to the Broken Tusk Bar for a drink and to recruit a contingent of white mercenaries for his force. This was a new role for him, one that he openly relished. White mercenaries looking for work made daily treks to haunts like the Broken Tusk to learn if someone was hiring. Renaud himself had done that often. Now he was the man with the contract; he was the one hiring. The Broken Tusk was a dingy clapboard storefront in the warehouse district. A single bare lightbulb illuminated the doorway and the peeling sign over the door. Inside, it was a standard workingman's tavern with a tattered wooden bar, high stools, and a scattering of tables. The fixtures and furnishings were yellow with grease and cigarette smoke. Behind the bar was a small kitchen grill where a black man in a camouflage-pattern beret and dirty apron dealt out a surprisingly palatable array of dishes. He had cooked for many of those who frequented the Broken Tusk in the South African Army. The owner was a disheveled man in his late seventies with bloodshot eyes and skin baked to the color and texture of rawhide. He had served with Mad Mike Hoare and Black Jacques Schramme during the Congolese wars, and had the stories to prove it. No one knew his real name; he simply answered to the name of Gunner. Few could remember when he was not behind the bar at the Broken Tusk. It was late afternoon when Renaud made his entrance, and the Tusk was a little more than half full.

"Well, look what the warthog just dragged in," Gunner observed when Renaud walked in. He had no high regard for Claude Renaud, but a customer was a customer. Gunner could not remember what war story he had last told, but if he had served someone at his bar only once, no matter how long ago, he never forgot what they drank. As Renaud eased himself onto a stool, Gunner set a mug of Castle Lager and a bar scotch chaser in front of him. Renaud laid ten 100-rand notes on the bar.

"A round for the lot, mate," Renaud said. Gunner raised an eyebrow. He also remembered who bought and who didn't, and Claude Renaud had never paid for anyone but himself.

"The bar or the house?"

Renaud savored the question for a long moment before answering. "Make it for the house."

"So you say," Gunner replied neutrally and set about building drinks.

Those who provided mercenary services had long referred to themselves as PMCs—private military companies. It was the custom for the hiring agent of a PMC to buy a round for the house when he had a contract and needed men. A house round announced that Claude Renaud was hiring. Not a few in the Broken Tusk looked puzzled when another of what they were drinking was placed in front of them. Most could not fathom that Claude Renaud had a contract. But the chance for work, however remote the prospect, could not be ignored. Even from the likes of Renaud.

"Why, hello, Claude. How have you been keeping?"

The speaker was a painfully thin man, with stringy blond hair and a muskrat-like mustache. He wore a black T-shirt, jeans, and military boots. He had been an eighteen-year-old trooper in the Rhodesian Light Infantry when he volunteered for the Selous Scouts. He and Renaud had entered the training together; Renaud had made it, but he had not.

"Well, Reggie. Quite well, in fact. You fancy a game of darts?"

"Absolutely," Reggie replied.

They took their drinks to the rear of the Tusk. As if to document his intent, Renaud ignored the three notes that remained on the bar. There were two dartboards on the rear wall—no pool tables or pinball. The two began to pitch darts. Reggie was in fact quite good, but he played down to Renaud's game. Then, one by one, men began to push away from their tables or drop from their bar stools to join them.

It took Renaud the better part of two months to get his group assembled—fifty blacks and ten whites in all. Arming and outfitting men, even a force as small as this, was no small undertaking. But Mr. Frémaux seemed to anticipate his every move. It was always a different shipping agent and a different receiving dock, but when Renaud called Frémaux with an order, it was air-shipped within days to Harare, usually in crates labeled as tools or building supplies. The AKM assault rifles, with a generous measure of training ammunition, were indistinguishable from those carried by the Zimbabwe Republic Police. The uniforms, less badges and insignia, were also the same. For static-defense weapons there were two .50-caliber machine guns and several Russian-made RPD light machine guns. The only thing with a substantial punch were twenty Czech-made RPG-7s. Renaud as of yet had no idea how he might use the rockets, but no mercenary force that he had ever been with were without them. Every mercenary soldier in Africa could use an RPG-7. They could make short work of a reinforced bunker or an armored car.

The mechanics of the mercenary or PMC business usually required a long apprenticeship and a great deal of local knowledge. The new African nations had a long and contentious affair with armed intervention and mercenary force. Therefore there were strict laws governing the sale and ownership of guns, let alone military weapons. One had to know when to follow the rules, what rules could be circumvented, and what officials to bribe. Fortunately, the corrupt nature of fledgling African bureaucracies and deteriorating economic conditions made almost anything doable if you had the money. Renaud felt that none of these problems were beyond him, but it was as if the mysterious Mr. Frémaux did not want him to be involved with these details. He had only to ask, and the requested items magically appeared. Men and materials were ferried to the camp by a small fleet of Toyota 4x4s that Renaud had bought at a premium from a defunct shooting safari concession near Kariba. From the technicals in Mogadishu to Al Qaeda irregulars in Afghanistan to park rangers in Kenya, they had all learned from experience that Toyotas were the toughest, most easily maintained off-road vehicles in the world. Renaud had managed to procure a Mercedes stake truck for moving large pieces of equipment over unimproved roads, and a newer Land Rover for himself. He somehow couldn't picture Mike Hoare in the cab of a Toyota 4x4.

Pavel Zelinkow, who Renaud knew as Georges Frémaux, trusted Renaud neither to provision his force nor to make sure the proper officials in Harare were taken care of. Zelinkow paid a former executive with Sandline, a well-regarded British PMC, to make the arrangements. He had been on the procurement side of Sandline's operation and knew his business. The man had no idea where or for whom the weapons, ammunition, and material were destined; he simply delivered the needed arms and equipment to a shipping agent in Nairobi who was paid to forward them to Harare and not to question the contents of the crates. Nor did Renaud have any clue who was so capably equipping his force. Frémaux had never given him a company name, and even if he had, it almost certainly would have been a phony. Cutouts and shell companies were a part of the PMC business. Really, all Renaud knew was that he would command a group of seasoned mercenary professionals, and that he would be well paid to do it. Questions that might or should have occurred to him were lost as his long-held dream materialized.

Once in camp, Renaud called his company to quarters and addressed them. He told them that their duties would be to provide security for a hotel/research complex and to patrol the immediate countryside to ensure there was no local or governmental interference with the work to be conducted there. They were also told that they would have to monitor the volunteers who would be participating in the research effort. Like all paid mercenaries, the assembled soldiers received this information with stoic indifference. They did not particularly like, and certainly did not trust, Renaud, and they had no illusion that this venture was legal. But then they always worked in the shadows, with or without host government sanction. All they wanted to do was to collect the balance of their fee, which in this case was more than a standard wage, and live to spend it. All else was secondary.

For six weeks Renaud put his men through their paces. The blacks didn't need the conditioning work, but most of the whites did, including himself. Renaud understood that for an integrated unit to function, there had to be some shared effort and pain. This was as true among the ranks of soldiers for hire as for national military units. Even pros need time in the field to bond. And at his core, Renaud was nothing if not a professional soldier. He knew what it was to get down to business; now for the first time he was the drover, not part of the herd. He was their paymaster, and that made him their leader. For all his leadership inexperience and bravado, he was determined not to squander this opportunity. So he positioned himself at the head of the column on the conditioning runs, and he stayed there. He led them in calisthenics, and took his turn on the ranges during shooting drills. When it came to tactics, he divided his force into ten six-man teams. In charge of each team was one of Renaud's handpicked white mercs. They were all good men, experienced in tribal warfare. The blacks, while often more capable and more experienced, were content to follow their white team captains, up to a point.

Renaud drove them hard, perhaps harder than necessary, but this was his long-awaited opportunity to lead a band of mercenaries. He wanted to make the best of it. In the calculus that now drove him, he truly believed that this could be the beginning of his own PMC, the Renaud Scouts. And word would get around the tight-knit mercenary community that there was something of the Selous Scouts still in Claude Renaud. At the end of their training period, he presented each man with a crimson beret with a silver pin that bore more than a token resemblance to the osprey emblem of the Selous Scouts. If some in the assembly on the makeshift parade ground thought this odd or frivolous, they kept it to themselves. Renaud was, after all, their paymaster.

As Helmut Klan approached the makeshift bar in the improvised tavern, the men at the bar melted away to join the dozen or so soldiers playing cards or at the billiard table. Klan thought about asking Renaud to step outside to make his request, but he was anxious to be done with it and get back to his quarters.

"Good evening, *Herr Doktor*. May I get you something to drink?"

This meant a glass of that god-awful beer, as Renaud permitted nothing stronger in the garrison. "No, thank you, Claude. I have some late work to finish, and it will only make me sleepy."

"Perhaps another time," Renaud replied amiably. He was in a good mood, as he usually was when he drank with his men, but as Klan had again observed with much relief, Renaud drank often but was never drunk. "I've just spoken with the head of my medical team, and things are going well. They anticipate that their research experiments will be concluded soon, perhaps within the next few weeks. But we will need more test subjects."

"How many more?" Renaud inquired.

A few weeks after the clinical team had begun their work, there was a need for a steady stream of "volunteers" for test purposes. To ask for these volunteers in Kariba or the smaller outlying communities would announce their purpose. So Renaud and his men were instructed to make the disappearances appear random, trying not to take too many from one locale. They often traveled a hundred miles or more on one of these sweeps, hiding during the day and making their abductions at night. For these procurements, Renaud was paid 2,000 rand per head, half of which he shared with the team leader responsible for the body snatch. Jerking people from their huts at night was almost second nature to the veterans of the bush wars and, to some extent, to the civilian population, who had known little but war for the better part of three decades. At first they had released those who were sick or showed no symptoms of the testing. They were blindfolded coming and going, so they had no knowledge of where they had been, and they were too scared to talk. When the testing had moved into a phase where the subjects became contagious, the test subjects never left the complex alive.

"We will need a dozen."

"A dozen," Renaud replied. "And how soon do you need them?"

Klan did not like to tell him how to do his work, but said, "As soon as you can deliver them, but we need them all by the end of the week. If it makes the task any easier, these should be the last."

Renaud considered this for a long moment. "What would make it easier would be a 3,000-rand bounty for each we bring in. This is merely a request, but for this number I will have to scatter three teams over a large area to take care of it that quickly. Word is getting out, and it is only a matter of time before we are met with clubs and spears on entering some remote village hut."

"I see," Klan said. He knew he was being extorted, but then this was the last of the test hosts, and it was, after all, not his money. "Agreed. Bring them in and handle them in the same manner as you did the others."

"As you say, *Herr Doktor.* I will get two of the teams away this evening, and the third will leave after sundown tomorrow."

Klan excused himself and headed back to the hotel bar for another schnapps. Renaud sat pondering whether to split the additional bounty with his team leaders or keep it all for himself. After another glass of beer, he settled on the latter.

Two nights later Matta Mimbosa had just got the last of her children to sleep and had set out the meager rations of corn and oatmeal for her husband's and oldest son's breakfasts. After they left for their work, she would prepare the morning meal for the other children. Matta and her family lived in a group of huts just east of the village of Karoi. There were five dwellings at the end of their road, but only three were occupied. One of their neighbors had gone to South Africa to look for better work, and the other had gone to Botswana for the same reason. There were few jobs in rural Zimbabwe. Unemployment in the nation was 50 percent, and higher in the countryside. Wages were low, and usually a worker's first month's pay had to be given over as a bribe to the foreman or overseer. With her oldest son now working with her husband in a cement factory, things had been better—not good, but considerably better, now that there were two wage earners in the family.

They were Ndebele, and with the older son now working, her husband was now thinking of taking a second wife. A man's status and measure of respect was greatly enhanced by a second wife. Matta was indifferent to the matter. A new wife meant someone younger than herself—someone who would occupy a more favored position regarding her husband's affection. So be it. After bearing ten children, six of whom were still alive, let him rut with someone younger and stronger. It was his home, and he could do as he pleased. And another pair of hands to help with the house chores and the garden would not be unwelcome. Matta had born eight sons and only two daughters. Neither girl had lived past her first year, and two of the boys died in their second, which meant she had six sons. This delighted her husband, for having many sons reflected well on him, even more than having many cattle. But Ndebele men did no work at home, so Matta was both mother and servant, and as the boys grew older, she became less the former and more the latter. They quickly learned that all the work around the house was women's work. Men sat, drank, swatted flies, and talked. It was the way it had always been.

They had electricity—not all of the time, but this evening the power was on. Moving in the shadows cast by a single bare bulb, she tidied up the room and put away the dishes she had washed earlier from the evening meal. The men and boys had gone to bed, and there was a symphony of snoring from the sleeping rooms. Matta was accustomed to dragging her mat into the kitchen to sleep. She would be the last to go to bed and the first to rise. The house had plumbing and tap water when the electricity was on to run the pump, but the flush toilet had not worked for some time. She and the younger boys had dug a privy a short distance from the house, but they needed to fill the pit and dig a new one. Perhaps soon. Matta splashed water onto her face in the kitchen sink and blotted herself dry with a soiled dishtowel.

Stepping from the house, she paused a moment to take in the night sky. There was the Southern Cross, the Dove, and many other constellations she once knew but had long since forgotten. She walked past the outhouse, seeking the brush that edged the field that abutted their small plot of land. Often when it was late and quiet, she sought the bushes rather than the noxious smell and fly swarm of the privy. She had just hiked up her one-piece, ankle-length shift and squatted when an arm gripped her waist and a hand closed over her nose and mouth. She was jerked roughly to her feet, even as she lost her urine, wetting her thighs and dress.

"Listen closely, mother," a harsh voice said in her ear. The man who held her spoke in her native Sendebele. "Because what you say and what you do will determine how many of your family will live to see the sun rise."

Bound and gagged, Matta was marched back into her house, followed by four heavily armed men. They took her oldest son and blindfolded him, with his wrists bound and his elbows tied behind his back. It was between her husband and the son, and they elected to take the son. This was the decision of the black team sergeant; there were plenty of boys in this household.

Matta stood dazed in the middle of her kitchen, surrounded by prone black bodies, their faces down with their hands bound behind them with nylon snap-ties.

"Do not worry, mother," the harsh voice said as he backed to the door, sweeping the room with the muzzle of his weapon, "you still have many sons."

The door closed gently, and in the silence that followed, Matta Mimbosa lowered her head. Tears ran down her ebony cheeks. Another child lost. She thought of the boy who had been taken away and the boys bound on the floor of her home. Unconsciously, she rubbed her belly to feel the life that stirred there. She knew, as she always had before, that it was a boy.

6

DEPLOYMENT

"All right, I'm going to need your undivided attention for the better part of the next two hours. This will constitute the jump-off briefing for this operation. Since there is a lot we don't know and much that we yet need to know to accomplish this mission, this will be a phased deployment—one thing at a time. The first phase will entail getting what we think we might need into the region in a way that will provide us as much flexibility as possible. We still don't know what kind of a nut we have to crack, let alone how to crack it. Once we are on the ground, we tackle the next phase; getting people and assets into position to move against the target objective. Right now, we are obviously short of specific target data. And finally, the takedown of this objective. It's not going to be easy. We have to stage assets, move into position, and make our attack without alerting the locals or the opposition. We have a border crossing to make. And then we have to repatriate everyone and everything, leaving no footprint—or, as Steven would often have it, leave the footprint behind that we want read. In my opinion, it can be done, but as with any semi-denied-area operation, we will have to move carefully—one step at a time. Again, there's a lot we don't know, but hopefully, we can fill in many of the blanks along the way."

Janet Brisco stood behind a small elevated table that served as her briefing platform. They were assembled in the Kona operations building. The exterior was plywood prefab, with a corrugated metal roof; a post-and-pier construction with two feet of latticed crawl space under the single main flooring. There were thousands of similar buildings in Hawaii. Inside, it was part modern office space and part space-age military planning center. There were seven in her audience: Steven Fagan, Garrett Walker, Akheem Kelly-Rogers, Dodds LeMaster, Bill Owens, Tomba, and another of his Africans, a small ferret of a man with aquiline features, hooded eyelids, and a calm intensity. His name was Mohammed Senagal, the only Somali among the Africans. He was quite different in appearance and manner from Tomba, but both men seemed to radiate a quiet forcefulness. They had that measure of deadly serenity that only years of soldiering in extreme conditions could form in a man. In spite of their primitive appearance, both men spoke excellent English, and both were reasonably well versed in the application of modern technology to military applications. Brisco spoke a little slower in her briefing than normal, but she did not talk down to them. All eight of them had indexed briefing folders in front of them.

"Okay, let's start with what we do know." She touched a keypad on the table in front of her, and a satellite image emerged on the two-by-three-foot plasma display behind her. There were no cords from her laptop; the system functioned on a wireless local area network. She stepped to one side so everyone had a clear view.

"This is the area in northern Zimbabwe we have to penetrate. Mostly high veld cut by deep ravines and heavily wooded areas. There is worse country to cross, and there will be challenges if we have to move overland with any equipment. This is where we think we will have to go." She tapped the keyboard several times. A series of increasing magnifications and lower-resolution images resulted in the grainy outlines of a hotel complex. "This is it, gentlemen, the Makondo Hotel." She quickly outlined the Japanese-Saudi history of the structure, and what they knew of its most recent history. Then she flipped through several subtle variations of the same image. "You will note that there are very few vehicles about the complex, but those we do see are very inconsistent with a luxury hotel operation. About half of them are small pickup trucks, probably set up for off-road travel. Note that the gatehouse is positioned on the only improved road into the area. From all appearances, it's a normal security gatehouse—all hotels have them, right? Well, take a look at the emplacement off to the right of the guard shack." The image grew, larger and more grainy, then suddenly clarified. "With some computer enhancement by our friend Dodds, we have what appears to be a machine gun emplacement—a fifty-caliber machine gun emplacement. One of the problems in this part of Africa is that anything that is nice is very well guarded, sometimes even guarded with automatic weapons. But a fifty-caliber? If they have fifties, then it would follow they probably have RPGs, perhaps even mortars. That means they are probably prepared to deal with light armor and helicopter gunships. Something is going on there, and I'd wager it is more than elegant dining and Swedish saunas. Hotels in Africa do need security, especially those in remote areas, but a fifty-cal. is over the top.

"We have a set of architectural plans coming, but the French firm who designed the place turned out to be a little stingy about sharing their work. Damn Frogs made it necessary to go through a consulting engineering firm in London, pay them a fee, and sign a licensing agreement if the plans are used for future construction. Of necessity, we have to go slow, as we don't want to surface any unusual or urgent interest in the place. I should have them in forty-eight hours, so we will have them for final assault planning.

"Now take a look at what we just got in from the NRO. Langley finally got them to bring one of their high-resolution satellites across Lake Kariba. Here we have two vehicles parked out in the middle of nowhere, covered by camouflage netting. Who in the hell cammies up their vehicles in the daytime? The safari concessions don't do this, and there are no Zimbabwean military units in the area. Poachers, maybe, but I doubt it; they look too disciplined. We can't make the kind of vehicles, but the dimensions match a Toyota 4x4. Now look at this." A slightly oblique image showed two blurry, upright figures. Both had what appeared to be dark headgear. "Something look a little strange about these two?"

"They're both wearing berets," AKR offered.

"Exactly, and look at their arms. One is definitely black. The other is either a light-skinned black or a very tanned white guy. What do you make of this, Tomba?"

Tomba studied the image for a long moment before answering. "It has all the appearances of a long-range scouting party, one that moves at night and laagers up during the day. And it's a military unit. See the dark smudge well off to the right side of the lower vehicle?" Brisco marked it with a laser pointer. "Yes, there," Tomba continued. "That seems to be where they built a fire for their rations. It is also near a stand of bush willows, which provide good low cover for men in a laager. Men in a scouting party will seek shade away from their vehicles. Perhaps from habit and training, all men in scouting elements fear helicopters. If helicopters find their vehicles and attack, they will be able to engage the helicopters from a relatively safe location, or if the attack is overwhelming, fade into the bush. I agree they are not poachers. Poachers would have a single flatbed truck, and they would cover it with canvas and brush, not military netting. And no safari, photographic or shooting, would take these measures." Tomba glanced at the Somali, who blinked slowly and slightly lowered his head in agreement.

"Excellent. Thank you for that. So it seems we have located the center of activity, and it appears to be guarded by a professional, mobile military force, one that can, or has reason to, range well away from their base. Other than that, we know very little about the threat environment from a conventional perspective. Since we suspect biological activity, this brings on a whole other layer of consideration. If it comes to moving on this complex, resistance from what appears to be a security detachment with light infantry capability may be only a part of the problem. Needless to say, we need a lot more information. We will begin to deploy assets immediately. The planning process will be ongoing and will have to be flexible enough to account for new information. Under almost any other conditions, we would not even consider a regional deployment with this scant amount of knowledge, but the danger that this threat represents may be time-critical, so we move now. That said, let's get into your briefing materials."

AKR opened his packet, turning it forty-five degrees to read the tabs: Topography, Country Profiles, Indigenous Peoples, Military Orders of Battle, Phase One Equipment Listings, Loading and Movement Schedules, Cover Documentation, and the list went on—some nineteen tabs in all. It was the size of a phone book for a small city. He leaned close to Garrett.

"Is she always this anal?" he whispered.

Before Garrett could answer, she was on him. "You have a problem, Kelly-Rogers?"

"Oh, no problem at all, madame planner. I was just remarking to my colleague what a comprehensive set of materials you've assembled."

"Okay, then, let's get to it." She glanced at her watch. "We don't have a minute to lose if we're going to begin to move personnel and gear by day after tomorrow. Everyone turn to the first tab."

There was an immediate rustling of pages. Like gradeschool boys kept after school, they dutifully complied.

Judy Burks was waiting for Elvis Rosenblatt when he emerged from the jetway into the Delta concourse at Dulles International. Most Americans now meet new arrivals at the security screening exit, but if you happen to have an FBI credential, you can go right to the gate. He walked into the concourse wearing cargo pants, a tan bush shirt with button-down epaulets, and sand boots. He had a small underseat backpack swung over one shoulder. During all his time with the CDC and for all his expertise with exotic disease, he had been to Africa only twice, and on both occasions it was to address gatherings sponsored by the World Health Organization, usually at a four-star hotel. His talents lay in his research product, and research was best done in a well-equipped laboratory. There were none better than those at the CDC. Rosenblatt was strictly, in his words, a lab rat. The prospect of an actual field expedition was all very exciting.

"Oh, my God," Judy Burks said under her breath as she spotted him. "This is going to be a charming trip."

"Hey there, Agent Judy. Good to see you again."

"Hello, Elvis. Nice outfit."

He lowered his voice. "It's my bwana cover. You like it?"

"Sure, it's just great. Look, we have the better part of an hour before they call away our flight. Let's get a cup of coffee, and I'll brief you into the problem, or as much as I know about it."

Breaking a key CDC epidemiologist away from Atlanta had not been easy. They were very parochial about their staff and not anxious to let him go, especially since they had been told nothing—only that the services of Dr. Rosenblatt would be needed for an indefinite time to consult on a classified project. Sensing that this must have something to do with infectious disease, they wanted details. It took a call from the President to the Secretary of Health, Education, and Welfare and a second call from HEW to the head of the CDC before Rosenblatt was allowed to leave. In order not to leave the Center totally in the dark, they were told that their man would be working with GSI on a critical project. Guardian Services International, while becoming a niche player in the corporate security world, did some contract work for the government. But the link between GSI and IFOR remained closely held. Only a handful in government knew of it, and those that did were at the very highest level. All but Judy Burks.

Elvis Rosenblatt had been asked if he would volunteer to help with a problem in Africa. He was told only that he would serve as a consultant and advise on how to handle a contagion that had surfaced intermittently in Central Africa. He was also told that this investigation was privately funded and that help in this particular area was something of a pet project for someone high up in the administration. He was, however, asked to make a list of field equipment that he might need if he were to conduct an on-site investigation, the tools he would need should they uncover some form of pathogen. Rosenblatt was immediately caught up in the excitement. He worked most of the night to deliver a detailed listing of everything he would need to do field work on a variety of viral agents. His bags checked through to Hawaii held an array of personal test equipment, some of them scaled-down versions of larger instruments he had personally modified. He told his colleagues at the CDC he was going on a bug safari.

"Okay," Judy Burks said after they found a table in the crowded concourse just outside of Starbucks, "here's the deal as I understand it. We are going to be met by some people in Hawaii. They will give you a more in-depth briefing as to exactly where you will be going and what to expect. The NGO that is funding this effort has chartered an aircraft to ferry you and your supplies to a forward operating base where you will—"

"Forward operating base," he said, cutting her short. "That sounds kind of military."

Judy Burks recalled the last time she had gone forward with an IFOR deployment. She had waited in a Quonset hut in Diego Garcia while an IFOR probe, led by Garrett Walker, was infiltrated into the Afghan-Iranian border region.

"It's just a figure of speech. You will probably be set up in some kind of field lab, probably in a regional clinic, maybe even in a hospital."

Rosenblatt considered this. He didn't like hospitals; he was a bug detective, not a healer. Hospitals could be full of distractions in the way of viruses and bacteria that had nothing to do with the bugs he might be looking for. He called it background noise.

"And you were able to get all of the equipment—everything on my list? Y'know, Agent Burks, that was a pretty expensive set of gear."

"I've been told that every item will be waiting in Hawaii and that it will all travel with you."

"No fooling," he replied skeptically. Some of the items he requested were not only expensive but sometimes very hard to find. And a few pieces of the metered test equipment could be obtained only in Germany. He would be very surprised if they had managed to pull it all together in such a short time.

"So what's your role in all this, Agent Burks? I thought people like you were supposed to be out catching crooks."

That was one question she could answer truthfully. "How many times do I have to tell you, the name is Judy.

And I'm strictly a liaison officer. I'm the link between the U.S. government and the NGO funding this research. If government assistance is needed to support this work, then I'm the person that sees to it. And believe me, there are times when I'd much rather be out chasing crooks."

"Why, Agent Burks, how—"

"Elvis!"

"Okay, Judy, but look at it this way. Dangerous felons are a dime a dozen. We may have the chance to catch a really dangerous bug. Don't you find that unbelievably exciting?"

"Positively stimulating," she deadpanned.

Once at the gate, they boarded early with the other first-class passengers bound for Honolulu International. "You work for the same government I do, Judy, and we never fly first class."

"I was told to take good care of you, Elvis, so I flushed my frequent-flyer piggy bank. Consider it my treat."

"Y'know, for a cop, you're a pretty decent human being."

The flight was long but comfortable. En route, Judy got a detailed history of the Centers for Disease Control and Prevention and of Africa's contribution to the world of deadly viruses, specifically AIDS and Ebola. When they arrived, they were greeted by an unassuming man in slacks and a quiet aloha shirt. He was not an FBI agent, but somehow he still managed to meet them at the gate.

Pavel Zelinkow sat on his balcony in a teak Adirondack chair, watching the evening shadows play across the rooftops of the crowded, ancient dwellings below him. It was the balcony of the spacious flat that had sold him on the property; it seemed to float high above the western out-skirts of Rome. The structure was a jutting, cantilevered platform, with an ornate iron railing that afforded him an unobstructed two-hundred-and-seventy-degree view. The flat was just outside the metropolitan boundaries of Rome, near the municipality of Eur. This was his favorite time of day, and he had positioned himself to take advantage of the magnificent panorama to the west. The offshore breeze that usually came in the afternoon had carried most of the pollution down and away from his hillside perch. Those noxious fumes that choked most major cities, including Rome, would soon filter the last rays of the sun and set the world that stretched before him ablaze. In the mornings, before the haze from the city materialized, he could glimpse a broad section of the Mediterranean. The eternal smog of the Eternal City made that impossible after mid-morning. Occasionally he would catch a flash of reflected sunlight from one of the planes queued up for landing at Leonardo da Vinci International Airport. Later that evening, a procession of evenly spaced landing lights would mark the staggered patience of those waiting their turn to land.

He had never been a small man, but his girth had broadened since he came to Rome just a little over a year ago. Zelinkow was two people. One was a meticulous manager of clandestine activities—a chess master who reveled in the manipulative, dangerous world of covert action. Once he had done this for his country, but now, as a stateless person, he did it for the money—that and the thrill of what he called the Grand Game. He was Russian, and that was a condition of one's soul, not a mere nationality. Zelinkow missed Russia, much as he missed his mother, who worked herself into an early grave to raise him after the father he never knew died of cancer. Both the woman and the nation, he reflected, were hard, no-nonsense, inflexible, and demanding. They were both gone, and nothing would bring them back.

The other Zelinkow was a connoisseur of food and wine and a patron of the arts. He glanced at his watch, noting that the Tuscan amarone he had opened to breathe a few hours ago would now be ready. He poured himself a splash and swirled it gently in the glass. It had an excellent nose and good legs. He held it up to the remnants of blue sky overhead and savored the deep, rich magenta color. The taste more than justified its other superb physical properties. With the tones of the wine still echoing in his mouth, he carefully set himself to preparing his afternoon cigar. It was an unhurried ritual, one in which he took a great deal of pleasure. Through a rolling cloud of blue smoke, he inspected the glowing tip of the Lonsdale to ensure the uniformity of the burn. You could tell a lot about a cigar by the way it took the flame. As he slowly blew a mouthful of smoke into the evening air, he once again revisited the African matter in his mind.

He had set a number of forces into play, and any one of them, if it went awry, could prove disastrous to the project. This assignment, as he referred to it, once again put him in the uncomfortable position of having to deal with people of questionable reliability and integrity. For the most part, these individuals did his bidding for the money. In those few cases where money was not the driving force, or just one factor in their participation, he had to be careful to balance the payment with their particular form of idealism or motivation. Such was the case for the mercenary Renaud. He needed money, but he also wanted the chance to prove himself. He was a contemptible man— totally amoral and self-absorbed. But Zelinkow had needed just such a man for this particular assignment, though he was relatively incompetent in many aspects of his profession. That was why he kept a close watch on Renaud's movements and had set up separate procurement channels to support his force. Zelinkow rightly marked Renaud as an ambitious bully. He was a man who would guard the project site and do the heinous chore of finding test subjects because he saw himself as a mercenary leader of stature. He had chosen Renaud because no responsible PMC would have taken the work, at any price. But Zelinkow did not kid himself. In Renaud, he knew he was dealing with a loose cannon.

He was far more comfortable with the choice of Helmut Klan to manage the project site. For Klan, the issue was certainly money, but it was also the job. Any queasiness he may have had about the objectives of the project was quickly overcome by the fee he was being paid. Any lingering doubts about the morality of the undertaking were quickly erased by the organizational challenge of running the operation. Perhaps it was the Teutonic mindset or some latent Germanic gene that allows someone like Klan to attend to the mechanics of an operation like this and somehow divorce himself from the outcome. How is it that a man can do that? Zelinkow thought. He took a sip of wine and further reflected on it. How is it that I can do it? he wondered. I suppose to one degree or another, all men continue down the path on which they took their first steps as a boy. Such is the inertia of life.

The members of the medical team he had assembled for the project were no less puzzling than Helmut Klan. They were a mixture of refugees and renegades from various academic and medical establishments. Each was undeniably brilliant in his own right, but research today was driven by research teams, and few of these men were team players. They also lacked the political skills to succeed in modern research efforts, which were driven by a quasi-academic bureaucracy fraught with political maneuvering. And there was the certain childlike naïveté that often accompanied a really fine mind. At least to some degree, they were blinded by their own brilliance. Zelinkow had gone to great pains to

learn about these men and assess their intellectual gifts as
well as their personal and emotional shortcomings. It was
to Klan's credit that he could keep them all working together toward a common goal. And, if he could believe
Klan's progress reports, the work and the clinical trials were
very much on schedule. But Zelinkow was not one to allow
good news to disturb his focus or his skepticism. He knew
he could not relax his vigilance until the project was complete and the product shipped—safely in the hands of
those who were paying him. Then he would take on a
whole new set of challenges.

And then, of course, there was the issue of the people he
worked for. Zelinkow had initially been contacted by Abdel
Moski, a man who described himself as a broker for a consortium of unnamed individuals who wished to retain his
services. They wanted him to oversee a project for them.
That Moski even knew how to get an e-mail through
Zelinkow's elaborate electronic screening protocol had
been disconcerting. Through a series of cutouts and trust-
building measures, the two had finally met in Cairo. It was
a short meeting, and both men knew it would be their last.
No business was concluded; Moski told him what his principals desired, and Zelinkow said he would consider it. The
two men then went on to resolve two issues: communications and money transfer. When it came down to it,
Zelinkow's interaction with a principal was quite simple.
He had to be tasked, and he had to report his progress on
this tasking, both of which required a secure, untraceable
method of communication. Fortunately, corporate America had developed all that was needed in the way of secure
communications technology. It was for sale to U.S. military
forces, intelligence agencies, government entities, and corporations, which meant it was for sale to him. Usually the
people that hired him were not so sophisticated, and
Zelinkow had to see to the upgrading of their systems for

the protection of all concerned. As it was, Abdel Moski had a state-of-the-art system, and he assured Zelinkow that his principals did as well.

However, the transfer of money was not so easy. It would always be a spy-vs.-spy game. The people who wanted to move funds with no attribution and the bankers who wanted to accommodate these transfers worked together against those who wanted to be privy to their dealings. Basically it was the whole world, from the terrorist to the taxpayer, against the United States of America, with a little help from the Brits and the Japanese. This did not mean that it was a one-sided affair. Zelinkow had long ago learned never to underestimate the American intelligence and counterintelligence services. For Zelinkow, this only put more of an edge to the Grand Game. And it kept a lot of amateurs out of the game. They were quickly and easily caught and put out of business.

After his meeting with Moski, Zelinkow began combing his many sources to learn the identity of Moski's clients. Not that Zelinkow really needed to know, but he was more than just curious. The effort it took to learn their identities would go a long way toward documenting Moski's professional credentials. It proved to be much more work than Zelinkow expected, which elevated Abdel Moski in his estimation. As Zelinkow suspected, it was an Al Qaeda–sponsored operation with Saudi financial backing. Most dedicated acts of terror were. There was no need to peel the onion back further and try to learn which Saudi organization, or which member of the royal family put up the money. He had no doubt that the pockets were deep.

After much consideration, he had accepted the commission, taken the retainer, and agreed to see the project through. It was certainly no casual undertaking; this would not be an easy task, nor would its successful completion be pretty. Had he not been thoroughly embarrassed by the Americans on his last major endeavor, he might not have taken this job. Two years ago, he had been asked to penetrate the Pakistani nuclear weapons stockpile and remove two of the weapons stored there. He had done this and made careful plans to bring the two bombs into Afghanistan. There they were to be detonated, causing little loss of life and crippling the construction of the Trans Afghan Pipeline, a massive project designed to bring Caspian oil to a deepwater port in Pakistan. The pipeline was underwritten by an American-backed consortium of Western oil companies with security provided by the U.S. military. Its destruction would have caused a great deal of embarrassment to the United States and further drawn America into the tarbaby of Southwest Asia. But it was not to be. Zelinkow considered himself a careful planner, someone who accounted for all eventualities. But something happened; a force he had not counted on, nor even knew the existence of, had intervened. This force had prevented the nuclear detonations and recovered both bombs. It was the first time he had ever been denied an objective—ever. This mysterious organization had also found a way to track his incoming payments and dispersals, eventually causing the French Sûreté to raid his home. He had lost everything—everything but his life and the sums of cash he had stashed in discreet banks around the world, banking sanctuaries he had once thought safe.

Nine/11 was a mistake. He had said so when he was hired to help Mohammad Atta and the others to attack New York and Washington. Americans respond when attacked. Now they controlled Afghanistan and might yet Iraq, and their influence in the region was many times what it was. By attacking America, Al Qaeda had called forth an American resource that was usually content to deal in commerce and commercial enterprise—American ingenuity. The fundamentalists thought America was fat and complacent, and 99 percent of Americans were exactly that. But it was the other 1 percent that made all the difference. Zelinkow was convinced that it was the efforts of that 1 percent that had defeated him in Afghanistan. That bitter defeat still troubled him. But what bothered him more was that he still did not know who these people were. Given their unorthodox methods and uncharacteristic brutality, he was sure they were some form of nongovernmental entity. No American congressional oversight committee would sanction what they had done; no American president would countenance that kind of activity unless he had complete deniability. No, Zelinkow concluded as he puffed thoughtfully on the Lonsdale, this was something new and out of the ordinary. Somehow they had bested him in that adventure in Afghanistan, and he had never been able to find out who they were or how they accomplished it. Africa was a whole different business, he told himself. Or was it? One thing was very clear to him, and probably to those who had hired him. He could not afford another failure.

The people who had denied him success in Afghanistan, whoever they might be—he figured he owed them one. As they were undoubtedly American, then it would be America that would pay.

Zelinkow poured himself a final glass from the bottle of the marvelous amarone. Two things seemed apparent to him. One of them was that the people who had hired him hated the United States. They consistently raised the ante with each project he undertook for them. And now that the Americans had established a presence in Iraq, their hatred knew no bounds. If accomplished, the Afghan venture would have done much to destroy American credibility in the region. The second: if this venture now germinating in Africa was seen through, it would destroy America as an economic superpower, and quite possibly as a military superpower. He was quite sure America would retaliate with everything it had. Even a crippled America would be formidable. Zelinkow had never played the Grand Game for these stakes. It both intimidated and exhilarated him. If he was successful, it would leave a huge power vacuum on the world stage. Perhaps Russia, with its emerging economy and vast store of natural resources, could fill that vacuum. Anything was possible.

He rose from his chair, draining the last of the wine from his glass. High stakes, indeed, he reflected. Zelinkow was a man who could work tirelessly for any length of time, focusing his not-inconsequential intellect and experience on a project. He could also totally segregate that part of his being, and devote his attentions to that which gave him pleasure. Nearly matching his passion for his work was that which he reserved for the arts. A superb string quartet was touring European capitals, and he had box seats for this evening's performance. Not only that, he had reservations at an exquisite Neapolitan restaurant. He would be joined by a ripe, round, middle-aged widow who enjoyed music and food almost as much as he did. For now, the collapse of the so-called leader of the free world would have to wait. Zelinkow headed for his bath with a subtle spring in his step, collecting a glass of sherry along the way.

It was now late in the day, several hours after Janet Brisco had held her deployment briefing. She was still in her office reviewing personnel and equipment lists, along with a host of other details that accompany the secret movement of men and material. As was always the case, she had to continually remind herself to concentrate on the immediate concerns of logistics and staging. Naturally, her mind fast-forwarded to the tactical considerations, but she disciplined herself not to get too far ahead—first things first. Experience had taught her that too much tactical thinking early on in an operation restricted flexibility. A good planner knew that tactical decisions made too early in the game were inevitably changed due to better and updated intelligence. In most situations, there were really only so many ways to assault a target. She remembered the old army saying: Amateurs talk about tactics; the professionals talk about logistics. Once her people and equipment were in place, then she could deal with tactical issues. And hopefully, by then they would have a better picture of what they were up against.

Zambia, Zimbabwe's neighbor to the northwest, presented its own set of challenges. It was about the size of Texas, and like Zimbabwe, the nation had massive social problems. Zambia had only half the population of Zimbabwe, about eleven million, and only one in five Zambians had AIDS, where in Zimbabwe it ran as high as two in five. The Zambian economy was only slightly better off than their neighbor's. The nation depended on copper exports, but low copper prices for the past several years had stagnated the economy. Zambia had all the problems of a struggling African state; high inflation, high infant mortality rate, high unemployment—about 50 percent—and a huge national debt. On the positive side, it was a reasonably functioning democracy, and that political stability made Zambia one of southern Africa's more popular tourist destinations.

There were two Zambias—rural Zambia and the capital of Lusaka. Lusaka was a modern city of some 1.3 million souls that offered a higher standard of living and more opportunity through an emerging service economy not available to rural Zambians. But it also had big-city problems. Like many black African capitals, it ran the gamut from the modern to the wretched, but at four thousand feet, it enjoyed one of the more temperate climates among African cities. There was also a fully staffed American embassy, including a Peace Corps representative and an officer on loan from the Centers for Disease Control and Prevention. For Janet Brisco, it was a jumping-off place for her force. It would be a place to hide and to stage equipment. Fortunately, they were well funded and had the Simpson Foundation to use as a cover for their activities.

In basic terms, Janet Brisco had to get Tomba and his Africans from Kona to Lusaka with all the equipment they would need to conduct an assault on a heavily defended position some hundred and fifty miles east of Lusaka in Zimbabwe. She had to get her command and control element there as well, not only to Lusaka but to a position where it could support the operation. And both the command and assault elements had to be equipped for a number of infiltration and recovery scenarios. Critical decisions had to be made. Too much equipment could raise their profile, and the lack of a critical piece of gear could put the mission at risk. Garrett and AKR continually shuttled in and out of her office to answer questions about what they might or might not need. Except for each man's individual kit and personal weapons, she made all final decisions.

As Janet wrestled with these dilemmas, there was a soft rap at the door. On the third series of knocks she finally looked up from her desk, an uninviting scowl on her face.

"Come!"

"Excuse me, miss, you wished to see me?"

She immediately softened. "Yes, Tomba. Please come in."

He made his way into the office and stood by the desk. Janet Brisco had worked in a man's world, a special operations man's world, for close to two decades. Her work often dictated that she take the measure of a man in short order—could he do the job? Could he cut it, or would he come up short? It was not an issue of battlefield bravery or judgment. Her world was one of command and control of men in the field. A bad decision by a controller could jeopardize a mission or get men killed just as surely as a bad decision in the field. As the senior planner and controller, she had to know about the men she ordered into battle—the warriors in the fight. And Brisco felt that this Turkana warrior was something very special.

As part of her preparation, she read the dossier of each of the African recruits. They came from all over central and southern Africa. They all had formal military training of some sort. Most of them had served as mercenaries at one time or another. Some were working as security guards when they were recruited, and not a few were game park rangers. All had some connection with Tomba, yet he was the only Turkana among them. The only common thread she could find from her review of their files is that they were all literate, all spoke English, and all seemed to be stateless. Tribalism had a strong influence on most Africans, and it often created problems. She was surprised to see that these men were recruited from such diverse tribal groups.

"I need a few minutes of your time," she said. "Can I offer you some coffee? Tea?"

"Some tea would be nice."

The Gurkhas recruited for IFOR had made a tea drinker out of her, but only when she was in camp, and only the tea made by the Gurkhas. She kept a carafe of it on her desk. She carefully poured him a cup and then warmed her own. He accepted the mug and quietly sipped at it. "Thank you," he said, relishing the strong, dark brew. "It is the first thing our British mentors taught us—how to make good tea. Yet only a few of us have had British training; I need to send some of my men over to the Gurkha camp to learn their method."

She watched him carefully. Tomba was lean, with long, hard muscles, a thin waist, narrow hips, and an oversized shoulder girdle. His hands were like heavy work gloves. He was not shy but soft, in his manner and his speech, and very polite. But all her senses told her that this was a very disciplined and capable man. Like many of the men in his unit, he was hardened by years of fighting. In Tomba's case, decades of living and fighting in the bush.

"Tomba, we are assembling the needed equipment to support you and your men in the field. I'll need some help in completing this deployment package, but first, tell me how you selected your men. And how is it that they work so well together? I know some of them come from tribes who have been historical enemies."

Tomba took a measured sip from his mug before he answered with a warm smile. "You have to understand, miss, that Africa today is not the Africa of Kitchener or Rhodes or Livingston. The forces of colonialism, Communism, and capitalism have swept through the continent and"—he paused to search for the right word—"rearranged things. This has happened in other societies, but most other societies are more uniform; change settles on a much larger group—a conquered or occupied nation makes the change as a nation. It is not that way in Africa; we are too diverse. Loyalty to one's tribe is not a bad thing, but it is out of step with the national boundaries set by colonial powers, and out of step with the world today. There is no going back. My men and I love Africa, yet Africa means different things to each of us. Tell me, miss, what did you do when you left the service of your nation? Did you go home?"

She smiled. "Why, yes, I did. I went back to St. Louis to be with my family."

He met her smile with his own. "It is the same with us, although for most of us, home as we knew it from our youth is gone. But we hold these images in our hearts. We are warriors from many different tribes, but for now, we are brothers. And we will fight as brothers from the same tribe. Was it not the same when you left your home to serve in your military? Did you not join a tribe of warriors in uniform? When we finish our service here, we will go home, each of us in our own fashion." He paused for a long moment, and she waited, knowing he was not finished. "Many in Africa long for the old times and the established order of things. I do not, and neither do my men. We respect the old customs, but you in the West, for all you have taken away, have given us something much more valuable. It is that a man is not bound by the restrictions of his tribe or his station in that tribe. And a tribal chief is no longer free to brutalize his subjects. Now, if a man is clever and brave and works hard, he can advance himself. And that is the biggest change of all. Many in the West think the whites destroyed Africa. In some ways they did. Painful as the transition from the old to the new has been, I believe they have liberated Africa."

She was not convinced. "Would you not, had you the chance, want to live in an Africa with none of the influence of the white man?"

He shrugged. "Possibly. Not all that the white man brought to Africa was good. Smallpox, as an example, devastated many parts of Africa. But the white man did not bring the AIDS virus. Western knowledge and medicine are the only hope of stopping this terrible disease. What if AIDS had come to Africa three hundred years ago? How many Africans would there have been left to exploit in the nineteenth century? The river of life moves on; we can only play our given roles as best we can. I do, however, envy Bijay and his Gurkhas. They come from a small nation in a remote part of the world that has been left alone. There are no diamonds or farmlands or metal ores that draw outsiders to their lands. When they return home, they can live much as their fathers and grandfathers once did."

"Where will you go, Tomba? Where is your St. Louis? Is there someone who waits for you?"

This brought a chuckle. "I have many choices, and in some ways all of southern Africa is my home. There are many men I have trained and fought with who live throughout the area. Some have become successful and wealthy. I will always be welcome at someone's kraal, if not my own."

"So there is no one who waits?"

A shadow seemed to pass across his rugged features. "No, miss, there is not. I have had two wives, but they are both gone, as are the children from both." He said this with a certain finality that brooked no response on her part.

"Tomba, we will probably move to a forward location the day after tomorrow. We have found some airport space at the Lusaka International Airport that is secure. You and your men will be able to stage from there, if and when we receive the order to move on this. Are your men ready to move out?"

"We are. Their kit is in good order, and our combat support equipment, well, it is of such a quality that we are very well equipped indeed. And the various uniforms are in place. We can dress out as a Zambian Army unit, Zimbabwe Republic Police, or just a roving band of bush fighters. The men can also pass as laborers if required." He smiled. "The men are very excited—so many uniforms and so many different weapons. They are used to going on a patrol with an assault rifle, six or eight extra magazines, a canteen, and a bag of cornmeal. With that they can stay in the bush for many weeks. Now, we have so much. Have we learned any more about our objective?"

"No, we haven't. Perhaps when we get on the ground in Lusaka we will have a better idea of what we're up against. We have a number of sources providing us with information, but this is a very unusual and remote target."

"May I make a suggestion?"

"Of course!" He had her full attention.

"*Nkosi* Akheem says we may be up against a unit that is similar to the old Selous Scouts. Is that correct?"

"Yes. And I understand you once served with the Selous Scouts."

"In another lifetime," he said easily. "But I have been thinking about this. If that is truly the situation, then these men are recruited mercenaries, and there is only one place where a mercenary force with both whites and blacks can be raised. South Africa. My men are in all respects ready for travel. Perhaps I should leave now and spend a few days in Johannesburg and rejoin you in Lusaka. I have many contacts in Johannesburg. If such a force was recruited, I may be able to learn something of their number and the contract for which they were recruited."

Janet considered this. Her first notion was that it was an excellent idea, and the second was, Why hadn't she thought of it? Or why hadn't Akheem Kelly-Rogers thought of it? Both of them should have.

"How do you propose to travel?"

"I have spoken with Mr. Owens. He recommends a British passport. I can fly from here to Japan, then on to Johannesburg. He can provide documentation that I am a travel agent employee. Getting to Johannesburg is not a problem. As a travel agent representative I will have no problem getting from Johannesburg into Zambia. I shouldn't be more than a day or so in Johannesburg, and perhaps a day in

Pretoria. It will not take long to find out what we need to know."

She thought about it a moment and concluded that it made perfect sense, feeling a little embarrassed that they had not thought to make better use of this resource.

"Yes, go ahead and prepare to leave at once. I will speak with Akheem and Mr. Fagan, but it seems an excellent idea."

"And another thing, miss. I would also—"

"Tomba, I would be most grateful if you would call me Janet. We are colleagues; it is only proper that you do so."

He paused and seemed to draw himself more upright, if that were possible. "You honor me, Janet. Thank you. If you will permit me, I have another suggestion. One of my men, Benjamin Sata, grew up in Lusaka and has relatives there. He is both intelligent and an excellent bushman. Would it not be a good idea to send him on ahead to spend a few days with his family? We may need some local assistance there. It will be easier for him to help us if he has been with his family for a short while before we task him with any requirements. As an intelligence officer and planner, miss—I mean, Janet, you understand the value of local knowledge and information."

Brisco considered this. Tomba was one thing, but one of his men going home, a man who was probably known to those in his extended family as a soldier of fortune . . . As if reading her mind, he continued.

"Benjamin will be discreet about our work and his role in this venture. His father is old, and it is quite natural for a son to visit to pay his respects. I have trusted him with my life many times, and he has never failed me. It could prove quite valuable to have someone who knows Lusaka and has contacts there."

"Again, Tomba, that makes perfect sense. Let me speak with Akheem about it."

*   *   *

Judy's eyes lit up when she saw him. "Steven, thank you for meeting us here at the gate. I'd like you to meet Dr. Elvis Rosenblatt, from the CDC. Elvis, this is Steven Fagan. He will be coordinating this investigation."

"Dr. Rosenblatt, it is a pleasure to meet you," Steven said, extending his hand. If he thought Rosenblatt's outfit a little strange, he gave not the slightest indication. "I hope you had a pleasant flight." He chatted amiably as he led them from the gate down the concourse, but he could sense Rosenblatt's growing anxiety. Steven Fagan was nothing if not a careful observer. Just before they reached the main terminal, he stopped and turned to Rosenblatt. "Doctor, I know you have a thousand questions. No doubt you are wondering just who we are and what we do. One of my jobs is to see that all your questions are answered fully and to your complete satisfaction. We have booked a room for you at the Hyatt, just a few minutes from the airport. I've arranged for your bags to be sent over there. There's a car waiting to take us straight to the hotel. I hope that will be acceptable? And before I forget," he added politely, "there are any number of people who appreciate your traveling here to help us with this matter. It is the opinion of our government that we may be facing a dangerous and potentially devastating situation. It is imperative that we learn more about it."

Rosenblatt wondered just who this agreeable, soft-spoken man was, but he was content to wait until he got settled in and received a proper briefing. Fagan put Judy Burks and Rosenblatt in the back of the sedan and climbed in the front with the driver for the short stint to the hotel. He tipped the bellman and told him to have Dr. Rosenblatt's bags sent up to his room. The room turned out to be a four-room luxury apartment with a small kitchen, a generous sitting room, and two bedroom-bath suites bracketing the sitting room. Steven held the door for Judy and Rosenblatt, and followed them in. Inside the main sitting room, a tall man in blue jeans and a bright aloha shirt was mixing himself a drink at the bar.

"You must be the good Dr. Rosenblatt," he said, crossing the room to offer his hand. "I'm Garrett Walker. I was just fixing myself a scotch. Can I build one for you?"

Rosenblatt took in the room, the bar, and the Magnum P.I. look-alike with a drink in his hand. "Only if it's a single malt," he replied, taking Garrett's hand.

"Is there any other kind?" Garrett said, turning back to the bar. "Judy? Steven?"

Judy Burks opted for a rum and tonic, while Steven deferred. Garrett handed out the drinks and dropped into one of the easy chairs that, along with a long high-backed divan, surrounded an ornate mahogany cocktail table. He hung a leg over the arm of the chair and waited for Steven to begin.

Fagan suddenly rose and retrieved a Perrier water, then took a seat on the opposite end of the sofa from Rosenblatt. He twisted off the bottle cap and poured a measure into a short crystal glass. Just what to tell Rosenblatt and what to withhold had been on Steven's mind, but he wanted to meet the man before he came to a decision. There was a great deal the doctor didn't need to know, but there was risk in withholding information from a key player in the operation, someone who might well be risking his life in the venture. Which secrets to share and which to withhold fell within his discretion and his expertise.

"Doctor," he began, "I think the best way to do this is to tell you a little about the organization that Garrett and I work for. We are a privately funded organization that is sometimes called in to deal with problems that our government cannot address, or where the presence of the U.S. government would either be counterproductive or inappropriate. When I said we are privately funded, I meant just that; we are not a government contractor, nor do we function with any kind of a retainer. Miss Burks is not formally part of our organization. She serves as liaison officer to the Federal Bureau of Investigation, the intelligence community, and the executive branch as needed. I should also like to point out that only select, key people in the government even know of us and what we do. The President of the United States is one of those people. Neither the Surgeon General nor the head of the CDC are cleared to know about what we do, or that we even exist, for that matter." Steven went on to outline IFOR's ability to project limited force and their semi-official, deniable relationship with the U.S. government.

"So," Rosenblatt interrupted, "you might say that you are kind of the opposite of the Peace Corps. Instead of sending in people to do good things, you send in people to do difficult and bad things—Mission Impossible stuff."

Steven's reaction was one of thoughtful consideration. "I never really looked at it quite like that, but perhaps your assessment is not entirely inaccurate. Maybe the current example will help to clear things up a bit. We believe, from a variety of sources, that a group or organization is developing and testing biological agents in a remote part of Zimbabwe. The facility where this is taking place, a small resort hotel, seems to be guarded by a mercenary force that exerts control in the immediate area and has been terrorizing the local population." He watched Rosenblatt carefully as he spoke. "We even suspect they are doing human testing." Steven paused to refill his glass. "We have trained a team of Africans who we plan to put into the area to observe the facility and, if needed, to neutralize it."

"Let me guess," Rosenblatt said, "these are also mercenary soldiers, only they are our mercenary soldiers, right?"

"I can see that you're grasping the concept," Steven said mildly. "Tell me, Doctor, have you heard of a man by the name of François Meno?"

"François Meno! You don't mean the French microbiologist!"

"The very one, I'm afraid," Steven replied. "He, along with the two scientists Miss Burks spoke about with you a few days ago, is nowhere to be found. As I am sure you know, he was dismissed from the Pasteur Institute several months ago over a dispute with Institute policy. Due to the controls now in place to monitor certain airports, we know that Professor Meno flew from Paris to Kuwait City and then on to Djibouti. From there he must have left under a different identity, but a number of flights connect from Djibouti to central and southern Africa. We don't know where he is, but it seems he may be headed toward our mysterious hotel." As he spoke, Steven watched Rosenblatt carefully. "Dr. Rosenblatt," he continued, "I'd be preaching to the choir if I were to tell you the level of havoc these men could create if they are working in concert in the same rogue laboratory. Modern genetic research has put some frightening capabilities in the hands of those who know how to modify and manipulate genetic material. Of course, they could simply be off working on cures for diseases using nonstandard methods and human testing. But we don't think so. We must know what is going on at that facility, and we need to do it quickly. You know better than anyone what these people are capable of." Again, Steven paused to measure his man. "If there is even a small chance that these people are trying to bring about the unthinkable, we simply have to do something about it."

Steven Fagan was very skilled in dealing with others. He knew when to speak as well as when to be silent. Now he held Dr. Elvis Rosenblatt in an open, patient gaze. On the other side of the table, Garrett watched all this play out. He had seen Steven Fagan perform this velvet rope-a-dope with others; he exuded warmth, trust, and sincerity with great skill.

Slowly, Rosenblatt nodded his assent. "So what can I do to help?"

Fagan did not miss a beat. "Doctor, as I mentioned, we are planning to put a small force into the area to find out what is going on. It would seem that we have a military problem as well as a potential biological problem. We need your advice in planning an assault on a biological complex and what precautions our men need to take. And should we be able to secure this facility, we will need someone with your experience and training to evaluate the situation."

Rosenblatt nodded again. He had suspected it would be something like this; in fact, he had long known it was only a matter of time before the proliferation of genetic research took an evil turn. When Agent Burks called and the head of the CDC told him his services had been requested by "senior government officials," he knew this might indeed be what many at the CDC feared most—a genetically engineered biological weapon in the making. Rosenblatt knew, as few people did, the difference between a bioterror weapon and a biological weapon. A terror weapon was designed to terrorize. These were things like anthrax or ricin. Biological weapons, ones that were now possible through genetic engineering, were designed to cause mass depopulation. But under this sober analysis, the prospect still excited him. They were after bugs, perhaps some new and rare bug he had never seen before.

"It seems my services are needed, and I'll help in any way that I can."

Before he could continue, Steven held out his hand. "Thank you, Doctor, thank you." Rosenblatt hesitated, then took his hand. "Speaking for all of us, I can say that we all feel an element of relief with your particular expertise aboard."

"Well, thank you for your confidence; I'll do my best." He paused, feeling a little flustered at this kind of attention. "I do have a few questions, however."

"Of course," Steven replied. "Please go ahead."

"If it is as you describe, there could be a catastrophic stew being brewed at the place. And given that this facility is well guarded, it would seem more appropriate that a battalion of Army Rangers should be storming the place rather than some private army. Why you? Why us?"

Steven smiled. "This is a remote facility in very rough country. Rangers, good as they are, are still light infantry, and their presence would signal an American invasion of a black African nation. It would be difficult for Rangers, or Special Forces or SEALs for that matter, to achieve the needed surprise. We believe that surprise may be essential in safely attacking this facility so that we can investigate what is actually going on there."

"What makes your army better than Army Rangers or Special Forces?" Rosenblatt asked.

"Our group is not like any in the U.S. military. They are all African bush fighters—seasoned professionals who won't stand out in the way an American military unit would. That's why we will be looking into this, not the U.S. Army."

Rosenblatt considered this. "Even so, breaking into any laboratory that is experimenting with biological material is a hazardous business, let alone one in some remote location. I'm not a military guy, but I can help with the evaluation. I gave Judy a list of equipment needed if I have to do a field analysis as well as necessary protective clothing. There would be little that I can do without them."

"We have a rather efficient procurement organization. The items you requested are on pallets at a transshipment facility at the airport, ready to be airlifted to Africa."

"All of them?" Rosenblatt questioned in disbelief. Had he submitted that kind of a requisition at the CDC, it would have taken the better part of a year for the paperwork to be processed, bids let, and the order filled. He had asked for the best and the smallest, most portable test equipment available, which meant the most expensive. He didn't expect to get even half his list.

"Doctor," Steven replied, "we provide our small force with the best weapons, communications, and combat support equipment in the world. Your work is no less important, so we certainly would do no less for you. It's been a long day, but first thing tomorrow morning, we'd like you to inspect and inventory the equipment and make sure it is satisfactory. And should you determine that more is needed, you only need to ask."

"That's—that's great. I can't wait to see it. So then what?"

"Along with the rest of our people, we will need to get you into the area as quickly and as quietly as possible. Garrett, maybe you should explain what we have in mind."

Garrett lifted a shiny aluminum case from the side of the sofa, laid it on the table, and lifted the lid for Rosenblatt's inspection. "Tell me, Elvis, do you like animals— lions, tigers, rhinos—that sort of thing?"

Rosenblatt grinned. "Are there any other kind?"

"Wonderful," Garrett replied, taking out a Nikon camera body and snapping a 400mm telephoto lens into place. "You and I are going on safari."

* * *

Later that evening, Janet Brisco was at her desk, deep into a recent set of satellite images. There were two mugs on her desk, one tea and one coffee, and an ashtray full of cigarette butts. Now that most of the logistic flow for the deployment of her small force was in place, she was free to begin to build a target package and think about the tactical problems that they might face. There was a soft rap on her door.

"Come— Oh, hello, Tomba. Please come in."

He crossed the room with several noiseless strides. "I will be leaving in a few hours. As you know, *Nkosi* Akheem will be going with me. There will be a private jet to take us to Nairobi, where we are booked on a commercial flight to Johannesburg."

At first Janet had questioned the necessity of having AKR accompany Tomba, but she had to admit that he could move in African cities as well as Tomba, and should there be a need for contact or assistance from the U.S. embassy in Pretoria, then his presence would be useful. It had been Steven's call, and on reflection, she realized it was a good one.

"My men are ready to travel in all respects; just give them the word when the time comes. I am here for two reasons. One is to thank you for all you are doing as we prepare for this mission. The other is to ask if you will join my men and myself for a few minutes. It is customary for African warriors to share a drink before we depart our base camp for an operation. I know you are very busy, but it would mean a great deal to my men—and to me."

She was on her feet without thinking. "I would be honored, Tomba."

They were seated around a small fire, dressed in T-shirts, long trousers, and sandals. All rose as she and Tomba approached.

"*Nkosi* Janet has come to join us for a drink. Please make her welcome at our fire." There was a murmur of agreement among the men around the circle. Suddenly, AKR was at her side, handing her a wooden cup. He inclined his head in a show of respect, and he smiled warmly.

"I see you, *Nkosi* Janet," he said as he solemnly raised his own cup and took a drink.

"What the hell am I supposed to do now?" she said under her breath.

"Enjoy the moment," he replied quietly. "This is an honor seldom given to one outside their number."

He gently guided her through an opening in the circle and paused in front of one of the men.

"I see you, miss," he said, raising his cup to drink.

"And I see you," she replied and drank. The brew was strong, bitter, and not altogether unpleasant.

With AKR's guidance they made their way around the circle and back to Tomba.

"I see you, *Nkosi* Janet."

"I see you, Tomba." She paused to swallow before continuing. "I, uh, thank you for this honor, Tomba. This is, well, it is very special."

He simply smiled and motioned for her to take a seat on one of the benches. They talked for the better part of an hour and passed around a wooden pitcher of the rich African brew. Then Tomba and AKR rose and quietly withdrew. Akheem gave her a gentle squeeze on the shoulder as he passed behind her. After what seemed to be another hour, she listened as the Africans talked quietly about wars past and the upcoming mission in Zimbabwe. Occasionally they spoke in a dialect she did not understand, but for the most part they conversed in English. Finally she rose, a little unsteady on her feet, and thanked them for including her. Mohammed Senagal seemed to materialize at her side. He escorted her from the circle and thanked her for taking time to be with them. On her way back to the operations building she passed close to Bijay, who was watching from the shadows.

"Good evening, Miss Brisco, or should I say *Nkosi* Janet?"

"Have you been here long?"

"A while," he replied, looking back at the men by the fire. "They are truly fine men, Miss Brisco, and they have done you a great honor. Take good care of them."

"I will, Bijay. Good night."

"Good night, miss."

Back in her office, she found her way to her desk. Dodds LeMaster looked up from his computer to watch her cross the room.

"You all right?" Bill Owens stopped sorting documents to also look up.

She nodded. "Did I ever thank you for helping with the training of Tomba and his men?"

LeMaster cast a curious glance at Owens.

"As a matter of fact, Janet, you didn't."

"Well, I am now. Thank you both." She took a deep breath. "And now Dodds, I would be in your debt if you would get me a strong cup of coffee and three aspirins. And then I want to go over these latest satellite images with you."

7

FORCES IN PLACE

Benjamin Sata moved along the back streets of Lusaka with his hands thrust into his trouser pockets and his head down. He had arrived that morning on a flight from Maputo, and it was now midafternoon. His soiled white shirt and scuffed shoes said that he was probably a laborer or an out-of-work miner. There were a great many of those in Lusaka. In his small knapsack he had a Mozambique passport and a work visa that identified him as Tilyenji Nkhoma, as well as some toilet articles, a change of clothes, and, stitched into the lining of the bag, a large sum of U.S. dollars and Zambian kwachas. As he made his way into the housing project, no one gave him a second look, but he was very aware of his surroundings. Unnoticed, he made his way through the suburb of Burma Road along Nzunga Avenue. He cut down a side street and stepped into an alley. Finally, he arrived at the back gate of a modest one-story home. Glancing around to make sure he was still unobserved, he slipped through the gate and stepped onto the back porch. The low growl of a small dog greeted him through the screen door.

"Hey, Kimba, it's me, Benjamin," he said quietly. "Don't you remember me, girl?"

The dog sniffed him cautiously but conceded nothing.

"Who's there? May I help you?" A shriveled, wizened black woman in a print smock approached the door. There was the patient, quiet dignity about her that was common to those few who reach advanced age in Africa. She was well into her eighties, but even she did not know exactly how old she was. Like the dog, she was alert and cautious.

"You may indeed, Grandmother," Benjamin replied in Bemba, the language of his tribe. "May a weary traveler find shelter and a place by your fire?"

"Benjamin? Good Lord, is that you?"

"Yes, Grandmother. May I come in?"

She lifted the lock, and he quickly slipped inside. He stepped away from the door and stood looking back into the alley to make sure his arrival was unobserved. After a moment, he turned from the door to formally greet his grandmother, in the Bemba fashion. He was the youngest of her grandsons, but there were still proper greetings to be exchanged. This was not the first of his infrequent visits home, and as on the others, he would have to balance courtesy with vigilance. It was known that he had served in the South African Army, and that he had been an employee of Sandline and deployed with the mercenary force that Sandline sent to Papua New Guinea. While not technically a criminal, he was unwelcome in Zambia to the local authorities and especially the national army police. The Zambian army distrusted anyone who had served in the South African Army or a mercenary force.

"How is he, Grandmother?"

"Not good, Benjamin. A man needs his sons around him, but now there is just you and David. He doesn't seem to want to live anymore. It's good that you have come. He will be glad to see you. You were always such a joy to him."

Benjamin Sata's mother had died during childbirth, along with his infant sister. As the youngest of his siblings who lived, he was raised by his older sisters. His father had worked since he was twelve in the copper mines. Only after he had become too old to work had they moved from the Copper Belt in the north to Lusaka. Close to half a century in the mines had left him a mere shell of the big, wide-shouldered man Benjamin remembered as a boy. Benjamin watched as his brothers went off to the mines, but when it was his time to go, the copper mines in Zambia weren't hiring, but the diamond mines in South Africa were. Two years of working the big hole in Kimberly were enough. Soldier's pay was not as good as miner's, but Benjamin knew in his heart he was an aboveground person. He joined the South African Army and went on to become a sergeant in the notorious 32nd Battalion, where he mastered the skills of a professional soldier. Following intermittent work with Sandline, he was hired as a park ranger in Kenya. It was there that he met Tomba, which ultimately led to his becoming a member of IFOR.

In the Sata home, as with most African families, there were lots of kids—six girls and four boys. There would have been eleven had Benjamin's younger sister survived. But now there were only two left, Benjamin and his brother David. His second oldest brother had been killed in a mining accident, and one of his sisters had died of meningitis. The other six had died of AIDS. His brothers and sisters left twelve orphaned children, all scattered about with grandparents and his father's two sisters. In Zambia, as in Zimbabwe, Mozambique, and much of sub-Saharan Africa, a whole generation was vanishing; there were only the very old and the very young. Benjamin learned about AIDS in the army and was told that if he contracted the disease, he would be discharged. Now all the contract mercenary firms tested for HIV; if you were found positive for the virus, you could not work. His brother David had married a devout Baptist and found a job as a bank teller. Monogamy and celibacy were the only sure ways to avoid AIDS in Africa. Protected sex was not fashionable, even in the cities.

Benjamin followed his grandmother into the cluttered

living room, where his father sat in a wooden rocker with a quilt across his lap. Anderson Sata was barely sixty-five, but he looked much older. He was painfully thin, and his eyes seemed more deeply recessed in his skull than Benjamin remembered. Benjamin quietly approached the rocker, pulled a stool up next to the chair, and eased himself onto it. There he waited for his father to wake. Fifteen minutes later, the old man's eyes fluttered open. He focused on Benjamin for a full minute before he spoke.

"I see you, my son."

"And I see you, my father." He lowered his eyes in a show of respect.

Anderson Sata's body was failing him, but his mind was sharp. "Is it safe for you to be here, my son?"

His father well knew how his son made his living. He also knew his youngest son was the brightest and most capable of his ten children, and it pained him that he had chosen to become a soldier. Yet the money Benjamin sent home on a regular basis kept the household going, as Anderson Sata had no pension from the mines. David and his wife gave to their church, but not to the care of David's father and grandmother. Yet upon their father's death, the house would belong to David; he was the eldest, and that was the custom.

Anderson Sata also understood that while his son was not a criminal, if the local police knew he was here, they would surely arrest and deport him. It was unlikely that anyone in the project where they lived would turn him in, but one could never be certain. What pained him most was that they would have to remain indoors while it was light, not sit on the porch and drink beer as he did with David. To sit in front of his home with his sons and grandsons, there for all to see, was all Anderson Sata had ever asked out of life—and now, all that was left to him.

"I am safe enough, Father. Look, I brought you something, so you will know when it is time for tea and when it is time to eat."

He handed his father a gold pocket watch, wound and set to the correct time. It cost what the average Zambian made in a year. Benjamin had purchased it with his IFOR signing bonus. He watched his father inspect the time-piece, as a broad smile slowly creased his weathered features. To hand a gift like this to his father in person was something he had wanted to do for many years. He was fortunate that the needs of his employer brought him to Lusaka. Even so he was not sure that he would be allowed to make a visit to his family. *Nkosi* Akheem had sent him ahead with specific instructions and duties. But he had talked it over with Tomba, and Tomba had told him to visit his father, then proceed with his IFOR taskings.

That evening his grandmother killed a chicken, and they dined on mullet and hen. After it was dark, he took his father out onto the porch, and they sat and talked while his grandmother cleaned up after the meal. Just before midnight, he helped his father into bed and kissed him gently on the forehead. The gold watch lay open on the bedside table. Benjamin left as he had come, making his way back into Lusaka.

Garrett Walker and Elvis Rosenblatt faced nearly twenty hours in the air between Honolulu and Mombasa, with a change of planes at Narita Airport in Tokyo. Their passports said they were John Naye and Greg Wood respectively, two Canadian tourists who shared a passion for photography, on their way to Zambia for a photo safari. Their documentation was prepared by Bill Owens and, like that carried by Benjamin Sata, impeccable. The two were booked in business class all the way except for the final jump from Mombasa to Lusaka. The long flight gave Garrett an opportunity to get to know Rosenblatt. They ate, drank, and spent time reading up on long-range photography. Both had top-of-the-line Nikon equipment. For Rosenblatt, it was a grand adventure—a chance to get away from the office, travel to a novel place, and chase bugs. The cloak-and-dagger aspect of the venture only added to the excitement. For Garrett, it was all business. His job was to make sure Dr. Elvis Rosenblatt was prepared and able to do his job when the time came.

"I'll have another scotch, rocks," he told the flight attendant as his empty glass was collected. They were over the Indian Ocean and still two hours out of Mombasa. "How about you, Doc?"

"Maybe a refill on the coffee," Rosenblatt replied.

Garrett was gratified to see that the doctor drank sparingly, and while he was something of a big kid in his exuberance about the trip, he was measured and professional when it came to talking about disease and pathogens. The attendant returned immediately with the scotch and the coffee.

"So, pretend you are a bioterrorist," Garrett said, sipping frugally at his drink, "and you're at some makeshift lab in Africa. What kind of a bug would you be trying to grow to turn loose on some Western city?"

"Interesting perspective," Rosenblatt said. "But before we talk about bugs, let's talk about the players in this game. I'm an investigator—a bug detective. I know the game, but I play defense. The guys that you said were missing also know the game, but they are offensive players. And they are some of the best offensive players. My training and experience are mostly with natural pathogens, but recently, with the emerging bioterror threat, we at the CDC have had to think about these offensive threats—unnatural, man-made threats. And that means we have to think like terrorists, which is not all that easy. Let me break this down for you.

There are three basic threat areas: bacteria, toxins, and viruses. For simplicity, we'll not consider HIV and some of the exotics like bovine spongiform. Now, do you want me to kill a lot of people, or just terrorize them?"

"There's a difference?"

"Sure. Take the anthrax scare right after 9/11. Not that many people died, but it terrorized a nation—people were afraid to go to the mailbox. Some still are. Anthrax is a great terror weapon, but it's not contagious, and it's very hard to weaponize—to get the spores small enough to stay airborne. That's a problem, because it takes about twenty thousand anthrax spores to infect a person. As a terrorist, you have to personally infect every victim. If I have anthrax, I can't hurt you. Now let's say you could weaponize a hemorrhagic fever, like Ebola. Now you've got a real killer. It's highly contagious, killing about seventy percent of those who contract the virus. It's a horrible death. Of course, if you kill a lot of people, you also create a lot of terror."

Garrett considered this. "Okay, you're in Africa, you're in a good lab, and you want to kill a lot of people. How would you go about it?"

"If I were going to use a bacteria, I'd probably use inhalation anthrax or melioidosis. Melioidosis can be some pretty bad stuff. It's rare and mostly confined to animals. Most cases found in humans are confined to Southeast Asia, Thailand, and northern Australia. If you can culture enough of the stuff and get it into an aerosol, you can kill a lot of people. It's ninety percent fatal, and there is no known antidote. But it's hard to transmit, and the bacteria doesn't do well in colder climates. Anthrax, even though it isn't contagious, is another good bacterial choice for an offensive player. And, as I said, you would have to somehow weaponize it—make it an aerosol—which takes some skill and some technology. If you could do that, you could also kill a lot of people. The nice thing about anthrax spores is that they last a long time, and if you have a refined aerosol process, you can keep them aloft long enough for people to breathe them. The Russians had lots of anthrax, tons of it in fact, and we have no idea what happened to most of it. Not sure you could decimate a population with anthrax, but you could sure kill a lot of people in Times Square on New Year's Eve or at a football bowl game. A small explosive and a few pounds of weaponized anthrax, and you could rack up forty or fifty thousand—no problem.

"Then there are toxins. These are natural poisons, as opposed to man-made poisons, like VX nerve gas. There are numerous forms of botulinum, there's ricin, and there's mycotoxins. Ricin and mycotoxins are both good candidates—there is no antidote, and both are almost always fatal. But both have delivery problems. The nice thing about ricin is its availability; it's made from castor beans. But getting it to a large number of people could be very difficult. Mycotoxins, and there are dozens of them, can be very effective in aerosol form. They can be synthesized from fungi. Just mix up a batch, find yourself a crop-spraying aircraft, fly over a crowd, like the New York Marathon or maybe a rock concert. Mycotoxins are what were supposedly released from an aircraft in the 'yellow rain' incidents in Laos, Cambodia, and Afghanistan. The incident in Afghanistan was probably a real one; the Soviets got pretty desperate right before they left. There have been mycotoxins in any number of military arsenals. If I were using a toxin and had a good source, I'd favor a mycotoxin."

"So you'd be growing fungi to make a mycotoxin in your African lab?"

"Now, did I say that? I said *if* I were going to use a toxin, I'd go with a mycotoxin. But why use a rusty knife when there is a shiny sharp scalpel available? I'm talking about a virus. Viruses are Cadillacs of microbial killing machines. We often don't understand how they live, move, and even kill in nature, let alone if someone in a laboratory is helping them. Viruses have been the scourge of the last two centuries. The flu epidemic of 1918 probably killed thirty million people before it ran its course; HIV is well on its way to killing twenty million. Smallpox decimated the American Indians and all but annihilated several smaller, isolated cultures that had no natural immunity. The viruses that cause hemorrhagic fevers are nasty little guys. Ebola is just one of the hemorrhagic fever viruses. Viruses were nasty, but over the years, we've pretty much gotten a handle on them. We have vaccinations against smallpox and tetanus, so they are controlled. Those we can't control, like Ebola, are rare and, so far, geographically isolated. But then we began fooling around with genetic engineering. The mapping of the human genome was a huge step forward. With these techniques, and the emergence of nanotechnologies, we can modify genetic material and literally create new forms of life, or at least significantly modify existing forms of life. A team of biologists created a polio virus in the lab—from scratch. The Armed Forces Institute of Pathology was able to re-create the exact same strain of a flu virus that swept through North America and Western Europe in 1918. So you see, any of the existing nasty little viruses that we have controlled or are very rare could, through genetic manipulation, be made resistant to current vaccines or made more robust, so they are no longer rare. We are into the age of designer bio-weapons. We can make bugs that are immune to existing vaccines or that so depress the human immune system that a common cold could take you out. On the ugly end of the scenario, they have the ability to depopulate whole regions, even continents. It could make the bubonic plague seem like a case of the sniffles."

"Y'know, Elvis, you must be a conversational treasure at a dinner party. Keep this up, and I'm going to need another drink."

"Hey, you asked. Think it scares you? I'm supposed to be a key player on the first-team defense, and it scares the hell out of me."

The pilot announced that they were beginning their descent into Mombasa. There were thunderstorms in the area, so the attendants hurried through the cabin to collect glasses and trash. Garrett put his tray table up but held on to his drink.

"So, Doc, you're in your lab in Zimbabwe. You want to kill a lot of people—a lot of Americans. How do you go about it? You're on the offense now. Which bug are you going to go with?"

Rosenblatt pursed his lips. "Since it's Africa and I have the right equipment, I think I'd go with viral hemorrhagic fever. Ebola is pretty elusive, so I'd probably try to get my hands on some common form of yellow fever or dengue fever, and then morph it into something resistant to current vaccines and give it a little more staying power in northern climates—maybe get some transmission medium other than the mosquito. Of course, you'd want to build in some human immune suppressant characteristics. If I had the ability to conduct human testing, I'd try to give the bug a higher transmission rate, perhaps even give it the ability to beat a HEPA filtration system. That way I'd be able to kill a lot of health-care workers and epidemiologists before they could figure it out, and without the caregivers and the epidemiologists, you can get to pandemic proportions in a hurry."

"You could do that?"

"Probably. I can assure you that those virologists and microbiologists that you can't find, if they are in a lab equipped for genetic engineering, sure as hell can. Look,

Garrett, there's no way to sugarcoat this. It's serious shit—
really serious shit."

The aircraft began to buck and yaw as they slipped
down into the dense, warm air coming off the African
mainland. "Elvis, you're one happy thought after another.
You know, the idea of spending a week with you on a
photo safari is rapidly becoming a bleak prospect."

Rosenblatt grinned at him. "I'll probably be a pain in
the ass while we're taking pictures of wildlife, but if we
have to go on safari for some killer microbes, you'll be
glad I'm on your team."

Garrett considered this and returned the grin. "You
probably got that right." He drained the last of his scotch
as the 767 broke through the overcast and banked for the
Mombasa airport.

François Meno sat in his office in the basement of the
Makondo, reviewing the data on the last group of test subjects. This was taking longer than he had anticipated, but
there was no way around it. Their pathogen was now a
contagion and had to be handled with care. The specifica-
tions called for an infectious period of a week, and that
had been done; the period between infection and the first
symptoms was now ten days or more. An incubation
period of two weeks with a highly contagious disease
meant that the infection would spread that much further
before anyone detected it. In a highly mobile, Western
population, a contagion spread almost exponentially with
time, if there were no symptoms of the disease to sound
the alarm. The longer the incubation period, the harder it
would be to check the reinfection rate. He smiled. This was
a potent weapon, and he relished his part in creating such
power. But the longer incubation period they had engineered now meant that it would take more time to check

the transmission rate among their test population. He was beginning to experience an uneasiness about the necessary extended time to complete this project and close the operation down. He wanted to be away from here; they all did. Meno was deep in thought when a quiet knock sounded at his door.

"*Entre,*" he said with ill-concealed irritation.

"François, I hope I am not interrupting?"

Meno scowled and motioned him in. He did not particularly like Hans Lauda, but Lauda, he admitted, had allowed him to do his work and keep the distractions at this godforsaken place to a minimum. And Lauda had proved a master at deconfliction. Among the talented rogues assembled for this project, there were some monstrous egos. Lauda himself was not without ability and experience, but his main talent was to keep this hastily assembled team focused and on schedule.

"A minute of your time, if I may?" Meno's German was much better than Lauda's French, but Meno insisted on French unless it was unavoidable, or as in the case of the Russian team member, the accent was simply too atrocious.

"What can I do for you, Hans?"

"I wanted your opinion," Lauda said diplomatically. He knew that the project was headed for success, in no small part because of this brilliant and volatile Frenchman. Lauda was there not only for his opinion but to also stroke Meno. "With the results of this most recently infected group, I think we will have taken this pathogen about as far as we need to, or about as far as we can without more research and testing, and a great deal more time. Unless there is something unforeseen that surfaces in these tests, I'd like to have Lyman and his team begin production on this last strain. What would be your opinion?"

A part of Meno wanted to continue the work, even though he was anxious to get out of this hellhole. The power that he felt in the art of genetic manipulation of a virus had a definite hold on him. It was God-like. They had altered their virus so that no known vaccine would be effective in controlling the disease. They had also engineered it for a longer incubation period—no small feat when dealing with this particular pathogen. With more time, he could make it a truly super disease, one that effectively suppressed the victim's immune system, like the HIV virus. Or he could give his virus the ability to quickly mutate so as to defend itself against the battery of drugs that would surely be thrown at it. Some of the best pathologists and epidemiologists in the world would be called in to stop his creation. Meno smiled at the thought. Some of them were clever, but not as clever as himself. It would be very interesting if he just had a little more time to build a disease that reflected his full range of talent.

Meno was a Frenchman. The French were superior, and he considered himself all that, and more. As the handsome only son of a prominent Parisian physician, he had enjoyed privilege and all the pleasures of Paris. At seventeen, he was sent to the Sorbonne in Geneva, where it was discovered that he was something of a prodigy in mathematics. Encouraged by his father, he had taken a degree in medicine, but he had no intention of ever becoming a healer. After school he spent a year in Nice, where he became a society favorite on the French Riviera. That ended with an expensive paternity suit by a wealthy New York socialite who had brought her sixteen-year-old daughter to Monaco for her coming-out. Back in Paris, and with the help of his father, he won an appointment at the Pasteur Institute. There, for the better part of five years, he distinguished himself as both brilliant and extremely difficult to work with. His job at the Institute was not unlike that of Elvis Rosenblatt at the CDC. When he was not offending his colleagues or some senior research fellow, he was capable of brilliant research.

His specialty quickly became tropical disease, and he was considered one of the Institute's leading specialists on the subject. François Meno was just thirty when his father died of a massive stroke in the arms of his mistress. His father, as it turned out, had far more debts than assets, so François was suddenly made to balance a practiced, extravagant lifestyle with his less-than-generous salary from the Pasteur Institute.

François Meno's understanding of World War II came solely from those in his liberal and medical circles. He was aware only of the shame it had brought to France. From his perspective, the France of his parents' era had been humiliated by the Germans, and now his France was being continually humiliated by the Americans—the Americans and their toady surrogates in Europe, the British. It appeared to him that the influence of the United States was heaping one indignity after another on France. The massive oil reserves in Iraq had been largely under contract and the control of TotalFinaElf, the French oil consortium. Had the Americans not interfered, those resources would still be under French control. Energy was the key to national prosperity and influence, and that had been taken away by the Americans' unilateral intervention in Iraq. Meno hated Americans, much as he hated the narrow-minded, politically driven bureaucracy at the Pasteur Institute.

In the summer of 2004, the juxtaposition of two events drove Meno from the Institute. The first was the appointment of a woman as his department head. In his opinion, she was a large, bovine creature, physically unattractive and his intellectual inferior. That she was a competent, proven administrator was beside the point. The second came when they instituted the practice of random drug testing. Meno ran with a crowd of recreational drug users, and he felt that what he did when he was away from the Institute was his own affair. If he had been smart, he would have simply resigned and, like his father, entered private practice, where the compensation was more in keeping with his habits and lifestyle. Instead, he devised a vitamin-rich herbal drink that masked any drug residue in his system. He might have continued to deceive the inspectors, but he couldn't resist bragging to one of the lab techs about his ability to fool the system. His new department head, who was not as dumb as Meno thought, managed to get her hands on his drug-masking concoction, and the drug screening procedures were altered accordingly. One Monday morning, François Meno tested positive for cocaine and was summarily dismissed from the Institute. The fact that this woman had beat him at his own game infuriated him. His only consolation, both financially and personally, was that he was able to sell his formula to an American consulting firm that specialized in advising professional athletes on how to avoid detection in the use of performance-enhancement drugs. The proceeds got him back on the Riviera for the summer, and in the company of bored, wealthy women. He was essentially living as a kept man when he received a call from Helmut Klan in September. They met, and Klan had only one question for him: Was he interested in a genetic engineering project that would pay him a great deal of money? He didn't have to tell Meno that it was illegal. Meno knew it instinctively.

Meno regarded Lauda across his desk. As much as he would love to take this virus a step further, he, like the others, was tired of Africa and the isolation. And he was also anxious to take his money and get back to the good life in the south of France.

"I think what we have will achieve our goals quite

nicely, and I can't imagine that these final tests would cause us to alter the product. These are simply confirmation tests. Tell Lyman to begin his cultures."

Lauda left Meno's office and set off down the long central corridor. On one side were the laboratories, and on the other were the isolation chambers where the wretched test subjects spent their final days. With some care and thought, the isolation wards had been soundproofed so that the researchers did not have to hear the agonized screams of the infected. A strange thing, Lauda mused, it was not so much the sight as the sounds of suffering that affected the staff. He wondered if that were true of those who presided over the Holocaust, or if it was just a peculiarity of this particular research cadre. No matter, he concluded; they would be finished very soon. He did not know the ultimate destination of their product, whether it was for blackmail or actual use. It didn't matter. That was none of his concern, he concluded, just as it had not concerned I.G. Farben what Hitler did with the Zyklon-B gas that Farben had developed.

Lauda did find it interesting that the senior members of the medical research team all seemed to share a dislike of America, and a great need for money. He often wondered if they had been selected for just those reasons. Yet they all somehow focused on their resentment of America as the primary reason for their participation in the project. That was a lot of idealism, Lauda mused, since each of them was being paid $1 million U.S. for a few months' work in this remote laboratory. He, Lauda, was not so inclined to use ideology as a crutch, but then he was being paid closer to $1.5 million for his part in this venture.

"Lyman," he said in German as he entered the office of Lyman Hotch, the team's pathologist. Lyman was the only one who habitually left the door to his office open, as if he somehow knew better than the others that the deadly virus they were perfecting could just as easily find its way through a closed door. "I believe it is time for you to begin farming the most recent strain of our virus. I'm on my way to see Helmut about the final production details, but I believe that you can now begin your cultures."

"Does that meet with the approval of Himself?" Meno's personality was no less abrasive to the research team at the Makondo than it had been to his coworkers at the Pasteur Institute.

Lauda grinned. "As a matter of fact, it does, so the sooner you are able to make what we need, the sooner we can leave this garden spot and return to the congestion and pollution of some overcrowded city."

"*Jawohl, Herr* Lauda," Hotch replied. He rose and, tossing an explicit pornographic magazine on the desk, donned his lab coat.

Elvis Rosenblatt had been a little off the mark, but not by much. The Makondo team had in fact developed a virus that was hemorrhagic in nature. Their virus was resistant to all known vaccine stocks, and designed with a much higher mortality rate than in its naturally occurring form. Oddly enough, it was a deadly disease that had been entirely eradicated by modern medical science—the last case on record in the United States was in 1949, and the last documented in the world was in Somalia in 1977: smallpox. The disease had been effectively wiped out by vaccine. So complete was the eradication of smallpox that vaccination was no longer necessary. Older Americans still bore the small, circular smallpox vaccination scars, but it was rare for anyone under forty to have one; smallpox simply did not exist in the general population. Only small quantities of the pathogen had been retained by the Soviet Union and the United States, just enough for medical research and antibody testing should there ever be another outbreak of the disease. Those held by the United States were in a secure facility at the Armed Forces Institute of Pathology, while those formally held by the Soviet Union were thought to have been destroyed in the transition that led to the formation of the Russian Republic. Most had been, but one of the vials of the disease had fallen into private hands. This one individual had been contacted by Dimitri Muschovia and persuaded, for $16 million, to surrender the deadly vial.

The Soviets had done half of the work for Helmut Klan's team. This particular vial of smallpox contained an enhancement of the more prevalent smallpox, variola major. At one time there were more than fourteen thousand scientists and clinicians working in the Soviet bio-weapons effort. They had isolated and refined a particularly deadly naturally occurring strain of smallpox—hemorrhagic smallpox. The eradicated variola major strain of smallpox was 30 percent fatal; hemorrhagic smallpox was 99 percent fatal. So really, all the Makondo team had to do was to genetically alter this strain of pox so it was immune to the highly effective stocks of smallpox vaccine that were kept on hand. They also engineered their virus to extend the incubation period and to make it a little more contagious. Normal variola major was most contagious at the onset of the rash, when the infected person was usually very sick and immobile. Someone infected with the Makondo-developed strain of this pox was highly contagious during the final ten days of the extended incubation period, when the carrier was still freely moving about and had yet to exhibit any symptoms of the disease. What Klan and his team had developed was a depopulation agent perfectly suited to thrive in a Western, urban society. It would frustrate and confuse the epidemiologists who would have to deal with it until the pandemic was completely out of control.

* * *

It took Garrett Walker, aka John Naye, close to five minutes to negotiate the fare for himself and Dr. Elvis Rosenblatt, aka Greg Wood, from the airport to the Intercontinental Hotel in downtown Lusaka. English was the official language of Zambia, spoken by almost everyone in the capital. The negotiation took longer than needed, since Garrett felt that there was nothing like a good bargaining session to get the feel of the people, even though price was not really an issue. Garrett used a few words of Swahili that the cabdriver seemed to understand, which finally got them to a mutual agreement on the fare. Swahili, like Zulu, Shona, and close to five hundred other languages, was of the Bantu language family. Garrett learned that their driver was Lozi, and from the large cross that hung from the rearview mirror, he assumed that he was Christian. More than half of Zambians were Christian, while something less than half were Muslim and Hindu. With their business concluded, they made the twelve-mile, forty-minute drive from the airport to the Intercontinental with a running commentary on current events in Lusaka. Elvis Rosenblatt observed the squalid approach to the city without comment.

They checked into their rooms, which were clean and modern, even by Western standards, then met on the terrace at the entrance of the Savannah Grill. They had gained a day and lost some six hours during the trip from Hawaii. When going west, Garrett always did his best to stay awake, then retire early evening, local time. It was now 7:00 P.M., so a good night's sleep would hopefully wash out most of their jet lag. When the menus arrived, Garrett chose some native dish that he had never heard of, while Rosenblatt simply told the waiter to bring him the closest thing they had to a cheeseburger. Both ordered the best scotch in the house. While they waited for their food, Garrett's Iridium satellite phone vibrated against his hip with a soft purr.

He snapped the phone open. "Yes?" He listened for a moment, then said, "We're on the ground and on schedule. The day after tomorrow we'll be on the Zambezi as planned, or we can stay in Lusaka another day.... Tomorrow? That's good to hear . . . and have you heard from AKR? . . . Don't worry, he'll be checking in soon. . . . Thanks, Janet; we'll talk tomorrow after I've spoken with Benjamin.... Good luck to you as well.... Good-bye."

"E.T. phone home?"

"Something like that. The rest of the team will be airborne tomorrow and are scheduled to arrive just after dark. If all goes well, they will leave the following morning, shortly before we leave for the Zambezi. Steven Fagan will be here early tomorrow to do the advance work at the airport." Garrett hesitated, not wanting to withhold needed information from Rosenblatt, but reluctant to tell him everything about their cover story. "Elvis, we plan to stage our people out of a vacant hangar at the airport. We will be using the cover of two NGOs to stage men and equipment. We have a proprietary relationship with one of these NGOs. The other knows only that we have deep pockets and that we will help to ferry some well-drilling equipment into the bush for them. Many of these NGOs operate on a shoestring and are glad for any financial or material assistance that they can get. However, the NGO that we work directly with does not have that problem. Our initial objective is to get our men and support equipment, along with your medical equipment, to Lusaka and safely in our hangar. Then we will take up the problem of getting across the Zambezi and to our objective in Zimbabwe. It might look like we're making this up as we go, but that's not the case. You haven't had the pleasure of meeting our operational planner, but she is one of the best in the business. She and her team of planners have been working the issues of getting across the border into Zimbabwe and the mechanics of approaching the target. When it comes to breaking into the laboratory proper, she is going to want your help as to how to safely go about it. But that's still a few days off. For now the drill is to get our people, equipment, and air assets in place at the airport. That done, we will move out into the bush as quickly as possible."

"So we have aircraft?"

"We do. A special C-130 from Bahrain will bring in most of the men and equipment. Two Bell Jet Rangers will be here as well. All three aircraft will be available to us. When we're not using them, they'll be tasked with a variety of humanitarian and community support duties to support our cover story. And candidly, they will do a lot of good when they're not working for us."

"Transport aircraft. Helicopters," Rosenblatt replied. "You must have backing with some very deep pockets. You sure Uncle Sam isn't paying for this?"

Garrett smiled. "Elvis, I may not be able to tell you everything, but I wouldn't lie to you. We are privately funded. This also includes the use of commercial communications satellites with dedicated, secure comm channels. As a matter of fact, you're our biggest security risk."

"Me!"

"That's right. A secret government-sponsored operation is almost an oxymoron. Money and people on the government payroll are hard to conceal or lie about. We didn't want to be in the business of dodging GAO inquiries or misleading congressional oversight committees, so we are a private organization—one that is only known to very few in the government. You are our only government employee, so we're going to take good care of you."

"I should hope so," Rosenblatt said. "But if I'm such a liability, why didn't you just hire some microbiologist from Johns Hopkins?"

"You're unique. No one has your experience in dealing with disease. Your security clearance has allowed you to see things in the lab that few civilian researchers have access to. And there's no one with your background even at the Armed Forces Institute of Pathology. You da man, Elvis."

Their food arrived, and they ate in companionable silence. "How was the burger?" Garrett asked after the waiter cleared the table.

"Well, for my first Zambian cheeseburger, it was okay. The quality of its cheeseburger says a lot about the culture of a nation." He glanced around the restaurant. "For me, it's a leading indicator. How was your . . . whatever it was?"

"I have no idea what it was, but it was delicious."

Rosenblatt sipped the last of his drink, trying to imagine just where they might be in another week. It was exciting, and somewhat scary. "Who is Benjamin, if I'm allowed to ask?"

"Benjamin Sata is one of our African retainers. His family lives on the outskirts of Lusaka. He arrived yesterday and is looking into a few things to help with the planning effort. There will probably be a need for some local arrangements, and he can do that without attracting attention."

Rosenblatt nodded and took the last of his drink in a single swallow. "I'm bushed. Think I'll turn in."

Garrett signed John Naye's name to the bill and walked back to the lobby with Rosenblatt. The concierge greeted them by name. John Naye and Greg Wood were important guests, as were all Western businessmen on holiday. Were someone to check on them, they would learn that the two were employed by a Toronto-based commercial real estate firm that did business across Canada. They were here to photograph wild animals, and their passports and visas were in perfect order. By Intercontinental Hotel standards, they were wealthy, but not super wealthy. Rosenblatt headed for the bank of elevators, but Garrett held back.

"Not coming?"

"Think I'll take a walk. See you in the morning."

"In the morning, then."

Garrett made the three-mile round-trip to the shopping district at a leisurely pace. He had never been in southern Africa, and he wanted to get the feel of it, even though Lusaka, in many ways, was just another big city. Yet each city had its own flavor—its own ripe blend of smells. For most, the odor was noxious; for Garrett it was simply a whiff of life. Zambia was a nation the size of Western Europe and, with eleven million people, the least densely populated nation in Africa. The population was concentrated in two areas—Lusaka and the Copper Belt, which ran across the northern part of the country along the Zambian-Congo border. That left large tracts of relatively uninhabited land in the central and southern plains. There were two main industries in Zambia: mining and tourism. Tourism centered around the game parks and Victoria Falls. From what Garrett had read, Zambia had done better than most in protecting its wildlife, which was the key to its tourist trade.

Garrett also needed to walk off his frustrations. For the first time, either as a Navy SEAL or as an employee with IFOR, he was relegated to a support role. Usually he was at the forefront of the action. He fully understood the reason; he was a white man, and white men simply don't move well in sub-Saharan Africa, where, outside South Africa, whites accounted for just over 1 percent of the population. There were only so many ways a white man could move about. Even with a good cover story, he would stand out due to the color of his skin. AKR was right; this was a job for Africans, at least in the initial stages of the operation.

His job for now was to babysit Dr. Elvis Rosenblatt. The fact that Rosenblatt would more than likely be a key player in the operation did not make his assignment any easier. And the task would not be a simple one. He was to see that Rosenblatt and his equipment got where they were needed, when they were needed. Presumably, that would be when any of the fighting that took place would be over. Given what they might be dealing with, the dangerous part could be only beginning after the guns fell silent.

Garrett got back to his room a little after 11:00 P.M. As in all modern hotels, his room was equipped with high-speed Internet access. He broke out his laptop and tapped in the privacy code to turn it on. Then he engaged the cryptographic circuitry. He logged onto the IFOR site and began to download message traffic from Janet and Steven. There was even a message for him from AKR.

Akheem and Tomba had been in Johannesburg for almost two days. Johannesburg, or Joburg as the mercs called it, was the mercenary capital of the world, even though section 2 of the South African Foreign Military Assistance Act forbade the hiring of mercenaries in what amounted to a constitutional ban on mercenary recruitment. There were two reasons for this. The first was the availability of the right kind of talent. Most mercenary requirements arose in Africa or other equatorial areas, where black men could move easily and fight under the harsh conditions often found there. The transition from white to black rule in South Africa had also put a great many superbly trained black troops out of work. The second was that South Africa was one African nation where whites comprised a sizeable minority, and a white man could move about easily and conduct business. The private military companies that hired mercenaries were basically color-blind. They paid for experience and reliability, but most PMCs were themselves corporations based in Western nations with largely white management and recruiters. And, as with seasonal farm labor in the United States, it was often hard to get whites to do the work; former black South African regulars not only were willing to put their guns out for hire but did as they were told and asked few questions. Many white soldiers of fortune were outcasts or expatriates, and usually came with a lot of baggage.

AKR and Tomba had taken a room in a nondescript motel a few miles from the airport. They entered South Africa from Nairobi with British passports and visas that said they were travel agents. An impressive pair in their pleated trousers, sport coats, and turtlenecks, they might have been taken for two professional athletes in the United States. Once through customs and checked into the motel room, Tomba set about to change their image. AKR had already shed his dreadlocks and the Rastafarian look that had served him so well in the Caribbean. Both of them changed into short-sleeved white shirts, dark trousers, and low-cut leather walking shoes. They were still two tall, handsome black men, but now they had the look of two off-duty security guards.

"So now what's next?" Akheem asked as they pulled out of the motel in their rental car.

"Now, my brother, we seek employment."

Tomba drove them to a restaurant between Johannesburg and Pretoria called the Wildebeest, a large, busy establishment that specialized in beef and wild game. They slipped into the adjoining cocktail lounge and took a small table in the corner. The lounge was barely half full. Both ordered beer. Horned animal heads adorned the walls of the dimly lit interior, and the clientele seemed to be equally balanced between black and white. The room was heavy with cigarette smoke. They had barely waited fifteen minutes when a white man, dressed much as they were, approached.

"G'day, gentlemen," he said with an easy smile. "May I join you?"

"There is always room at our table for one more," Tomba replied.

The man set his own beer on the table and slid into an empty chair. He had a ruddy complexion and unruly brown hair. AKR noticed that he smiled with his mouth, not with his eyes, and that he had huge hands and forearms, with tattoos of dragons buried under the forearm hair. He reached one of his massive paws across the table.

"Tomba, it is good to see you again. How long has it been, three—four years?" His accent was that of an Australian stockman. Tomba took the outstretched hand.

"Perhaps four. And I would like you to meet Samuel. Samuel, this is Irish. I'm not sure if that is his real name, but it is what he is called. Perhaps it is his nom de guerre."

"Too right," Irish said with a chuckle as he took AKR's hand in a crushing grasp. "Happy t' meet ya, Samuel. Are you Turkana as well?"

"My roots are Masai, but I have not been back to Kenya for a while."

Irish studied AKR a moment, as if trying to catalog him, and turned his attention back to Tomba.

"I was delighted t' get yer call, and t' hear that you might be looking for work," he said carefully. "I was given to understand that you had found work with an American security firm. Is that no longer the case?"

"It was a contract to train some people for executive protection duty in African cities. The Americans are deeply engaged in security considerations right now, as you can imagine. It was a short contract, and work there is completed." Tomba's explanation had a final tone. Now he leaned forward to address the Aussie. "And I am given to understand, Irish, that you are no longer with Sandline but represent a new organization. Can you tell me about it?"

Irish glanced at AKR, and Akheem sensed that the man would have been more comfortable discussing this one-on-one with Tomba. Tomba was known and respected by those who hire professional soldiers, and in the closed fraternity of mercenaries, he had the respect of others who hired themselves out as professional soldiers. Reputation was everything in the mercenary trade.

Sensing his reluctance, Tomba continued. "You may speak freely in front of my brother Samuel. I can vouch for his discretion as well as his ability as a fighter."

Irish again forced a smile. "Very well, then. I'm now working for Northbridge Services Group out of the UK, and we have ongoing requirements for experienced men. We do a number of things—demilitarization of warring factions, mine clearance, and counterterror operations—standard fare. It's a good firm. We pay the going PMC wage and, for supervisory personnel like yourself, a generous bonus." He chuckled again, and this time it seemed genuine. "And for the most part, our operations have the blessing of the Pommy foreign secretary."

"Forgive me for questioning you," Tomba said pleasantly, "but that didn't seem to be the case in Ivory Coast."

Irish took on a deeper shade of red. "True, but I think his lordship, Mr. Jackie Straw, was forced t' say what he did for political reasons. Our firm was on solid ground going into Ivory Coast, and those buggers at Whitehall knew that."

"I understand," Tomba said neutrally, but he had put Irish on notice that he knew of Northbridge and their activities. In fact, few PMCs did things without government approval, both from the host nation where the work was done and from the resident nation of the PMC. Great Britain was one of the more lenient western nations regarding mercenary activity. After all, had they not used Gurkhas for close to two hundred years?

"Samuel and I may be looking for work," Tomba continued, "but we would prefer to stay out of West Africa. Are there other areas where our services might be needed?"

They talked for another half hour. Tomba indicated that they might be available later in the spring, and Irish replied that there were a number of contract negotiations in the works that could result in a hire. Irish's job, as Tomba well knew, was to stay close to the mercenary community and to know who was available. Experienced, reliable retainers were the key to a successful private military contract. Tomba gave Irish a piece of paper with an international cell phone number, and Irish gave him a card with phone, telex, fax, and e-mail contacts. Soon the talk drifted to past wars and some of the colorful, dysfunctional expatriates who called themselves soldiers of fortune. As they were about to leave, Tomba paused and, almost as an afterthought, turned to Irish.

"I was told something a few weeks back by a friend from the 32nd Battalion. It made little sense to me, but perhaps you may know something of it. It seems that someone was recruiting for a force to return to Zimbabwe. Is someone thinking about mounting an insurgency against Mugabe?"

Irish smiled ruefully as he leaned closer and spoke in a low voice. "If they are, they couldn't have chosen a worse bugger to lead it. From what I hear, Claude Renaud hired between fifty and sixty men for some job in Zimbabwe or

Mozambique. A good many of them were from the 32nd along with a handful of white expats."

AKR felt Tomba stiffen at the mention of Claude Renaud, but he quickly recovered. "Renaud?" Tomba managed. "But who would hire a man of his reputation?"

"Who indeed," Irish replied. "Certainly no legitimate government or mining consortium, and most of the white farmers have quit the country. Perhaps it was Mugabe himself. Then he can claim the colonial powers are still picking on him. What a bloody cockup he's made of that country. The Pommies should never have let him make himself president-for-life in that poor nation. It's their fault, mind you. As I recall, you served in the Rhodesian Army, didn't you, Tomba?"

"I did," Tomba said, regaining his composure, "but that was a long time ago, and I was a very young and foolish man." He rose and offered Irish his hand. "Thank you for speaking with us. Please keep us in mind if there is work you can send our way."

The lounge was now almost full. They left Irish at the table and threaded their way through the tables to the door.

"This Renaud is our man, is he not?" AKR said as soon as they were in the parking lot. He spoke carefully, as there was a murderous look on Tomba's normally tranquil features.

"He is," Tomba replied. "How soon can we be on a flight to Lusaka?"

Pavel Zelinkow had been out late the previous evening to the theater, but up very early that morning. There was a great deal to do. The previous afternoon he had taken a call from Helmut Klan in Zimbabwe. The development and testing of the product were nearly complete, and they were now about to enter the production phase. As Zelinkow understood it, growing the smallpox virus they needed was a relatively simple task compared with what they had done in the genetic modification and testing process. They were now only days from having the final test results. Those results would validate the pathogen they were already starting to produce. When they had their disease, they could begin to close down the Makondo project. And then he would be free to complete his final task: shipping the product to the location specified by the people who hired him—and to the man who would use the pathogen. Now that the African end of the project was in its last few days, it meant another trip to Tehran. His only consolation was that it would be his last, at least for a while.

Closing down the Makondo operation would be a big relief. It had not been difficult to bribe those in Harare to cooperate, but that kind of money only bought so much time. The sooner the product was out of Africa, the better. An undertaking such as this meant opening doors to get things done. To conclude the operation, he would have to close those same doors, carefully wiping his fingerprints off each handle and latch. He had just booked his flight from Rome to Tehran through Cairo when one of his lines rang. He checked the caller ID, but it registered a blank.

"Yes," he said cautiously.

"Good morning, Pavel Zelinkow. I hope I am not disturbing you at this early hour."

"Not at all, Boris Zhirinonovich," Zelinkow replied warmly, relieved and gladdened to hear the old man's thick Russian. "I can think of no better way to start my day than to hear your voice."

"You are much too kind to an old apparatchik. Pavel, how secure is the connection at your end?"

"As secure as that where you are," he replied. He did

not want to offend his former mentor by saying that his communication suite was far more state-of-the-art than anything in Moscow. Technology and high-speed encryption had made secure communications commonplace in corporate practice. There were no longer the delays and voice distortions of the past.

"Very good, but nonetheless, I will be brief. There is, it seems, a covert organization in America that was responsible for the recovery of the two stolen Pakistani nuclear weapons. This is a deduction our people have made, since it appears that no one in or associated with U.S. military or Western intelligence services seems to have been involved. Yet we have it on authority from a number of sources that it did happen with American knowledge and limited American military support. It appears that this organization is not sponsored or funded by the U.S. government, or we would have more information on it. Our sources close to American intelligence confirm that this is neither a military special operations unit nor a part of the CIA Special Activities Division. It would seem that it is some kind of corporate security element that operates with very limited official contact, and probably with complete denial of the U.S. government." Zelinkow heard the older man chuckle. "Perhaps this is what makes them so dangerous; there is no collateral political damage to fear from their actions or overzealousness.

"At any rate, we understand that they may be active and again have operatives in the field. I wish I had more for you, but that is all we know. One would think that they are able to move assets and people in ways we used to do in the heyday of the Ninth Directorate. If I learn any more, I will contact you. . . . Are you still there?"

"Yes, yes, I am here. I was just absorbing all that you have told me. Boris Zhirinonovich, may I ask you for a favor?"

"Certainly, Pavel, you may ask." Again the chuckle. "And I will do what I can for you."

"Could you ask our residents in sub-Saharan Africa to let you know if they have any unusual activity in their capitals, something out of the ordinary in the way of non-military activity that could be used to support a military operation?"

"Our reporting assets in that region are not what they once were, but we have a few options. And there are men not unlike yourself who occasionally make inquiries for us. I'll see what I can do. In the meantime, you be careful, Pavel."

"*Da*, I will be careful, and thank you for your assistance."

Zelinkow rang off and sat looking at the dawn that was just beginning to reach out over the Mediterranean. He felt a sudden chill and, without thinking, reached out and cradled the cup of espresso for warmth. The instincts that he had refined to almost a sixth sense in KGB's Ninth Directorate under Zhirinon now screamed at him. Something was not right. Zelinkow did not know who or what, but some force or entity was out there, and somehow he knew it was stalking him. They had surprised him in Iran and Afghanistan, and he was resolved not to let that happen again. He turned the matter over in his mind for five minutes while finishing his espresso. Time, always his enemy, was now becoming very dangerous. Then he made two calls. The first was to Helmut Klan. Zelinkow instructed his project director to conclude the project with all haste and to put his security detachment on full alert. With no further need to range out into the countryside to procure test subjects, they could be pulled in for added security around the hotel complex. His second call was to move up the date and time of his flight from Rome to Tehran.

8
BOOTS ON
THE GROUND

The bored customs officer took the man's passport with a surly gesture. "Purpose of your visit?" he droned impatiently.

"I am with Siemens, AG and here to work with CAPC, the Central African Power Corporation, to assist with your electric power supply. I believe my papers to be in order, are they not?" The German electrical giant worked throughout Africa and was, in fact, also contracted to repair and expand the telephone system in Iraq.

The customs officer's whole demeanor immediately changed. "Of course, Mr. Schultz. Welcome to Zambia."

Steven Fagan, who had arrived on the morning flight from Nairobi, proceeded to clear customs and recovered his single piece of luggage with no further delays. Bill Owens had him well documented as a consultant with the German firm under contract to provide engineering services for CAPC. Dodds LeMaster had managed to hack into the Siemens HR database and list a Herman Schultz as one of their field engineers. Steven had a working knowledge of engineering and German, but few spoke German in Zambia, the former British colony of Northern Rhodesia. The closest former German colony was Tanzania. Zambia and Tanzania shared a section of border where the black surrogates of Germany and Britain had fought a bloody conflict during World War I.

CAPC employees and any foreigners working with CAPC enjoyed privileged status in Zambia. Revenue from the copper mines and tourism came and went, depending on metal prices, exchange rates, and the world economy. Hydroelectric power generation was a constant. Zambia exported close to two billion kilowatts of electricity, primarily to South Africa. It was an important source of revenue, and since this was Africa, it was also a source of under-the-table payoffs to key members of the government. Currently, the name not withstanding, those members belonged to the ruling Movement for Multiparty Democracy, which held a slim majority in the Zambian National Assembly and controlled the presidency. Steve Fagan, aka Herman Schultz, sported a pair of clear-rimmed glasses and a white plastic shirt-pocket protector that, along with his mild, inoffensive manner, said he was a man who was interested in technical matters and the transmission of electricity.

Steven also carried papers that identified him as a regional director for the Joseph Simpson Jr. Foundation. For what he needed to do in support of the operation, he had to be two people in Zambia. Once outside the terminal, he hit a redial number on his satellite phone.

"Garrett."

"Hello, Garrett. I'm on the ground and heading for the hangar. It's on the civil aviation side of the airport, hangar B-5, as in bravo, five."

"Hangar B-5, got it. See you there in about an hour."

"In an hour, then," Steven replied and snapped his phone shut.

He caught a cab that took him to the civil aviation complex, which was far more utilitarian than the main passenger terminal. He was anxious to see the hangar and to ensure that it was suitable for their needs. Things were going to begin to happen fast. An employee of the Joseph Simpson Jr. Foundation had made the arrangements through an intermediary—a hangar between eight and ten thousand square feet, suitable for general aviation purposes, with shop space, power, and water—a tall order in southern Africa. He had also asked that the facility be remote, if possible, and secure. Steven handed the guard at the gate to the complex a 50,000-kwacha note, about $10 U.S. He checked Steven's Simpson Foundation ID and gave him a ring of keys and directions to hangar B-5. After a short drive down a dusty road, they came to a hangar served by two smaller outbuildings. From the outside, it looked perfect. He paid off the cab and began a careful inspection of the facility. Close to an hour later, another cab delivered Garrett Walker. He found Steven inside, and they greeted each other warmly.

"What is that god-awful smell?"

"Chemical residue. Apparently the hangar was once used to support a crop-dusting operation. They grow a lot of corn and sorghum north of here. It probably wouldn't meet OSHA criteria, but I think it will do nicely for our purposes. There's a head and shower facility in one of the outbuildings, and some crude office space in the other. No matter, we won't be here all that long."

"When do the others arrive?" Garrett asked

"Just after dark. We'll unload and get set up. Janet wants to get them across the Zambezi as soon as possible, but no later than dawn day after tomorrow. Have you heard from Benjamin?"

"We talked by phone this morning, and I plan to see him this afternoon. He says everything is in order. How soon will you be moving from here?"

Steven paused to consider this. "If we can manage it, I'd like to see the equipment and main group move at first light, but that will be Janet's call. We both agree we'll be a lot safer when we are dispersed and away from the capital. I know she wants the assault element out of Zambia as soon as possible."

"How about Tomba and AKR?"

"They will be here sometime late this afternoon or this evening. Can you get back here before dawn tomorrow morning for a jump-off briefing?"

"No problem," Garrett replied. "I've got a cabdriver on retainer until we leave. You want the doctor here?"

Again, Steven was not quick to answer. "I don't think so. We'll probably talk about a lot of things that he has no need to know about. We don't want to scare him, but then again, I don't want him too surprised at what may be taking place. My sense from our meeting in Hawaii is that he's a pretty solid man. How do you feel about him?"

"I think he's good to go—physically, for sure. We got up this morning and went for a run. When I left him, he was heading for the hotel health club to lift some weights. On the flight over we talked at length about what might be happening at the hotel in Zimbabwe, and it's some pretty scary stuff. You don't have to worry about Rosenblatt not taking this seriously. He's pretty keyed up. Judy still due in tonight?"

"She'll call you as soon as she gets to the hotel. I understand her appointment at the embassy is for sometime late tomorrow morning."

Steven showed Garrett quickly around the hangar complex, and they shook hands before Garrett climbed back into the waiting cab. He rode up front with the driver, and they maintained a running conversation all the way back to Lusaka. They spoke mostly in English, but the driver was astonished at how easily this white man picked up on the few words he used in his native Kaonda.

While Garrett Walker made his way back into Lusaka, Claude Renaud was sitting in Helmut Klan's office, slouched in a chair across the desk from him.

"So, *Herr Doktor,* your research is about finished. I'm sure you and your colleagues will be happy to return to the comforts of Europe."

Klan smiled tightly. He couldn't wait to be out of Africa, but he was not going to admit that to Renaud. "Actually, Claude, it's been an interesting experience. Perhaps," he lied, "I can return at some point for a visit that is purely pleasure. At any rate, I've asked to meet with you, as my principals have informed me that there may be a dedicated threat to our work here. What I'm saying is that someone or some force may attempt to intervene."

Renaud leaned forward, suddenly very alert. "You don't mean that someone would attack us here, at the Makondo? But that is impossible. You yourself said that the authorities in Harare had been well paid to leave us alone as well as to alert us if someone comes nosing around. Who could get to us without someone sounding the alarm?"

"I really don't know," Klan said patiently. "All I know is that I was told to complete our work as soon as is practical, and that I was to instruct you to have your men be extra vigilant. Apparently there may be a small American unit that has the ability to project force globally. It seems that they can move with great speed and striking power. I think we can be finished with our work in five days, perhaps less. Your job is to keep us safe until that time."

"I know my job, *Herr Doktor.* I'd like to see someone try to interfere. I've trained these men myself, and they are the best group of fighters on the continent. No, *Doktor,* you go about your business; we will see that you are not bothered." Renaud was now slouched back in his chair. "And if someone does come nosing around, we will see that they get a warm reception."

Klan started to warn him about complacency and overconfidence, but he knew it would be a waste of time—better to flatter. "Very well, Claude; I have complete confidence in you and your fighters. But we have come a long way, and we are very close to finishing our mission here. If we are not successful, neither of us will collect our completion bonus. Think about that as you go about your duties."

Renaud had no intention of losing out on his bonus. As soon as he left the hotel, he went to find his team leaders to discuss additional security measures. Renaud would have liked the project to go on a little longer. He was enjoying the power of heading his own mercenary band, not to mention the weekly sums that were deposited to his account in Maputo. He had never had such a financial cushion. But he knew it would have to end sometime, and there was the bonus—three hundred thousand American dollars. With that kind of money he could return to Johannesburg, find himself a comfortable apartment, and buy a new car—perhaps a new Land Rover. And when he went back into the Broken Tusk, he would be a man with a mercenary contract under his belt—a man who had led his own commando. While he was sure that their position at the Makondo was unassailable, he again walked the grounds to inspect their perimeter security. Since there was no longer any need to procure test subjects, he was free to concentrate all his men on security. He doubted that any American force could suddenly appear in the heart of southern Africa. The Americans could not move without jet transport and a huge logistics train. True, the Makondo had a helo pad, but it was only suitable for light-duty helicopters, not troop transports. Still, he would locate a machine gun to cover the pad. If an uninvited helo did try to land, he would cut it to pieces. But this was all conjecture. If there were such a force, he would hear of it long before they got to the Makondo. That's why he kept two men in the town of Kariba, and had paid the constables in the villages along the road that led to the hotel complex to alert him if anyone approached.

As Claude Renaud was walking the security perimeter of the facility, stopping occasionally to chat with the men in their security outposts, François Meno inspected the final group of test subjects held in the basement of the Makondo. That's how he and the others referred to them— test subjects, or hosts. They were in small rooms—cells actually, two to a room. Most of them were men, but there needed to be a few women to ensure that the pox was not somehow gender-selective. When the genetic composition of a virus was altered, almost anything could happen, and any number of unintended side effects could accompany the modified organism. Meno would have liked a more even ratio of men to women, but the teams that procured his subjects brought in mostly men, even though he and the others on his team repeatedly asked for more women. Meno was aware that African men have a low regard for women. Perhaps, he thought, they felt that taking women captive was beneath them, or they wished to leave women behind because they performed virtually all the manual labor around the home. No matter, the pathogen they had developed was aggressive and lethal beyond their expectations to either man or woman.

"Which one do you want to examine, Johann? And this is the last, right?"

"It is. I think we need only see the man in this room."

Johann Mitchell was a pathologist with a great deal of experience in internal medicine. It was his job to gauge the progress of the disease and the intervening time between exposure and death. He was also tasked with the critical issue of contagion—how long did it take an individual, once infected, to become contagious? How long was an infected person contagious before they became ill and exhibited symptoms? With the more common variola major smallpox, a victim was not contagious until the onset of symptoms, when he or she was too sick to move around. The Makondo strain of hemorrhagic smallpox they had developed acted very differently.

The man they were about to examine was ambulatory and appeared healthy. Only the drugs that were administered with their meals kept him quiet and semi-catatonic. Meno and Mitchell entered the room and locked the door behind them. During the initial testing, before the use of sedatives, they would not be able to work like this without guards present. Still, Meno carried a pistol. The man was sitting docilely on his cot. Mitchell asked him to lie down, and he quietly obeyed. Meno remained standing while Mitchell pulled a stool alongside the man's bunk. He talked to the man in reassuring tones while he drew blood and thoroughly examined him. Bedside manners, even in this macabre setting, were a matter of reflex for most physicians. Then, with wooden-handled swabs, Mitchell took cultures from the man's nose and throat, sealing them carefully in special ziplock bags. If the man thought it strange that two men encapsulated in yellow spacesuits were visiting him in this way, he didn't show it. He merely smiled vacantly up at them through a drug-induced haze.

"No symptoms yet?" Meno asked.

"None," Mitchell replied. There was a rubber diaphragm in the airtight suits that allowed them to communicate with only slight distortion. "It's been nine days since he became contagious, and if it were not for the sedatives, he would be up and about with no abnormalities. It's incredible."

As they left the room, they passed the cot of a woman who was moaning softly. Her symptoms had begun the day before. She was drenched in sweat from fever. A few lesions were beginning to appear on her forehead. The sedatives that had been administered to keep her quiet and passive would alleviate some of her suffering, but only for a while.

The decontamination process took longer than the examination. Those tasked with developing and refining this deadly strain of smallpox were able to cut corners that would have been unthinkable in a normal clinical setting. Decontamination, however, was not one of them. First they passed through a shower of a sodium hypochlorite solution to thoroughly wash and disinfect their suits. Then they passed into an ultraviolet-lighted room with heating elements to dry the suits and remove moisture from the air. From the drying room, they moved to a disrobing area, where they carefully removed the suits and pulled on respirators. They kept the respirators on until they got into the shower room, where they could fully scrub down. The whole process took close to half an hour.

The blood samples and swabs they had taken were then sent to the lab, where a masked and gowned lab tech handled them in a Plexiglas isolation chamber with holes in the glass for rubber-gloved access to the sealed and sterile environment. An examination of the cultures would ensure that the few seemingly healthy subjects were still infected and contagious. An hour's work by the lab tech confirmed that the swabs contained hemorrhagic smallpox, still virile and very deadly. He called Meno in his office with the results.

"It's confirmed, Johann," Meno said as he hung up the phone. "The healthy-appearing ones are just as contagious as those manifesting the advanced symptoms. So it would appear from the last infected group of subjects that we can expect a victim to be a contagious carrier seven to nine days before he becomes sick—perhaps longer. And our carrier, depending on his health and level of activity, will become contagious about forty-eight hours after becoming infected. Very impressive, Johann. Very impressive indeed. I think we're there."

Mitchell nodded. With this last strain, a carrier would have a week, perhaps more, to move about and contaminate those with whom he came into contact. He would still be contagious after he fell ill, but those with the outward symptoms of smallpox—fever, malaise, vomiting, and body aches—were seldom ambulatory. The symptoms of smallpox were reasonably well known, and those with symptoms could expect to be quarantined.

"With these last cultures, we can expect them all to be showing overt symptoms within forty-eight hours," Mitchell said. "I, uh, prepared some lethal injections should we want to help them along. It's probably best all around, don't you think?"

Meno considered this. The final stages of this strain of smallpox were not pretty. It usually began with a fever, followed quickly by the first lesions. Then it was a quick progression from lesions to pustules, with the fever causing the pustules to scab over. Most of their test subjects experienced several days of fever, dehydration, internal bleeding, and a great deal of pain. Death was welcome. There are few more painful ways to die than from hemorrhagic smallpox.

"I don't think so," Meno replied. "I'd like some more data on the average length of time between the onset of symptoms and death. Let's let the disease run its course. It will give us a better idea of the length of time between the first symptoms and death. We know that they will still be highly contagious when they're sick, and that they will have to be cared for. Even when quarantined, they will be dangerous, and they will clog up any health-care system.

A lot of resources will be consumed trying to put off the inevitable."

Mitchell nodded. "If that's the way you want it." He promptly left Meno's office, trying to hide his displeasure.

By noon the next day, all of the eight subjects, five men and three women, three Shona and five Ndebele, were racked with fevers ranging to as high as 105 degrees. Most of them had begun to throw up, and all but two had lesions. It took them about two days to die once the symptoms appeared. The entry in Dr. Meno's medical diary recorded it as two days, four hours, and thirty-seven minutes—on average.

As the sun slipped behind the horizon on the broad Zambian plain, a Lockheed C-130J Hercules crabbed in toward the Lusaka airport, fighting a strong crosswind. The pilot skillfully touched down and taxied to the general aviation area, pausing some fifty yards from hangar B-5. The plane was met by a jeep with two uniformed officials. With two of the four engines still turning over, a tall, commanding woman stepped down from the hatch just behind the flight deck and walked a short distance from the nose of the plane to the jeep. She towered over the one official who slid from the open jeep's passenger seat. They talked for a few moments, then she handed him a manila folder. The man began to inspect the paperwork inside. From the shadows next to the hangar, three men tensely watched this mini-drama unfold.

"We have already paid the senior customs official and the airport manager," Steven Fagan observed. "She should only have to present loading documentation and the forged manifest."

"Perhaps this official was not a party to that which was

paid to his superiors," Tomba said. "It would seem that he is awaiting what he feels is his due."

"That guy better clear that aircraft and do it soon, or he's going to get his ass kicked," AKR offered. They watched as she handed him a letter-sized package. The official touched his cap with a riding crop and climbed back into the jeep. "The man doesn't know it," AKR continued, "but he just survived a near-death experience."

The three stepped from the shadows and into the dull glare of the bare bulb over the single sliding door of the hangar. Janet Brisco immediately saw them and began walking toward the hangar. The big Hercules pivoted and followed her.

"You seem quite intimidated by Miss Brisco, are you not?" Tomba asked.

"Quite," Akheem replied. "That lady scares me. I'm just glad she's on our side—at least, I think she's on our side."

The turbine whine of the two Allison turbofan engines cut short any further conversation. Brisco joined them, and they watched as the aircraft made a tight hundred-eighty-degree turn to bring the rear loading ramp to face the hangar. The aircraft was painted all white, with "Joseph Simpson Jr. Foundation" blocked onto the tail in neat black letters. The pilot cut power to the two engines as the tail ramp began to grind down. Janet Brisco walked under the tail section and called up into the bowels of the aircraft.

"All right, people, let's get this aircraft unloaded."

In the orderly confusion that followed, the C-130 was quickly emptied. First, two white vans were driven down the loading ramp and into the hangar. They looked like nine-passenger shuttle vans, but there were no windows—just a number of wire antenna whips projecting from the van roofs. Tomba's men were all dressed as laborers—dark tan trousers and short-sleeved, collared shirts. About half of them wore hard hats; they looked like any work crew at an African airstrip. Two small forklifts charged from the belly of the plane with the first of the palleted equipment. The two machines shuttled loads while the men formed a brigade for bags and small boxes. Some of them were stamped, "Medical Test Equipment—Handle with Care." In less than forty minutes, the Hercules was unloaded. When the hangar doors were closed, the aircraft began to spool up the four big turbofan engines and crawl back out to the airstrip. It taxied to the main runway, where it hesitated for only a moment before beginning its takeoff roll. The big six-bladed Dowty composite propellers bit into the African night, and the Hercules gathered momentum quickly. Using less than half the allotted runway, it rotated and climbed steeply, banking to the north.

The inside of the hangar was a hive of activity. Janet Brisco roamed the interior with a clipboard, seeing that everything was staged in accordance with her planning diagram. Two 10kw generators were set up behind the hangar, with thick umbilicals leading inside. Lights on tripod stands were set out to augment the dimly illuminated space. Two of the Africans in the shabby attire of contract security guards lounged about in front of the hangar, seemingly inattentive to their duties. When all was in its assigned place in the hangar, the men recovered their personal bags and began to set up their operational equipment. Two of them began to pry the lids from the weapons and ammunition boxes.

"This is right out of *The Dogs of War*," AKR said with a grin. "To hell with the mission; let's take Zambia."

Janet Brisco scowled at him. They were joined by Tomba, Steven, Dodds LeMaster, Bill Owens, and Mohammed Senagal, who had taken charge of the men in Tomba's absence.

"Okay, everyone, we are on time and on schedule. The

C-130 is on its way back to Nairobi to refuel and wait for any further tasking. The two Jet Rangers will be here just before dawn to begin ferrying men and equipment to the staging areas." She looked at her watch. "It's twenty hundred now. Tomba, I'll want you, Akheem, and your men ready to move out by zero three forty-five. The final mission briefing will be at zero four hundred. Dodds, I want a full functional test of the vans' communications and support electronics between now and then. Let me know if there are any problems. Steven, was Benjamin able to make the needed arrangements?"

"Garrett met with him this afternoon, and all was said to be in order. Garrett will be here for the mission briefing."

"And the doctor?"

"He will not be here. As I understand it, he and Garrett will go forward tomorrow afternoon and wait for the assault element to do their work."

Janet nodded, then turned to the small, hickory-skinned man standing next to Tomba. "Are you and the men sufficiently rested to begin tomorrow? They may get a few hours' sleep tonight, but not much more."

The men had flown commercial from Honolulu, taking a variety of flights and connections into Nairobi. There they had rendezvoused with the equipment and the C-130J. Janet noticed that they fell asleep immediately on takeoff and awoke only when the plane touched down. They were like gundogs, able to sleep anywhere and awake immediately.

"They will be well rested and ready, miss," Mohammed Senagal replied, meeting her gaze. Senagal had none of the shyness of the other Africans, but then he was a Somali. He was polite, but there was an imperiousness and arrogance about him that was absent in the others. "But thank you for asking."

"That's about it. As we take inventory and test equipment, I will want to know immediately if there are any problems. Thanks, everyone, for all your hard work. And now, Tomba, I'd like a word with you and Akheem."

"I will be with you in a moment, Janet," Tomba said formally.

He individually greeted each of his men and had a quiet word with Senagal, then joined Janet and AKR in the corner of the hangar. Dodds LeMaster had a pot of coffee brewing on a propane camp stove. There, Janet listened without interruption as Tomba told her about their meeting with Irish near Johannesburg, and what might be waiting for them at the target.

This was not Pavel Zelinkow's first trip to Tehran, and each time he found it taxing. On this trip he was Philippe Poulenc, a French expatriate living in Algeria. On his last visit, he had been a French businessman in the olive oil export/import business. This time he was a representative for Bouyges Telecom, a French wireless provider, here to sell digital cell phones to the Iranians. Even though Zelinkow found it too dangerous to live in France, it did not mean that he could not convincingly masquerade as a Frenchman. The beauty of being French, Zelinkow often mused, was that no one took you too seriously. You could appear greedy or ill-mannered or arrogant, and if you were French, it was accepted. His last visit here had been to meet in secret with Imad Mugniyah, the security chief for Hezbollah. The personal security for Mugniyah had been tight, but it would be even tighter for this meeting—tighter and much more discreet.

The plane was an older A320-200 Airbus operated by Orca-Air, an Egyptian carrier out of Cairo, but it managed to arrive exactly on time that evening. His papers were in perfect order, so he quickly and easily cleared customs. As he stepped out of the building, he was unprepared for the cold, damp wind that swept in from the Elbruz Mountains to the north, still carrying moisture from the Caspian Sea. Tehran was actually farther south than Rome, but the Caspian was not the Mediterranean. There had been no one waiting to pick him up, so Zelinkow approached the first cab in the queue waiting for fares outside Mehrabad Airport. The cabdriver stood holding the door open for him, then quickly slid in behind the wheel.

"The Shohreh Hotel in Tehran, please," Zelinkow managed in Farsi, which was far from his best language.

"With your permission, sir," the driver replied in very good English, "my instructions are to take you to the city of Chahar Dangeh. It is only about ten kilometers south of here. A private residence there has been reserved for you. It is perhaps not so elegant as the Shohreh, but more private, and hopefully to your satisfaction."

Zelinkow was momentarily taken back, but realized that there was now nothing he could do but agree to go. He had always found it safer and less conspicuous to be in a crowded city than in some out-of-the-way place. There were many reasons that a secret, private meeting was better carried off in an urban setting. But Chahar Dangeh was indeed a city, one that passed for an industrial city in Iran. Above all, he could understand why the man he was going to meet might want to stay out of Tehran, and well away from public view.

It was only ten kilometers, but in the afternoon traffic it took them close to forty minutes to reach the residence, a neat one-bedroom stucco structure, clean and most unremarkable. The cabdriver said he would call for him in an hour and that the meeting would be a dinner meeting. Once inside, Zelinkow locked the door and made a quick inspection of the premises, making sure the back door and windows were closed and locked. He tossed his carry-on bag on the bed and headed for the bath. It was nothing fancy, but it was adequate. Having left Rome very early that morning, he was grateful for the time to shower and shave. The flight from Rome to Cairo and the flight from Cairo to Tehran were both about three hours. With a two-hour lay-over in Cairo, it made for a long day. His plans had him back in Rome tomorrow evening by way of Istanbul, but first there was the business at hand. The driver returned exactly one hour later, and another short cab ride brought them to a second private residence, albeit a slightly larger one. Zelinkow understood that a man of his international reputation would need to be kept from public view, but in as comfortable a dwelling as possible, subject to security considerations. Indeed there was a $25-million reward on his head. The cabdriver opened the door for Zelinkow but made no move to follow him to the door. It was a neat, above-average home, probably one that could have housed a professional or government worker, but indistinguishable from others on the street. Zelinkow started to knock, but a hard-looking man in traditional Arab dress opened the door. He stepped into a dim interior, thick with cigarette smoke. A man in casual Western attire rose awkwardly from the settee to greet him.

"Mr. Poulenc. It is very good to make your acquaintance. Thank you for coming such a long way to meet with me."

"Not at all," Zelinkow replied in Arabic. "Thank you for making time for me. It is an honor to finally meet you."

The politeness was feigned on both their parts. Neither of these men particularly cared for the other; it was not a personal dislike but a cultural one. Also, each had his own agenda, and each was highly suspicious of the other. They had been thrown together only by necessity. Both were wanted men, but Zelinkow had been the one to travel because no one in the West, or Tehran for that matter, really knew his identity. That was not the case for Abu Musab al-Zarqawi; he was one of the most wanted men in the world. Before events in Iraq propelled him to the senior tier of Al Qaeda leadership, he was Al Qaeda's top biological weapons expert. Technically deficient by Western standards perhaps, he was nevertheless totally committed to the use of biological agents against the infidel, specifically the United States of America. After the collapse of the Taliban in Afghanistan, he had slipped out of Tora Bora and crossed the Afghan/Pakistani border. He made his way through Karachi to Baghdad and from there to the Ansar al-Islam bio-weapons facility in northern Iraq. Then the Americans came again, and after a narrow escape from Kurdish partisans, he was given sanctuary in Iran. But sanctuary did not mean freedom of movement, though he occasionally slipped in to Iraq to meet with insurgent leaders. Al-Zarqawi was in many ways a liability. The Americans wanted this man very badly. The Iranians still struck a defiant pose, but the manner in which the Americans had dispatched the Iraqi army and occupied the country gave them pause. Iranian president Mohammad Khatami and the governing mullahs had their hands full with dissident students and disillusioned citizens. The last thing they wanted was a provocation that would launch an American armored column toward Tehran. The Iranians knew they were less of a match than Saddam Hussein for such an armored thrust. Not only did they not trust the American president; more importantly, they feared him, and with good reason.

Abu Musab al-Zarqawi was born in a Jordanian refugee camp in 1966, and had known nothing but poverty and terror his whole life. He had a special grudge against

Americans. In February 2002 he was meeting with an Al Qaeda cell in eastern Afghanistan when a JDAM scored a direct hit on the building where the meeting was held. All were killed but for al-Zarqawi. He was wounded in the leg, a wound that eventually cost him the limb. He now had a prosthetic leg and walked with a pronounced limp. The loss had only stiffened his resolve. He had since been linked with numerous terrorist attacks in Britain, France, Georgia, and Chechnya. He was credited with the assassination of Lawrence Foley, the American diplomat killed in Amman, and the toxic ricin plot that was foiled in England. In addition to directing the insurgency in Iraq, he could link bio-weapons development in Iraq to Saddam Hussein, making Zarqawi a prize catch. Pavel Zelinkow had resisted a meeting with this high-profile terrorist, who must surely be watched by agents of the Iranian Intelligence Ministry, the successor to the notorious SAVAK. But like many in Al Qaeda, al-Zarqawi had a phobia of using cell phones and trusted few intermediaries. Indeed, so many Al Qaeda operatives had been brought to an untimely end by their cell phones that many resisted using them, even with encryption.

Once greetings were exchanged, al-Zarqawi motioned Zelinkow to a low table where a simple meal of rice, fruit, and *khoresht* waited. Zelinkow had removed his shoes and now took his place at the low table. Many in Al Qaeda used the funding of the Arab charities to live and eat well. Al-Zarqawi was not one of them.

"I am given to understand," al-Zarqawi began, "that the weapon is almost ready."

"It is," Zelinkow replied. "I am told that within the week it will be fully tested and ready for delivery."

"And in what form will that delivery be made?"

Zelinkow was careful in his reply. "There will be enough material to infect twelve people by direct injection. It will be packaged in twelve syringes and hidden in an attaché case. A courier will take it from Harare to Riyadh, where he will deliver it as you have instructed. At that point, my part of the project will be complete."

Al-Zarqawi considered this. "I understood that the delivery would be made by diplomatic pouch from the Zimbabwean capital to Riyadh."

"And it is my understanding," Zelinkow said politely, "that those officials in Saudi Arabia who said they would do this, while still sympathetic to our cause, feel it is too dangerous for this kind of overt official help. They will assist you with a safe haven and allow your people to move freely, but they will not put themselves in a position where they cannot deny the help given. Using the diplomatic pouch is something they will not risk. We will have to trust this to a courier."

Al-Zarqawi slowly nodded. "You have the name and arrival date of this courier?"

"I do," Zelinkow replied. He took a single piece of paper and wrote from memory a name, flight arrangements, and date, then handed it to al-Zarqawi. The Arab stroked his beard and studied the information.

"You have done well, Mr. Poulenc, and you have earned the right to know what we will do with this weapon you have provided."

Pavel Zelinkow did not want to know what was to be done with this pathogen he had helped to create, but it would have been unthinkable for him to refuse to listen. So he listened stoically as al-Zarqawi outlined his fanatical plan.

After dinner, they were served harsh Turkish coffee, which Zelinkow loathed and al-Zarqawi seemed to relish. Zelinkow stayed only long enough to be polite, then rose to leave. Al-Zarqawi limped to the door to see his guest out.

"You must understand," al-Zarqawi told him before he left, "it is for the cause that we must attack the infidel, but for me personally it is life itself. If I do not get them, these Americans who now chase us like a pack of dogs, they will surely get me."

Zelinkow was returned to his quarters and caught his flight the next morning without incident. He was not in the habit of drinking while traveling unless courtesy demanded it, but on the leg from Istanbul on Air Anatolia into Rome, he asked for a double Courvoisier, straight up. Al-Zarqawi's plan was simple and essentially foolproof. And it would lead to a pandemic such as the North American continent had never seen—such as the world had never seen.

Janet Brisco paced about the hangar amid the bustle of activity. Periodically, she paused to look at her watch and to light another cigarette. She saw everything but said nothing. If anything soothed her, it was the professional way in which Tomba and his men prepared for the mission. They slept as one between 10:00 P.M. the previous evening until 2:00 A.M.—2200 to 0200 in military time—and promptly arose to begin preparing their gear. Their weapons, ammunition load, and operational gear were displayed and inspected by Tomba and Mohammed Senagal. AKR had his equipment laid out for inspection as well. Then Tomba picked two of the men at random to inspect his own combat load as well as Senagal's. Once the inspections were complete, the gear was stowed in individual waterproof duffel bags, the weapons in the center of the bags, with softer gear packed around them. Each duffel was then carefully weighed, staged, and strapped to pallets. The men themselves were once again turned out in the uniform of the African laborer—leather shoes or sneakers, dark cotton trousers, and white shirts. In America, a lean group of fighting men cannot pass unnoticed in a population that is largely overweight. In Africa, nearly all men have that lean, purposeful look to them. Only a close inspection would identify them as soldiers. No announcement was made, but a few minutes before 4:00 A.M., everyone assembled in the corner of the hangar where Janet Brisco stood before an easel with a large-scale map of the Lower Zambezi, with the Zambezi River bisecting a section of Zimbabwe and Zambia, west-southwest to east. Just before she began, Garrett slipped through the side door of the hangar. He looked tired, having just quietly left the room of a federal agent at the Intercontinental Hotel to get to the briefing.

"This is it, people," she began in a clear, commanding voice. "Today it begins, and tonight the assault element will cross the Zambezi and begin their advance on the target. I have zero four hundred in fifteen seconds . . . ten seconds . . . five, four, three, two, one—mark, zero four hundred. Today is day one of the mission. This is also the last time we will all be together before we meet at the final extraction site. This is the objective." She flipped over the Zambezi area map to reveal a grainy black-and-white overlay from a satellite image. "This structure is the Makondo Hotel, which we believe is being used for bioweapons research. Our mission is to defeat the security forces that now guard this facility and to capture it intact, or as intact as possible. Once that is done, we will bring in a medical specialist to evaluate what may or may not be going on there. The Makondo Hotel complex is just over a hundred and forty miles from here as the crow flies. The first hundred miles will be relatively easy; the last forty are over some of the most difficult terrain in Africa. It will be a formidable journey, to say the least.

"This is a better look at the target." She again flipped the sheet to show a precise layout of the Makondo compound. "This is a composite rendering of the site from the architectural drawings and landscape design. You will see marked in red—here, here, and here—what appear to be security positions with machine gun emplacements. This outbuilding here is where we think the security element keeps itself when not on duty. Apparently their barracks are inside the hotel. This is all we have from the limited satellite coverage of the area. Given the size of the guard force, there have to be more security emplacements than we are seeing here from these few fixed defensive positions.

"There will be five phases to the operation. Phase one will be the approach to the target. This will comprise of getting the assault force across the Zambezi to the target, and to get the support assets in place. Akheem, this will give you two full days to get through the mountains. Phase two will be a twelve-to-twenty-four-hour period to observe the target and make the final refinement to the assault plan. Phase three will be the actual assault, which is planned for zero four hundred four days from now. With the facility secure, we will begin phase four, a careful inspection of the hotel for signs of bio-weapons activity. Phase five will be the extraction to the forward operating base. If all goes well, we will be clear of Zambian airspace and on our way to Nairobi in a little more than four days from now—if all goes well. I will be your tactical controller, and I will do my level best to see that it does.

"We have an hour and a half before the first helicopter arrives. By noon, I want this hangar empty, except for the vans, and completely sanitized. Questions so far?" There were none. "All right, let's get started with the details of phase one."

The briefing lasted for a little over an hour. It was

designed primarily for the Africans; Brisco would conduct separate briefings for the aircrews and support elements. Steven Fagan stood alongside Garrett while she detailed the infiltration to the target area. They listened carefully; both had been in the business of covert and special operations long enough to know a brilliant operational plan when they saw it. Two Bell Jet Rangers would arrive shortly after dawn, along with a stake truck driven by one of Benjamin Sato's cousins. The operational equipment and most of the men would be loaded onto the truck, while the medical boxes were put on the Jet Rangers with the remaining Africans. The helos would return mid-morning and begin ferrying pumps and water purification equipment out to projects managed by Africare and Water Aid International. Jet Rangers are the most common helicopters found in Africa, used extensively in moving equipment too fragile for the primitive roads, and for flying tourists out to see wild game and to view Victoria Falls. A military version of the Jet Ranger, the OH-58 Kiowa, had been used by militaries around the world for four decades. These two aircraft were owned and operated by the Simpson Foundation, but flown by contract pilots with extensive military special operations experience. One of the first things Janet Brisco had done when it became apparent that they would stage out of Zambia was to get two of these helicopters headed for Lusaka along with crack maintenance crews. Until they were again needed, the helos would fly humanitarian sorties for NGOs working in Zambia.

Early that afternoon, the two vans left hangar B-5, which was again as deserted as it had been only twenty-four hours earlier. Both vans bore the logo of the Zambia Electricity Supply Company, Ltd., or ZESCO, and had the documentation to prove it. They were headed for the rural area of southeastern Zambia to survey for a new power line that was to run from the Central African Power Corporation generation site at the Kariba Dam, across Zambia, and into Tanzania. Since the prospective power lines were to run across the Lower Zambezi National Park, the route had to be carefully chosen. Steven, Dodds LeMaster, and Bill Owens all had CAPC documentation. Two of Tomba's men who were with them had ZESCO identification as vehicle drivers. Since it would be odd for a Zambian woman to have technical expertise, Janet was identified as an American consultant with the Zambia Media Women's Association, visiting the area with the survey crew in the hope of catching a herd of elephants or zebra. The documentation didn't have to be all that good, so long as they had something to hand a curious constable along with a 50,000-kwacha note.

Late that afternoon, Garrett and Elvis Rosenblatt arrived at Chiawa Camp in the Lower Zambezi National Park. One of Africa's top safari camps, it carried a five-star rating in the guidebooks. The camp, if it could be called that, was on the northern shore of the Zambezi River. The grounds were spacious and well tended. Guest accommodations consisted of large tents with slatted teak floors, queen beds, high-draped mosquito netting, cushioned rattan armchairs, and Victorian nightstands complete with a large porcelain bowl and water pitcher. There were fine cotton sheets and chocolates on the pillow. It was a setting that Katharine Hepburn, filming *The African Queen*, would have been quite comfortable with. And it was also just the kind of place that would attract two wealthy Canadian real estate brokers.

"Now this is what I call roughing it. And here I thought we'd be out in the bush with the tsetse flies and the hyenas. This is really cool," Elvis Rosenblatt happily remarked as he surveyed the camp surroundings. A black man in shorts and a sparkling white T-shirt with the Chiawa

Camp logo, two Cs superimposed with an elephant in the center, arrived with their luggage. Giving his name as Alfred, he placed a bottle of Crown Royal on the table next to the cut-crystal glass service and ice bucket. Alfred addressed them as "bwana," and explained that he would be their personal helper while they were in camp. They could come to the main lodge for dinner, he explained, or he would bring it to them. They told him that they would dine in.

"Bwana," Rosenblatt said after Alfred had departed with Garrett's bag to deliver it to the tent-bungalow next door. "I've always wanted to be called that. This is great. And you can be my manservant and gun bearer. 'Oh, Walker. Please bring up the Mannlicher big-bore. I think blighter is about to charge.'"

"Don't push it, Elvis," Garrett replied.

Ten minutes later they were sitting on director's chairs under Garrett's tent fly, sipping Crown Royal and watching the broad, muddy Zambezi flow past them, right to left. Garrett, who was no stranger to wild splendor, had never seen anything quite like this. They sat in an awed silence.

"I've gotta get out of Atlanta more often," Rosenblatt finally said. Garrett freshened up their drinks.

In the manner of two businessmen on African safari, they had left the hotel for Lusaka International midmorning and been flown by air charter to the Jeki airfield deep inside the National Park. It was a half-hour flight into the dirt strip, and two hours by Land Rover to the camp. The drive should have been only an hour, but they stopped to observe and photograph a herd of elephants and a family of giraffes.

Alfred arrived, quickly set up a camp table, and served them a groundnut stew over a bed of jollof rice and ashanti chicken. A traditional sub-Saharan meal does not include appetizer or dessert. Alfred left them with a carafe of hot coffee and withdrew.

"Is this typical spy work? You do this kind of thing all the time?"

Garrett's mind was across the Zambezi, up in the rugged Mavuradonha Mountains, where AKR, Tomba, and the others were soon to cross. It would be a brutal forced march with very little sleep, but he would trade his luxurious setting in an instant to be with the assault team.

"This is about it, Elvis. Another continent, another five-star outing. Just one patch of tall clover after another."

"So what do we do while we wait? They've got everything here—river cruises, canoe trips, game drives, fishing, you name it. After all, we have to maintain our cover, right?"

"I don't want to be more than a couple of hours from camp and the helo pad. We wait in luxury, but we have to be ready to move. I've booked us on a series of day bush walks with one of the camp rangers. He carries the gun, we carry cameras and photograph game."

"Then we come back here for drinks, and Alfred brings us dinner?"

"That's it. War is hell, but someone has to do it. We'll have to earn our keep soon enough, but for now, we'll just have to tough it out in this hellhole."

Rosenblatt poured coffee, and they sat in silence, watching the clouds at the foothills of the mountains on the Zimbabwean side as they were set afire by the last rays of the sun.

The two vans, with their ZESCO markings, were led by a battered Toyota pickup truck over mostly unimproved roads southeast from Lusaka. The Toyota was driven by

Benjamin's uncle on his mother's side, along with his son. They knew the roads and were able to find their way, even after dark. Two hours after sundown, about the same time Garrett Walker and Elvis Rosenblatt were pouring themselves a nightcap, the dirt-covered vans and their escort arrived at the Jeki airfield. This was some eight hours after the air charter that had delivered the two Canadian businessmen had departed on the return leg back to Lusaka. Tomba and one of his men were there to meet them. They had set up a small base camp across the dirt strip from the ranger shack that served as the runway office. Janet and Steven got out, stretched, and began to inspect the area by lantern light. They could hear hyenas howling in the distance. Charter aircraft and a few intrepid private pilots used the 3,000-foot-strip at Jeki several times a week to shuttle guests to Chiawa Camp and for other national park business. It was a natural place for a survey crew to spend a few days. Resupply by Jet Ranger would be in keeping with their business.

"Welcome to the bush, Miss Janet, Steven." Tomba said in greeting. "I believe you will be safe here, and no one will bother you. A park ranger is assigned to monitor traffic at the airstrip, but he has been paid and knows you are with CAPA. He may come around out of boredom, as he has very few duties to keep him busy. Once we are away, Benjamin will be back here with you to oversee your camp. He and one of my men will remain with you, along with his uncle and cousin. A few of the local people may come from the bush and approach, perhaps to beg for food or out of curiosity. Benjamin will be here to deal with them."

"The medical equipment?" Steven asked. There was more staged than would probably be needed, but they had planned for all contingencies.

"The helicopter delivered it as planned, and it is cached

under that tree over there, along with the other supplies. The rains are late this year, but they could come at any time. Everything is on pallets and in waterproof containers, and covered with a tarpaulin. So," he said, smiling as he turned to Janet. "How do you like Africa?"

"It's a little like what I expected, but I was not prepared for the vastness. Somehow, I didn't imagine that it was so . . . so empty."

"I know you and the others will be busy with your duties, but as they permit, ask Benjamin to take you on a walk in the bush. It can be very settling. But do not go without him."

She looked around to where the lantern light was lost in the blackness of low scrub. "I think you can count on me not taking five steps from camp unless he is with me."

"Excellent," Tomba replied. "And now the others and I must leave. Benjamin will return before first light. Allow him and his relatives to deal with the park rangers and others who are curious. And relax. Africa can be a frightening place, but it is not as dangerous as one might think."

"Good luck to you, Tomba."

"And to you, Janet. If all goes according to your excellent plan, I will see you back here in less than four days." He formally offered his hand to Steven and left them.

Tomba, the two who had served as drivers, and his other fighter climbed into the pickup and drove away. The others busied themselves around the small camp. Benjamin's uncle, a silent man of undetermined age named Godfrey, and his son, Christian, started to erect tents and tended the small fire. Dodds LeMaster and Bill Owens began to get the two vans set up. As survey support vehicles, they could be expected to have some creature comforts along with some electronic gear, but that was not the half of it. The two vans were crammed with state-of-the art, solid-state components and microprocessors. The vehicles were connected with thick umbilical cables, and two small satellite antennas were set out a short distance away, each camouflaged with canvas drape. Inside each van were two consoles served by flat-plasma screens and a host of computer-driven electronics and communication equipment. The genius of Dodds LeMaster and the miracle of microtechnology had given these two dingy-looking vans the capability of a large, well-equipped military command center.

Steven found Janet by the fire. He took a canvas stool and pulled it alongside her as Christian approached and quietly handed them each a mug of tea. There were night sounds, but they were comfortably in the distance. It was cooling off nicely, and the canopy of stars was breathtaking.

"You've done a great job with the planning and logistic flow," Steven said, "and in an amazingly short period of time. Thanks for all your hard work."

She smiled. "I appreciate your saying so, but isn't that what you pay me for?"

"I suppose so. But I do have a question for you." She sipped at the sweet, strong tea as he spoke. "With the dedicated satellite links and the technology of the vans, you could be controlling this operation from our base in Diego Garcia, or from the embassy compound in Nairobi. Or even from a warehouse in Lusaka. Why out here?"

Janet Brisco considered this. On Tomba's advice, they had decided to remain in Lusaka no longer than necessary and to get their small force broken into small groups as soon as practical. Much of what they were doing looked like mercenary activity or a smuggling operation, and would invite official and unofficial attention. Their presence at any embassy compound would have had to come at the expense of some State Department knowledge and approval. Most embassy staff were hardworking professionals, but they did talk. In African capitals, the embassy compounds were well-guarded American ghettos, where everyone seemed to know about everyone else's business. They had previously used Diego Garcia to control IFOR activity, and it was both secure and very private. But during that mission, they were operating in Iran and the operation was totally black—no one knew who they were or why they were there. Africa was more like operating in Arizona or New Mexico, only the officials were bribable. But it was more than that.

One of the reasons Janet had come out of retirement to serve as planner and tactical coordinator for IFOR was the freedom and trust afforded her by Steven and the others. He could have asked this question back in Hawaii when they were putting this together, but he hadn't. That he was asking now was a matter of curiosity, not trust.

"The operational security of what we do, given our lack of official portfolio, is always going to be something of a tradeoff. Out here our OPSEC is probably as good as anywhere else. Since we don't know what or who we're dealing with, they could have agents just about anywhere, especially in large cities. And it's imperative that our men get there unobserved and undetected. Moving like this— hiding in plain sight—seemed to be the best way." She was silent for a moment, and Steven, always the careful listener, did not intrude. "Since this is our first operation with the Africans," she continued, "I thought it would be important for them and for us that we're out here with them. Of course, we'll not be doing what we are asking them to do, but they see it as our sharing some of the risk. I believe our being here, even in the safety of camp, will help the mission."

Steven nodded. "I agree with you that it will most likely help the mission. Tell me something else. You're African; how does it feel to be here? Were you not drawn back to see something of Africa, out of curiosity if nothing else?"

"You mean the roots thing and all that?" She smiled and lit a cigarette. "Steven, I grew up in East St. Louis. I'm used to the city, the smog, the lights, and all the creature comforts of the mall. I drive a Lexis, and I have a big-screen TV. When I'm not with you running special operations, I'm going to PTA meetings or getting my nails done." She suddenly became serious. "When the operational considerations put us here, I was excited; I thought perhaps there would be some movement in my soul about 'returning' to Africa—the land of my people and all that. Well, it ain't happened. It's beautiful—dramatically beautiful—but in all honesty, it's foreign. I'm an American, just like you. I just have black skin. When the job is done, I'm going to want to go home to America. Still, from what I've seen of it, it's beautiful and very peaceful."

Dodds LeMaster stepped into the glow of the campfire. "Am I interrupting anything?"

"Not at all, Dodds," Janet replied. "Pull up a stool."

"I've just run a complete set of diagnostics on all the electronics," LeMaster continued after he was seated by the fire, "and we have a clear satellite link—full communications and full backup. All the gear is up. We're ready to go to work."

"How about comm checks?" Suddenly, she was all business.

"I have AKR on satcomm and HF backup. He's good to go. Garrett and Miss Burks are on encrypted sat links on both our dedicated channels. Bill has the first watch and is guarding all channels. I'll relieve him midnight to four."

Sat phone technology was satellite communications technology. It was clear, secure, and reliable. Through Guardian Services International they had contracted for commercial satellite time with a dedicated primary channel and one for a backup. In the highly unlikely event of the failure of their satcomm links, they could always revert to old-fashioned high-frequency radio.

Janet nodded and relaxed. "Good job. So now we wait for Tomba and the others to make the crossing and watch for indicators." Then, turning to Steven, "So what's on the menu this evening?"

"Sandwiches and soup today and tomorrow. Then we're going to be eating like the troops."

"MREs?"

"MREs."

Janet considered this. "I'll save my sandwich for when I relieve Dodds at 4:00 A.M. I think I'll have an MRE right now. Want to join me?"

"Why not?" Steven said easily. "It seems like a good way to begin this venture." Dodds LeMaster readily agreed. MREs, or Meals, Ready to Eat, were the standard field ration of the U.S. military, similar to hiking rations but with a packet that chemically heated the meal. Loaded with calories, and reasonably tasty, a single ration could keep a man in the field for an entire day.

They set about preparing their MREs in companionable silence, eating them from the foil packets like containers of Chinese takeout. Dodds relieved Bill Owens from his comm watch so he could join them for something to eat. Steven had seen Janet Brisco run an operation before. She was normally tense, prowling about like a nervous cat; thus far, she had been no less vigilant about her duties, but she seemed far more settled and centered than he would have expected her to be. Perhaps Africa was reaching out to her, even if she was not reaching out to Africa.

Several miles east, and upstream of where Garrett Walker and Elvis Rosenblatt were so elegantly encamped, a group of men and several trucks gathered on the bank of the Zambezi River. They were on an uninhabited stretch between the Kafue and Chonga Rivers, which ran circuitously north to south into the Zambezi. They all worked quietly, showing no lights. One of the easiest, most popular, and accessible ways to see the Lower Zambezi is by canoe, so there are a number of concessions along the river downstream from the town of Chirunda that serve the Lower Zambezi National Park on the Zambian side and the Mana Pools National Park on the Zimbabwean side. Now that they were going into the wet season, Mana Pools National Park was accessible only by canoe. One of Benjamin Sato's many cousins owned a concession that provided guided canoe tours on the Zambezi. These range from single day paddles on the river to canoeing safaris that lasted up to a week. The Zambezi from Kariba, through Chirunda and the two national parks, to the town of Karryemba, near where the Zambezi flows into Mozambique, is one of the most spectacular waterways in the world. Since the damning of the Zambezi to form Lake Kariba, the water levels have been controlled and consistent for most of the year, except for the runoff late in the wet season—generally March and April. It is a land of dramatic beauty and contrast. On the Zimbabwean side the land rises to rugged mountains. On the Zambian side, it is a hot, flat, malarial flood plain.

At first, Benjamin's cousin had not been keen on the project. A concession on the Zambezi and the license to operate tours was his livelihood, but when Benjamin offered him three times what he made in a year, with half up front in South African rand, he agreed. A flotilla of eight safari canoes had been assembled on the bank. The assault team contained a dozen men plus Tomba, AKR, and their two guides. Crossing the placid Zambezi and drifting downstream toward the Mana Pools National Park on a moonless night did not appear to be a difficult task for a band of seasoned bush professionals, but the Zambezi could be dangerous. There were shifting sandbars and islands that were often hard to distinguish from the permanent shoreline, even in the daylight. Then there were several pods of hippopotamuses, mostly on the Zimbabwean side. A rampaging hippo could easily take out half of the little fleet of canoes; more Africans are killed by hippos each year than by lions. Then there was the matter of navigation. Tomba and his men were well equipped with GPS receivers, but the GPSs did not mark where the Mana Pool rangers might be camped along the river, nor did the exact trail that would take them into the hinterland have a set of GPS coordinates. To avoid park rangers and find the right trail, they needed guides with local knowledge.

The men had their individual gear stowed in waterproof bags, two men and two bags to a canoe. They were all dressed in dark clothes and black sneakers for the crossing, the canoes lined up on the bank, the men standing by their craft.

"All is ready, sir," Benjamin's cousin said to Mohammed Senagal, who had organized the crossing and had the small force ready to move when Tomba and the others arrived.

"And the guides understand exactly where we need to be on the Zimbabwean side?"

"Yes, sir." Senagal exuded a quiet, powerful presence that Zambians seemed to respect and fear.

"Then we will be away. Thank you for your work here." He handed him a bag filled with hundred-rand notes. "This is the balance of what is owed for your services. If something unplanned is waiting for us on the other side, then I will be back for the money and your life."

Benjamin almost spoke out, but held his tongue. Senagal was not a man to be contradicted, at least not by him. Then Tomba joined them, placing one hand on Senagal's shoulder and the other on the cousin's.

"Benjamin has vouched for this man, so I am sure his

services are in order and his guides will see us to the proper place in Zimbabwe. Still, it will be unfortunate if Mohammed has to return to Lusaka. Let us be about our business." AKR stood to one side, allowing Tomba to handle the matter.

Benjamin and his cousin watched as the expedition eased themselves into the eight canoes and pushed off from the shore. Another of the Africans, a quiet Zulu named Msika, had been detailed to stay with Benjamin and to keep an eye on the Jeki camp. Both Tomba and AKR agreed that neither Benjamin nor Msika should be away from the camp at the same time. Both men understood their duties and did not complain, but both desperately wanted to be away with the assault force on the Zambezi.

One of the guides was in the bow of Tomba's craft, the other with AKR. The canoes formed two loose groups of four as they paddled easily out from the shore, and the gentle current swept them off to the northeast. It was a very dark night, so both Tomba and AKR had Chemlights tied to the stern of their canoes. They were not visible from the shore, but the dull, lime green lights allowed the others to keep them in sight. In addition, one man in each boat had a small squad radio and was fitted with an earpiece and a small boom mic. Mid-channel, Tomba inventoried his flock with a radio check as they proceeded at a leisurely pace toward the Zimbabwean side of the river while the current carried them to the section of shoreline within the boundaries of the Mana Pools National Park. The string of canoes made their way around several islands and across a shallow bar where they could touch bottom with their paddle blades. On one occasion they could hear hippos snort and blow from shallows near the shore. Shortly before 3:00 A.M., they coasted into a marshy indentation on the shoreline. Tomba told them all to wait in the shallows while he and the lead guide beached their craft and scouted ahead.

They were back in twenty minutes; this was the proper insertion point.

"Our trailhead is fifty meters in from the shoreline," he whispered into his boom mic. "We will secure and hide the canoes as briefed and meet at the rally point."

One by one, the men dragged their craft through the bed of papyrus reeds to the shore. They left the canoes in the water, nestled in the reeds, but hefted their gear bags onto solid ground. Once at the trailhead, the men began to change into their operational gear and prepare for land travel. At the shoreline, Tomba gave each of the guides a large tip and left them with the canoes. While the men melted into the bush to form a security perimeter, AKR dropped to one knee and shifted his squad radio to the designated satcomm frequency.

"Home Base, this is Unit One, over."

"This is Home Base, Unit One. Go ahead."

"Unit One, here. We are feet dry at point alpha and proceeding, over."

"Home Base, Unit One. Understand feet dry at point alpha and proceeding, over."

"Good copy, Home Base. Unit One, out."

There was no need for strict radio procedure—their satellite channel was shared by no one else and fully encrypted—but proper procedure ensured a clear understanding, and it was a habit. Dodds stepped from the van to pass the news along to Janet. It was time to wake her, as she was to relieve him at 4:00 A.M. She was not in her tent, but he found her sitting by the fire, gazing at the riot of stars in the African sky.

As the dawn spread across the Zambezi, two men, each paddling a canoe and towing three others, worked their way out into the slow-moving river. Soon an aluminum boat with a large outboard came downstream to meet them. They tied the eight canoes together in a line astern and began to slowly work their way back upriver. This activity went unobserved, with the exception of a single white man, a Canadian real estate executive badly in need of a shave, sitting in a director's chair at Chiawa Camp on the Zambian side. After they labored past him, he rose, stretched, and walked back into his tent.

9

DANGER CLOSE

The American Embassy in Lusaka was a large complex on the corner of Independence Avenue and United Nations Avenue. In spite of the impressive address, it was still an armed compound, as were most American embassies in Africa. The morning was quickly warming, and a brief shower had momentarily purged the streets of the ever-present stench of sewage and decay. Across from the embassy at a sidewalk café, a waiter had just brought Judy Burks a pot of tea. Both of them were steaming. She had just come from the embassy, and had taken shelter at the café to wait out the rain and try to figure out what to do next. Per her instructions, she had presented herself at the embassy gate at ten o'clock that morning to see the ambassador. First she was made to stand outside for close to half an hour while the marine sentry hit on her. She was then thoroughly searched and finally, after signing in at the guest registry, allowed to enter the main building. There she waited for another half hour before an embassy staffer came to ask what she wanted. She presented her FBI shield and credentials and informed him that she was there on official business, and it was important that she meet with the ambassador as soon as possible.

"He has a frightfully busy schedule. Could you please tell me what this is about?" He was a first-tour Foreign Service officer who had graduated from Georgetown only the year before.

"I am here on Bureau business, and I have been given instructions to speak directly with the ambassador and the ambassador only. He should be expecting me."

"Well, I don't know about your instructions, Agent Burks," the staffer said with a patient, there-there-little-girl attitude, "but we are instructed to screen all audiences with the ambassador, even official ones."

"Please understand that I am here on official business. This is a classified matter," she said tightly, "and one that involves national security."

"I'm sorry, Agent Burks, but you will need to tell me exactly what this—"

"Excuse me, but as I have already told you, I am instructed to speak only with the ambassador. Does Ambassador Conrad even know that I'm here?"

The junior FSO sat up and regarded her coolly. "The ambassador is not in the habit of being notified about every single person—"

"Stop right there." Suddenly she was on her feet. "I didn't come halfway around the world to be hassled by the likes of you. I have a job to do, and you seem determined to keep me from doing it. In the meantime, Mr. Schoolcraft," she said, squinting at his ID badge, "I suggest that you go back through your message traffic and look for my clearance. I'm authorized to speak only with the ambassador." She rose and pulled on the bottom of her suit jacket as she took a deep breath. "I'll be at the Intercontinental." When you pull your head out of your ass, she almost added, but held back. She turned and headed for the door.

She took a cab from the café back to the Intercontinental and went straight to the bar, ordered a martini, and dialed Steven's sat number. After a short wait, the ciphers clicked into place, and he came on the line. She explained what had happened at the embassy. Steven listened without comment.

"So what next?" she asked.

"Does the hotel where you are have a nice pool?"

"What!"

"I said, do they have a pool there at the hotel?"

"Well, yes, they do."

"Good. Why don't you take the day off and sit by the pool. Take in some sun and treat yourself to a cocktail."

"Uh, I'm already working on the last one."

"Good. Let me make a call or two, and why don't you plan on returning to the embassy again tomorrow. Maybe things will turn out differently."

"You think so?"

"Perhaps. We need to bring the ambassador into this, but whether it's today, tomorrow, or the next day doesn't really matter. Go enjoy yourself, and give it a try tomorrow."

Judy rang off and turned her attention to her martini. She sipped cautiously at her drink, noticing that a man having lunch a few stools down was watching her. He wore a poorly tailored suit, and must have just come from the airport, as his bag was sitting on the tiled floor by his stool.

"What?" she said, a little too loudly, and he immediately went back to his lunch.

She took Steven's advice and spent the day by the pool, reading magazines. The next morning at 10:00 A.M. sharp, she presented herself to the same marine lance corporal at the gatepost. She wore makeup, but it didn't quite mask the raccoon look she had acquired from falling asleep in the sun by the pool with her sunglasses on. This time there was a sergeant alongside the corporal at the gate. Both snapped to attention, and each rendered her a parade-ground salute.

"Good morning, Miss Burks," the senior marine offered. "I'm Gunnery Sergeant Hallasey, ma'am, and I'm to be your escort. If you will just come with me, my orders are to take you directly to Ambassador Conrad's office. We'll bypass the security and sign-in this morning. You're good to go."

She followed him inside and up to the second floor. Without hesitation or any word of announcement they strolled past Mr. Schoolcraft, intently working at his desk. He never looked up. The marine sergeant opened the heavy wooded door to Ambassador Donald Conrad's office, allowing it to swing inward. He again snapped up a salute.

"You have a nice day, ma'am."

"Thank you, Sergeant," she replied, and added quietly, "It's already looking better."

The large black man who came around the desk was dressed in a crisp white shirt, red tie, dark pleated slacks, and polished black shoes. He was a fit, handsome, younger version of James Earl Jones—same deep, gravelly voice. Judy had envisioned an overweight political hack; this man was anything but that. The ambassador held out a chair for her in front of the desk. She formally handed him her credential. He studied it with measured care and handed it back to her.

"First of all, Miss Burks, let me apologize for yesterday. That said, I now understand that your visit was to be low-key, and that your business is with me alone. The message we received a few days ago announcing your arrival was of routine precedence and routed to one of the junior staff. I now gather that your business here is not purely routine." He folded his hands on the desk, looking very ambassadorial. "Please understand, I run a good embassy here. It's not London or Paris, or even Nairobi for that matter, but we do our job. And I might add that this is the first time I've been woken in the middle of the night and had my butt chewed by the Secretary of State." He handed her an official card across the desk. "My private number is on the back. In the future, should any of my staff not be up to the task, call me directly, day or night. Now, what is it that I can do for you?"

"First, I should apologize for any inconvenience to you," she began. "Given the closely held nature of the matter that brought me here, I have very few official points of contact up the chain of command. I am sorry it came to your attention in the manner that it did. I'm here to brief you on an issue that is, for want of a better word, a matter of courtesy. I can tell you only that which is required should you have to function as the president's representative. The situation is this. We have become aware of a serious weapons-of-mass-destruction threat in neighboring Zimbabwe. As we speak, a small, covert paramilitary force is being launched from Zambia to investigate this threat and take action. I don't want to seem overly dramatic, or oblique for that matter, but this force operates independently of the U.S. government. They have no official portfolio, but their involvement is a closely held and guarded understanding with our government. My relationship with this force is strictly that of a liaison officer." That triggered a flashback to Garrett's clandestine visit to her room the night before last, and she could feel a blush surfacing through her sunburn. She paused and cleared her throat. "It was decided at the very highest level that you and you alone were to be made aware of the situation, since the force is being infiltrated from Zambia, and controlled from here. As I understand it, if things go as planned, no one will even know that they were even here. However, if all does not go well, our government will officially deny any knowledge of the event. As I mentioned, I am here to extend a courtesy so that if something does go wrong, you can be properly surprised and privately not be caught unaware of the situation." She paused for a moment. "Just between you and me, this kind of unconventional activity would not be taking place if there was not a significant risk to our national security. Past that, you just gotta have faith."

Neither of them spoke for a long moment. "I'm not sure I have that kind of faith, Miss Burks," Conrad replied, "but I do have my instructions. I assume the information that you have shared with me so far is the extent of what I am allowed to know?"

"That is correct, sir."

Another silence. "Do you require anything more of me or the embassy and my staff?"

"No, sir. I will contact you again if I am directed to pass along any more information. You will hear from me by phone, or if there needs to be another face-to-face meeting, I'll ask for another appointment. Hopefully, the next time we talk I will be informing you that this force has completed its mission and is no longer in Zambia."

Ambassador Conrad slowly shook his head, deep in thought. "I have a thousand questions, Miss Burks." He sighed and exhaled his concern through steepled fingers. "But I'll only ask one. Can I at least provide you with an embassy car to return you to your hotel or wherever you may need to go?"

"No, thank you, sir," she said, rising and offering him her hand. "I'll catch a cab."

That same afternoon, a file of fourteen men made their way up yet another escarpment of the Mavuradonha Mountains and down into yet another drainage. The Mavuradonha Range forms the backbone of Zimbabwe and is part of what is known as the Great Dyke, which runs along the same fault line as the Great Rift Valley. The file of men had long since left the lower reaches of the Mana Pools National Park area along the Zambezi and were now crossing some of the most rugged terrain in Africa. This was the easiest and hardest part of the journey. It was easy, in the sense that this mountainous part of the Mavuradonha Wilderness Area was totally uninhabited. Centuries ago it had been a part of the Bushman and Monomatapa empires, but now it was a restricted wilderness area. Aside from isolated ancient ruins, the only vestige of civilization was the Kopje Tops Lodge, a rustic bush lodge used by the few safari concessions that lead treks into the Mavuradonhas during the dry season. Now the lodge and the few outlying bush camps were deserted. But the going was hard. In some places it was hand-over-head scaling rock outcrops, and on climbing lines to descend from steep areas. On top of the ridgelines they halted briefly to plan their next descent, and at the bottom of the ravines they strung lines to safely cross the fast-moving streams. Every two hours, they paused for about twenty minutes. Two men remained awake while the others simply squatted on their heels, and with heads on folded arms across their knees, fell immediately asleep.

The file moved for the most part in a straight line toward the objective, as there were no man-made roads and few game trails. They walked on a compass bearing, periodically checking their position by GPS and on computer-generated topographical maps. The task of their point man was only to make the job of the others a little easier. A Ndorobo and a skilled tracker, he moved well in any terrain, and ranged out in front of the laboring column. Periodically he dropped back in to speak with Tomba, pointing to where a game trail might make the going a little easier for a short while or where there was a detour around a rocky outcropping. Occasionally they would flush a bushpig or a small pack of wild dogs, but the *miombo* woodland birds were always with them. They heard cheetah, but never saw one of the elusive cats. The only real danger was from the thorns of the acacia trees while moving at night. They only had forty miles of terrain to cross, but they had to walk twice that, dealing with the elevation gains and losses and negotiating their way around obstacles.

Each man in the fourteen-man patrol carried between fifty and sixty pounds of gear. In addition to rations, sleeping poncho, and personal weapons, they were all laden with ammunition. Since there was no local population, there was no need to dress like locals. They wore a combination of standard special operations combat dress, modified to carry their individual load across the mountains, and bush-fighter clothing of their own choosing. All wore leather gloves and had short machetes and garden pruning shears to get through the brush. Most wore Danner jungle boots, but a few, including the Ndorobo scout, wore *velskoen*, three-quarter boots with heavy hide soles, a favorite among bush fighters. At dawn of their second full day on the trail, they arrived on a ridge that peered into the *mana* or valley they were seeking. The Makondo Hotel rested in the lower reaches of this drainage. The travel would be easier as they descended into the valley. The force was now only three hours' steady march from the target. AKR quickly set up an antenna and aimed it in the general direction of a geosynchronous satellite that patiently waited 22,000 miles above the earth. The antenna was needed for data transmission. He slipped on the earphone-boom mic appliance and hit the autodial on the Blackberry display. It was answered on the second ring.

"Owens, here," came the reply, as clear as a number dialed in an urban area.

"Hello, Bill. It's AKR; is Janet there?"

"Akheem. Good to hear your voice. Wait a sec, and I'll get her."

A few moments later her voice crackled over the headset. "Brisco here."

"Janet, this is AKR. We just arrived at Point Bravo. GPS has us about two and a half miles from the objective. Tomba wants to rest his men for a few hours before we begin our approach."

"How are the men holding up?"

"It was a walk in the park for them, but I'm a little tired. Tomba feels we will have the target in sight within a few hours of leaving here, but they will take that much time or more to cover the last four hundred meters. Depending on what we find as we approach the target, we will be ready for the assault just before first light tomorrow. Any more intelligence?"

"Nothing concrete," she replied, "but the recent satellite passes show increased vehicular activity, and we have found two more weapons emplacements at grid D-11 and M-6. They should be plotted on your download. M-6 looks to be a machine gun dug in near and above the helo pad."

"Understand D-11 and M-6. We'll put them in the assault plan. When do you launch the bird?"

"About zero nine hundred your time, so it will be overhead late afternoon for the duration."

"And the packages?"

"The packages are aboard."

"Excellent. I'll check in when we've established a forward observation post later today. Still enjoying the camping trip?"

She ignored his last question, but he noticed her voice had softened. "I'll relay all this to Steven and Garrett. Be careful, and good luck to all."

"Good-bye, Janet."

"Good-bye, Akheem."

That was the first time, he reflected as he restowed the

antenna, that she had called him Akheem. Normally it was Kelly-Rogers, or something less endearing. Perhaps, he mused, a little time in the bush, even a bush camp, was softening some of her edges.

At dawn Alfred brought coffee, rolls, and fresh fruit to a small portable table near the riverbank. The sun was just peeking over the Mavuradonha Mountains, giving the Zambezi a touch of gold before its return to its normal light chocolate color. Dr. Elvis Rosenblatt arrived at the table fresh from eight hours of solid, uninterrupted sleep, scrubbed and freshly turned out in tan walking shorts and a clean bush jacket. Garrett had been up for over four hours and had probably slept no more than that the previous night. He was wearing what he had on the night before. In fact, he had slept poorly ever since Tomba, AKR, and the others had crossed the Zambezi and begun their trek into Zimbabwe. His need to be with the assault element had been so great that he had almost petitioned Steven to let one of the Africans stay with Rosenblatt, masquerading as his native guide. But he hadn't. It made sense that he stay with Rosenblatt, and bring him to the party at the right time. Yet that was just a small part of it. The real reason was that his presence would undercut AKR's role as the ground controller and Tomba's role as assault leader. This band of Africans were proud of their ability to fight, and a white man in their midst would be an affront to that pride. It was a matter of trust. And finally, while they did not expect to encounter anyone in this uninhabited area, a white face would only raise questions. As Alfred withdrew, Garrett stood with his hands thrust deep into his cargo shorts, gazing out across the Zambezi, into the mountains.

"Will you come and sit down, for Christ's sake? You're making me nervous."

Garrett turned from the river and slumped into a canvas chair. His eyes were red slits from the lack of sleep, and he hadn't shaved in two days. Gratefully he poured himself a steaming cup of coffee.

"Y'know, you look like shit. If we're supposed to be on a safari vacation, you're blowing our cover, big-time."

Garrett shrugged and then grinned. "You're right. I guess I'm just not good at waiting while there is a team in the field."

"What are they doing now, or is that still a secret?" Rosenblatt had been told little of the tactics of the operation, only that he would be brought in when the objective was physically secure and the issues before them were medical in nature.

"They should be in the mountains above the hotel complex about now. They will rest for a while, then make their way down to predetermined observation posts this afternoon. From there, they will move into position for the final assault, which is scheduled for just before dawn tomorrow."

"You say those mountains are rugged?"

"Some of the most challenging terrain in Africa," Garrett replied.

"There has to be a road into this place. Why didn't they just sneak up the road at night? Probably a lot of guards, huh?"

"You can bet on it. Did you see the movie *Lawrence of Arabia*?" Rosenblatt nodded. "Lawrence and his desert tribes were heavily outnumbered and outgunned by the Turks at Aqaba, but they won a decisive victory. Know how they managed it?"

"They came in from behind them, from the desert?" Rosenblatt ventured.

"Exactly. The Turks thought they would attack from the sea—that no force could cross that desert. So they fortified the harbor defenses and left the back door open. It was the same for the British in Singapore; they relied on the jungles of Malaya to defend Singapore from the north. So the large British garrison surrendered to a much smaller Japanese force. Sixty thousand men, and they surrendered almost without a fight. So you see, surprise is everything. The men that will soon be creeping down that escarpment to the hotel will be outnumbered four to one. As far as we know, the security force there is not expecting an attack, but if they are, they will look for one along the access road—at least, that's the theory. If we achieve surprise, we will do well. Surprise and a few other goodies we have in store for them."

"These guys, the ones who are going to do this—they pretty good, are they?"

"The best."

"Think they can do it without you?"

Garrett grinned again. "Oh, yeah. They don't need me to be there half as much as I need me to be there. They'll get along just fine."

"Then why don't you finish your coffee, have a crumpet, and go get yourself a shave and a shower, and find some clean clothes."

"Is that the doctor's advice?"

"That's the doctor's advice."

Garrett drained his cup and grabbed a piece of fruit as he stood up and stretched. "I respect your medical opinion; I'll do just that."

When he returned a half hour later, he found Steven Fagan in his seat, with Benjamin squatting a few feet away in the shade. Benjamin was dressed as a laborer, and Steven had his CAPA identification card in a laminated carrier clipped to his shirt pocket. Garrett shook hands with Steven, waving him back into the seat as he dropped to his heels next to Benjamin, greeting him, to Benjamin's surprise, in Bemba. Steven thoughtfully sipped his coffee, then turned his attention to the others. They were quite alone sitting along the bank of the river, yet he still addressed them in a guarded voice.

"The assault force made the mountain crossing without incident and are now about two and a half miles to the northwest of the hotel complex. They'll rest the balance of the morning before moving into position for the final thrust. All indications are that they are undetected although there seems to be some stepped-up activity around the main hotel building itself. If all goes as planned, the bird will be here to pick you up about midnight. If they are detected, they will attack immediately, so you had best be ready to move by midafternoon, just in case. All else is in place. Dr. Rosenblatt, please be assured that we will not put you on the ground until the complex is secure."

"I understand," Rosenblatt said. "And the equipment is ready to go?"

Steven glanced at his watch. "The portable equipment is aboard the helicopter, which is now waiting at the Jeki airstrip. The backup gear you wanted will be standing by in case you need it. Hopefully you won't; we'd like to get in and out of there as quickly as possible, but we won't leave until you are finished with your investigation. From here, it will take about fifty-five minutes to get to the staging area. From there it will be another ten-minute flight to the objective. Any other questions?" There were none. "Good. Then we wait while the men on the ground do their job. But let me say again, Doctor, that we appreciate your part in all this. If this is what we believe it to be, then your work will be critical." He looked around. "I trust you haven't been inconvenienced by having to wait it out in this little safari camp? It seems to be a great deal more accommodating than our bush camp by the airstrip."

Steven again wished them well, and he and Benjamin made their way back toward the battered pickup truck. He stopped by the Chiawa Camp office to pick up a handful of brochures before they drove back to the Jeki airstrip.

"Hello, fellow campers. May we join you?"

As they had done the previous mornings, Clark and Maria Gerhardt joined them early on to talk about the day's activity. The Gerhardts were from the San Francisco Bay Area. This was their third safari to Africa, only this time they had brought their two sons, Nicholas and Miguel, along. They were the only other North Americans at Chiawa Camp. The Gerhardts, proficient photographers, found the two Canadian businessmen eager to learn game photography. The boys, nine and eleven, showed no interest in exotic wild animals and were content to chase about the camp, playing with the native children of the camp attendants.

"I hope we aren't intruding," Clark Gerhardt said. "We saw you had a visitor."

"Not at all," Garrett said. "Just a contractor from Toronto out here to help with the electrical power system. We Canadians keep a lookout for each other. Please, sit down." Alfred had anticipated their arrival with a plate of fresh fruit and another carafe of coffee.

"Are we ready to go after that black rhino today?" Maria Gerhardt asked as she took a seat. "Our guide said they spotted several of them just across the Chonga River in the Game Management Area. If we can get a rhino, we'll have done the big five." The big five were elephant, lion, leopard, buffalo, and rhinoceros. "You fellows are bringing us luck. We've never done the big five on a single trip."

"I'm afraid you'll have to go without us today," Garrett said. "Greg is having some stomach problems. He was up most of last night with a case of the trots. I think we'll stay in camp today." Rosenblatt shot him a questionable look.

"So sorry to hear that," she replied, turning her attention and sympathies to Rosenblatt, who was now doing his best to look like a diarrhea victim.

"Tough luck, old man," Clark said empathetically. "It can take it out of you. I know from personal experience. You sure you won't join us, John?" he said to Garrett. "Perhaps Alfred can see to him."

"Thanks," Garrett replied, "but I better stick around. He was pretty sick last night."

The Gerhardts left with their guide later that morning, but not before Maria Gerhardt returned with a bottle of medicine. She would not be persuaded to leave until Elvis Rosenblatt, aka Greg Wood, had taken a spoonful of the dark, vile-tasting liquid while Garrett Walker, aka John Naye, looked on with benevolent approval.

For the past week, Guardian Systems International and the Joseph Simpson Jr. Foundation had been working on a jointly sponsored project. GSI had a short and successful history in adapting military drone aircraft for basic security work. They had contracts, bid well below their cost, to provide surveillance for large, high-security government facilities like the Idaho National Engineering and Environmental Laboratory and the Air Force secret test facility known as site 51 in southern Nevada. A single drone or unmanned aerial vehicle, UAV for short, could survey large tracts of land and sound an alarm if there were intruders on the property. These facilities were still patrolled by military units and contract security forces, but if the concept proved out, the drones could eventually replace costly vehicle patrols and electronic sensors.

Their work in Africa was a pilot program to see if drone aircraft could help with the tracking of game herds. In addition, sensors aboard the UAVs could collect a host of migratory and environmental data to help with wildlife and game management. Given the growing sophistication of these sensor packages, it was envisioned they might also be able to spot poachers and direct park rangers and army units to intercept these outlaws. Poachers with automatic weapons were still the biggest threat to the elephant and rhino populations in Africa. Each morning one of the two UAVs took off from Kilimanjaro International Airport and began to make a long, lazy figure eight over Kenya and Tanzania. Soon the air traffic controllers began to ignore the slow, high-flying aircraft. The drones were easily able to stay aloft for a full twenty-four hours. They used a blend of synthetic aperture radar and electro-optical sensors during the daylight and primarily relied on infrared imagery at night. The drones were, in the words of the attending technicians, maintenance pigs that required an hour of work for every hour in the air. But once in the air, they had proved highly reliable. By working in shifts, the ground crew was able to get one of their two drones airborne moments after the other landed.

The surveillance project was not cheap. Each Global Hawk UAV carried a price tag of $15 million. Along with the two supporting C-130Js at $70 million a copy, and the various support equipment, there was close to a quarter of a billion dollars tied up in the project. Several of the technicians tending the two Global Hawks had only two years earlier been tracking enemy tanks and SAM batteries during Operation Iraqi Freedom. These were men who were, in the words of the supervising GSI program manager, queer for the gear. It didn't matter if they were tracking an Iraqi armored personnel column or a herd of giraffe. For them it was a grand video game. In the spring of 2003, these talented technicians and their sophisticated UAVs not only generated tactical targeting information but provided fast-look target assessment of designated weapons impact points to lower civilian casualties. The Global Hawks were essentially low-hanging satellites. They could provide dramatic pre- and poststrike imagery as well as serve as a reliable communications relay platform.

Early that morning, *Cheetah* was rolled out of the small hangar provided by courtesy of the Kenyan government and given her preflight checks and avionics inspections. (One of the technicians was a Northwestern graduate and had put a wildcat decal on the bulbous nose of the drone, hence the name.) On this particular morning, two cylindrical packages were fitted to the bird, one under each wing. Each had an infrared sensor in the nose and looked benign enough, yet a few of the techs gave one another knowing looks. They could only assume it was some black government program that GSI had taken on to defray some of the cost of this venture. Fine. They were being paid, and paid well, to track critters, and track critters they would. It wasn't as exciting as killing tanks, but many, especially the younger ones, felt it was a better use of the technology. Right after *Antelope* landed, *Cheetah* began her takeoff roll and gently lifted into the air. The launch/recovery team watched as it climbed out of sight.

The UAV took a leisurely thirty minutes to reach 50,000 feet, well above any commercial traffic. *Cheetah* headed east to the edge of the Masai Mara before turning south and crossing the Serengeti Plain. From there it continued south toward the Selous Game Reservation in southern Tanzania and set up in a lazy orbit just 150 miles from the Indian Ocean. The data began to stream in as *Cheetah* got her bearings and began to look for game movement on the ground. Up to that point, it had all been routine. Suddenly, the data link from the UAV was broken, and most of *Cheetah*'s electronic suite went silent. The tech on duty immediately called the GSI project manager.

"What's the problem?" he asked as he climbed into the semitrailer that served as their mission control headquarters.

"I don't know," the senior controller on duty said. "The secondary indicators say that all avionics and flight control systems are fine, but I've lost the sensor datalink and navigational presentation. Looks like it's still flying a racetrack over the Selous Reservation, but I can't be sure. It's almost like *Cheetah* has taken it into her head to do what she wants to do and not tell us about it." The other techs in the van listened but said nothing.

The project manager put his hand on the controller's shoulder. These were very smart people; you could withhold information from them, but it was unwise to lie to them or to try to fool them.

"That's an interesting way to look at it," the project manager said in a conversational tone. "Let's, for now, just work on the assumption that she, in fact, has some other business to tend to. Perhaps when she finishes, she'll check back in with us. Just keep monitoring the systems and let me know if anything changes."

"Should we alert the air traffic control system that we're having a problem with the UAV?" a tech asked.

"I don't think that will be necessary. Let's just keep an eye on things. Perhaps *Cheetah* will come home when she's finished."

After the project manager left, the watch team cast knowing glances about and returned to their scopes. Two of them, sensing that it would be a long wait, began to play pinochle.

Cheetah was not a particularly small cat, with a wingspan of 116 feet and a length of 44 feet, but she was amazingly quiet—electronically speaking. Her outer skin was made of a composite absorption compound that might not elude a military search radar, or even a Western air traffic control radar, but this was Africa. A man in another van some eleven hundred miles southwest gave a new set of instructions to *Cheetah,* and she was only too happy to comply. The UAV climbed to her maximum altitude of 65,000 feet, crossed Lake Malawi into Zambia, and flew down the Muchinga Mountain Range, neatly bisecting the distance between Lubumbashi, Zaire, and the Malawi capital of Lilongwe. The controllers at those local airports saw nothing that caused them alarm. Staying well west of Lusaka and north of Harare, she descended to 40,000 feet and took station, unnoticed, over the Mavuradonha Mountains.

While the others rested, the Ndorobo scout made his way down the escarpment that led into the valley of the Makondo Hotel. He did not approach the structure, but observed from a rise above the hotel complex for a long while. His name, or the one he answered to, was Robert. His task was to find an easy, quiet route by which to bring the others down. Like most who had learned tracking from their fathers and uncles, Robert did not seem to need sleep, and when he did, fifteen minutes was as good as several hours. Most trackers knew the land but had difficulty in relating the ground they saw to the features on a map. Robert could do both. When he made his way back into the security perimeter of the little force, he went straight to Tomba, who greeted him in Masai; the Ndorobo language is almost extinct. AKR joined them.

"Our best line of march is to follow this stream drainage down from here," Robert said in English as he ran his finger along a sharp break in the contour lines of the computer-generated map. "At this bend, the bed of the stream cuts to the right of the shallow plateau where the hotel is located. If we leave the streambed here and break into our attack groups, we can easily move close behind and to the side of the complex."

"And you saw no security precautions along this line of approach?" AKR asked.

"No, *Nkosi*, but then per my instructions, I did not get too close. I was able to see the sentries along the road and observe some of them as they came and went into the small, flat building that seems to be their headquarters. From what I saw, it is my belief that they are guarding against a threat along the road—against a force that would approach along the road that serves this hotel."

"We have learned of two additional gun emplacements, here and here," Tomba said. "Could you see anything of them?"

Robert studied the map, mentally overlaying what he had seen from his perch above the hotel on the map laid out before them. "I saw only one. It was an RPD emplacement with a good field of fire to cover the helicopter pad. They have not taken the time to properly conceal it. I was not able to see the other one. Of the other three that are on the map, I saw only two. The one here is also an RPD, and the one near the guard post by the road is a fifty-caliber machine gun. And again, they are manned, but from what I could see, they are sloppy and inattentive to their duties. It seems," he added without emotion, "that many of them are our old comrades. But as I have said, they are lax and not attending properly to their duties."

"Thank you, Robert," AKR said. "We are indeed fortunate to have a scout with such keen eyes and good judgment."

Tomba thanked him in Masai and squeezed his arm. Robert withdrew to where his pack and weapon were resting; he had taken neither on his scouting mission. Tomba and AKR leaned over the map.

"It would seem that they are not on high alert, nor are they expecting us to approach from this direction," Tomba said. "Unless there is a change, we may achieve total surprise."

AKR nodded, studying the map. It appeared that the long march across the mountains had served them well. When he looked up at Tomba, he saw in his eyes a warrior's fierceness that had not been there a few moments ago. He was a man who expected a fight, even welcomed it.

"Robert spoke of old comrades," he said gently. "Will that be a problem?"

Tomba smiled. "We Africans, as you collectively call us, have always fought among ourselves—tribe against tribe, the people of one river valley against another. Since the colonial wars, it has often been brother against brother. Which is better—or worse? To choose the side on which you will fight, or to fight on the side on which you were born? We have made our choice. Those who guard the hotel have made theirs. That we may have at one time fought on the same side or shared a fire together is of no concern. The issue now will be how well you fight for the side you have chosen. Perhaps this is as close as we Africans get to democracy, at least in this lifetime." He smiled, raising his M-4 rifle from between his knees. "We vote with this."

"Then we prepare for battle," AKR said, surprising himself at the emotion in his voice. He had always prided himself on being an Englishman and a professional military soldier. But here, with these men, he felt a strange sense of savagery, and in spite of himself, he found it pleasingly intoxicating. Akheem Kelly-Rogers was no stranger to combat, but he knew this was to be different. Still, amid this new, infectious near-lust for combat, he knew that technology and unit discipline would be key in overcoming the odds against them. How easy it would be, he admitted to himself, to simply give himself over to the fight—to allow himself to be carried forward on a rush of adrenaline. But that was not his role. He took a deep breath and mentally projected their small force around the hotel complex, positioned for the assault. Then he asked Tomba to assemble the men around the map.

"We are here," he began, "and this is our objective. Robert has found a way to the target from our current location, a route that will take us there while masking our approach. Now, for the last time, we will go over our movement to the target and review our actions once we have broken into the assault groups."

AKR spoke softly and clearly for close to twenty minutes. Then he asked a man from each of the assault teams, not necessarily the team leader, to outline his duties when the attack began. Looking around the circle of warriors, he knew that they were ready; they would carry out the mission, or they would die trying—or both. After a radio check with their personal transceivers, the men shrugged into their packs and checked their weapons. Then Tomba called them in close.

"My brothers, we have worked and trained together, and *Nkosi* Akheem has given us the tools to succeed. Remember what we have learned and use these things well. But do not forget that when the battle is upon us, the victory will belong to those warriors with the greatest hearts. When that time comes, remember your training and fight hard. Then it will be victory or death, my brothers."

"Victory or death," they echoed as one, with quiet determination. And as one, they turned and looked to AKR.

"Victory or death," he repeated, his voice charged with emotion. "It is a privilege to go into battle with warriors such as you. Together, we will win the day. Thank you for counting me as one of your own. I am deeply honored."

Tomba nodded to Robert, and he led them down from the escarpment toward the Makondo Hotel.

*　　*　　*

Late that afternoon, François Meno found Helmut Klan in the bar, a small box in a plain brown paper wrapping under his arm. It seemed, Meno noted, that his colleagues on the clinical staff began drinking a little earlier each day. Klan was having a schnapps at a quiet table in the corner with Hans Lauda. These Krauts stick together, Meno thought. He didn't entirely trust them. That Lauda was put in charge of the medical team had at first angered him, but given the administrative duties of the team leader, Meno had been content to assume the role of primary researcher. Klan was a bureaucrat and Lauda, at best, a medical cheerleader. He, Meno, was responsible for the development of the pathogen, and they all knew it. And after all, there would be no credit given for this effort in the medical journals. The money was important, but Meno still felt cheated by the lack of recognition. No matter, the Frenchman reasoned. After the pandemic he developed had ravaged North America—perhaps the world— then he, the brilliant François Meno, would come to the rescue. Meanwhile he would have to deal with these German cretins, Klan and Lauda.

"Ah, François," Klan said as he approached. "Please join us. Hans here was just telling me that we will soon be ready to ship our product."

Our product, indeed, Meno thought. "More than ready, Helmut." He tossed an eight-by-ten-by-six-inch package on the table. "Here it is. There are fifteen hypodermic syringes filled with toxin and ready for injection—a few extras in case some of them are mishandled. They are standard dosages of two milliliters for ease of administration. Not nearly that much is required, since the pathogen is, by design, quite contagious. Only a few microbes is enough to create an infection." The two men sat staring at it. Meno chuckled at them. "There you have it, *meine Herren,* all in a shock-resistant container."

He took up the package and tossed it to Klan, who juggled it, almost spilling his drink, before wrestling it to his lap. The surprised and rattled project director took the package and gently returned it to the table.

"That's—that's wonderful, François. So it's finished; it's all here?"

Meno permitted himself a condescending smile. "That's right, gentlemen. The civilized world's worst nightmare, all in that single small container."

"Marvelous," Lauda said, "simply marvelous. You are to be congratulated. Without your effort and skill, this would not have been possible. Shall we call it the Meno Pox?" Lauda knew Meno needed to be stroked, and he was not without a sense of humor.

"Charming thought, Hans, but I think not. No, it is done; I am done, and I want no more to do with it. I will need a few hours to clean out the lab spaces and to pack my things. I will be ready to leave this godforsaken place by tomorrow afternoon." He looked at Klan. "Now that you have your epidemic, I assume we are free to leave?"

"Of course. I will see to the arrangements, but we will probably not be able to get you out of here until the morning after tomorrow. First," Klan said, nodding to the package on the table, "I must deal with this. Those who pay us are anxiously awaiting delivery."

Suddenly Lauda, who was on his second schnapps, began to clang on the side of his glass with a knife. "Your attention," he said as he pushed himself to his feet. "May I have your attention, please. *Achtung,* for those of you from the fatherland." He raised his glass. "It seems our project is complete; our mission here in the Heart of Darkness, finished. Please raise your glass to a successful effort and to our imminent return to civilization. Gentlemen, a toast."

"Here, here!"

"To success!"

"To going home!"

There was a round of clinking glasses, and several of those in white coats made for the bar to recharge their drinks. François Meno merely rose and excused himself. He had a single bottle remaining from the case of Petrus 1996 Pomerol Bordeaux he had brought with him when they arrived almost six weeks ago. Tonight he would enjoy it in the privacy of his room while he packed his things. But before that, there were still a few matters he must attend to in the lab.

After a second round of toasts, Helmut Klan sat looking at the box for several moments. He rose and tucked it under his arm. There was still time to get it out that evening, and have it aboard the last flight out of Harare. But that meant trusting it to the roads at night. Or he could send it out the following morning. Either way, the sooner it got to its destination, the sooner they would be paid. Back in his room, he placed a call to the mysterious Maurice Baudo. Baudo told him to get the package to the airport in Harare as soon as possible, taking all precautions for its safe arrival. Helmut Klan was given explicit instructions on how and where someone from the lab was to meet with the courier who would be receiving the precious cargo.

In his Rome apartment, Pavel Zelinkow breathed a sigh of relief. It was 7:00 P.M., an hour behind Harare and all of Zimbabwe. All that remained now was to make a good delivery. When the product was in Riyadh, he would have fulfilled his commission, and he'd be done with this risky business. He poured himself a cognac and dialed a number in Harare. It was answered on the second ring. He gave the man instructions in Arabic and had him repeat them back.

He had personally chosen this man for this particular job. He was not an experienced courier, but for his purposes that was to the good. Cell phone intercepts by Western intelligence agencies had led to the capture or killing of a great many terrorists. So the terrorists, primarily Al Qaeda and their operatives, had taken to using couriers. Now those same intelligence agencies had begun targeting known couriers. Zelinkow's man was a Saudi businessman, driven by his faith to put his services at the disposal of Al Qaeda. He traveled frequently in his work, but had never been used in an operational capacity. He was a perfect choice.

Zelinkow swirled the cognac in his glass a moment, savoring its aroma. He took a measured sip—excellent. Then he called Claude Renaud. The man had obviously been drinking, but when Renaud heard the voice of Georges Frémaux, he became instantly alert. Frémaux had Renaud repeat his instructions as well.

The rule of the Nyati was that they drank only beer when not on duty, but since it was his rule, he felt he could break it, and this evening he felt he needed something stronger. Claude Renaud stepped outside into the cool mountain air and took a flask from his pocket. It was gin, and he drank greedily. It was like dropping a burning coal into the pit of his stomach, but after the initial sensation, it seemed to steady him. He glanced around the hotel complex; all was quiet. The African night, like the dawn, came quickly. A faint afterglow still silhouetted the mountain to the west. There were lights burning in the main building, and the generators hummed as they kept a steady flow of power to the facility. Looking down the road, he could just make out the outline of the guard shack and the glimmer of a cigarette. Normally he would have stormed down and disciplined the offender; smoking while on guard duty was not allowed. But not tonight. It would be their last night here. The job was over, save for one final task that they were to complete tomorrow afternoon. He took one last look at the dark ridge of mountains that walled off the hotel from the valley that opened below and to the southwest. Then he pocketed his flask and went back inside the spa building.

At the bar he opened a beer and motioned for his white team leaders to join him. They all knew the project would soon be over, and while the pay was good, they were anxious to leave. Like Renaud, they didn't know exactly what was going on inside the main hotel building, but they knew it was not good. These were hard men, but dragging people from their homes and subjecting them to medical experimentation was an unsavory business, even for them. And the whites knew that the blacks liked it even less than they did. Well, Renaud thought, the blacks will have their chance to make it right.

"I want the bar closed in an hour," Renaud told his team leaders. "The job here is finished; we leave tomorrow afternoon. I want the lorries and transports packed out at first light. We'll be on the move just after midday. From here we'll go back to the training camp and demobilize. Everyone will be paid off there, and we'll begin the repatriation from the camp."

"What about the others?" one of his lieutenants said, jerking his head toward the hotel.

"They're not our concern. Other arrangements are being made for them." The lieutenant shrugged. "Now, if you'll all get something in your glass, we'll have a drink on it. Tomorrow we'll be away from here and out of it. Gentlemen, you've done well. To you, the Renaud Scouts."

The others mumbled an agreement and drank with their leader. There was nothing else to do. The blacks, while they had been told nothing, sensed that this was their last night in garrison and quietly passed out bottles of beer. The whites at the bar gradually left their leader and found their men. While they would never mingle with blacks in Capetown or Johannesburg, they were brothers while in the field, and the whites sought out their black teammates, almost in preference to other whites.

Renaud was again by himself. He desperately wanted another gulp of gin, but he resisted and poured himself a second beer. The instructions from Mr. Georges Frémaux had been clear. Before they left, they were to kill everyone in the hotel and burn it to the ground with the corpses inside. He smiled ruefully. It would be just like the old days, when the colonial powers and the Communists fought for control of southern Africa. Kill and burn, burn and kill. Frémaux had been very specific about not looting, but who would know? After all, the boys had earned it. Renaud pushed himself from the bar and headed for his quarters in the wing of the hotel reserved for himself and his men. He promised himself another tote of gin once he had packed out his kit.

At first, Robert led them down toward the Makondo Hotel at a brisk walk. When they closed to within a mile of the objective, he began to move at a much more cautious pace. He ranged out in front of the file, moving fifty to a hundred meters ahead while the others waited. Once well out in front, he would freeze like a gundog on point, using all his senses to look for danger or something out of place. When he was satisfied, he thumbed the transmit key on the pistol grip of his rifle.

"You may move," he whispered into his boom mic.

"Moving," came Tomba's voice in his earpiece.

When the Africans came to the Kona training facility, they were already soldiers and competent bush fighters.

Tomba had selected them for their experience and courage. But they were weak on teamwork and technology. Under AKR's tutelage and Tomba's firm hand, the teamwork came rather quickly, but most of the men were several generations behind in technology. At first there were problems with change—the transition from AK-47s to the M-4 rifles. Then they had to learn to use the M-4 rifle and attached M-203 grenade launcher as a weapons system. Most were good combat shooters and proficient at close-in fighting, but their long-range shooting skills needed work. They were good at setting ambushes, but they had to be taught fire-and-movement tactics, and the selective use of force and firepower. And there were a number of other technologies, most of them common to American special operations soldiers, they had to master. The complex assault plan drawn up by Tomba and AKR would challenge their newly learned skills. Fortunately, much of the advanced technology was highly user-friendly.

Just before dark, they reached a position four hundred meters from and just above the perimeter of the complex. There the men dissolved into four groups of three, with Tomba and AKR forming a fifth, two-man control element. They faded into the bush and waited in total silence for close to fifteen minutes—time enough for everyone to become accustomed to the sounds and smells near the hotel. Tomba called his four team leaders in close. He unfolded a map and orientated it in relation to the actual complex before them. The map glowed under the red hooded lens of his penlight.

"Here we are, and here are the buildings before us. Each of you has your assignment. Are there any questions?" No one spoke. "Good. And you know your route from here to your positions for the assault?" Tomba looked each of the four men in the eye as he nodded his assent. "Very well, we are ready. Trust your instincts, but listen to your radio; if contacted, do exactly as you are instructed, just as we did in training on Kona. We are warriors, so let us now be about the business of warriors." He held their eyes a moment, then said quietly, *"Awusipe namhla isinkwa."*

"Awusipe namhla isinkwa," they murmured in return. It was a Zulu prayer for victory in battle—"Give us the day."

The four three-man teams melted into the bush and began to move toward their objectives. True to their training and breeding, they moved like incense through bamboo, making no sound and leaving the ground over which they traveled undisturbed. After they were gone, AKR keyed his radio.

"Home Base, this is AKR, over."

"Go ahead, AKR," came Janet Brisco's immediate response.

"Janet, AKR. Teams are away. Dodds should have them on the plot now, over."

"Understand teams away, stand by."

A moment later, Dodds LeMaster's voice came over AKR's headset. "Dodds here. I have you and the four teams. They should be on your presentation as well, over."

AKR and Tomba crowded behind the notebook computer connected to a tiny six-inch wire-whip antenna. With the UAV overhead, there was no reason to look for a satellite. The picture was sharp and identical to the one LeMaster had before him on the large plasma monitor in the van. Their restriction was only the size of the presentation. Both the van and the men in the field had a real-time overhead presentation of the hotel complex, courtesy of *Cheetah,* silently prowling the sky some 25,000 feet over their heads. Overlaid on this real-time image was a computer-generated schematic of the facility. The known defensive gun emplacements and guard posts were marked on the schematic. There were five blips, one red and four yellow. The red blip was their location, and the four yellow ones marked the transponders carried by each of the four teams. Thanks to Dodds LeMaster's modification of the surveillance program, while *Cheetah* circled above, the image remained stable and orientated to their position on the ground.

"We have a good picture, Dodds. How about a close-up of our posit?"

"Coming down," Dodds replied.

The picture began to zoom down on their location as their red blip began to grow in size and fade in intensity. While Tomba stared in amazement, AKR looked up and waved. There he was on the Global Hawk candid camera.

"It is magic," Tomba whispered.

"No," AKR said with a grin, "it's just our own personal video-games geek."

"I heard that," came a sharp voice over both their headsets, but it was laced with good humor. The image on the screen zoomed back out to include the yellow blips that were slowly moving around the perimeter of the Makondo complex. "What else can I do for you?"

"Keep an eye on the teams while we move into position. Let us know if anything develops. AKR out."

"Good hunting, AKR. Dodds out."

While Tomba led AKR closer to the hotel, Dodds LeMaster remained glued to his scope—zooming in, zooming out, searching the ground in front of the teams as they moved into position. Only once did he interfere.

"Senagal, this is Control, over."

"Uh, this is Mohammed Senagal, over." The voice was clear, but there was hesitation in it.

"Senagal, this is Control. Hold where you are. There is a roving sentry moving across your line of travel, left to right, ten o'clock to two o'clock. You should see him soon, over."

A dubious Mohammed Senagal and his two men froze and waited. Soon an armed man came into view fifteen meters away, crossing their line of travel and disappearing along the perimeter of the complex.

"Senagal, Control. The way ahead appears clear. Proceed as you were, over."

"This is Senegal. We are moving again. Thank you, Control."

The three bush fighters exchanged a brief, incredulous look. They had rehearsed this at the Kona training facility, but only half believed this kind of thing was possible. They were beginning to be convinced, even the taciturn Mohammed Senagal.

"I can't believe you're still having a problem. This medicine was given to us by a Kikuyu tribal healer; he said it was made from fermented wildebeest parts. It's always worked for us before. Maybe you should try a little more." Maria Gerhardt stood poised over Elvis Rosenblatt, bottle and spoon in hand.

"Wildebeest parts, you say. Perhaps just one more dose," Garrett offered, trying to suppress a smile.

"I think we might hold off for a bit," Rosenblatt said, looking pointedly at Garrett. "This could be more serious than I thought. Perhaps it's time to take our friend up on his offer for the use of the helicopter—before I get any worse. Yeah, I think it's about that time."

"Helicopter?" Maria asked, capping her medicine bottle and setting it aside.

"That's right," Garrett replied. "The gentleman who was here this morning said, if he wasn't better by this evening, to call him. He has a helicopter at his disposal and offered to fly Greg out. Maybe we should go ahead and take him up on it."

"You think?" Rosenblatt said, his voice laced with sarcasm.

"Well, it's that, or more of Maria's medicine." Rosenblatt's eyes narrowed. He came up on one elbow, and Garrett put a hand on his shoulder. "Take it easy, Greg. I'll call him right now."

It was well after dark when the Jet Ranger set down gently on the Chiawa Camp helo pad. John Naye and Clark Gerhardt helped a moaning Greg Wood into the cabin of the helo. The camp director had followed them anxiously to the pad. A sick guest was cause for concern— not for the health of the guest, but for the reputation of the camp. Alfred handed up their bags, and Garrett secured them in the rear of the cabin. The helicopter lifted into the night air and eased itself out over the Zambezi. The pilot ran along the riverbank to the west until he was several miles from the camp, but instead of turning north for Lusaka, he rolled the Jet Ranger on its left side and turned south across the dark river into Zimbabwe.

Clark and Maria Gerhardt stood on the pad for a while after the helo had left. "I can't understand it, Clark. The medicine has always worked before. And he was such a healthy-looking man."

Clark shrugged. "Who knows. Maybe he was just sick of Africa and wanted to get out of here. There are some people who are like that, you know. Boys asleep?" She nodded. "Then, c'mon, the moon won't be up for a while, and the stars are at their best. Let's go have a whiskey by the river. Tomorrow we'll get our rhino."

All the teams were in place when a quarter moon rose high enough to peer over the rim of the mountain ridge to the southeast and into the valley. It was just after midnight. Accepted special operations doctrine called for a thorough reconnaissance of an objective before conducting an assault.

Thanks to the technology IFOR had at its disposal, the recon of the objective was done as the assault teams made their approach. *Cheetah* provided an eye in the sky that could monitor ground activity with amazing clarity. Dodds LeMaster maneuvered the drone over and around the Makondo complex to get diagonal as well as overhead looks at various emplacements around the facility. Depending on natural and artificial lighting conditions around the complex, *Cheetah* used a blend of optical, radar, and infrared sensors to gather specific target data. En route to their positions, the assault teams had each placed two or three remote video cameras along their route and, under AKR's guidance, aimed them to cover various aspects of the complex. Once in place, the small mini-cams could be selectively interrogated, and the images displayed to AKR or flashed back to the two control vans where Dodds LeMaster, Janet Brisco, and Bill Owens had a near-total surveillance of the Makondo Hotel grounds. They visually patrolled the grounds, passing all movements to the men on the ground who waited at their assigned positions. One man in each of the four three-man assault teams had been assigned a combat support role. Two of them would serve as snipers, while the other two were armed with shoulder-fired rocket launchers. Their various perches had been selected to provide overlapping fields.

Tomba and AKR had positioned themselves on the rise right behind the main building. From this point they had a clear view of the guard post at the main entrance gate, the hotel building, and the principal outbuilding, which was the spa complex. Tomba searched the area from their vantage point with night vision goggles—or NVGs. AKR, well concealed in the brush, was glued to the computer screen as he interrogated the various mini-cams and periodically checked *Cheetah*'s presentation. Along with the four deployed teams, they and the others waited, watching the movement patterns of the guards on duty and looking for anything that might be useful for the assault. They would continue to gather information right up to the moment of the attack.

"AKR, this is Dodds, over."

"Go ahead, Dodds."

"From what we've been able to observe, the guards coming on duty and going off duty go into either the west wing of the hotel or the spa building. We know from previously monitored activity that the spa building is probably their off-duty hangout. And we've felt all along that the west wing serves as barracks. Can you confirm this? Over."

"Roger, Dodds. Wait, out."

Tomba had heard the same transmission, and the two men exchanged glances. Neither could see what was going on inside the wing from their location, although they did see several of the guards entering and leaving. Tomba slipped off his pack.

"Let me approach for a closer look," he whispered. "I will be back in a few moments"

Before AKR could respond, Tomba had vanished into the brush in front of them. All AKR could do was alert Dodds and the other men on the ground that one of their number was on the move inside the perimeter of the complex. A half hour later, Tomba returned as silently and as abruptly as he had left.

"I was able to slip inside unnoticed and see into the ground-floor hallway," he said as he shrugged into his pack. "This is the part of the hotel where the soldiers are billeted. And from what I could see, they are preparing to leave. I was able to see several rucksacks in the hall outside of the rooms and a pile of sleeping bags. This is a force that is preparing to be on the move soon. If we wish to catch them here, we may not have too much longer."

AKR considered this a moment and glanced at his watch; it was just after 2:00 A.M. The original plan was for them to attack just before dawn, when the sentries were least alert and they would have some filtered daylight to inspect the camp. The extra time that day had been allowed for the force to make their way to their assigned assault positions. They were now already in place. And there was always the unlikely chance that a sentry would run across one of the assault teams, and that in itself would precipitate an attack. If they were preparing to leave, at dawn more of the guard force would be up and about. Little could be gained by waiting, AKR reasoned. He keyed his radio.

"This is AKR. You with us, Janet?"

"Right here, Akheem. What do you have?"

"Looks like the security force is preparing to leave. They probably won't move until first light, but we can't be sure. Recommend that we attack as soon as Garrett is ready to move, over."

"Understand you want to attack ASAP. Give me a minute. Brisco, out."

Janet Brisco was seated behind her console in the van with an infrared presentation of the Makondo Hotel filling the large flat-plasma screen before her. Steven stood behind her, watching and listening on the net, but he said nothing. He was in charge of the operation, but he had delegated tactical responsibility to Janet Brisco; it was her show. Without taking her eyes from the screen, she shifted frequencies and keyed her radio. Like Dodds LeMaster and Bill Owens in the other van, she wore a headset with a mic boom that swung down from one of the earpieces.

"Gopher Two Seven, this is Control. How do you hear me? Over."

* * *

A little more than thirty miles to the southeast on the high Zimbabwean plain, a Jet Ranger sat quietly in a clearing on the veld. The two pilots pumped the last of the jet fuel from two fifty-five-gallon drums, prepositioned there the night before, into the tanks of the helicopter to top them off. The aircraft had the legs to make the journey unrefueled, but by topping off, they could, if need be, fly clear of Zambian or Zimbabwean airspace into Tanzania or South Africa. While the pilots attended to the fueling, Garrett Walker and Elvis Rosenblatt climbed into black rubber-and-vinyl suits designed to protect them in a hazardous chemical or biological environment, equipped with state-of-the-art charcoal and ionic filtration systems. The suits were lightweight and only mildly restrictive, but very warm.

"How come these are black?" Rosenblatt asked. "Normally these are bright yellow."

"Because our guys have been told it's okay to shoot at yellow," Garrett replied, "but not black."

"Oh, good idea."

Garrett and Rosenblatt now looked like astronauts with their full-body suits, holding their helmets under their arms. After a final check of each other, they sat on the open deck of the helo compartment with their legs hanging over. Both men had earpieces with microphones held in place with elastic headbands. The pilots, finished with their refueling, had climbed back into their seats up front. Both had NVGs fitted to their flight helmets, and if they thought it strange that they had just gassed up in the middle of Africa with two moon men in the back, they didn't show it. Like most GSI pilots, they were former military special operations crewmen, and they relished a bit of tight flying as much as the men waiting around the Makondo Hotel relished a good firefight.

Janet's voice crackled in Garrett's earpiece. "This is Gopher Two Seven," he replied, "Garrett here, Janet. Go ahead."

"Garrett, AKR wants to move up the attack, as there are
signs that the guard force may be preparing to pull out. I
concur. Are you ready?"

Garrett cut the two men up front into the circuit. "You
guys ready to rock and roll?" One of the pilots turned to
look back at Garrett and gave him a thumbs-up, as did
Rosenblatt. "We're ready and standing by when needed.
Tell AKR and Tomba to kick some ass."

"Understand you are ready. Stand by, and I'll keep you
advised. Brisco out."

Garrett looked at Rosenblatt and shrugged. It wouldn't be
long now, but they could still do nothing but sit and wait.
Garrett and Rosenblatt did so impatiently and in silence. The
two pilots up front debated the need for a realistic salary cap
in major-league baseball and the merits of the designated-
hitter rule. Experienced special operations pilots were practiced at waiting while events on the ground ran their course.

Janet Brisco looked over her shoulder to where Steven
Fagan sat on a stool. Before him was a large screen that displayed the Makondo complex along with the five blips rep-
resenting the men standing by for the order to attack. Like
Garrett, Steven would have liked to be a little closer to the
action. He had initially thought of going along on the helo,
but he was not needed there. Steven Fagan's job was to
keep a careful watch as events unfolded. He was the mission commander. Janet would run the tactical picture,
AKR would coordinate the ground assault, and Tomba
would lead it. Garrett, when he arrived, would see that
their medical expert took stock of the situation. If something went wrong or a strategic determination had to be
made, it would be a critical decision, and Fagan alone

would make it. He made eye contact with Janet and imperceptibly nodded his head.

"Akheem, this is Brisco, over."

"AKR here, Janet, go ahead."

"Green light, I say again, green light, over."

"Understand green light. Tallyho. Dodds, you there?"

"Right here, AKR."

"Okay, make your drop. As planned, give me a countdown to impact."

In the next van from Janet and Steven, Dodds LeMaster made a few calculations on a slide rule. Some dated technologies, like vintage carpentry hand tools, were still useful and pleasurable. "I will make the drop in about ten minutes and give you a countdown from there, over."

"Roger, Dodds, understand ten minutes to drop and count down."

"Akheem, Brisco, over."

"Right here, Janet."

She hesitated a second, then keyed her transmit button. "Garrett says for you and Tomba to kick some ass."

"Did he now. We'll see what we can do. Thanks to all; AKR, out."

10

THE PANDEMIC

Judy Burks had returned from her meeting with Ambassador Donald Conrad feeling relieved and vindicated, and a little humbled. The ambassador was quite a man. That afternoon she had taken a long walk around Lusaka. She had found the city mildly disgusting and the people wonderful. Late that afternoon she was back out by the pool, reading a Patricia Cornwell novel. She was there to serve as an official go-between should something go wrong, but until it did, there was really nothing for her to do for the next two or three days but wait. There were any number of tours and side trips that might have been an option, but cell phone coverage—to the embassy or Washington, with the exception of Steven—was iffy outside Lusaka. She was reasonably sure that whatever was going to happen, it would happen the day after tomorrow, though that was nothing more than a guess on her part. After dinner at the hotel dining room, she went back to her room to read, finally putting her book aside and falling asleep a little before midnight. Garrett was with her in the dream, and the two of them were sitting on the patio of a coffee shop in Coronado when suddenly it started to rain. She was trying to get him to come inside, but he insisted it would stop; he just sat there drinking his coffee, soaked to the skin, as the rain fell harder and harder. The rain was so distracting that she never heard the two men slip the lock and move silently into her room. Suddenly, the rain began to choke her. She was awake for only a moment, struggling against the alcohol smell that filled her nose and mouth. The struggle lasted only a moment, and she was back asleep, only it was dark, she was alone, and it was no longer raining.

The two men were dressed like hotel employees, and both were black. They dumped the sleeping Ms. Burks into a linen-hamper cart, bending her double as if she were folded into a loosely strung hammock. They wheeled her to the service elevator, took her straight down to the loading dock, and loaded her, laundry bag and all, into the back seat of a Peugeot driven by an older white man. He handed the two men in hotel-employee uniforms a fist full of rand, and the Peugeot sped off.

Cheetah continued to roam over the Mavuradonha Mountains, reporting everything she saw. The UAV had flawlessly made the transition between daylight and nighttime, keeping her sensors locked onto the Makondo Hotel complex. Sometimes she flew out several miles away and dropped down a few thousand feet for a better angle on the objective, but basically she ran a racetrack pattern overhead. Then she received a command to take an easterly heading, pushed along by a mild tail wind. She complied, and when she was well away from the area, she was ordered back to the target on a westerly bearing. Without being told, *Cheetah* made minor course adjustments to keep the Makondo square on her nose. About a mile from the center of the complex, the two cylindrical packages under *Cheetah*'s wings came alive, electrically speaking. The sensors in the nose of each powered up, and in a few nanoseconds, both knew precisely where they were, not just over the Mavuradonha Mountains—*exactly* where they were on the face of the globe, and their *exact* altitude. A half mile out, the tail cones of each underwing package dropped away, and the cylinders sprouted fins. As if to flex stiff joints, servo-motors cycled the fins within a narrow range of motion and came back to a neutral position. The program that had sent *Cheetah* downwind from the target and back released the two packages exactly a half second apart, and they fell away from the UAV into the night. All this was a little disturbing to *Cheetah,* whose life centered around her sensor suite and an avionics package that demanded precise adherence to altitude and heading. The turbulence caused by the jettisoning of the tail cones and the unannounced, uneven dropping of the packages had forced her to make altitude and heading adjustments. She was much happier now that they were gone.

"Weapons released," Dodds LeMaster reported.

"Understand weapons released," AKR echoed.

"Damn, I hope I got those coordinates right," he replied. It prompted a grim smile from AKR who looked up into the canopy of stars. Death was on its way.

Moments before, he had alerted the teams to stand by for an impact. On the intersquad tactical net he had tried to sound confident and routine, but this was all new to him. He had called in fire before, but not like this, and not so close. The team leaders all acknowledged, coolly and professionally.

LeMaster's voice startled him. "Ten seconds."

"Copy ten." His eyes were locked on those of Tomba, who immediately keyed his intersquad radio. "Five seconds, brothers; five seconds. Tomba out."

The fourteen men on the ground turned away from the target, put their hands over their ears, closed their eyes, and opened their mouths. Before AKR assumed this position, he made brief eye contact with Tomba. He couldn't be certain, but in the dim moonlight, he thought he saw a look of amusement cross that man's handsome features.

WHUMP—WHUMP!

It was almost a single explosion. For those arrayed in a semicircle just outside the perimeter, it was like two rapid, vicious jabs in the kidneys. For those inside, it was much worse. The packages were modified three-hundred-pound, precision-guided bombs. Like their big brothers, the 2,000 JDAMs that had ravaged the Taliban in Afghanistan and the Republican Guard in Iraq, these baby smart bombs, directed by their onboard GPS receivers, struck within a few feet of their aim points. A half-microsecond delay allowed them to penetrate the roof and explode inside the buildings. One detonated just over one of the card tables in the bar-spa, the other in the center of the hallway on the second floor of the hotel barracks wing.

Eight of the Renaud Scouts died instantly in the spa, along with another twelve in the barracks. Seven more in the barracks, most of them in the first floor of the two-story wing, had their internal organs so mauled that they would never regain consciousness. Three crawled from the rubble of the destroyed wing bleeding from their nose and ears, unable to walk. Before the assault had begun, half the security force had been taken out of the fight. Those who were outside or away from the impact points had fared better, but none totally escaped the effects of the blasts. Many were knocked to the ground, and more than a few were temporarily blinded by the flash. Yet most of those left had experienced mortar bombardments and rocket attacks before. They recovered, some more quickly than others, and began to look for a place of safety, if not a place from which to fight.

Elsewhere in the complex, there was shock and confusion. With the exception of an all-night poker game, the clinical staff had been shaken from their beds, a few of them literally. Most thought it was an earthquake, followed by a quick realization that perhaps there was some kind of an explosion in the medical spaces, and that, more than anything else, prompted them to scramble to their feet and to look for a way out. Down in the basement medical facility, the effect was least felt, but nonetheless terrifying. Two technicians were in the process of disassembling the lab equipment, some of the more expensive and portable test equipment for transport, the rest for destruction. The two on duty paused to absorb the shock wave that passed through the medical spaces, exchanged a terrified look, and headed for the stairs. Throughout all this, the lights flickered but remained on. That was quickly taken care of when one of the Africans on the perimeter sorted himself out, shouldered his rocket launcher, and took out the two generators that had weathered the explosions. The two mini-JDAMs had, by design, started no fires. When the complex was plunged into darkness, the assault force pulled on their NVGs and began to move along preassigned routes into the complex. All but two. Joshua Konie and Pascoal Mumba remained in their perches, camped behind the IR sights on their SR-25 Stoner sniper rifles.

"Garrett?"

"Garrett here,"

It was Bill Owens; both Janet Brisco and Dodds LeMaster were glued to the tactical picture. "It appears that the initial strikes were dead on. AKR has initiated the ground assault. The generators are out, and the complex is dark. Time to rock and roll."

Garrett grinned at that. Owens watched too many war movies. "Roger that, Bill. We're on our way."

Garrett caught the pilot's eye and rotated his index finger in the air as a signal to start turning, but the pilots had heard the transmission and had already started to spool up the single engine of the Jet Ranger. A moment later, the blades began to turn.

"Don't you think we should wait until the place is secured?" Rosenblatt yelled over the turbine whine.

"And miss all the fun?" Garrett retorted. "Are you nuts?"

As the Jet Ranger lifted from the veld, Garrett and Rosenblatt clung to the aircraft with one hand and held onto their helmets with the other. Once airborne, they got a radio check. Rosenblatt had a single earpiece and could hear only Garrett. By pressing a button on his wrist, Garrett could speak to Rosenblatt, AKR, or both. He noticed that his doctor was starting to look a little pale. He reached over and squeezed his knee.

"Tell you what, buddy. You don't get me sick, and I won't get you shot. Deal?"

Rosenblatt managed a grin. "Deal."

A review of the video tapes later confirmed that the first individual kill during the assault belonged to Dodds LeMaster and Pascoal Mumba. LeMaster picked up an infrared image moving from the guard post on the road back toward the main building.

"Sniper One, this is Control. Can you hear me?"

"This is Mumba, Sniper One. Yes, I hear you very well."

"There is a man moving up the road toward the large building. He should be in your view any moment."

"Yes, Control. I see him now. May I shoot?"

"Mumba, Control. You may fire; you may fire, over."

"Very well, I have him, out."

Mumba had memorized the ranges from his shooting perch to various points in the compound. He judged it to be about 150 meters, which for the SR-25 was point-blank range. The man's IR signature was clearly humanoid, but not clearly defined. He decided against a head shot and settled the cross hairs on the center of mass. The gun had been around for a while, but the ammunition had not. It was a new variant of armor-piercing, low-penetration 7.62 match-grade ammo. The round APLP bullet is designed to penetrate steel but not pass through a human torso. When the bullet entered into the flesh of the guard moving along the road, the heavy 192 grain round simply exploded. Mumba's round caught the guard in the chest and blew off his head and left arm. LeMaster's mouth fell open as he watched the expanding heat bloom from the scattered flesh. Then squirts of flame registered on his presentation screen as the .50-caliber near the guard shack opened up. They were firing at nothing, because they could see nothing. All they did was attract attention. Both snipers began to send rounds into the gun pit, and a moment later an LAAW rocket slammed into the emplacement, killing anyone still at the heavy machine gun.

Inside, the medical staff began to gather in the halls in various stages of partial dress. A few of them had flashlights. The stairwells and hallways were dimly lit by emergency battery lighting.

"What is it?"

"Are we under attack?"

"Where are the guards?"

Only one of them had any military experience—the Russian, a microbiologist who had worked with the Soviet and Russian bio-weapons effort. He waved the bottle of vodka he had been nursing most of the night, declaiming, "All can all kiss our sorry ass good-bye—All can all kiss our sorry ass good-bye."

Then Helmut Klan appeared. "I believe we are under attack, but there is nothing we can do. Go back to your rooms. The security force will beat them back, or they will not. We'll just have to await the outcome. Now go." Some did as they were told; others didn't, wanting only to escape the building.

Klan, dressed in his robe and slippers, went to his office and began setting out files for destruction. How he was going to accomplish this, he had no idea, but it seemed the logical thing to do. He was so intent on the task that he failed to notice François Meno enter the office. Meno was smoking a cigarette.

"So here we are in the führer's bunker, and the Russians are pouring through the gates." Meno held the cigarette backward in a theatrical Teutonic fashion, palm up, as he took a puff. "So, ve can say, ve vas yoost following orders? Eh? I don't think so, *mein Herr.*" He peered carefully from the office window, which was cracked in several places. "I wonder who they are, anyway?"

Klan suddenly realized there was nothing to be done but wait for it to be over. He sat down at the desk and stared at the Frenchman. "If we're lucky, they are a local African force, and perhaps Renaud and his men can deal with them," he said to Meno, "but I rather think it is some kind of contract special operations force." Suddenly remembering there was one thing he could do, he took his cell phone from the drawer and punched in the number for Maurice Baudo on his speed dialer. A single ring was followed immediately by a high-pitched squeal as *Cheetah* picked up the outgoing call and flooded the frequency with a jamming signal. Then a series of explosions sent them to the floor amid a shower of broken glass and dust.

Claude Renaud had packed his gear, had another belt of gin, and then tumbled into his cot, but had not been able to sleep. He finally gave up and, taking another pull from his flask, decided to return to the spa. After quickly downing another beer at the bar, he had started back to the barracks when the two mini-JDAMs struck. He was immediately blinded by the flash, and the concussion brought him to his knees. Most of the explosive force was absorbed by the structures, leaving him unhurt but unable to see for a few moments. Instinctively, he knew he must get to cover if he were to stay alive. He crawled until he was able to stand up and stagger to a stake truck parked well away from the buildings. Renaud threw himself under it, and from this relatively safe spot watched rocket and small-arms fire pour in from the perimeter. He was enough of a soldier to know that the RPD emplacements and guard posts were well targeted by incoming fire. After just a brief burst from the .50-caliber machine gun, there was little or no return fire from his men. He knew with sudden clarity that this must be the Western special operations force that Klan had warned him about. He also quickly realized that they had not come up the single road to the hotel complex. For a brief moment, Renaud was angered that his force was being so systematically destroyed, but that anger was quickly replaced by his need for self-preservation. He was absolutely certain that his only chance for survival was to get away from the area, which was rapidly becoming a killing field. When there was a lull in the firing, he crabbed his way to the other side of the truck and scurried off into the brush.

When Judy Burks awoke, she was puzzled—at first because she was on top of the bedcovers, not under them, and then because the light was on. Or was it morning sun that seemed to scald her eyes? She distinctly remembered that she had closed the curtains before she undressed for bed. And was that cigarette smoke that she was smelling? This is all wrong, she told herself as she tried to sit up. It was then that she realized that she couldn't move. Her hands and feet were tied down to the bed. As her eyes slowly adjusted to the light, she could now see that it wasn't sunlight but a strong, shaded floodlight suspended at the foot of the bed. She took a moment to inventory her situation. Think back to what you last remember, she demanded of herself. As the sleepy fog started to clear, she had the icy realization that it hadn't been a dream at all. She had been taken from her hotel room, removed from her bed. She didn't know how or by whom, but she probably had a good idea why. Simultaneously, she was very angry and very scared.

"Okay, jokes over. I got no money, and you'd have to be crazy to harm a United States federal agent. I'd suggest that you might rethink this whole thing and just let me go. We'll forget that it ever happened." She raised her head and saw the glow of a cigarette in the shadows behind the light. "Really, I'm not worth the effort. C'mon, talk to me."

Vadim Karpukhin was from the old school, the old First Directorate to be exact, and he was feeling uneasy about this woman. Karpukhin had been a specialist in foreign operations and foreign internal security affairs. Retired for more than a decade, he now headed a thriving semi-legal corporate security business. On occasion he was contacted by Boris Zhirinon with a special request. Karpukhin was a busy man, and rapidly becoming a wealthy one, but he would never say no to Boris Zhirinon. KBG operatives are often portrayed in the West as thugs or ideologues, but in reality most are principled professionals. Karpukhin took no money for these special requests; it was a matter of honor and respect for what had once been—that and the fact that he occasionally called on Zhirinon for a favor of his own. He had initially been sent to Harare with the ambiguous instructions to look for evidence regarding some kind of Western interventionist force in Zimbabwe. After a few inquiries he had concluded that something was going on in the province of

Tonga, but since he was not able to travel there, little more could be learned in Zimbabwe. On his own, he decided to fly to Lusaka and do some probing in the Zambian capital. He found that little was to be gained from the Russian legation. The KGB was gone. None of the old guard, like Karpukhin, trusted the new spies of the Foreign Intelligence Service. And if one of the old KGB hands had in fact been assigned to the Lusaka residence, how good could he be, to have been posted to Lusaka? A little legwork on his own, a few bribes, and the fact that Vadim Karpukhin was a true pro from the old school quickly produced some results. He soon learned that there had been a brief flurry of activity at hangar B-5 at the airport. Then a hotel clerk tipped him off that there was a female registered at the Intercontinental Hotel with a red official U.S. passport. He had asked himself, Are the two connected? Karpukhin knew that you could no longer just grab a U.S. federal agent off the street, even in some neutral third-world capital, without good reason or as some kind of retaliation. And there really was no cause for such retaliation, since the CIA and KGB called it quits in 1991. The only excuse for such an action was that Vadim Karpukhin didn't want to disappoint Boris Zhirinon.

"Miss Burks. I'm sorry it was necessary to abduct you like this, but I must have some information. A large transport aircraft and two helicopters arrived and left a deserted hangar at the Lusaka general aviation terminal a few nights ago. It was about the same time you arrived. I believe that these two events are somehow connected. I would like you to enlighten me on this matter."

Judy Burks's mind was racing. She could see nothing beyond the white beacon at the foot of the bed except a cloud of cigarette smoke that lazily drifted through the light. She was reasonably sure that she was in some kind of a bedroom; it was air-conditioned, and that meant

Western comforts, but she sensed it was not a hotel room. Her interlocutor's English was practiced, and she could detect an accent that was probably German or Slavic. She was reasonably sure it wasn't Middle Eastern. The voice wanted information, not money, so it wasn't ransom. She was still dressed in her nightgown, so it wasn't sexual, at least not yet. What to do? She could scream, but since he hadn't gagged her, it probably wouldn't do any good. Maybe she could get very emotional and break down crying. Not a whole lot of options.

What the hell, she thought. "Eat shit and die, you pervert," she yelled in a loud voice, proud of herself that it didn't crack. "I don't know what the hell you're talking about. So get these restraints off me and let me the hell out of here. Do you hear me, you asshole?"

Holy Mother of Russia, Vadim Karpukhin said to himself, shaking his head. So she's not going to make this so easy. He had done the arithmetic; it would take a day for anyone to miss her, and another day for the embassy staff to go on the hunt for her. Bribes in the right place might put them on his trail by the third day. He figured he had a safe forty-eight hours. He had hoped she might turn out to be one of those whiny Western bitches that fall apart when they break a fingernail. So far, that didn't appear to be the case.

Tomba and AKR watched the systematic dismantling of the Makondo Hotel. All of the known and fixed RPD emplacements were rocketed and raked with well-aimed fire. In a few instances some unfortunate guard managed to shoot back, to be immediately met with lethal counterfire. After about five minutes, the firing died away, as the men on the perimeter were finding no more targets.

"Dodds, this is AKR. See anything?"

LeMaster had brought *Cheetah* down to some ten thousand feet over the target—about a mile and a half overhead. *Cheetah* flew figure eights over the complex, crossing and recrossing, looking for any sign of movement. Now that the firing had stopped, the thermal sensors had began to sort out the picture on the ground.

"Nothing that would . . . hold on, I have something near grid G-6, over. I'm marking it now."

"Roger, grid G-6. Wait, out."

On his notebook display, AKR saw the cursor on his screen float to a single thermal image near a small storage shed behind the hotel. Probably someone walking perimeter patrol at the time of the attack was now trying to slip back into the compound. AKR pointed it out to Tomba, who immediately keyed his radio.

"Joshua, we have a man moving on the south side of the storage shed that is in front of you and to your left. You may have to move to get a shot at him."

"I understand. I am moving now to a position where I can see him." Tomba let all know that one of theirs was moving inside the perimeter of the complex. *Cheetah* zoomed on the drama, and they watched one thermal image move in relation to the other. Then Joshua stopped, and a brief bloom on the scope marked his muzzle flash. He made the shot from about thirty yards, and in a few seconds it was followed by a burst of heat on the scope. They heard the report of an explosion.

"He was carrying a grenade with the pin pulled," Tomba observed to AKR. "We often do that when close fighting is at hand." Then on the radio, "Are you all right, Joshua?"

"I am well. I have a piece of shrapnel in my thigh, but it is not deep. I will hold here until the final assault."

Joshua moved to the modest cover of the storage shed

and waited. AKR, with Tomba on his shoulder, watched Cheetah's view of the complex. Occasionally they looked up, snapping on their nightvision goggles for a ground-level look. Both of them had led raids and assaults; neither had done this with the tools IFOR had placed at their disposal. The technology had given them a great advantage, and as always, surprise is everything, but clearing and securing the facility would be low-tech, basic infantry work.

"What do you think, Akheem?" It was Janet Brisco. She could recommend they move in, but as ground commander, it would be his decision. He glanced at Tomba, who nodded his consent. Once more AKR slowly swept the area with the image intensifiers. There was nothing. But he knew, as well as Tomba, that any guard force remaining who still wanted to fight would have gone to ground and be waiting. Any more delay would not necessarily make moving in any less risky.

"Okay, Janet, we move now. It's Tomba's show. Silence on the net unless it's tactical and it's critical. AKR out." Then he turned to Tomba and put a hand on his shoulder. "*Awusipe namhla isinkwa,* my brother."

"Victory or death, my brother," Tomba replied. Then he keyed his radio. "Assault teams, move out. If you leave your assigned corridors as you approach the target, I must know." He paused while the four team leaders acknowledged the order; then, clutching his rifle, he turned and melted into the bush, moving down and toward the hotel.

It was with some sense of relief that Tomba crept toward the objective. He was back in his element. He eased the earpiece slightly off his ear so as to better listen for enemy movement. Tomba and the four two-man teams began to clear the outlying buildings and guard posts as they closed on the hotel. Twice Dodds LeMaster alerted a team of potential danger, one of them leading to a kill. For the teams with the use of night vision devices, it was like flushing game birds from low grass. If they moved, they were dead. The Africans moved steadily and professionally, calling their shots. Then tragedy struck. An RPD machine gun in the back of a canvas-covered truck had remained hidden from *Cheetah* and from the attackers until it was too late. As one team moved across the last stretch of ground toward the entrance of the hotel, the RPD caught them in the open.

The truck and the two men manning the machine gun became an instant magnet for automatic-weapons fire and 40mm grenades. Then a rocket slammed into the vehicle and turned it into a burning pyre. In the glow of the fired truck, the complex fell silent. Tomba directed the three remaining teams to security positions around the downed men and went to them. One was dead and the other mortally wounded. Tomba dragged him to safety, checked his wounds, then plunged a morphine syringe into his thigh. The man, a Masai, had taken three of the AK-47–type rounds in his bowel and stomach, and another in the chest. He was in terrible pain, but he did not cry out. It took only a moment for the man's features to relax from the drug, and he was gone. Tomba took a moment to lightly touch the Masai's bloodstained face and close his eyes. He then quickly directed his attention to the remaining teams, directing them to close and secure the doors to the hotel. He himself covered the entrance.

"We are in position," he radioed to AKR. "The hotel is secure. Two men dead, no others wounded."

"Understood. I will be there in a moment." AKR wanted to ask which of his men were killed, but this was not the time. "Janet, are you there?"

"Right here, Akheem."

"Hotel and complex secure for now. We're ready for Garrett. Two men KIA."

"Understand two KIA. Stand by for an ETA on the helo." Her voice was neutral and controlled; this was not the first time she had lost men in an engagement under her tactical control. A moment later she was back to him. "Akheem, Brisco, over."

"Right here, Janet."

"The helo will be there in about four minutes. Do you want the helo to remain in air while you check out the hotel?"

AKR thought for a moment. The ambush by the RPD had been a surprise, and there could be others. Even one man with a rifle could wreak havoc on a stationary helo and crew. And they had no seriously wounded men, only dead.

"Negative. Have the helo drop Garrett and the doctor and clear off. Have them return to their refueling site. We'll call them back when we need them."

"Understood. They will drop their passengers and wait off-site. Brisco, out."

They didn't hear the helo until it was on top of them. The pilots did their military flying with the 1st Special Operations Wing and knew how to fly a tactical approach. They made a downwind approach, flying close to the hardwood canopy and flaring only for the landing at the last moment. The Jet Ranger paused at the helo pad, a small piece of level ground fifty yards from the hotel. They stayed only long enough for the two men in the back to scramble from the cargo bay and pull off their equipment bundles. Garrett and Elvis moved as quickly as possible, limited somewhat by their protection suits and gear. The helo jerked into the air, paused a moment as if to regain its bearings, and rolled away into the safety of the night sky.

* * *

Back at the Jeki airstrip Steven Fagan had followed the
action from a console in one of the vans. They were air-
conditioned for the sake of the equipment, yet he found
that a rivulet of sweat was making its way down his temple.
It had been a while since he had been this close to a ground
action. As a young Special Forces sergeant, he had led a
contingent of Montenyard tribesmen on the Plain de Jar-
res in Laos toward the end of the Vietnam War. That experience had left him with an appreciation of the desperate,
fast-moving, life-in-the-balance struggle that is a firefight, even a one-sided one. For Steven, the thermal images
and computer-enhanced presentations conveyed emotion.
Even without the audio play-by-play, this was much more
than a video game. So intently was his focus on the scope
that he almost failed to notice the vibration of the sat
phone vying for attention in his pocket. Once he became
aware of it, he stripped off his headset and flipped open
the phone. The caller ID was blank, and that in itself puzzled him. "Yes?" he said, holding the phone to his ear.

"Steven, this is Jim Watson."

"Sir, what can I do for you?"

"Steven, I can only guess that you are very busy right
now, but something has come up in Lusaka that you need
to be aware of. I want you to call this number there in
Lusaka; are you ready to copy?"

The connection was excellent, but Steven read the
number back to him to be sure he had it right. "And who
am I to ask for?"

"Only one person will answer," Watson said. "It will be
Ambassador Donald Conrad."

* * *

"AKR, Garrett. We're on the ground and at the helo pad, over."

"AKR here. Stay where you are, and I'll send a couple of the men to bring you down."

AKR was now with Tomba near the entrance to the hotel. Tomba detailed one of his snipers and one of his rocketeers to bring the two spacemen down. Both Garrett and Rosenblatt carried their helmets. The two Africans who escorted them to the entrance flanked them to either side and kept them well in the shadows. Each shouldered one of Rosenblatt's packs. Garrett carried an M-4 assault rifle.

"Everything all right?" Garrett asked as he dropped to one knee beside AKR.

"We lost a team—two men. Otherwise it's gone well."

"Tough break. Any movement inside?"

"None. If you're ready, let's move. I don't want to give them time to recover."

AKR nodded to Tomba, who called up one of his men, a Zulu they called Wilson because his tribal name was too difficult for westerners, even Garrett, to pronounce. The two astronauts put on their helmets—they were now ready to battle microbes. AKR and Wilson pulled on gas masks and gauntlet-type gloves that they had brought with them for this purpose. They hadn't the protection of Garrett or Rosenblatt, but they were there primarily for security support. The four men moved into the foyer and lobby in a diamond formation, Garrett in the lead, flanked by AKR and Wilson. Rosenblatt brought up the rear. Tomba remained outside for external security with the rest of the force. The nine remaining Africans stayed in static positions at observation points around the hotel, all with good fields of fire. Their objective now was to hold and protect the main hotel building and the helo pad just long enough for the men inside to do their job.

Above, *Cheetah* remained on the prowl. The ever-vigilant Dodds LeMaster reported what she saw to Tomba.

Per his instructions, Rosenblatt stepped to one side while the other three men moved quickly through the lobby area and cleared it. They were about to take the stairs to the basement when a disheveled man entered the lobby. His hands were thrust into his bathrobe pockets, and he had obviously been drinking.

"May I ask what you are doing here? This a medical research facility, and—"

Three rifles swung on him, but only AKR spoke. "On the floor, now! Do as you are told or we will shoot to kill!" Helmut Klan went to his knees and eased himself to the floor. "Cross your ankles! Look to your left! Hands behind your back!" Klan did as he was told. Wilson pounced on the prone man, cuffed him, quickly searched him, and jerked him to his feet. Garrett and AKR kept their eyes moving around the room. Wilson unceremoniously dumped Klan into a lobby armchair and took a security position across the lobby. Garrett dropped to one knee in front of Klan, whose eyes were wide with fear even though he had nearly drained a bottle of schnapps while the battle had raged outside. Rosenblatt approached and squatted beside Garrett. He had been briefed to keep his head down when possible, at least no higher than those around him. Garrett put the muzzle of his rifle under Klan's chin, raising his jaw, but not so high that Garrett couldn't look at him through the Plexiglas shield of his helmet.

"Who are you, and what is your job here?" Garrett asked in a low voice. He assumed the man was doped up, dazed, or drunk. He pushed on the rifle a little harder; he wanted to see if the man could be controlled by pain. He accomplished that and more. Klan was immediately convinced that the man behind the Plexiglas shield would end his life if provoked or if it pleased him. Yet he had one gambit that he hoped would save his life.

"I—I am the director here or, what I mean to say, I *was* the director here. Our project is finished. We—we were about to leave."

Garrett glanced at Rosenblatt, who had taken up a station on the other side of Klan. "You were developing a bio-weapon here," Rosenblatt said. "Where is it?"

"No, no—you have it wrong, please. We came to develop a drug for AIDS, that is all," Klan managed, spouting his much-rehearsed story. "And we were successful; we developed a vaccine that has great promise." Then he played his last card. "We shipped the vaccine out just last night; we were about to close the lab down. I admit that we were using HIV-positive members in the local population for testing. That is why we had a security force here. It—it was not right, but it was in the interest of science. You have to believe that!"

Rosenblatt was now within a few inches of Klan's face, his heated voice partially fogging the faceplate. "Just another German obeying orders—doing what he was told, is that it?"

"Yes, yes. It was medical research."

"You're just another Nazi shit," Rosenblatt spat. "Your father was probably one of those bastards that made soap out of my relatives."

"You want me to kill him?" Garrett asked.

"Sure. Blow his fucking head off," Rosenblatt replied coldly.

Garrett pushed on the barrel of his rifle, causing Klan to gag.

"No, please, it was not me," he gasped. "I am not a researcher; I am only the facility manager. I did not know what went on in the basement. You must believe me." And then he fainted, from fear and from the pressure of the muzzle on his carotid artery.

"Damn," Garrett mumbled, not wanting him to lose consciousness. But then he was suddenly aware of AKR and Wilson moving at the same time. Coming down the staircase was a man in khaki slacks, collared shirt, and a windbreaker.

The newcomer smiled and held his hands out from his sides. "May I join you?"

Garrett glanced at Rosenblatt and nodded. Both of them rose. The man moved across the lobby, still holding his hands out from his sides—still smiling. AKR tracked him with his rifle, while Wilson covered the stairs and the hallways that opened into the lobby. Garrett lifted his weapon, and the man stopped.

"He's lying, but then you already know that." The newcomer's English was good, with only a hint of a Parisian accent. He directed his comments to Garrett, assuming he was the one in charge. "We have in fact developed a bioweapon, and it's a bad one—very bad. One might say it borders on the diabolical. I know; I developed it. But our fearless director here"—he looked at the unconscious Klan with a sneer—"was right about one thing. We shipped it out yesterday. I couldn't tell you where it is right now, but it's probably somewhere over the Indian Ocean or the Mediterranean by now."

"So why are you telling us this, Dr. Meno?" Rosenblatt said. "You've just admitted to a monstrous crime."

"Ah, so you know who I am," Meno said, beaming as he turned to the second astronaut. "This makes it easier. *Parlez-vous français?*" Rosenblatt did, but shook his head no. "American, no doubt," Meno replied, his voice dripping with condescension. "A pity. Then let me break it down for you in English. You see, I have developed a pathogen that is like nothing known to man. It is robust, and it is deadly, and it will take months of effort by the best geneticists in the world to develop a vaccine. And more time still to produce it in quantity." He eyed Rosenblatt closely, now rightly assuming that the smaller of these two was the brains and the other, the muscle. "I have no doubt that your Centers for Disease Control or the bumblers at Johns Hopkins could in time develop such a vaccine," he continued, but when he mentioned Johns Hopkins, the sneer returned. They had denied him a fellowship. "But I know this germ. Trust me when I say that tens of thousands will die most unpleasantly before you even clear clinical trials. And if this pathogen evolves, as it has the ability to do once established in a large population, many more thousands will die."

"So what are you saying?" Rosenblatt asked coldly.

"What I'm saying is that for safe passage and ten million of your dollars, I will *give* you the vaccine. Once I am safely away from here, of course. You see, I developed the vaccine along with the pathogen. It's much easier, genetically speaking, to design the cure while you design the disease." The condescension was back, along with a measure of triumph. "It's not here, if that's what you were wondering. It has been sent along to a location that is known only to me." He turned and sat in a nearby armchair. "That's it, gentlemen. You Americans like analogies, so take your pick. The genie is out of the bottle; Pandora's box has been thrown open; or it is the time of the locusts." Meno languidly propped his feet up on a low magazine table and put his hands behind his head. He exuded confidence. "Of course, I know you will need time to talk with your people. Take your time, but remember, the clock has already started."

Rosenblatt looked at Garrett and, in a tone of voice

that Garrett had not heard before, said, "Get this scum away from me." The look on his face was even more terrible. They had agreed that when it came to handling the medical staff, Rosenblatt was to set the agenda. Garrett and the others would take their cues, if not direct orders, from him. So Garrett swung his rifle up to the port-arms position and cracked Dr. François Meno in the mouth with the barrel, not doing him serious damage but carrying away his front teeth. He took the stunned Frenchman by the collar, dragged him into the cocktail lounge area, and dumped him into one of the Naugahyde chairs. Surprised and stunned, Meno tried to speak. Garrett hit him sharply with an open hand, and he passed out. He cuffed him to a nearby stanchion with nylon snap-ties and returned to the lobby. Rosenblatt was now hovering over Klan. He had found some water and splashed it in Klan's face. This brought him around, and his eyes again grew wide.

"Whether you live or die depends on what you tell me next, so it better be right. Is the man who was charged with the culturing and manufacturing of this bio-toxin still here?" Klan bobbed his head in the affirmative. "Then take me to him."

While Garrett Walker had been rearranging François Meno's dental work, a Citation Encore chartered to a Saudi multinational corporation landed in Nairobi. It had taken the aircraft a little over three hours to make the 1,200-mile trip from Harare. A swarthy man with a briefcase in one hand and a small package in the other disembarked, paid the customs agent a bribe in keeping with the plushness of the small corporate jet, and caught a taxi for the commercial terminal. The Citation's pilot took on fuel and filed a flight plan for

Aden. He was airborne and crossing into Ethiopian airspace as the sun was coming up. The Citation's single passenger, per his instructions, took the package to the FedEx counter and paid for it to be sent overnight.

"My name is Tamay," he said to the man at the counter. "I believe you have something for me."

"Mr .Tamay?" he replied. "Yes, I believe this is for you."

The counterman, per *his* instructions, handed over an envelope. It contained a key to one of the airport lockers. Tamay quickly found the locker and removed an even smaller package stuffed with rand. It looked to be all there, but he hadn't the time to count it; he had to hurry to catch his flight to Dubai. The briefcase held medical samples and nonpointed instruments, in keeping with his documentation as a pharmaceutical rep. In the false side of the case, entombed between two thin sheets of padding, was a row of syringes with the needles removed. Security was lax at the Jomo Kenyatta International Airport, but then he would have also passed unchallenged through the TSA maize at JFK.

Vadim Karpukhin was not having a good time of it. He was a professional, and he knew from experience that his best course of action was to use the least amount of physical force to achieve the desired result. This meant disorientation, bondage, sensory deprivation and/or overload, and the threat of mutilation, but no real bodily harm. Failing that, there were drugs, but he had left Moscow on short notice, and he had no drugs available. He had been dispatched quickly and neglected to prepare the vials of thiopental sodium for travel. It was not difficult; he only had to prepare the needles and serum to appear to be the medication of a diabetic. But he had not taken the time, and now he wished that he had. In most cases, especially with westerners, only one in ten even needed to be drugged. When he first saw her at the hotel pool, oiling her body and repeatedly turning herself in the sunshine, like some ripe female rotisserie, he was certain that there would be no need for drugs. He went so far as to speculate that with a few hours' work, this slip of a girl would quickly tell him what he needed to know. Then he could make his phone call and be on his way back to St. Petersburg. But so far it had not worked out that way.

Karpukhin looked at his watch. He had used just about every trick he knew—all his skill and technique. Had he the drugs, he would now be rolling her onto her stomach and stabbing her skinny tush with a hypo. Why, he wondered, did American men seem to want their women to be so thin? And why did the women starve themselves for their men? He peered at her from behind the light without emotion. He lit a cigarette and considered how to proceed; he hadn't much time left in the two days he had allotted to complete his job. Then the odor of excrement hit him.

"You sonovabitch! Damn it, I couldn't hold it any longer, so I just shit the damn bed. You fuckin' pervert! I may have to lay in it, but you, you asshole, have got to smell it!"

He drew heavily on the cigarette, sucking the acrid smoke deep into his lungs. Vadim Karpukhin was becoming concerned. Not all people responded to torture, and this little lady might just be one of them. Well, he had one more thing to try before he had to get rough; it might work, and again, it might not. But he had no choice; failing Zhirinon was not something he cared to think about. He rose, took a last draw on the butt, and dropped it to the floor, grinding it out with the sole of his shoe. Then he snapped off the light and moved toward the bed.

* * *

Pavel Zelinkow knew the Citation had made the flight from Harare to Nairobi without incident; the pilot had called an exchange and left a message that he had delivered his passenger and was out of Kenya. He also knew that the courier, presumably with his lethal cargo, was now on a flight from Nairobi en route to the Saudi capital. Pavel Zelinkow was totally unaware, however, that the courier had agreed, for a very generous gratuity from someone else, to carry the package from Harare to Nairobi and deliver that package to the FedEx counter at Jomo Kenyatta International. Feeling confident and close to success, Pavel pushed himself away from his desk and went to the side counter for a second cup of espresso. This morning, in celebration of the product having been safely shipped, he poured a bit of anisette into the strong brew and, selecting one of his better Dominicans, went out onto the balcony. It was a warm morning, and he was quite comfortable in his fleece-lined slippers, pajamas, and robe.

From the compound of some fundamentalist cleric near Riyadh, Zelinkow mused, Abu Musab al-Zarqawi would put his plan into action—and what a fiendish plan it was. As horrible as the projected outcome of this venture was to be, Zelinkow could only marvel at the simplicity of al-Zarqawi's plan, now that the bio-weapon was, or soon would be, in his hands. In Saudi Arabia, there waited a dozen young men who would be injected with the deadly virus. They would become biological suicide bombers. These lethal individuals would then fly to Paris and London, and then on to the United States, each to a major city—New York and Los Angeles had been targeted for two each. Upon arrival in their target cities, they would draw large sums of money and indulge themselves. Zelinkow drew thoughtfully on his cigar and reflected on the irony of it. Most suicide bombers were promised forty virgins if they gave their life for the cause, but their reward was in the *next* life. These dozen men in America would, as the Americans were fond of saying, be able to have their cake and eat it as well. These highly contagious young men were to take their large bankrolls and buy as much sex on the American market as their libido could stand. Their instructions were to literally screw themselves to death, and in doing so, they would figuratively screw America.

He tapped the ash from his cigar and watched the Eternal City bask in the early-morning sun. When the pathogen reached Riyadh and was safely in the hands of an al-Zarqawi agent, he would be finished with this business. All that remained were a few housekeeping chores in Zimbabwe—unpleasant chores, but housekeeping nonetheless. He glanced at his watch. Perhaps it was time for Mr. Frémaux to call Claude Renaud to see how that end of the business was going. Renaud would be one of those loose ends that usually followed an undertaking of this kind, but that couldn't be helped. If he carried out his instructions at the Makondo Hotel, he would be the only loose end. Zelinkow fully expected Renaud to start talking once he went through his money, but who would listen? Who would he implicate?

Zelinkow suddenly felt a chill. The morning, though spectacular in promise, was not yet as warm as he had imagined. He set the Dominican in a stone ashtray to burn out and went back inside. Knowing that Renaud, if he had not yet completed his final task at the Makondo, might need some prompting, Zelinkow dialed Renaud's cell, the one with a dedicated line to the mercenary leader. He dialed twice but got only static—no ringing, and no indication of the absence of a signal. Strange, Zelinkow thought; he had spared no cost in making sure that the cell coverage that supported his operations was both secure and reliable. Very strange indeed.

A terrified Lyman Hotch led Elvis Rosenblatt and Garrett Walker down the corridor of the basement lab. The explosion in the far wing of the hotel had not visibly disturbed the lab, but a fine coating of dust had been jarred loose from the structure as the shock wave passed through the building. They were still in their sealed suits. It was possible that some of the pathogen or dangerous materials in the lab spaces could have been released by the blast.

"I cannot help you," Hotch wailed. "It is all gone." He turned to plead his case, but Rosenblatt pushed him down the corridor. Both he and Garrett had powerful lanterns.

"I want to see where you made the stuff. Keep moving."

Hotch led them to a laboratory space that was set up to culture viruses. To Garrett it looked like something from a TV commercial for a pharmaceutical company. Rosenblatt walked over to the desk, which was littered with Swedish pornographic magazines. He began to rifle the drawers. Suddenly he whirled on Hotch.

"Your notes? Where are your notes?"

"I told you, it's all gone. We were told to destroy everything. I burned my ledgers and doused all the culture mediums and laboratory plumbing with bleach. We were told to leave no evidence behind. I told you, there is nothing left."

With this declaration, Hotch slumped down a wall and lowered himself to the floor. Rosenblatt sat on a lab stool, lost in thought.

"I can see what they did and how they were accomplishing it. With his help and some time, I could probably replicate the process. Maybe reverse-engineer how they produced it to come up with a vaccine."

"But if that Frog is right, Elvis," Garrett said, "time is something we may not have."

Rosenblatt went back to searching the lab. "There has to be something they left behind, some clue." He was beginning to sound a little desperate. "Could you have someone bring down my equipment? I'm going to need it." Then he added, "I think it's safe enough, but have them wear a mask."

Garrett was about to call up to AKR when his voice came over the circuit. "Garrett, AKR. Can you hear me?"

"Garrett here, what is it?"

"I need you up here now. Something's come up. I'm sending Wilson down to be with the doctor."

Garrett didn't question him. "The doc needs his equipment; have Wilson bring it. I'll be up as soon as he gets here."

Moments later, Garrett saw Wilson struggling down the dimly lit corridor with the equipment bundles. He helped unburden him, then was off at a jog to find AKR. He found him waiting in the lobby.

"Steven will be here in a few minutes in the other Jet Ranger. He wants you waiting at the pad. Something's happened, but he didn't say what. He just said for you to be waiting when he sets down." Garrett nodded and headed for the front entrance. Once outside, he was met by Mohammed Senagal.

"Where is Tomba?" he asked, removing the helmet of his suit.

"There was a matter that needed his attention," Senagal answered neutrally.

Garrett was about to question him further, but he heard the rotor beat of an approaching helicopter. He raced toward the helo pad. The Jet Ranger touched down, and Steven appeared in the doorway. He motioned Garrett aboard. Garrett hesitated, wondering what could be so urgent that he was being called away. Then he realized that he was not in command of the operations; that was AKR's job. He vaulted onto the helo, and they lifted immediately into the air.

In the basement of the lab, Dr. Elvis Rosenblatt was unpacking his test equipment, a small but highly effective spectrometer, a portable electron microscope, and several pieces of metered test equipment. Perhaps, he thought, I can find some residue of the virus on one of the ampoules. Even a dead virus might give him the clue he needed. It was a long shot, but there seemed no other way.

"*Nkosi,*" Wilson said, "there is someone coming down the corridor."

The newcomer approached with his hands at his sides. There was a sense of purpose as well as a resignation that made him unafraid. He gently pushed the barrel of Wilson's weapon aside and entered the lab.

"My name is Johann Mitchell," he said in a barely audible voice, "and I helped to create this monster. Perhaps I can be of service."

In the road that led from the main compound, a solitary figure was moving slowly and carefully through a grove of *mopane* trees. There was a Toyota 4x4 parked just below the now-destroyed sentry post that had guarded the access road to the complex. It might still be serviceable; if he could reach it, he could make his escape.

Claude Renaud had watched the systematic destruction of his force by the invaders. They were obviously a disciplined, Western military force. When he saw two of them illuminated by an explosion, he was surprised that they were both black. He saw them only briefly, but there was something familiar about them. No matter, he had to get away. His force had been beaten, and beaten almost without a fight. He clearly heard the distinctive chatter of an RPD, but it was quickly silenced by a volley of fire and an explosion. Instead of using this brief stand of resistance to rally his men, Renaud had taken the advantage of the exchange to scurry away from the complex to safety. So much for the completion bonus, he thought, but there were still the funds that had been building up in his Maputo bank account. All that mattered at this moment was to use the remaining darkness to make his escape.

Renaud managed to work his way past the rubble of the guard shack. There were two charred bodies, but only one was recognizable. He stepped past them without emotion, peering into the darkness for the dim outline of the Toyota. As he moved along the side of the road away from the complex, his heart almost sang as he caught a glint of the setting moon off a windshield. Renaud plunged toward the vehicle, praying that it would run. The pickup was parked on an incline, so he could allow it to roll for perhaps a hundred yards before he had to start the engine.

Reaching the truck, he leaned through the driver's side window, releasing the brake and taking it out of gear. He braced his shoulder against the window post, and the Toyota began to move. He had hoped to leave the Makondo in the comfort of his Land Rover at the head of a column of his scouts—the Renaud Scouts—but obviously that was not to be. At least he would be leaving with his life, perhaps the only one of his force to do so. Then his head seemed to explode, and he was thrown to the dirt and scrub of the valley floor. Dazed, he managed to raise his head and watched helplessly as the Toyota rolled across the road and slowly nosed into a deep ditch on the far side. He felt the pistol in his belt holster being jerked away. Then he was aware of a tall form standing over him.

"W-what the hell is going on? Who are you?" The waning moon was full on the man's face, and his features were vaguely familiar. It must be one of his blacks—or was it? The blow he had taken to the side of his head was now beginning to swell, threatening to close one eye. Then the man squatted and looked him full in the face.

"You do not remember me?" Renaud looked at him, fighting through the throbbing pain in his head to try and bring the man into focus. Yes, he did know this man, but he could not quite recall the time or place.

"Think back to your last day as a Selous Scout."

The realization exploded over him. "You!" he exclaimed.

A cold hatred instantly overtook him. He had not thought it possible after so long a time. It had been over twenty years. But squatting there beside him was the same Selous Scout warrant officer who had beaten him in front of the other men and then watched as he was dismissed from the Scouts. His hate for this man knew no bounds; it now overwhelmed his pain and his judgment.

"You black bastard! Go ahead and do whatever it is you're going to do! You were a bloody kaffir then, and you're still a bloody kaffir." Renaud immediately regretted the words, but they had come from deep within his soul.

Tomba regarded Renaud for a long moment. "I will not only do with you what I please, but I will tell you about it." He paused while he took a length of duct tape and wrapped it around Renaud's mouth and head to effectively gag him. "I'm going to drag you back into that thicket of blackthorn trees, far enough so no one can see or hear you from the road. I'm going to tie you to a tree and hamstring you. Then I'm going to castrate you. You will bleed to death, but probably not before the hyenas and bushpigs find you."

And that's what he did.

Garrett struggled out of his anti-exposure suit as the Jet Ranger sped over the Mavuradonha Mountains toward the Zambezi and Lusaka.

"What's up?" he yelled over the whine of the turbine. He could tell from experience that the helo was making its best speed, which was close to 140 knots.

Steven helped him pull the suit from his legs. Garrett was wearing jeans, a T-shirt, and sneakers underneath the chem-bio suit.

"I'm sorry to have to tell you this, but it appears that Judy Burks was kidnapped from her hotel room."

"What! When?"

"Two nights ago. It seems that she was abducted in the early-morning hours and taken to a private residence outside Lusaka. The good news is that we have the home under surveillance."

"Under surveillance! And nothing's been done! How long have you known about this?"

Steven placed a hand on his arm. "I just found out. Now sit back, and I'll bring you up-to-date. As you know, Judy was waiting out the operation in Lusaka in the event she was needed in a liaison capacity. She briefed our ambassador that an operation was being launched from Zambia, but gave no specifics. Nor was State brought into the picture with any detail. Fortunately, the ambassador put her under surveillance as a precaution. Once she was taken, he really had no option but to report the event back up the chain of command. It took two days for it to get from State to the CIA. Once the Director was made aware of what had taken place, Jim Watson called me direct. That was about an hour ago."

"So what are we going to do?"

Steven grinned. "Get her back, of course. Our embassy in Lusaka is thinly staffed, and there is no station or CIA presence in Zambia. But I'm given to believe that they can and will help us."

"Help us how?"

Again, Steven grinned. "You're not going to believe this, but they're going to provide some muscle."

François Meno had recovered somewhat, but he was still shaken. He was seated in a lounge chair with his back to a stout wooden post that was there as much for decor as for support. His hands were strapped behind him and around the post. He was now starting to lose the feeling in his arms. Meno had grown up with affluence and privilege. It was the first time in his life that he had been in a situation over which he had no control. And it was also the first time in his life that he had been struck. Typical American ruffians! Not long ago he had paid to have his teeth straightened and whitened. Now his mouth was ruined. The tall man in the chem-bio suit was nothing but a vicious bully. Meno salved his anger and fear with the revenge he would demand for this insult and personal attack. These people, he seethed, clearly did not know who or what they were dealing with.

Bottom line, they needed him. Without the vaccine, perhaps hundreds of thousands would die, and only he had the antidote. These bastards, he vowed, would pay! Thanks to the rough stuff, the price for the vaccine had just gone to $20 million.

Suddenly a man in a chem-bio suit walked briskly into the lounge. A stab of fear gripped Meno until he realized that it was not the one with the rifle who had dealt him the cowardly blow. He had removed the helmet, so Meno had a clear look at his face. His hair was matted with sweat, and he wore clear-framed glasses set slightly askew on his thin face. He looked like another of the faceless lab rats who populated research facilities around the world. One of the nobodies who scurried about it—white coats doing menial tasks.

"So you have inspected the laboratory spaces?" Meno said, trying to control the lisp he now had by virtue of broken teeth and swollen lips. "And as you can see, there is nothing for you to learn there. And if there were, there is nothing that you could do about it. You must do business with me, or many, many thousands will die. Only thanks to your brutal friend, the price of my vaccine is going to be much higher."

"So you have the vaccine?" Rosenblatt asked.

"I do. I have a small quantity that I manufactured myself, and the detailed process by which more can be made. But it is in a safe place—somewhere known only to me."

"And you're sure it is an effective vaccine?"

Meno managed to wipe his mouth on his shoulder and give Rosenblatt a look of pure disdain. "I developed it myself. It's as effective in managing this pathogen as are the vaccines for variola major smallpox or polio."

"Well, I certainly hope so, for your own sake," Rosenblatt replied. He wore surgical rubber gloves and held up a hypodermic syringe at eye level, the needle pointed up. "Because you're going to need it."

Rosenblatt shoved a knee into Meno's groin, pinning him to the chair. Meno tried to resist, but there was little he could do. He watched in horror as Rosenblatt plunged the needle through his jacket and into his arm, feeling the knot of serum disperse into the muscle tissue of his shoulder. When Rosenblatt removed the needle and stepped back, Meno saw Mitchell for the first time.

"Johann?"

"Yes, it's me, François. And no, not all of the pathogen produced by Lyman was given to you or destroyed. I kept back a small amount, just in case." Mitchell closed his eyes a moment and took a breath. "This was a terrible thing we did, François. I didn't realize how wrong until I watched those wretches in the isolation cells suffer from this pox. Now I will do all in my power to undo the damage and prevent a pandemic from taking place."

"And how long will it be before he becomes contagious?" Rosenblatt said, assuming a clinical tone.

"About forty-eight hours, give or take," Mitchell replied, standing well back from Meno. "Then he will be quite contagious, and perhaps beyond help for his vaccine. Once this pathogen takes hold, the outcome is quite irreversible."

"Then we mustn't delay," Rosenblatt said, holding up a vial of amber liquid. "We have an active strain of the virus, Dr. Meno, so that should give us a start on replicating your vaccine. It will be too late for you. I doubt even my colleagues at the CDC, even with a total effort, can save you from the fate of those poor devils you put to death here." He turned from Meno to Mitchell. "We must get him to an isolation facility before he becomes infectious. With your help, using him as a test subject, we will learn something of the progress of this virus as it spreads through a host."

"No!" Meno screamed. "You can't do this to me!" He began to struggle wildly, causing the nylon snap-ties to bite into his wrists. The cut on his lip opened and again began to stream blood down his chin.

"What about his blood? Now that he has the virus, is his blood particularly dangerous?"

"I—I really don't know," Mitchell managed. "We were interested in the airborne spread of the virus, not the contaminating effects of blood."

"Hmmm." Rosenblatt carefully turned the matter over. "He's a little smaller than me, but we can put him in my suit while we're en route, to be on the safe side. With any luck at all we can have him in an isolation facility in fifteen hours. And the sooner, the better. We want to prolong his life as long as possible to study the evolution of the virus."

"No!" Meno screamed as Rosenblatt and Mitchell left the lounge. "NOOOOOO!"

Rosenblatt found AKR and gave him some very specific instructions, making the point that there was no time to lose. Meno continued to scream, but the screams soon dissolved into sobs and pleas for mercy. His voice grew hoarse and barely intelligible, what with the broken teeth, and he spoke in French, so Rosenblatt could catch only a word here and there. He continued with his pleas until he passed out from exhaustion.

11

THE SETTLING
OF ACCOUNTS

There was little time for Steven and Garrett to talk during the flight. Once the Jet Ranger had cleared the mountains and began the descent into the Zambezi basin, the pilot raced along at no more than a hundred feet to stay under the Lusaka airport radar. A lot of smuggling went on between the two countries, which meant that a lot of bribes were paid to customs officials—and to air traffic controllers. They were making a border crossing without the benefit of having greased the right palm. The Bell helo had no terrain-following radar, but the pilot had a great deal of stick time with the 1st Special Operations Wing. He wore night vision goggles, which enabled him to race along, dodging the occasional structure or acacia tree, but it made for a very rough ride in the back. Both Steven and Garrett were tightly belted in. As they began to pick up the lights of Lusaka, the pilot straightened out and did his best to appear like a helicopter on a routine mission for some NGO.

"We're going to set down at a small hospital. It's not far from where we need to be, and they are accustomed to helos coming and going. But the helo will drop us and go. I need to get this bird back to the Jeki airstrip, refueled and ready to support AKR. They should be just about ready to come out of there."

Garrett listened, but he was on the edge of his seat. He had all but forgotten about the events at the Makondo Hotel. When they did come to mind, he knew that AKR

could handle them. And after all, AKR was in fact the
ground commander. Right now, he wanted to be out of
the helo and on the ground. "Who did you say was going
to meet us?"

Steven put a hand on his shoulder. "I didn't say. I was
just told that two men would be meeting us, and that they
would take us to where they were holding Judy."

"But who are they; how much do they know?"

"Relax," Steven said in a reassuring tone. "From what I've
been led to believe, they know enough to be able to help and
not ask too many questions. Here." He handed Garrett a Sig
Sauer .45 and several loaded magazines. "Better leave the
rifle on the helo." Garrett pulled the slide of the pistol to
chamber a round and thumbed the hammer drop to safe the
weapon, all in a single fluid motion. He pushed the pistol
into his belt at the small of his back and pulled his T-shirt
over it.

The Jet Ranger came in hot, flared quickly, and neatly
settled onto the pad. Garrett was off running to the sedan
that was parked between the helo pad and the hospital.
Steven, after a word with one of the pilots, was right behind him. There were two men in the sedan. The one in
the passenger side was black; the man at the wheel, white.
Large, serious-looking men, they both emerged from the
car when the helo landed. As Garrett and Steven reached
the car, the helo rose, and for a moment the area was enveloped in blowing dust. The aircraft cleared off very
quickly and headed back, low and fast, to the east. In the
silence of the retreating helo, Steven held out his hand to
the black man.

"Ambassador, thank you for meeting us like this. I'm
Steven Fagan. I'd like you to meet my colleague, Garrett
Walker. Garrett, this is Ambassador Conrad."

"Ambassador?" Garrett said dubiously.

"Mr. Fagan, Mr. Walker, my pleasure. And I'd like you to meet Luther Hallasey."

Garrett noticed that both of them wore body armor vests, and both had sidearms. "Shall we get to the business at hand?" Conrad asked.

"Whoa, what's going on here?" Garrett demanded. "This is not a diplomatic mission. This is a kidnapping. What do you think you're doing?"

Conrad turned and face Garrett straight on. "Now you listen to me, Mr. Walker. This is a poor, sleepy African nation. I'm the ambassador here, the President's representative. A few days ago I get a federal agent on my doorstep, telling me, and no one else, that some private army is going to launch an invasion from my nation into another sleepy African nation. She says it's a matter of national security. Thinking this could have some negative consequences to my sleepy African nation, I have her discreetly watched by a local policeman I trust. And someone ends up bagging her. So what do I do now? It's supposedly a national security issue, but I have no one to call but my boss, the Secretary of State. He tells me to mind my own business; he says the people who cooked this up have made their bed—let them lie in it. I'm ordered to tell no one and do nothing. Well, sir, no one kidnaps an American in my nation. I can't call out the local constabulary, but I *can* and *will* do something about it."

Garrett softened. "Sir, I didn't know. And I do appreciate what you've done, probably more than you can imagine. You see, for me, this is personal. But why don't you let Steven and me take it from here? This is our job."

The driver who had come around the car to stand with his ambassador now spoke. "Look pal, maybe it's personal for us as well."

The ambassador intervened. "What Sergeant Hallasey

means is that we have a personal stake in Agent Burks's safety as well. And perhaps also in letting those up the line know that they shouldn't keep those of us here on the country team in the dark. Now, the sergeant and I are going to go get Miss Burks. You may come along or not, as you please." With that the ambassador climbed back into the front passenger seat.

"And don't worry about the ambassador," Hallasey added. "When he was in the Corps, he led the first recon team into Kuwait City. He's a helluva marine. I know. I was his radioman." He walked around the car and climbed behind the wheel.

Steven and Garrett looked at each other and shrugged. They climbed into the rear seat, and the car sped off. The African dawn was just making its way across the high Zambian plain to Lusaka.

At the Makondo Hotel, the sun would not clear the mountains for another hour or more, but it was now fully daylight. The Africans now guarding the main hotel building were extra vigilant, as they no longer had the advantage of seeing at night while their enemy couldn't. Tomba and AKR crouched at the lobby door of the Makondo peering out. Inside, fifteen members of the clinical staff sat on the floor, facing the wall as they had been instructed, while a wary Mohammed Senagal kept an eye on them. A few had chanced a look behind them and received a kick in the kidneys from Senagal. Most sat quietly resigned, awaiting their fate. Many assumed they would be killed, and several were weeping softly. In the lounge, Wilson sat with his weapon on François Meno and Johann Mitchell. Meno, now encased in Rosenblatt's black chem-bio suit, had his hands bound in front of him. Mitchell sat quietly, waiting for what might come next. Elvis Rosenblatt crossed the lobby under the weight of two packs—the test equipment he had brought, plus what notes and ledgers he could scavenge from the lab. He had also photographed everything with a small digital camera. When he reached AKR and Tomba, he slung the packs to the floor and dropped to one knee beside them.

"All set," he said without preamble. "I have what I need, and I'll want to take two of the scientists out with us—those two." He pointed at Meno and Mitchell. "Will that be a problem?"

AKR looked to Tomba. "The men we lost. Will we take their bodies with us?"

Tomba shook his head. "We will bury them here, where they fell. It is our way. I will need a few minutes to make them ready. We will find a place in the earth for them nearby."

"How about the guard force? Think they will give us a problem on the way out?"

"I doubt it," Tomba replied. "Their leader is dead, and they have been scattered by the attack. The few survivors, if there are any, will watch us from well out in the bush. They will come back and scavenge the area and get away as best they can."

AKR considered this and nodded, glancing at his watch. "Okay, our first bird will be here in a few minutes," he said. To Tomba, "Start pulling the men back toward the helo pad and get your burying detail to work." He knew he had fifteen men to extract from the area—that would be three loads by Jet Ranger. "Elvis, I want you to get the two scientists up to the helo pad. Take Wilson with you, and one other man that Tomba will assign to the first lift. The rest of us will finish up here, bury our dead, and be ready to leave as soon as the helos can get back for us." Tomba and Rosenblatt nodded. "Very well, let's make it happen."

Tomba began to give instructions to the men out on the perimeter. Wilson and Rosenblatt escorted Meno and Mitchell to the helo pad. Per Rosenblatt's instructions, Meno was bound, and a pillowcase covered his suit helmet; Mitchell walked free. Soon they heard the rotors of an inbound helicopter. The four of them, plus one of Tomba's Africans from the perimeter, boarded the Jet Ranger and lifted away from the complex. The helo struggled but gradually gained altitude and transitional lift and flew down the valley, quickly reaching cruising speed. Soon it began to climb toward the mountains in the west.

AKR saw the helo off and ran back to the hotel lobby. "Get them outside and away from the building," he said to Mohammad Senagal, and then set off to find Tomba.

Senagal began to herd the remaining medical staff outside and into the courtyard in front of the hotel, littered by the aftermath of battle. Two vehicles were still smoldering, beside the remains of a truck that had been dismembered by rocket fire. The bodies lying about the courtyard and access road were beginning to draw flies. There was the smell of burned rubber and death. Many of those filing from the hotel entrance recoiled from the scene, and a few tried to turn back, only to receive a blow to the ribs from Senagal. He drove them like sheep, making them line up under an acacia tree and kneel down. They were sure this courtyard was soon to become a killing ground. One man leapt to his feet and began to run down the drive, away from the hotel. Senagal took leisurely aim and put a bullet between his shoulder blades. Like all the M-4 rifles carried by the Africans, the rounds were APLP bullets. On impact, the bullet entered the man's chest cavity and literally exploded his heart and lungs, opening a huge hole in his side. He was dead before he hit the ground. Those under the acacia tree watched in horror. Senagal lowered his rifle and turned to them.

"You will probably die soon enough, but there is no need to hasten the event. If any of you so much as gets to his feet, I will shoot you where you stand."

No one moved.

In a stand of trees above the hotel, two of the Africans, stripped to the waist, dug furiously at an elongated pit. They were four feet into the rich, black soil, throwing shovels of dirt with the rhythm of two machines. Another kept watch with his rifle. Near the grave lay two forms, each wrapped in his sleeping blanket. A dark figure silently approached the two men at work.

"That is all we have time for, brothers," Tomba said. "Put them to rest."

The two men scrambled up from their work and helped Tomba ease the bodies into the hole. Saying nothing, they immediately began to shovel the soil back. Tomba turned to the man on guard duty. "When you have finished, fall back to the helo pad. We are soon to be gone." The lone sentry nodded and returned to his security duties. Ten minutes later, the two gravediggers tossed aside their shovels and recovered their rifles and field equipment. The three moved off in the direction of the helo pad in a file, with good spacing between them.

AKR walked down the main corridor of the hotel, tossing thermite grenades into one room, then another. When he reached the main entrance, he lobbed the final two—one into the lounge, and another behind the reception desk. The explosions were not loud, but they hurled bits of molten white phosphorus everywhere, setting fire to all they touched. By the time he had cleared the entrance portico, the belly of the Makondo Hotel was burning furiously.

AKR was standing behind the line of scientists. They had been stripped to the waist and all were barefoot. Mohammed Senagal passed in front of them with a small canvas bag, into which they were ordered to turn out the contents of their pockets. When he reached the end of the line, he had a sack full of money, watches, wallets, and personal identification.

"The vehicles?" AKR said to Tomba.

"They have been taken care of." While AKR had been firing the hotel, one of the other Africans had visited each car and truck not destroyed in the attack and put a small thermite charge on each engine block. All transport serving the compound had effectively been destroyed.

"Excellent. You and Mohammed head for the pad. I will be along in a moment."

"We are not going to shoot them?" Senagal said, rifle at the ready. There was a murderous look on his face. He genuinely wanted to kill them; there was no doubt that it would give him pleasure.

Tomba put a hand on his shoulder. "We do as the *Nkosi* says. Come with me." He led Senagal away. The faint beat of the second Jet Ranger could just be heard echoing down the valley.

"My men wanted to kill you here and now," AKR told them, "but there has been enough death in this place for the moment. And simply shooting you would be too good for you. You are free to leave this place. Most of you will be taken soon enough by animals or the African heat, or by the angry relatives of those who died at your hands. Those of you who survive the walk out of here will carry the shame of what took place here for the rest of your miserable lives. God have mercy on you, because Africa and the Africans will not."

Kelly-Rogers reached the helo pad as the Jet Ranger began to power up for takeoff. Aboard were five of the Africans, including Mohammed Senagal. Moments later they were airborne and hurtling down the valley. Tomba, AKR, and the three remaining Africans quickly filed out of the compound and began to climb back up the drainage away from the hotel. When a Jet Ranger was available to bring them out, they would find a mountain clearing where it could land. Twenty minutes later, they stopped on a ridgeline to look back. The hotel was now consumed in flames, and an angry pillar of smoke rose from the compound. They paused only for a moment before they were again on the move.

The miserable collection of men under the acacia tree watched the helo lift from the pad and disappear down the valley. So did a half dozen or so armed men well out in the bush, the remnants of the Renaud Scouts. They turned their attention to the ragged stream of white men that had begun to file away from the burning hotel and down the access road, wondering if they had anything of value on them.

This was probably Vadim Karpukhin's last chance to learn what this girl knew. Time was running out. He had led his blindfolded prisoner into a small bath with a shower and tossed in a T-shirt and a pair of men's jockey shorts. He told her that she had fifteen minutes to make herself clean. He knew from experience, especially in the interrogation of Western women, that they detested being dirty. He had learned that if you let them clean themselves up, especially after they had soiled themselves, the prospect of becoming dirty again caused them to crack. A little privacy and some hot water made them feel human again; then you took it away. But this was his last trick. If it didn't work, then he was going to have to start hurting her. The prospect of that distressed him—not that he minded hurting people, and especially not this American female agent. It just meant that he was down to his last option. She might respond to pain, but then again, he had thought she would have broken by now. He stood outside the door and heard the water running. Then, moments later, he heard her singing in the shower. She was a tough one, all right.

Exactly eight minutes later, Karpukhin found the central water shutoff valve and cut the water to the bath. The act of stopping the water was part of reestablishing control. Time to get her back into a vulnerable position. When he opened the door, he expected to find her wet and wrapped in a towel, but she was dressed in the T-shirt and shorts. She had turned off the light, so he did not see her clearly. She exploded upon him out of the dark, screaming with rage. She had a long shard of mirrored glass wrapped in a towel, holding it like a knife. In her other hand she had a section of pipe. The force of her charge caught him off guard, and they both went down. He partially blocked the shard dagger, but not before she cut his cheek and sliced away part of his ear. It took both of his hands to fend off the deadly weapon. He twisted the hand with the blade with both his own, but she would not drop it. Then the first of the blows came from the pipe. It was a short piece of iron plumbing with the U-joint still attached, and she wielded it clumsily in her left hand. The first blow only mildly stunned Karpukhin, and he continued to fight for the makeshift knife. The second blow brought his eyes to hers, and he saw for the first time the terrible rage and determination in her face. Again and again she hit him. He relinquished his hold on the knife hand, vaguely knowing that he must somehow stop this incessant pounding to his head. He tried to bring up his arms to ward off the blows, but he was becoming addled, and movement was difficult. When he again caught her face, he saw that the rage was still there, but now it was accompanied by an expression of triumph. Then things grew dim, and finally dark.

While in the bathroom, Judy Burks had turned on the

shower, rinsed off quickly, and then scrambled into the scanty clothes provided her. In the process, she took quick stock of her surroundings, looking for a way to arm herself. It had taken all her strength to move the locking threads on the sink trap, but it had come away and provided her with a rudimentary club. Wrapping the towel around her hand, she began to sing while she pounded at the mirror. It cracked long-ways, as she had hoped, and after sustaining some minor cuts to her fingers, she managed to extract a suitably long piece of the glass. When her captor cut the water to the shower and came for her, she was armed and ready. She gave no thought to the method of her attack; she knew only that she would rather fight and die than again submit to this man. So she had continued to hit him well after he had ceased to struggle. Only when she rose and stood over him did she realize that he wasn't moving, and that his face was distorted and beginning to swell. There was blood coming from his nose and mouth, as well as from the partially severed ear and the gash on his cheek.

Suddenly the front door exploded inward, away from the lock and hinges, down flat on the hall floor. She whirled around to see two men surge through the opening, one black and one white. Others were behind them. Her first impulse was that these were associates of her captor, and they had come for her. She then recognized the familiar form in the jeans and T-shirt.

"Oh, Garrett! Garrett!" Her voice was high-pitched and girlish, not the scream of the Valkyrie that had half beaten her tormenter to death. She rushed to him, flinging her arms around his neck. He held her close to him while the other three men quickly moved past them, pistols drawn.

"Clear in back."

"Bedroom clear."

"Kitchen clear."

They drew back to the hallway, where Judy still clung to Garrett. He safed the Sig and eased it back into his trousers. Then he gently peeled her away from him and guided her to a chair in the adjacent living room.

"Why don't you let us have these for now?" Garrett said softly. He slipped the towel from her hand. It was bloody and still holding the shard of glass, now broken off to half its former length. Then he eased her fingers from the pipe and set it aside. As soon as she released the pipe, she reached desperately for his hand.

"You got here—you got here just in time," she now babbled, somewhat in shock. "He was going to hurt me. Thank God you came. Thank God you got here in time."

Sergeant Hallasey rose from the still form of Vadim Karpukhin and turned to Ambassador Conrad. "Yeah, thank God for him. He's still breathing, but he needs to get to a hospital fast."

Conrad looked at the battered man on the floor and then at the diminutive figure who had again flung herself into Garrett's arms. "It's a good thing we let her back into the embassy, Sarge. She might have come after *us.*"

Janet Brisco lit a cigarette from the half-inch butt of the previous one and watched as *Cheetah* tracked the second Jet Ranger away from the hotel. Dodds LeMaster controlled the camera with a joystick at his console. He followed the helo down the valley and saw it bank away to the northwest for the Zambezi; then he slewed the camera back to the hotel, now fully engulfed in flames. Whatever had been going on there was now gone forever. Then he began to watch over the five men toiling up the valley, searching around and in front of them for any sign of danger.

"Where's our first bird from the target?" she said to LeMaster.

"It's inbound; it should be here in about five minutes."

"Good. After it lands with the first lift of our men, send it on to Lusaka. Tell them to refuel there and stand by for instructions from Steven and Garrett. As soon as the second one lands, get it back across the Zambezi for the last group."

LeMaster raised the pilots and gave them instructions. He passed control of *Cheetah* to Bill Owens in the next van. With things winding down, he had to see about getting his systems shut down in preparation for leaving. Owens continued to watch over the five men still on the ground.

"The C-130?" Janet asked.

"On station and orbiting over Lake Malawi. It's an hour away, no more."

"Let's get it here. I want it on the ground when Steven and Garrett get back, and the last helo returns from Zimbabwe."

LeMaster passed the instructions along to the aircrew of the C-130J. The pilot checked in with the controller at Lilongwe Airport and requested permission for the Simpson Foundation aircraft to continue with its humanitarian mission. The flight was quickly cleared into Zambian airspace. As with all NGOs who flew regularly into southern African nations, the foundation regularly paid controllers a small fee to ensure that its aircraft encountered no delays as they went about their business.

"Keep an eye on things, Dodds," Janet said, lighting yet another cigarette. "I'm going to meet this helo."

The Jet Ranger set down a respectful forty yards from the vans, but it still sent a wave of dust across the vehicles and into the camp. As soon as the five passengers were on the ground, it rose and headed on northwest toward Lusaka. Brisco watched as two Africans escorted a solitary figure from the helo to an isolated piece of ground near the camp. He was in a black suit and had his hands bound in front of him. There was a pillowcase over his head. Elvis Rosenblatt approached with another white man in tow.

"How'd it go, Doctor?"

"I'm not sure. We destroyed the place, but there's a good chance we got there too late to prevent the delivery of a dangerous pathogen. I'm afraid we're a long way from being out of the woods on this one. You know we lost two men in the attack."

"Yes. Are we bringing them out?"

"Tomba and his men are burying them there. This is Dr. Johann Mitchell. He was one of the clinical staff at the hotel, but he's decided to help us with this problem. So far, his help has been invaluable."

"Mr. Mitchell," Janet said, regarding him cautiously.

"Miss Brisco, how soon can we be on our way out of here?" Rosenblatt asked.

"The men we lost," Janet asked, ignoring his question, "I'd like to know their names."

"I'm sorry, but I don't know." Then, seeing her anguish, he added, "I wish I did and could tell you. I only know they were killed in the assault. There were a lot of people killed at that place. Now, please, this is important. How soon can we leave?"

Janet Brisco looked at her watch. "With any luck, Steven and Garrett will be back here in an hour or so. The C-130 will be on the ground in fifty minutes. We can break camp quickly, and the vans can be loaded as soon as the transport arrives. But it will take another two hours to get a helo back for the last of the attack force. What's the hurry? If we were too late, we're too late. We are configured as an assault force. What can we do about it now?"

"Maybe nothing, but we have to try. I need to get that man to Paris as fast as I can," he said, pointing to the solitary figure under guard with his head swathed in a pillowcase. "I don't have time to explain right now, but trust me when I say that we may have a chance to get back some of what was created in that lab. Now, I'm given to understand that you have long-range private jets available. Is that right?"

"Well, yes, but I—"

"Then get your best and fastest plane here as soon as possible."

"It certainly can't land here." She thought a moment. "Perhaps we can link up with it at another location. You say this is vital?"

"It's life and death," Rosenblatt said, "on a massive scale. Now, I need to get a call to the States. Can I do that from here?"

"See the fellow over there by that van?" LeMaster was folding up a portable dish antenna. "He can connect you to the pope if you need to talk to His Holiness."

It was a very busy day for the Jeki airstrip. Thirty minutes later, the second Jet Ranger approached. It did not even touch down. Five bush fighters leapt from the hovering helo, which quickly returned in the direction in which it had come—one more load. Fifteen minutes after that, a big Hercules C-130J crabbed out of the sky at stall speed and squatted onto the end of the dirt strip. It immediately reversed the big Allison engines, taking most of the dirt strip to bring itself to a stop. There was dust everywhere. The aircraft taxied over and pivoted a hundred and eighty degrees to present its open bay to the camp. The loading ramp grinded down. By the time the two vans were driven aboard and chained to the deck of the transport, the first Jet Ranger had come over the horizon from the west and delivered three people to the dirt strip. It turned on the ground for a few minutes, then headed back to Lusaka. Garrett and Steven made their way over to the transport with Judy Burks between them. She was wearing a long nightgown under a T-shirt that was spotted with blood. Janet spotted them first and rushed over to Judy, putting a motherly arm around her.

"Just what the hell have you been doing to this girl!" she said, looking sharply from Garrett to Steven and back.

"It's okay," Judy said with a lopsided grin. "We had to kick a little butt."

"Is that a fact? Well, let's get you aboard and cleaned up a little."

Steven Fagan left Judy Burks in the care of Garrett and Janet and went straight for Elvis Rosenblatt. He found him standing off to one side with another white man, talking quietly while the Africans helped break camp and load the transport. Steven glanced at a third figure who sat bound and blinded in a chem-bio suit. One of Tomba's men, the one they called Wilson, stood nearby with his M-4 rifle at the ready. During the trip to Lusaka, Fagan had been kept apprised of events at the Makondo Hotel—the successful attack, the regrettable loss of the two Africans, and the two scientists brought out from the hotel. He also had a sketchy report from AKR that the Makondo Hotel was in fact a bio-weapons development site. What troubled him most was that a biological weapon might have already left the site and be in the hands of the wrong people. If that were the case, then all their efforts—the training, the planning, the diplomatic risks, the superb performance by their assault element—were for nothing. Whether or not that lethal cat was or was not irretrievably out of the bag was known only to Elvis Rosenblatt.

He called Rosenblatt off to one side and, in his typically polite and self-effacing manner, asked for an accounting of events at the Makondo. Rosenblatt, under Fagan's mild, insistent gaze, complied. Fagan listened, interrupting occasionally to clarify a point or gently guide the doctor back to the central theme. When Rosenblatt

finished, Fagan thanked him for his service and report.
Moments later he was on his sat phone to Jim Watson.

Inside the belly of the big transport, Bill Owens still sat
at his console in one of the control vans. While Owens
and his van were being loaded, he and *Cheetah* guided a
helo to a mountain clearing where five men waited. Once
they were aboard the Jet Ranger, he gave *Cheetah* her instructions and released the UAV from her responsibilities
in Zimbabwe. With a little more than half her fuel gone
and nothing under her wings, she took a northerly heading and easily climbed back up to 60,000 feet. When she
was in Malawian airspace, she called home.

In the Global Hawk control van at Kilimanjaro International, a controller suddenly noticed a blinking light on his
console. It was from a transponder aboard *Cheetah.*

"Hey, Stan," he said to the other tech. "Looks like our
prodigal cat has returned to the pride."

Stan came over and peered over the controller's shoulder. "Where is she?"

"A long way off. She's over Lake Malawi, almost into
Mozambique airspace and heading our way."

"I'd sure like to know where she's been and what she's
been doing."

"I don't think she's going to tell us, and we probably
shouldn't ask."

"Probably not."

As the last helo lifted away from the Jeki strip, the C-130
powered up and began to roll. Tomba and the last three
Africans raced up the loading ramp as the transport
turned for the downwind end of the runway. AKR leapt
aboard, the last boots on the ground. The big Hercules

used every bit of runway, power, and pilot skill to claw its
way back into the air, turning north out over the muddy
ribbon of the Zambezi River. Four hours later it touched
down at Kilimanjaro, just ahead of a Gulfstream G550.
The two aircraft couldn't be more different. One was a
blunt, hulking giant of pure utility, the other as sleek as a
spaceship. Both had the logo of the Joseph Simpson Jr.
Foundation blocked on their tails. Eight people deplaned
from the Hercules and boarded the Gulfstream. One of
them was dressed like an astronaut and seemed, to the
Global Hawk technicians watching at a distance, to have
his hands bound. Both aircraft immediately took off. Five
hours later, *Cheetah* set down neatly onto the strip and
demurely taxied over to the control van.

Armand Grummell often slept in the apartment that
adjoined his office at the CIA headquarters building in
Langley. It was a spartan studio arrangement with a single
bed and shower. Whenever there was a potential crisis
brewing, which recently seemed to be about every other
week, Grummell liked to be near the building. It was not
his agency's elaborate information-gathering apparatus he
needed to be close to, nor his organization's extensive communications network. In a locked drawer of his very secure
office was a small Rolodex that was simply referred to by
his top aides as "the Director's File." In the Rolodex were
perhaps three dozen cards, and each one held two entries.
The first were the initials of an individual contact, and the
second was a telephone number. The cards were changed
as phone and contact numbers changed, but only occasionally was a new card added. The removal of a card usually meant the death or compromise of that individual.

Grummell had served as the Director of Central Intelligence for close to three decades. Administrations came

and went, but Grummell stayed. During some changes of administration, his status changed from DCI to interim DCI while a suitable replacement was sought. But once the new president and his national security team compared the old spymaster with a new appointee, however qualified, he was quickly reinstated as Director. There were many reasons for this—competence, patriotism, loyalty, experience, devotion to duty, to name a few. But the Rolodex was one of them. The names and contacts in that reference file represented decades of personal trust and respect. They were not something easily handed off to a successor, nor did any replacement have such a resource. The Rolodex was sitting on the desk at Grummell's elbow when Jim Watson came in. It was 5:30 A.M. on a Sunday morning, and Grummell, though freshly shaved and showered, was still in his bathrobe. It was obvious that he had been up for a while. Jim Watson himself had been at his desk for quite some time.

"So," the older man began after Watson took one of the two chairs in front of his desk, "it would appear that we are a day late and perhaps a dollar short. Coffee?"

"That'd be great, sir."

Grummell filled a mug and pushed it across the desk to Watson, then rewarmed his own.

"So bring me up to date." The tone was soft, but commanding.

"The IFOR assault on the laboratory in Zimbabwe was an apparent success. But it seems the bio-weapon developed there, a particularly virulent and lethal form of smallpox, from what I'm told, was shipped from the lab only the day before. A corporate jet under lease by a Saudi multinational left Harare, landed in Nairobi, and discharged a single passenger. A passenger matching that description boarded a Kenya Airlines flight for Dubai and then took a Saudi Air flight to Riyadh. The flight arrived at King Khalid International Airport about a half hour ago. We can only assume that this biological weapon is now in the Saudi capital."

Grummell was silent for several moments. "And the IFOR contingent?"

"Most of them are on their way to Diego Garcia, where they will break down their equipment and return to Hawaii. But Steven Fagan and some members of his team, along with the two scientists from the lab in Zimbabwe, are headed for Paris. As I understand it, they are tracking a lead there. Apparently one of the scientists who helped develop this pox is a French national."

Grummell began to thumb through his Rolodex, then picked up the receiver to one of his desk phones. Very seldom when he made one of these calls was someone else allowed in the room. Watson rose to leave, but Grummell waved him back to his seat. Grummell greeted the person on the other end in Arabic, then switched to English.

"Saeed, we have a problem—a very serious problem. This problem has just arrived in your country, so in a sense, it's also your problem, at least for now. I think it will take both of us working together if we hope to resolve it. Let me explain." Grummell spoke for several minutes and then listened without speaking to the short reply. Then a coldness Watson had never heard came into Grummell's voice. "How sure are we? Sure enough that I will ask my president to place Saudi Arabia under a no-fly restriction. That means all commercial or military aircraft attempting to leave Saudi airspace will be turned around or shot down." Again another pause. "I think that is very wise. . . . Thank you, Saeed. . . . Good-bye."

Grummell replaced the phone, and looked across the desk to Watson. "He says he will do what he can. I believe him, but only time will tell. And now, I had best bring the White House up-to-date. I'm not sure the President will be keen on imposing a no-fly zone on the Arabian Peninsula," Grummell mused, and Watson thought he detected a slight twinkle in the old spymaster's eye, "but our friend Saeed Al-Qahtani seems to think he might. Thank you for staying with this, Jim." Watson again rose to leave, and this time Grummell did not try to stop him. "Keep me apprised of events in Paris."

"Yes, sir, and thank you, sir."

In a well-appointed office in Riyadh, a man in traditional Arab dress set aside his Havana cigar and quickly made two phone calls. One resulted in the closing of King Khalid International Airport. It was not the first time that the airport just five miles north of Riyadh had been shut down due to a bomb threat. The other placed him on the calendar for a thirty-minute meeting with Crown Prince Abdullah that evening.

Al-Qahtani's quick action produced immediate results of a sort. Within minutes, security police were swarming over the airport. Only two people on the flight from Dubai had connected from Nairobi. One was an African diplomat whose papers were in perfect order. The other was a businessman who was stopped as he tried to leave the airport by taxi. When questioned, he proudly admitted that while he was not Al Qaeda, he supported Al Qaeda. And yes, he had brought a briefcase from Harare to Riyadh. He told them that per his instructions, he had set the case down next to the baggage claim and walked away. When the police raced there to find it, there was no case to be found.

When Pavel Zelinkow rose the following day, he was of two minds. He knew that he had delivered on his end of the contract and that the toxin for which he had been contracted had been produced and also delivered. A terse message left on one of his voice mails confirmed that. Technically, he was in compliance with his contract and had earned his fee. He also knew that there were any number of loose ends, and a man in his business did not live with loose ends. His contacts in Africa had gone silent, and any pursuit of information there, or in Iran or Saudi Arabia for that matter, would only invite attention to himself. Nothing was to be gained by asking questions. He could only guess that something, somewhere, had gone wrong. Late last evening he had placed a call to Boris Zhirinon. This old mentor, in so many words, said that he had asked an old colleague to go to Africa to look into the matter. But Zhirinon had heard nothing from the man in several days, and feared the worst. This did nothing to assuage Zelinkow's apprehension about the loose ends.

Bank transfers, even large ones, are overnight transactions. Since yesterday was Sunday, as well as the day he made delivery, he would not know if the funds, per his instructions, had been paid to his account until the following day, Tuesday, though authorization should have been given on Sunday. His only leverage to ensure payment was that he too could be a loose end, and those who had employed him would want him to quietly disappear with his funds. He would know tomorrow. Meanwhile, it was going to be a long day. Carefully sipping his morning espresso, he again went over it in his mind and again decided that his only option was to wait; nothing could be gained by further inquiries. He pushed himself from the table and retired to his bath. There he shaved, showered, and put on freshly pressed slacks, shirt, a tweed jacket, and comfortable shoes. He next called for a car to take him to the Colosseum. For Zelinkow, the only way to deal with uncertainty and apprehension was to surround himself with art. He would have preferred to lose himself in one or two of the many art galleries in Rome. But since Rome art galleries are closed on Mondays, he would have to content himself with ruins. This, he hoped, was not a portent of his fortunes.

The flight from Kilimanjaro International to Paris was about 4,300 miles, which made for close to eight hours of air time. Because of the limited services available at the Kilimanjaro airport, they had to stop in Cairo for fuel. They were finally over the Mediterranean just a little before midnight. Fortunately the Gulfstream G550 is a very comfortable aircraft. At $35 million a copy, it should be. The organization had two of them, one registered to the Joseph Simpson Jr. Foundation and the other to Guardian Systems International. The one that raced across northern Africa for the Mediterranean belonged to the foundation. Aboard were Garrett, Steven, Janet Brisco, Judy Burks, Elvis Rosenblatt, AKR, Johann Mitchell, and a bound and hooded François Meno. Even if Meno had not been confined to the crew galley, there would still have been plenty of room in the plush sixteen-passenger aircraft.

Settled side by side in a pair of tucked-leather seats, Garrett and Judy both immediately fell asleep. He was still in jeans and T-shirt. The crew on the C-130 had found Judy a small pair of overalls, and had dressed and bandaged the cuts on her hands. Janet had cleaned her up a bit with alcohol swabs and gauze pads. They looked like a longshoreman and his daughter taking a nap together. Rosenblatt had stretched out on the four-place divan and fallen asleep as well; AKR had done the same, simply flaking out alongside him in the aisle. Dodds LeMaster had immediately found the computer workstation, logged on, and gone to work. There was something bothering him and he could not rest until he had the answer. Steven and

Janet talked quietly at a small table, relishing a spinach quiche with toast and jam after close to three days of MREs. Mitchell kept to himself and sat staring out the window. Meno, on Rosenblatt's instructions, was kept isolated and hooded, sealed inside the chem-bio suit.

"Well, I'll be damned. I don't believe it," he said chuckling aloud. "I simply don't believe it."

This mild outburst from the normally taciturn Dodds LeMaster caused both Steven and Janet to push back from their food and join him at his workstation.

"What have you got?" Janet asked, resting a hand on his shoulder.

"I think I might have him."

"Him?" Steven asked, looking to Janet, who raised her eyebrows in conjecture.

"The guy who's behind all this, or at least the one who has been giving all the orders." Now he had their full attention. "You see, encrypted cell phones are very hard to decipher, not impossible but very, very hard. It takes a great deal of computer power, massive amounts. A lot more than we have in our organization. So I tapped into the NSA data bank. They probably have the most capable computing engine on the planet. We've taped all the calls made to and from that makeshift lab in Zimbabwe, hoping that someone would make a mistake or give us something that would allow us to break the encryption algorithm. Usually, if you can get a known piece of information or component of the conversation, then the computers can take that known bit of data and use it to defeat the encryption and break the code."

"And you've done that?" Steven queried.

"I've done nothing, but he made a mistake. On one of the calls, before the ciphering clicked in, we picked up the name of Poulenc. Just an accommodation name, I thought—one chosen at random. Most covert operators who have to deal with multiple clandestine contacts use aliases. They choose them at random and change them frequently. But this one had an indulgence." LeMaster paused, and permitted himself a triumphant smile. "Classical French music."

"French music?"

"Exactly. Poulenc was not chosen at random. Francis Poulenc was an eighteenth-century French composer. When I ran the encrypted cell phone intercepts against a listing of French composers and arrangers, I came up with several more names—Drouet, Boulez, Frémaux, Baudo, among others. All are French orchestral or operatic luminaries. Their names recur in the cell phone intercepts. These names, when matched with the recorded calls, provided the computers with enough data to begin to decipher the encrypted intercepts. It'll take a little more time; the NSA computers are grinding away as we speak, but we can read their mail. It will be after the fact, but we will know what they said."

"Excellent work, Dodds," Steven said. "Absolutely superb. Do you have any idea where this French music lover lives?"

"I do," LeMaster said, wreathed in smiles. "Rome."

Steven took a seat next to LeMaster, and they began to talk about how to use this information to their advantage. Janet worked her way through the aisle of the Gulfstream, waking people up. They were due into Charles de Gaulle Airport in a few hours. There were calls to be made and planning that had to be done if they were to execute what Elvis Rosenblatt had in mind.

The office, while exquisitely furnished, was not as opulent as the anteroom or the rest of the palace. Saeed bin Abdullah Al-Qahtani, head of security for all of Saudi Arabia, was admitted that evening to a private meeting with the effective ruler of Saudi Arabia, Crown Prince Abdullah bin Abdul Aziz. King Fahd had been ailing for so long that Abdullah had become the defacto monarch. He listened carefully as Al-Qahtani relayed the details of his conversation with Armand Grummell and the events at the airport. All air traffic in Saudi Arabia had been grounded. When Al-Qahtani finished, the crown prince rose from his desk and walked to the window, which opened to a magnificent view of an immaculately tended courtyard, bathed in artificial light. He did not feel the need to tell Al-Qahtani of his private conversation with the American president. If Grummell had been direct with the Saudi security chief, the President had been downright blunt with the crown prince. America would not tolerate another catastrophe that involved Saudi Arabia or Saudi Arabian nationals. In spite of Grummell's doubts, the President had declared a no-fly zone over the entire Arabian Peninsula until the pathogen that came into the country had been recovered. If it was not recovered, and this pandemic reached America, the United States would consider it an act of war. The President did not need to remind the crown prince how quickly the American Third Army could be in Riyadh. He turned to Al-Qahtani.

"Place the city, indeed the entire nation, under martial law. You will do everything in your power to find and recover this disease and anyone who may be infected with it. If you do not, the kingdom will cease to exist. Now go, and keep me informed of your progress."

When he stepped into the anteroom, General Saleh Ali Al-Mohayya, chief of staff of the army and, in effect, the head of the Saudi military, was waiting for him. He and Al-Mohayya were rivals; at best they treated each other with suspicion bordering on contempt. Nonetheless, Al-

Mohayya rose when he entered the room and stood at attention.

"My forces stand at your command."

"Thank you," Saeed replied politely. "Please come with me."

It took Judy Burks four calls, two to the Bureau and two to the American Embassy in Paris, before she was finally given his cell phone. She had rung his residence several times, but the calls had gone straight to the answering machine. Even then she had to call the cell twice before he picked up.

"Who the hell is this? Do you realize what time it is?"

Judy, who had no watch, looked up at the eight clocks on the bulkhead that led to the cockpit of the Gulfstream. "Wait a minute, I can do this." She found the one labeled "Paris." "Okay, got it; it's a quarter of two. That sound about right?"

"Who in the *hell* is this?"

"C'mon, Walter, you don't recognize my voice?"

The voice did in fact sound familiar. Special Agent Walter O'Hara was the FBI liaison officer to the French Gendarmerie Nationale, a job he detested; he hated the French. A little more than a year ago he had participated in the raid of a residence in Villefranche, supposedly the home of a man connected to Hezbollah. This man, he later learned, was a Russian-born, naturalized French citizen who had orchestrated the theft of two nuclear weapons from Pakistan. The information given to him, which he had passed along to the French, was gold-plated. Only a bungled raid by Les Unités d' Intervention, the French national SWAT team, allowed this master terrorist to escape.

"Agent Burks?"

"You *do* remember." She turned to Garrett. "He remembers me." Back to O'Hara. "Walter, how'd you like to do me and the Bureau a big favor and save the free world, all at the same time?"

"Just what exactly do you want?" he asked dubiously.

"We'll be landing in a Gulfstream at Charles de Gaulle in about two hours. I want you to meet us with a nine-passenger van. We need to skip customs, and we want no questions asked about the aircraft or the people on board. Then we need to make a trip to a villa about two hours outside of Paris."

"Uh, Agent Burks, this sounds like something that has to be cleared through the Director; it will take his intervention to make this happen. The French are wired pretty tight right now, and they don't like taking orders from a lowly liaison officer."

"Tell me about it," she replied. "I just spoke with the executive director. It's being done as we speak."

"So—so what do you need me for?"

"Walter, we need someone we can trust. We need you to drive the van."

"No gendarmerie along on this one?"

"No gendarmerie."

"See you when you get on the ground."

It was with no small degree of relief that Al-Qahtani was able to tell his crown prince that they had been successful in finding the mysterious briefcase, along with three of the fifteen syringes carried into the country. This had come just twenty hours after the flight from Dubai had landed. Now he waited at his desk for his call to Armand Grummell to be put through.

The search of Riyadh and the outlying areas had been unprecedented and overwhelming. It involved the local police, the local and national security services, and the army. Never before had there been such a concentration of force, and never before had they taken a search into holy places. The Saudi Army and the security services had looked for terrorists before, but the searches were limited because of the sway the fundamentalist clerics held over the people. This time there was no such restraint. Mosques and madrassas, normally exempt from this kind of scrutiny, were thoroughly searched. It was in the basement of the latter, near al-Jubaylah, that they found an Al Qaeda cell, the syringes, and twelve young men. They had taken their first step toward martyrdom; the twelve had all allowed themselves to be injected with the deadly serum. Per their instructions, the army unit that found them immediately called for the Saudi medical team assembled for that purpose. The area was cordoned off by a Special Security Forces national guard unit, and medically quarantined.

Al-Qahtani's call went through. "Yes, Mr. Grummell, we were successful—completely successful." Grummell asked for the details, and Al-Qahtani told him all they had done. Then Grummell told him what he wanted. Al-Qahtani lifted his eyebrows. "You say a team of epidemiologists and a special operations security element from the United States will be landing in Riyadh within the hour? Mr. Grummell, it is not within my power to authorize this. . . . They are talking as we speak. . . . I see. . . . Well, then, with the authorization of the crown prince, I will see they get everything they need. . . . No, Mr. Grummell, thank *you* for helping us to avert an unpleasant situation. . . . And you, sir, good-bye."

Moments later, Crown Prince Abdullah sent for him. He had just spoken with the President of the United States.

* * *

Just after dawn, the nine-passenger Dodge van, with eight passengers and the driver, pulled up to a small villa near Le Chatelet-en-Brie. It was an embassy vehicle O'Hara had borrowed from the Marine guard force, but with no official markings. The two-story stone house was dark and appeared empty. Meno claimed to have no key, so they had to break in. The oak door was stout, and it took both AKR and Garrett together to force the lock. Once inside, they made a quick search of the home. The housekeeper who came twice a week would not be there today, or so Meno claimed.

"So we wait?" Steven asked.

"We wait," Rosenblatt replied.

They wandered about the generous living areas and the well-appointed library, which was filled mostly with medical texts. Janet and Judy went to the kitchen to see what they could find to eat. They soon returned with tea and a plate of bread and cheese. François Meno was still in the chem-bio suit, but the pillowcase had been removed. His face shield was smeared and dirty, but he could now see. He sat by the window in the foyer, still bound, not taking his eyes from the driveway. About ten o'clock, a FedEx truck pulled into the drive. Meno was immediately on his feet.

"I better handle this," O'Hara said. "Keep him quiet." He handed Meno off to Garrett and stepped outside to meet the deliveryman.

"Package for Dr. François Meno," she said. The FedEx deliveryman was a woman.

"He's not available at present," O'Hara said in horrible French. "I'll sign for it."

"May I see some identification, *s'il vous plaît.*"

O'Hara showed her his FBI credential, which meant

nothing, and his Gendarmerie Nationale ID, which did. She gave him the standard French shrug and handed him a clipboard. He signed, and she handed over the package.

They all gathered in the dining room and watched while Elvis Rosenblatt carefully opened the package. Garrett kept a firm hold on Meno. Neatly packed inside were a half dozen ampoules of clear liquid.

"So this is it?" Rosenblatt asked.

"Yes, yes, that's it. Now you must let me have it. There's no time to lose!" Meno was becoming excited, fogging his faceplate. "Please! I've done all you asked!" Dancing before him were the death throes of the men and women who died in the soundproof cells at the Makondo Hotel.

"You're sure this vaccine is effective?"

"Damn you. Why would I lie? Give it to me! There are syringes in my office upstairs. Please hurry!"

"Okay," Rosenblatt said lightly, "I believe you."

Rosenblatt rose and walked around the table to Meno. He unsnapped the locking mechanism on the helmet, twisted it an eighth of a turn, and lifted it from his head. The smell that came from the confined reaches of the suit were overpowering.

"Wh—what are you doing?" Meno fully expected them to keep him in the protective garment and inject him with the vaccine through the fabric of the suit. "What is this?"

Johann Mitchell had not spoken a dozen words since they left Africa, but he spoke now. "We had no remaining pathogen in the lab. All of it had in fact been destroyed, as you had so ordered. You then claimed to have a vaccine. It was Doctor Rosenblatt who had the idea to scare you sufficiently so that you would lead us to it." For the first time in a long while, Mitchell actually smiled. "And so you did."

"You are a brilliant virologist, Meno," Rosenblatt observed, "but you're also a chicken-shit. Thanks for the vaccine."

Garrett Walker, like the rest of the IFOR contingent in the villa dining room, was as shocked as Meno to learn that Rosenblatt was running a bluff. So shocked that when Meno bolted for Rosenblatt, he slipped from Garrett's grasp. Rosenblatt was ready. The right hand wasn't thrown that hard, but Meno ran straight into it. It caught him square in the face, giving him a broken nose to go with his broken teeth. He went down like a sack of sand.

In the stunned silence that followed, they all stared at Elvis. AKR spoke first.

"Why, you sonova—"

"Hey," Rosenblatt said, holding up his hands, one of them sporting a bruised knuckle. "You guys have to keep your secrets; Johann and I had to keep ours."

EPILOGUE

Before they left the Meno villa, Garrett and AKR had a good look around. In the basement they found a well-stocked wine cellar, carefully assembled by François's late father. They took four cases altogether and packed them into the back of the van for the drive back to Charles de Gaulle Airport. The wine, they reasoned, would be a good complement to the African beer Tomba's men brewed at the Kona facility. Three of the cases went into the Gulf-stream, and one they gave to Special Agent Walter O'Hara, over his protest.

"Hey, I'm a Mick from New York," he said, "I drink beer."

"Give it a try," Garrett urged. "A little grape never hurt anyone, even an Irishman."

That evening, after a very long day, O'Hara inspected one of the bottles—a Petrus Bordeaux, the same as what François Meno had taken with him to Africa. He splashed some in a tumbler and took a gulp. Not bad, he thought, but it's not beer—maybe it needs to be colder. He poured out the remainder of the glass, set the bottle on a shelf in the refrigerator, and took out a can of Pabst Blue Ribbon. The next day he took an unopened bottle of the Bordeaux to work and gave it to his secretary. He recalled that she was always going on about wine.

"*Merci,*" she cried, cradling the bottle as if it were a newborn. It caused such a stir in the office that O'Hara did some investigation. It seems that a single bottle of Petrus 1996 Pomerol Bordeaux, if you could find one, went for around five-hundred dollars.

Dr. Elvis Rosenblatt took the vaccine to the Pasteur Institute in Paris, where he and a Franco-American medical team closely examined the work of François Meno. The politicians of France and the United States often find themselves at cross-purposes, but the virologists from the CDC and the Pasteur Institute get on quite well. Two days later, the three unused syringes of genetically altered smallpox arrived from Saudi Arabia. It would take some time for conclusive tests, but it appeared that Meno had indeed developed an effective vaccine for his pathogen.

A portion of this vaccine was sent to Saudi Arabia for the would-be bio-suicide bombers. They had been taken to an isolated medical facility under Saudi control and quarantine. Those at the Pasteur Institute thought all would be given the vaccine, but only half were inoculated. The half who did not receive the vaccine experienced the same fate as those unfortunate test subjects in Africa. Those who received the vaccine recovered fully. As soon as they were pronounced fit, they were promptly beheaded.

It was not until Tuesday morning that Abu Musab al-Zarqawi learned of the disaster outside of Riyadh. He was still in Iran, still safe, yet he knew that it would only be a matter of time until the persistent Americans caught up with him as well. Nonetheless, he left the house by way of the back door and was helped into a waiting van. It was on to yet another safe house.

* * *

At Charles de Gaulle International Airport, Steven Fagan and Dodds LeMaster immediately boarded the Gulfstream and took off, chasing the sun west across the Atlantic. They were met at Andrews Air Force Base by Jim Watson. From there Steven and Watson were driven to a private room at an exclusive Georgetown eatery. They were joined by Armand Grummell and Joseph Simpson. It was a rare meeting, one that in all probability would not be repeated. In keeping with the character of these men, they exchanged a brief round of congratulations, but beyond that, refrained from talking business. That would be handled through unofficial channels at another time. Most of the discussion centered around international politics, national security affairs, and the inability of the Redskins to make the playoffs—again.

"By the way," Simpson said to Steven in passing, "what happened to your lead computer technician, the one you think so highly of. Didn't he fly in with you?"

"He did," Steven replied. "With the help of Jim Watson here, we were able to get him a temporary clearance to the National Security Agency and drop him off at their headquarters at Fort Meade. He said there was a matter there that needed his attention."

The French authorities were waiting for Meno when the van returned to the airport. He was immediately taken into custody. After his broken nose was set and he endured a crude bout of dental reconstruction, he was placed in a cell to await trial. A week later, Meno concluded that another day of bland food, prison attire, restricted movement, and lack of privacy was unacceptable. France did not believe in capital punishment, so he faced a lengthy imprisonment, if not a life sentence. The French also wanted no unpleasantness in their jails, so lethal objects were kept out of the cells. But Meno, as he had so capably demonstrated in his medical career, was a resourceful man. That evening he quietly removed his trousers, placed his neck through the fly and tied the legs to an upper rung of the barred cell door. In this manner, he managed to hang himself, albeit slowly.

Mitchell was another story. With the pathogen and the vaccine in the laboratory spaces of the Pasteur Institute, he again proved his worth in helping to analyze the pox and accelerate the production of more vaccine, just in case. His contribution was evident to all, yet he had unquestionably participated in a great crime. Johann Mitchell had gone to Africa for the money; his wife had a heart condition that only a heart transplant could correct. But in the socialized German medical scheme of things, she was deemed too old—available organs were slated for younger recipients. Ironically, she had died while he was in Zimbabwe. Now the French didn't want him, and he had no desire to return to Germany. He was a superb internist, but he would never practice again, at least not in public practice. It was Steven Fagan who came up with the idea, and it was immediately endorsed by Rosenblatt, Garrett, AKR, and even Janet Brisco. There was no physician on staff with IFOR on Kona, and it was becoming increasingly inconvenient to take men to the clinic in Waimea for medical treatment. A resident doctor at the training facility would be most useful. As it was, Mitchell probably knew more than he should about the workings of IFOR.

When the matter was put to Mitchell, he readily agreed. Subject to final approval by Joseph Simpson, IFOR now had a staff physician. While he was completing his work at the Pasteur Institute, a package arrived for him from a Mr. Bill Owens of Guardian Services International. Enclosed was a passport and birth certificate for one Franz Suhadolnik, a German-born, naturalized American citizen. The passport photo was a good likeness of Johann Mitchell. Also enclosed was a first-class ticket on Delta Airlines from Paris to Honolulu.

Pavel Zelinkow did not sleep all that well on the Monday night following the Sunday delivery of the pathogen to Riyadh. His rest was not helped by news of the airport closures in Saudi Arabia. He could only assume that, while things had come apart in Africa, and all was not as it should be in the Saudi Kingdom, these difficulties had not materially affected the delivery of the product. There was no news of any terrorists being taken into custody.

He rose at the usual time Tuesday morning and resisted going to his computer until his espresso was fully prepared. It was with a great deal of trepidation that he turned on the machine and brought up the main menu of the Arzi Bank AG in Zurich. He logged onto the site and tapped in his personal ID code. The computer hesitated, but only for an instant, and there it was: $30 million!

Zelinkow closed his eyes, sighed, and then went to work. He had an established protocol for moving the money from Arzi Bank AG through a dozen offshore banks and private banking arrangements. Per his preprogrammed instructions, the money came and went through these financial institutions, the funds running their route like a border collie on an agility course. At each stop, a fee was charged, and the character of monies changed—euros became pesos, yen became rubles, and the amounts were forwarded in differing denominations. At each stop, the money became a little cleaner and a little harder to trace. The process would take several hours. When the $30 million, less fees, arrived at its final destination, it would be as clean as freshly fallen snow.

Zelinkow pushed back from the computer and permitted himself a broad smile. It was done. With these funds, he would never again have to take another contract, and certainly never have to soil his hands with business as dirty as that just concluded. He quickly changed into some walking clothes and, with visions of attending private parlor concerts by the now-retired Luciano Pavarotti, to the tune of ten thousand dollars a head, let himself out of the flat. After a short walk he was seated in his favorite bakery, trying to decide between a cannoli or a biscotti. He finally selected tiramisu and another cup of espresso and settled in behind the Italian edition of the *Paris Mondo Times*. He turned quickly to the entertainment section and tucked into the tiramisu.

Few people, including Pavel Zelinkow, knew to what lengths the Americans, in prosecution of their war on terror, had gone in tapping into the international financial markets. Dodds LeMaster was one of the few. He now sat at a console deep in the bowels of the NSA with three scopes in front of him. The lanky Englishman perched on his stool in an agreeable slouch. Periodically he rubbed his hands together in front of his face, like a fly on a bowl of potato salad. There were no certainties in this business, but he felt he had a chance. One of the screens held the same presentation as that in the office of Martin Klein at the Leeward Bank on Nevis in the Caribbean. For LeMaster it would be a waiting game, and he was prepared to wait as long as it took. The clearance LeMaster had been given came from very high up and allowed him total and unrestricted access to all NSA computing capability. He had the run of the place. Otherwise he would never be allowed to bring a stack of tuna on rye sandwiches, several bags of barbeque chips, and a cooler filled with Dr. Pepper into the pristine, antiseptic NSA computer control center.

* * *

The largest, most secure, and most remote money-laundering and electronic offshore banking facility in the world is on the South Pacific island of Nauru. This little speck of phosphate lies south of the Marshall Islands; its nearest and most famous neighbor is Tarawa, some four hundred miles east-northeast. Rich phosphate deposits were discovered there some hundred years ago, which made Nauruans and their little island nation dazzlingly wealthy. But the mining activity devastated the island, and mismanagement squandered much of the once-large Nauruan trust fund that had been amassed with money from phosphate ore. Ninety percent of the twelve-square-mile landmass is an arid wasteland of mining tailings. The thirteen thousand residents depend on imports for food, fuel, building materials—everything. In the face of declining phosphate revenues, the world's smallest republic turned to another industry: offshore banking and offshore corporate registration. Laws were written expressly to make legal what was illegal in most of the banking capitals of the world.

Nauru is isolated and secure. There is a dock to accommodate phosphate ore carriers, and a single airport, which handles but one flight a week. The "bank" is a low three-thousand-foot-square cinder-block building in the Yaren District near the airport that houses the computers; the "bankers" are computer technicians. The roof of the low building is populated by an array of dish antennas. The doors have stout locks, but there is no other physical security; there is no need on such a remote island.

While Garrett Walker and Akheem Kelly-Rogers were cruising the Caribbean, the USS Kamehameha (SSBN 462) silently approached the island of Nauru. The big nuclear submarine carried two small wet submersible SEAL delivery vehicles, piggybacked behind its sail. Well offshore in deep water, the big nuclear mother sub launched one of her SDVs, which made its way in close to Nauru. Under cover of darkness, four Navy SEALs bottomed their mini-sub and anchored it just outside the reef that surrounds Nauru. They swam the rest of the way on scuba and crossed the beach near the banking facility. With them was a skilled CIA technician and several bundles of electronic equipment. The SEALs easily defeated the standard door locks and entered the bank. The technician worked for most of the night while the SEALs kept watch. They left before dawn, leaving no physical trace of their visit, but within the data-processing infrastructure of this electronic financial conglomerate, some subtle and important changes had been made.

The technician who did the work was like an astronaut; he represented the visible component of a brilliant and dedicated team of engineers and scientists who had worked long and hard to develop the software patch that the technician had just installed. For the SEALs, it was an interesting but routine mission. They did it professionally and without complaint, but to a man, they wanted to be in Afghanistan or Iraq, where the real fighting against terrorists was taking place.

Dodds LeMaster watched from his perch at NSA while the international banking community rose to meet the new day. The volume of money transfers varied from country to country, but they were generally completed before 10:00 A.M. on a business day, as the flow of money followed the sun around the globe. Some banks, like the one on Nauru, never slept. Suddenly LeMaster uncoiled from his slouch and eased the half-eaten sandwich to the console.

"Well, hallo, luv," he said as his fingers raced over the

keyboard; his face was as animated as a child's on Christmas morning. "Gotcha!" he said aloud. "Make one more move, and you're mine."

The communication algorithms and decoding technologies were sophisticated and very, very fast. And there was a little bit of luck involved, not the least of which was a certain Russian's affinity for French music. LeMaster tagged the four transfers totaling close to $30 million as they entered and left the Leeward Bank on Nevis. When the funds, in different denominations and different currency, arrived on Nauru, he was able to deflect them to a bank account in the Caymans registered to LeMaster Trading Partners, Ltd. These funds then, through an even more complex series of laundering transfers, made their way in the form of a bequest to the Joseph Simpson Jr. Foundation. But for a brief moment in time, Dodds LeMaster had been a very wealthy man.

Pavel Zelinkow carefully wiped his hands before taking out his Blackberry handheld. He dialed his account tied to Nauru and punched in his PIN. The account was empty. *Can't be!* He dialed again, and got the same result. A cold feeling crept up his spine, replacing the warmth of the tiramisu and espresso. Could it be happening again?! Two more inquiries to banking accommodation addresses only confirmed the fact. His funds were gone. Then he heard the growing wail of sirens. He watched helplessly as several police cars and unmarked sedans, which meant the Detective Division of the Polizia di Stato, raced by the bakery in the direction of his flat. For the second time in as many years, it seemed, the Grand Game had taken a turn against him.

With some reluctance he took out his cell phone, sighed, and punched in the number he had hoped never to have to dial. There was a short ring, then a busy signal, followed by a dial tone. The call triggered a relay that activated a solenoid, letting acid into a small glass chamber with a thin wire. The wire quickly gave way, breaking the circuit and firing the primer charge. It was not a large explosion, designed only to scatter flammable material about the office. Within seconds the whole flat was in flames.

Pavel Zelinkow rose, left a generous tip on the table, and walked out into the warm Rome morning. He decided to walk, and a half hour later he arrived on the steps of a small, rather ordinary and quite legal Italian bank. From his safety deposit box he removed a briefcase that contained cash in several currencies, credit cards, a flask of fine cognac, a small traveling humidor with four Cuban Churchills, and a passport in the name of Jean-Paul Desmond. He took a cab to the airport and caught a flight to Athens and from there on to Frankfurt, where he changed planes for Buenos Aires.

As soon as the American medical team had arrived at the madrassa outside the Saudi capital, they took possession of the three syringes of genetically altered smallpox. The serum was immediately dispatched by special military aircraft to Paris. When tests at the Pasteur Institute were completed, it was taken, again by special military aircraft, to Robbins Air Force Base near Atlanta. The final leg of the journey to the CDC was by armored car. There, the first man-made pestilence took its place beside what was once thought to be the last remaining strain of variola major smallpox. Those in Riyadh, Paris, and Washington hoped this new addition was the entire remaining stock of the African smallpox, but only time would tell if this were the case.

*   *   *

Graham Burkett sat at his desk in Georgetown studying the balance sheets and cash-flow projections of Outreach Africa. Things were not good. The recent setbacks in Zimbabwe had strained the financial reserves of the foundation and several of the benefactors who supported Outreach Africa had shifted their normal bequests to help with reconstruction efforts following the Indian Ocean tsunami. In a very short time, Burkett concluded, his foundation would have to cut back on their clinical services and that meant more suffering. He was massaging his temples with his fingertips when Florence stepped in, without knocking as usual. She put a file in his inbox and paused as she turned to leave.

"Oh, by the way, Mr. Findley from Citibank called and wanted you to call him right away."

This sent up alarm bells with Burkett. They were low on funds, but he didn't think they were that low.

"When did he call?"

"Well, the first time was early this morning, but he's called back twice since then."

"And why didn't you tell me this before now," Burkett said evenly, trying to keep the edge out of his voice.

"Oh, well, I thought you might be busy," Florence mumbled, wringing her hands and studying the carpet, "and well, I thought you might not want to be disturbed."

Burkett sighed. "Thank you, Florence, and please close the door on your way out."

After she retreated to the foyer, Burkett took up the phone, sighed again, and hit the speed dialer. The receiver felt as if it weighed ten pounds. Kenneth Findley had been Outreach Africa's banker for some time, and often covered drafts for the charity while donor checks cleared. If we've overdrawn an account, Burkett thought, there is no check to clear and cover.

"Ken," Burkett said when Findley came on the line. He made no attempt to hide his concern. "Is there a problem I should know about?"

"On the contrary, Graham, on the contrary," the banker replied genially. "Congratulations on the donation."

"The donation?"

"Why yes, it arrived this morning. Thirty million dollars! Well done. I know you will see that it is put to good use."

"You are positive it was for us?"

"Absolutely. We don't make mistakes with that kind of money."

Burkett was dumbfounded. "But . . . but who was it from?"

"Hell, man, I thought you would know. The transmission letter just said, 'For some much needed and noble work'."

Burkett considered this. "Some much needed and noble work," he slowly repeated. It had a familiar ring to it, but for the life of him, he couldn't place it.

In a small, fashionable Paris bistro, two couples sat at the best table in the house and ordered dinner. There was no listing of prices on the menu; everything was outrageously expensive, and the normal clientele so affluent that cost was not even addressed. Garrett poured out the last of a bottle of Dom Perignon, flipped it into the air, deftly catching it by the neck, and in a smooth motion dropped it into the ice bucket, bottom end up. He signaled to the wine steward for another. He and AKR were dressed in slacks, open-collared shirts, and sport coats. Judy Burks and Janet Brisco had made a crusade through a half dozen high-end

Parisian boutiques and were dressed to the nines. Garrett raised his glass and was about to speak when Janet touched his arm.

"Maybe we should let the ground commander make the first toast."

"Madam controller, I think that is entirely appropriate. AKR?"

Akheem Kelly-Rogers raised his glass and, smiling broadly, looked at each of the other three in turn.

"Ladies and gentlemen—fellow warriors—to the Africans."

"To the Africans!"